Cupid in Africa

Table of Contents

Cupid in Africa

P. C. Wren

Part I: The Making of Bertram

CHAPTER I

Major Hugh Walsingham Greene

There never lived a more honourable, upright, scrupulous gentleman than Major Hugh Walsingham Greene, and there seldom lived a duller, narrower, more pompous or more irascible one.

Nor, when the Great War broke out, and gave him something fresh to do and to think about, were there many sadder and unhappier men. His had been a luckless and unfortunate life, what with his two wives and his one son; his excellent intentions and deplorable achievements; his kindly heart and harsh exterior; his narrow escapes of decoration, recognition and promotion.

At cards he was *not* lucky—and in love he … well—his first wife, whom he adored, died after a year of him; and his second ran away after three months of his society. She ran away with Mr. Charles Stayne–Brooker (elsewhere the Herr Doktor Karl Stein–Brücker), the man of all men, whom he particularly and peculiarly loathed. And his son, his only son and heir! The boy was a bitter disappointment to him, turning out badly—a poet, an artist, a musician, a wretched student and "intellectual," a fellow who won prizes and scholarships and suchlike by the hatful, and never carried off, or even tried for, a "pot," in his life. Took after his mother, poor boy, and was the first of the family, since God–knows–when, to grow up a dam' civilian. Father fought and bled in Egypt, South Africa, Burma, China, India; grandfather in the Crimea and Mutiny, great–grandfather in the Peninsula and at Waterloo, ancestors with Marlborough, the Stuarts, Drake—scores of them: and this chap, *his* son, *their* descendant, a wretched creature of whom you could no more make a soldier than you could make a service saddle of a sow's ear!

It was a comfort to the Major that he only saw the nincompoop on the rare occasions of his visits to England, when he honestly did his best to hide from the boy (who worshipped him) that he would sooner have seen him win one cup for boxing, than a hundred prizes for his confounded literature, art, music, classics, and study generally. To hide from the boy that the pæans of praise in his school reports were simply revolting—fit only for a feller who was going to be a wretched curate or wretcheder schoolmaster; to hide his distaste for the pale, slim beauty, which was that of a delicate girl rather than of the son of Major Hugh Walsingham Greene…. Too like his poor mother by half—and without one quarter the pluck, nerve, and "go" of young Miranda Walsingham, his kinswoman and playmate…. Too dam' virtuous altogether….

Gad! If this same Miranda had only been a boy, his boy, there would have been another soldier to carry on the family traditions, if you like!

But this poor Bertram of his …

His mother, a Girton girl, and daughter of a Cambridge Don, had prayed that her child might "take after" *her* father, for whom she entertained a feeling of absolute veneration. She had had her wish indeed—without living to rejoice in the fact.

* * * * *

When it was known in the cantonment of Sitagur that Major Walsingham Greene was engaged to Prudence Pym, folk were astonished, and a not uncommon comment was "Poor little girl!" in spite of the fact that the Major was admitted by all to be a most honourable and scrupulous gentleman. Another remark which was frequently made was "Hm! Opposites attract. What?"

For Prudence Pym was deeply religious, like her uncle, the Commissioner of the Sitagur Division; she was something of a blue–stocking as became her famous father's daughter; she was a musician of parts, an artist of more than local note, and was known to be writing a Book. So that if "oppositeness" be desirable, there was plenty of it—since the Major considered attendance at church to be part and parcel of drill–and–parade; religion to be a thing concerning which no gentleman speaks and few gentlemen think; music to be a noise to be endured in the drawing–room after dinner for a little while; art to be the harmless product of long–haired fellers with shockin' clothes and dirty finger–nails; and books something to read when you were absolutely reduced to doing it—as when travelling....

When Prudence Walsingham Greene knew that she was to have a child, she strove to steep her soul in Beauty, Sweetness and Light, and to feed it on the pure ichor of the finest and best in scenery, music, art and literature....

Entered to her one day—pompous, pleased, and stolid; heavy, dull, and foolish—the worthy Major as she sat revelling in the (to her) marvellous beauties of Rosetti's *Ecce Ancilla Domini.* As she looked up with the sad mechanical smile of the disappointed and courageous wife, he screwed his monocle into his eye and started the old weary laceration of her feelings, the old weary tramplings and defilements of tastes and thoughts, as he examined the picture wherewith she was nourishing (she hoped and believed) the æsthetic side of her unborn child's mind.

"Picture of a Girl with Grouse, what?" grunted the Major.

"With a ... ? There is no bird? I don't ... ?" stammered Prudence who, like most women of her kind, was devoid of any sense of humour.

"Looks as though she's got a frightful grouse about somethin', *I* should say. The young party on the bed, I mean," continued her spouse. "'Girl with the Hump' might be a better title p'r'aps—if you say she hasn't a grouse," he added.

"*Hump*?"

"Yes. Got the hump more frightfully about something or other—p'r'aps because the other sportsman's shirt's caught alight.... Been smokin', and dropped his cigar...."

"It is an angel shod with fire," moaned Prudence as she put the picture into its portfolio, and felt for her handkerchief....

A little incident, a straw upon the waters, but a straw showing their steady flow toward distaste, disillusionment, dislike, and hopeless regret. The awful and familiar tragedy of "incompatibility of temperament," of which law and priests in their wisdom take no count or cognizance, though counting trifles (by comparison) of infidelity and violence as all important.

And when her boy was born, and named Bertram after her father, Dr. Bertram Pym, F.R.S., she was happy and thankful, and happily and thankfully died.

* * * * *

In due course the Major recovered from his grief and sent his son home to his place, Leighcombe Abbey, where dwelt his elderly spinster relative, Miss Walsingham, and her niece, Miranda Walsingham, daughter of General Walsingham, his second cousin. Here the influence of prim, gentle, and learned Miss Walsingham was all that his mother would have desired, and in the direction of all that his father loathed—the boy growing up bookish, thoughtful, and more like a nice girl than a human boy. Him Miranda mothered, petted, and occasionally excoriated, being an Amazonian young female of his own age, happier on the bare back of a horse than in the seats of the learned.

Chapter II

Mr. Charles Stayne-brooker (or Herr Karl Stein-brücker)

When it was known in the cantonment of Hazarigurh that Major Hugh Walsingham Greene was engaged to Dolly Dennison, folk were astonished, and a not uncommon comment was "Poor old Walsingham Greene," in spite of the fact that the young lady was very beautiful, accomplished and fascinating.

Here also another remark, that was frequently heard, was that opposites attract, for Dolly was known to be seventeen, and the Major, though not very much more than twice her age, looked as old as her father, the Sessions Judge, and *he* looked more like the girl's grandfather than her father.

It was agreed, however, that it was no case of kidnapping, for Dolly knew her way about, knew precisely how many beans made five, and needed no teaching from her grandmother as to the sucking of eggs, or anything else. For Dolly, poor child, had put her hair up and "come out" at the age of fifteen—in an Indian cantonment!

Little more need be said to excuse almost anything she might do or be. Motherless, she had run her father's hospitable house for the last two years, as well as her weak and amiable father; and when Major Walsingham Greene came to Hazarigurh he found this pitiable spoilt child (a child who had never had any childhood) the *burra mem–sahib* of the place, in virtue of her position as the head of the household of the Senior Civilian. With the manners, airs, and graces of a woman of thirty, she was a blasé and world–weary babe—"fed up" with dances, gymkhanas, garden parties, race meetings and picnics; and as experienced and cool a hand at a flirtation as any garrison–hack or station–belle in the country. Dolly knew the men with whom one flirts but does not marry, and the men one marries but with whom one does not flirt.

Mr. Charles Stayne–Brooker was the pride of the former; Major Walsingham Greene *facile princeps* of the latter. Charles was the loveliest, daringest, wickedest flirt you *ever*—and Hugh was a man of means and position, with an old Tudor "place" in Dorset. So Charles for fun—and Hugh for matrimony, just as soon as he suggested it. She hoped Hugh would be quick, too, for Charles had a terrible fascination and power over her. She had been frightened at herself one moonlight picnic, frightened at Charles's power and her own feelings—and she feared the result if Hugh (who was most obviously of a coming–on disposition), dallied and doubted. If Hugh were not quick, Charles would get her—for she preferred volcanoes to icebergs, and might very easily forget her worldly wisdom and be carried off her feet some night, as she lurked in a *kala jugga* with the daring, darling wicked Charles—whose little finger was more attractive and mysterious than the Major's whole body. Besides—the Major was a grey–haired widower, with a boy at school in England and *so* dull and prosperous....

But, ere too late, the Major proposed and was accepted. Charles was, or affected to be, ruined and broken–hearted, and the wedding took place. The Major was like a boy again—for a little while. And Dolly felt like a girl taken from an hotel in Mentone and immured in a convent in Siberia.

For Major Hugh Walsingham Greene would have none of the "goings–on" that had made Dolly's father's bungalow the centre of life and gaiety for the subalterns and civilian youth of Hazarigurh; whilst Mr. Charles Stayne–Brooker, whom he detested as a flamboyant bounder, he cut dead. He also bade Dolly remove the gentleman's name finally and completely from her visiting–list, and on no account be "at home" when he called. All of which Dolly quite flatly and finally refused to do.

* * * * *

Mr. Charles Stayne–Brooker (or the Herr Doktor Karl Stein–Brücker, as he was at other times and in other places) was a very popular person wherever he went—and he went to an astonishing number of places. It was wonderful how intimate he became with people, and he became intimate with an astonishing number and variety of people. He could sing, play, dance, ride and take a hand at games above the average, and *talk*—never was such a chatter–box—on any subject under the sun, especially on himself and his affairs. And yet, here again, it was astonishing how little he said, with all his talk and ingenious chatter. Everybody knew all about dear old Charlie—and yet, did they know anything at all when it came to the point? In most of the places in which he turned up, he seemed to be a sort of visiting manager of a business house—generally a famous house with some such old–fashioned British name as Schneider and Schmidt; Max Englebaum and Son; Plügge and Schnadhorst; Hans Wincklestein and Gartenmacher; or Grosskopf and Dümmelmann. In out–of–the–way places he seemed to be just a jolly globe–trotter with notions of writing a book on his jolly trip to India. Evidently he wanted to know something of the native of India, too, for when not in large commercial centres like Calcutta, Madras, Bombay or Colombo, he was to be found in cantonments where there were Native Troops. He loved the Native Officer and cultivated him assiduously. He also seemed to love the Bengali amateur politician, more than some people do.... Often a thoughtful and observant official was pleased to see an Englishman taking such a friendly interest in the natives, and trying to get to know them well at first hand—a thing far too rare....

There were people, however—such as Major Walsingham Greene—who affected to detect something of a "foreign" flavour about him, and wrote him down as a flashy and bounderish outsider.

Certainly he was a great contrast to the Major, whose clipped moustache, bleak blue eye, hard bronzed face and close–cut hair were as different as possible from Mr. Stayne–Brooker's waxed and curled moustache over the ripe red mouth; huge hypnotic and strange black eyes; pink and white puffy face, and long dark locks. And then again, as has been said, Mr. Stayne–Brooker was only happy when talking, and the Major only happy (if then) when silent.

On sight, on principle, and on all grounds, the latter gentleman detested the jabbering, affected, over–familiar, foreign–like fellow, and took great pleasure in ordering his bride, on their return from the ten–days–leave honeymoon, to cut him dead and cut him out—of her life.

And, alas, his bride seemed to take an even greater pleasure in defying her husband on this, and certain other, points; in making it clear to him that she fully and firmly intended "to live her own life" and go her own way; and in giving copious and convincing proof of the fact that she had never known "discipline" yet, and did not intend to make its acquaintance now.

Whereupon poor Major Walsingham Greene, while remaining the honourable, upright and scrupulous gentleman that he was, exhibited himself the irascible, pompous fool that he also was, and by his stupid and overbearing conduct, his "*That's enough*! *Those are my orders*," and his hopeless mishandling of the situation, drove her literally into the arms of Mr. Charles Stayne–Brooker, with whom the poor little fool disappeared like a beautiful dream.

* * * * *

When his kind heart got the better of his savage wrath and scourged pride, the Major divorced her, and the Herr Doktor (who particularly needed an English wife in his profession of Secret Agent especially commissioned for work in the British Empire) married her, broke her heart, dragged her down into the moral slime in which he wallowed, and, on the rare occasions of her revolt and threat to leave him, pointed out that ladies who were divorced once for leaving their husbands *might* conceivably have some excuse, but that the world had a very hard name for those who made a habit of it.... And then there was her daughter to consider, too. *His* daughter, alas! but also hers.

CHAPTER III

Mrs. Stayne-brooker—and Her Ex-stepson

From Hazarigurh Mr. Charles Stayne–Brooker went straight to Berlin, became the Herr Doktor Stein–Brücker once more, and saw much of another and more famous Herr Doktor of the name of Solf. He then went to South Africa and thence to England, where his daughter was born. Having placed her with the family of an English clergyman whose wife "accepted" a few children of Anglo–Indians, he proceeded to America and Canada, and thence to Vladivostok, Kïaou–Chiaou, Hong Kong, Shanghai, and Singapore; then to the Transvaal by way of Lourenzo Marques and to German East Africa. And every step of the way his wife went with him—and who so English, among Englishmen, as jolly Charlie Stayne–Brooker, with his beautiful English wife? ... What he did, save interviewing stout gentlemen (whose necks bulged over their collars, whose accents were guttural, and whose table–manners were unpleasant) and writing long letters, she did not know. What she did know was that she was a lost and broken woman, tied for life to a base and loathsome scoundrel, by her yearning for "respectability," her love for her daughter, and her utter dependence for food, clothing and shelter upon the man whom, in her mad folly, she had trusted. By the time they returned to England *via* Berlin, the child, Eva, was old enough to go to an expensive boarding–school at Cheltenham, and here Mrs. Stayne–Brooker had to leave her when her husband's "duties" took him, from the detailed study of the Eastern Counties of England, to Africa again. Here he seemed likely to settle at last, interesting himself in coffee and rubber, and spending much of his time in Mombasa and Nairobi, as well as in Dar–es–Salaam, Tabora, Lindi and Zanzibar.

* * * * *

Meanwhile, Major Hugh Walsingham Greene, an embittered and disappointed man, withdrew more and more into his shell, and, on each successive visit to Leighcombe Priory, more and more abandoned hope of his son's "doing any good" in life. He was the true grandson of that most distinguished scholar, Dr. Bertram Pym, F.R.S., of Cambridge University, and the true son of his mother.... What a joy the lad would have been to these two, with his love of books and his unbroken career of academic successes, and what a grief he was to his soldier father, with his utter distaste for games and sports and his dislike of all things military.

Useless it was for sweet and gentle Miss Walsingham to point to his cleverness and wisdom, or for Amazonian and sporting Miranda Walsingham hotly to defend him and rail against the Major's "unfairness" and "stupid prejudice." Equally useless for the boy to do his utmost to please the man who was to him as a god....

When the Major learned that his son had produced the Newdigate Prize Poem, won the Craven and the Ireland Scholarships, and taken his Double First—he groaned....

Brilliant success at Oxford? What is *Oxford*? He would sooner have seen him miserably fail at Sandhurst and enlist for his commission....

Finally the disappointing youth went to India as private secretary and travelling companion to the great scientist, Sir Ramsey Wister, his father being stationed at Aden.

* * * * *

Then came the Great War.

Part II: The Baking of Bertram by War

CHAPTER I

Bertram Becomes a Man of War

Mr. Bertram Greene, emerging from the King Edward Terminus of the Great Indian Railway at Madrutta, squared his shoulders, threw out his chest, and, so far as he understood the process and could apply it, strode along with the martial tread and military swagger of all the Best Conquerors.

From khaki helmet to spurred brown heel, he was in full panoply of war, and wore a dangerous–looking sword. At least, to the ignorant passer–by, it appeared that its owner was in constant danger of being tripped up by it. Bertram, however, could have told him that he was really in no peril from the beastly thing, since a slight pressure on the hilt from his left elbow kept the southern end clear of his feet.

What troubled him more than the sword was the feeling of constriction and suffocation due to the tightness of the belts and straps that encompassed him about, and the extreme heat of the morning. Also he felt terribly nervous and unaccustomed, very anxious as to his ability to support the weight of his coming responsibility, very self–distrustful, and very certain that, in the full active–service kit of a British Officer of the Indian Army, he looked a most frightful ass.

For Mr. Bertram Greene had never before appeared on this, or any other stage, in such a part; and the change—from a quiet modest civilian, "bashful, diffident and shy," to what his friends at dinner last night had variously called a thin red hero, a licentious soldiery, a brutal mercenary, a hired assassin, a saviour of his Motherland, a wisp of cannon–fodder, a pup of the bull–dog breed, a curly–headed hero, a bloody–minded butcher, and one who would show his sword to be as mighty as his pen—was overwhelmingly great and sudden. When any of the hundreds of hurrying men who passed him looked at him with incurious eyes, he felt uncomfortable, and blushed. He knew he looked an ass, and, far worse, that whatever he might look, he actually was—a fraud, and a humbug. Fancy him, Bertram Greene, familiarly known as "Cupid," the pale–faced "intellectual," the highbrowed hero of the class–room and examination–hall, the winner of scholarships and the double–first, guilty of a thin volume of essays and a thinner one of verse—just fancy him, the studious, bookish sedentary, disguised as a soldier, as a leader of men in the day of battle, a professional warrior! ... He who had never played games was actually proposing to play the greatest Game of all: he who had never killed an animal in his life was going to learn to kill men: he who had always been so lacking in self–reliance was going to ask others to rely on him!

And, as his spirits sank lower, Bertram held his head higher, threw back his shoulders further, protruded his chest more, and proceeded with so firm a tread, and so martial a demeanour, that he burst into profuse and violent perspiration.

He wished he could take a taxi, but even had there been one available, he knew that the Native Infantry Lines almost adjoined the railway terminus, and that he had to cross a grass *maidan* [1] on foot.

Thank heaven it was not far, or he would arrive looking as though he had come by sea—swimming. A few more steps would take him out of this crowd of students, clerks, artisans, and business–men thronging to their schools, colleges, offices, shops, mills, and works in Madrutta.... What did they talk about, these queer "city men" who went daily from the suburbs to "the office," clad in turbans, sandals, *dhoties*, [2] and cotton coats? Any one of these bare–legged, collarless, not *very* clean–looking worthies might be a millionaire; and any one of them might be supporting a wife and large family on a couple of pounds a month. The vast majority of them were doing so, of course.... Anyhow, none of them seemed to smile derisively when looking at him, so perhaps his general appearance was more convincing than he thought.

But then, short as had been his sojourn in India, he had been in the country long enough to know that the native does not look with obvious derision upon the European, whatever may be the real views and sentiments of his private mind—so there was no comfort in that.... Doubtless the Colonel and British officers of the regiment he was about to join would not put themselves to the trouble of concealing their opinions as to his merits, or lack of them, as soon as those opinions were conceived.... Well, there was one thing Bertram Greene could do, and would do, while breath was in his body—and that was his very best. No one can do more. He might be as ignorant of all things military as a babe unborn: he might be a simple, nervous, inexperienced sort of youth with more culture and refinement than strength of character and decision of mind: he might be a bit of an ass, whom other fellows were always ragging and calling "Cupid"—but, when the end came, none should be able to say that he had failed for want of doing his utmost, and for lack of striving, with might and main, to learn *how* to do his duty, and then to do it to the limit of his ability.

A couple of British soldiers, privates of the Royal Engineers, came towards him on their way to the station. Bertram attempted the impossible in endeavouring to look still more inflexibly and inexorably martial, as he eyed them hardily. Would they look at him and smile amusedly? If so, what should he do? He might be a fool himself, but—however farcically—he bore the King's Commission, and it had got to be respected and saluted by all soldiers. The men simultaneously placed their swagger–sticks beneath their left arms, and, at three paces' distance, saluting smartly and as one man, maintained the salute until they were three paces beyond him.

Bertram's heart beat high with pride and thankfulness. He would have liked to stop and shake hands with the men, thanking them most sincerely. As it was, he added a charming and friendly smile to the salute which he gave in acknowledgment of theirs.

He passed on, feeling as though he had drunk some most stimulating and exhilarating draught. He had received his first salute! Moreover, the men had looked most respectfully, nay, almost reverentially, if with a certain stereotyped and bovine rigidity of stare, toward the officer they so promptly and smartly honoured. He would have given a great deal to know whether they passed any contemptuous or derisive comment upon his appearance and bearing.... In point of fact, Scrounger Evans had remarked to Fatty Wilkes, upon abandoning the military position of the salute: "Horgustus appears to 'ave 'ad a good night at bridge, and took a few 'undreds orf Marmadook an' Reginald. Wot?"

Whereunto Fatty had murmured:

"Jedgin' by 'is 'appy liddle smile," as he sought the smelly stump of a cigarette in its lair behind his spreading shady ear.

Enheartened, but perspiring, Bertram strode on, and crossed the broad grass *maidan*, at the far side of which he could see the parallel streets of the Native Infantry Lines, where lay the One Hundred and Ninety–Ninth Regiment, to which he had been ordered to report himself "forthwith." Yesterday was but crowded, excited yesterday, terminating in a wild farewell dinner and an all–night journey. *To–day* was "forthwith." ... What would to–morrow be? Perhaps the date of the termination of his career in the Indian Army—if the Colonel looked him over, asked him a few questions, and then said: "Take away this bauble!" or "Sweep this up!" or words to that effect. He had heard that Colonels were brief, rude, and arbitrary persons, sometimes very terrible.... Approaching the end of the first long row of the mud buildings of the Native Infantry Lines, Bertram beheld a sentry standing outside his sentry–box, in the shade of a great banyan tree. The man was clad in khaki tunic, shorts and puttees, with a huge khaki turban, from which protruded a fringed scrap of blue and gold; hob–nailed black boots, and brown belt and bandolier. His bare knees, his hands and face were very far from being black; in fact, were not even brown, but of a pale wheat–colour.

The thoughts of Private Ilderim Yakub were far away, and his eyes beheld a little *sungar*–enclosed watch–tower that looked across a barren and arid valley of solid rock. In the low, small doorway sat a fair–faced woman with long plaits of black hair, and, at her feet, crawled a tiny naked boy … and then the eyes of Private Ilderim Yakub beheld a British officer, in full war–paint and wearing his sword, bearing down upon him. By Allah the Compassionate and the Beard of the Prophet! He had been practically asleep at his post, and this must certainly be the Orderly Officer Sahib or the Adjutant Sahib, if not the Colonel Sahib himself! Possibly even the "Gineraal" Sahib (from the neighbouring Brigade Headquarters) having a quiet prowl round. It must be *somebody*, or he wouldn't be "in drill order with sword," and marching straight for the guard–room.

Private Ilderim Yakub (in the days when he had been a—well—a scoundrelly border–thief and raider) had very frequently been in situations demanding great promptitude of thought and action; and now, although at one moment he had been practically asleep and his wits wool–gathering in the Khost Valley, the next moment he had sprung from his box, yelled "*Guard turn out*!" with all the strength of his leathern lungs and brazen throat, and had then frozen to the immobility of a bronze statue in the attitude of the salute.

In response to his shout, certain similarly clad men arose from a bench that stood outside a large thatched, mud–built hut, another, wearing a red sash and three white stripes on the sleeve of his tunic, came hurrying from within it, and the party, with promptitude and dispatch, "fell in," the Sergeant (or Havildar) beside them.

"Guard!" roared that bearded worthy, "*'Shun*! *Present* arms!" and, like the sentry, the Sergeant and the Guard stood as bronze statues to the honour and glory of Second–Lieutenant Bertram Greene—the while that gentleman longed for nothing more than that the ground might open and swallow him up.

What on earth ought he to do? Had he not read in his newly purchased drill–book that the Guard only turned out for Emperors or Field–Marshals, or Field Officers or something? Or was it only for the Colonel or the Officer of the Day? It most certainly was not for stray Second–Lieutenants of the Indian Army Reserve. Should he try to explain to the Sergeant that he had made a mistake, and that the Guard was presenting arms to the humblest of God's creatures that wore officer's uniform? Should he "put on dog" heavily and "inspect" the Guard? Should he pretend to find fault? No! For one thing he had not enough Hindustani to make himself intelligible. (But it was a sign that a change was already coming over Bertram, when he could even conceive such a notion, and only dismiss it for such a reason.)

What *should* he do, in these distressingly painful circumstances?

Should he absolutely ignore the whole lot of them, and swagger past with a contemptuous glance at the fool Sergeant who had turned the Guard out? … It wasn't *his* fault that the wretched incident had occurred.… *He* hadn't made the mistake, so why should he be made to look a fool? It would be the others who'd look the fools, if he took not the slightest notice of their silly antics and attitude–striking… (Heavens! How they'd made the perspiration trickle again, by putting him in this absurd and false position.) … Yes—he'd just go straight past the lot of them as if they didn't exist.… No—that would be horribly rude, to say the least of it. They were paying him a military compliment, however mistakenly, and he must return it. Moreover—it wasn't the Sergeant–fellow's fault. The sentry had shouted to the

Guard, and the Sergeant had naturally supposed that one of those Great Ones, for whom Guards turn out, was upon them.

Should he march past with a salute, as though he were perfectly accustomed to such honours, and rather bored with them? Unless he were near enough for them to see the single "pip" on his shoulder–strap, they would never know they had made a mistake. (He would hate them to feel as horribly uncomfortable as he did.)

And if he did, where should he go? He must find the Officers' Lines, and go to the Officers' Mess and inquire for the Colonel. Besides, this was *his* regiment; he was attached to it, and these men would all see him again and know who and what he was....

Of course—he would do the correct and natural thing, and behave as though he were merely slightly amused at the sentry's not unnatural mistake and its results.... With a smart salute to the Guard, Bertram smiled upon the puzzled, imperturbable and immobile Havildar, with the remark:

"*Achcha,* [3] Sergeant. Guard, dismiss *karo*" [4]—upon hearing which barbarous polyglot of English and Hindustani, the Non–Commissioned Officer abandoned his rigid pose and roared, with extreme ferocity, in the very ears of the Sepoys:

"Guard! *Or*der–r *ar–r–rms*. Stannat *eashe*. Dees*mees*!" and with another salute, again turned to Bertram to await his further pleasure.

"*Ham Colonel Sahib mangta. Kither hai*?" [5] said that gentleman, and the intelligent Havildar gathered that this young and strange Sahib "wanted" the Colonel. He smiled behind his vast and bushy beard at the idea of sending a message of the "Hi! you—come here! You're wanted" description to that Great One, and pictured the meeting that would ensue if the Colonel Sahib came hastily, expecting to find the Commander–in–Chief–in–India awaiting him.

No—since the young Sahib wanted the Colonel, he had better go and find him. Calling to a young Sepoy who was passing on some fatigue duty, he bade him haste away, put on his tunic, tuck his long khaki shirt inside his shorts, and conduct the Sahib to the Adjutant Sahib's office. (That would be quite in order; the Adjutant Sahib could decide as to the wisdom of "wanting" the Colonel Sahib at this—or any other—hour of the day; and responsibility would be taken from the broad, unwilling shoulders of Havildar Afzul Khan Ishak.)

An uncomfortable five minutes followed. Bertram, longing with all his soul to say something correct, natural, and pleasant, could only stand dumb and unhappy, while the perspiration trickled; the Havildar stood stiffly at attention and wondered whether the Sahib were as old as his son, Private Mahommed Afzul Khan, new recruit of the One Hundred and Ninety–Ninth; and the Guard, though dismissed, stood motionless in solemn row beside the bench (on which they would sit as soon as the Sahib turned his back), and, being Indian Sepoys, emptied their minds of all thought, fixed their unseeing gaze upon Immensity and the Transcendental Nothingness–of–Non–existent–Non–entity–in–Oblivion, and tried to look virtuous.

Returning and saluting, the young Sepoy wheeled about and plodded heavily down the road, walking as though each hob–nailed boat weighed a ton. But pride must suffer pain, and not for worlds would this young man (who had, until a few months ago, never worn anything heavier than a straw–plaited sandal as he "skipped like a young ram" about his native hill–tops) have been without these tokens of wealth and dignity. What he would have liked, had the Authorities been less touchy about it, would have been to wear them slung about his neck, plain for all to admire, and causing their owner no inconvenience.

Following his guide through the lines of mud huts, saluted every few yards by passing Sepoys and by groups who sat about doorways and scrambled to their feet as he passed, Bertram found himself in a broad sandy road, lined by large stone European bungalows, which ran at right–angles across the ends of the Sepoys' lines. Each bungalow stood in a large compound, had a big lawn and flower–gardens in front of it, and was embowered in palm–trees. Turning into the garden of the largest of these, the young Sepoy pointed to the big house, ejaculated: "Arfeecers' Mess, Sahib," saluted, performed a meticulously careful "about turn," the while his lips moved as though he were silently giving himself the necessary orders for each movement, and solemnly marched away.

A pair of large old–fashioned cannon and a white flagstaff gave the place an important and official appearance. Beyond the big porch stretched to left and right a broad and deep verandah, in the shady recesses of which Bertram could see a row of chairs wherein lay khaki–clad figures, their feet, raised upon the long leg–rests, presented unitedly and unanimously towards him. Indeed, as he advanced with beating heart and sense of shy discomfort, all that he could see of the half–dozen gentlemen was one dozen boot–soles backed by a blur of khaki. Up to the time he had reached the flight of steps, leading up from the drive to the verandah, no one had moved. Mounting the steps, and coming to the level of the recumbent figures, ranged along the rear wall of the verandah and on each side of an open door, the unhappy Bertram, from this new standpoint, saw that the face of each officer was hidden behind a newspaper or a magazine.... Profound silence reigned as he regarded the twelve boot–soles, each crossed by a spur–chain, and the six newspapers.

Another embarrassing and discomfortable situation. What should he do? Should he cough—as the native does when he wishes to attract your attention, or to re–affirm his forgotten presence? It seemed a rather feeble and banal idea. Should he pretend he had not seen the six stalwart men lying there in front of his nose, and shout: "*Qui hai*!" as one does to call an invisible servant? And suppose none of them moved, and a Mess servant came—he had no card to send in. He couldn't very well tell the man to announce in stentorian voice and the manner of a herald: "Behold! Second–Lieutenant Bertram Greene, of the Indian Army Reserve, standeth on the threshold!" And supposing the man did precisely this and *still* nobody moved, *what* a superlative ass the said Second–Lieutenant Bertram Greene would feel! ... But could he feel a bigger ass than he did already—standing there in awkward silence beneath the stony regard, or disregard, of the twelve contemptuous boot–soles? ...

Should he walk along the row of them, giving each alternate foot a heavy blow? That would make them look up all right.... Or should he seize a couple of them and operate them in the manner of the young lady in the Railway Refreshment Rooms or the Village Inn, as she manipulates the handles of the beer–engine? The owners of the two he grabbed and pulled would come from behind their papers fast enough.... Bertram moved, and his sword clanked sharply against a pillar. None of the readers had looked up at the sound of footsteps—they were resting from the labours of breakfast, and footsteps, as such, are of no interest. But, strange to say, at the sound of a sword clanking, they moved as one man; six papers were lowered and six pairs of eyes stared at the unhappy Bertram. After three seconds of penetrating scrutiny, the six papers rose again as one, as though at the sound of the ancient and useful military order, "*As you were*."

Major Fordinghame beheld a very good–looking boy, who appeared to be taking his new sword and revolver for a walk in the nice sunshine and giving the public a treat. He'd hardly be calling on the Mess dressed up in lethal weapons. Probably wanted the Adjutant or somebody. He was quite welcome to 'em.... These "planter" cheroots were extraordinarily good at the price.... Lieutenant and Quartermaster

Macteith wondered who the devil *this* was. Why did he stick there like a stuck pig and a dying cod–fish? Still—if he wanted to stick, let him stick, by all means. Free country.... Captain Brylle only vaguely realised that he was staring hard at some bloke or other—he was bringing all the great resources of his brain to bear upon a joke in the pink paper he affected. It was so deep, dark and subtle a joke that he had not yet "got" it. Bloke on the door–mat. What of it? ... Captain Tavner had received a good fat cheque that morning, he was going on ten days' leave to–morrow; he had done for to day; and he had had a bottle of beer for breakfast. *He* didn't mind if there were a rhinoceros on the doorstep. Doubtless someone would take it into the Mess and give it a drink.... Cove had got his sword on—or was it two swords? Didn't matter to him, anyway....

Captain Melhuish idly speculated as to whether the chap would be "calling" at so early an hour of the morning. It was the Mess President's business, anyhow.... Why the sword and revolver? And mentally murmuring: "Enter—one in armour," Captain Melhuish, the *doyen* of the famous Madrutta Amateur Dramatic Society, returned to his perusal of *The Era*... Lieutenant Bludyer didn't give a damn, anyhow.... And so none of these gentlemen, any one of whom would have arisen, had he been sitting there alone, and welcomed Bertram hospitably, felt it incumbent upon him to move, and the situation resumed what Bertram privately termed its formerness.

Just as he had decided to go to the nearest reader and flatly request him to arise and direct him to the Colonel, another officer came rushing from the room whose open doorway faced the porch. In his mouth was a quill pen, and in his hands were papers.

"Lazy perishers!" he remarked as he saw the others, and added: "Come along, young Macteith," and was turning to hurry down the verandah when Bertram stepped forward.

"Excuse me," he said, "d'you think I could see the Colonel? I have been ordered to report to this regiment."

"You *could* see the Colonel," replied this officer, "but I shouldn't, if I were you. I'd see the Adjutant. Much pleasanter sight. I'm the Adjutant. Come along to my office," and he led the way down the verandah, across a big whitewashed room, simply furnished with a table, a chair, and a punkah, to a smaller room, furnished with two of each of the above–mentioned articles.

Dropping the pen and papers upon the table, the Adjutant wheeled round upon Bertram, and, transfixing him with a cold grey eye, said, in hollow voice and tragic tones:

"Do not trifle with me, Unhappy Boy! Say those blessed words again—or at once declare them false.... *Did* I hear you state that you have been ordered to join this corps—or did I not?"

"You did, sir," smiled Bertram.

"Shake," replied the Adjutant. "God bless you, gentle child. For two damns, I'd fall on your neck. I love you. Tell me your honoured name and I'll send for my will...."

"I'm glad I'm welcome," said the puzzled and astonished Bertram; "but I'm afraid I shan't be very useful. I am absolutely ignorant—you see, I've not been a soldier for twenty–four hours yet.... Here's the telegram I got yesterday," and he produced that document.

"Good youth," replied Captain Murray. "I don't give a tinker's curse if you're deaf, dumb, blind and silly. You are my deliverer. I love you more and more. I've been awaiting you with beating heart—lying awake for you, listening for your footprints. Now you come—*I* go."

"What—to the Front?" said Bertram.

"You've guessed it in once, fair youth. East Africa for little Jock Murray. We are sending a draft of a hundred men to our link battalion there—awfully knocked about they've been—and I have it, straight from the stable, that I'm the lad that takes them.... They go in a day or two. ... I was getting a bit anxious, I can tell you—but my pal in the Brigade Office said they were certain to send a Reserve man here and relieve me.... Colonel *will* be pleased—he never *says* anything but '*H'm*!' but he'll bite your ear if you don't dodge."

"I suppose he'll simply hate losing an experienced officer and getting me," said Bertram, apprehensively.

"He'll make himself perfectly miserable," was the reply, "but nothing to what he'll make you. I'm the Adjutant, you see, and there'll be a bit of a muddle until my successor has picked up all the threads, and a bit of extra bother for the Colonel.... Young Macteith'll have to take it on, I expect.... He'll bite your other ear for that..." and Murray executed a few simple steps of the *can–can*, in the joy of his heart that the chance of his life had come. No one but himself knew the agonies of mind that he had suffered, as he lay awake at night realising that the war might he a short one, time was rushing on, and hundreds of thousands of men had gone to fight—while he still sat in an office and played C.O.'s lightning conductor. A usually undemonstrative Scot, he was slightly excited and uplifted by this splendid turn of Fortune's wheel. Falling into a chair, he read the telegram:

To Second–Lieutenant Bertram Greene, A.A.A.

You have been appointed to Indian Army Reserve of Officers with rank of Second–Lieutenant, and are ordered to report forthwith to O.C. One Hundred and Ninety–Ninth Regiment, Madrutta. A.A.A. Military Secretary.

"Any relation to Major Walsingham Greene?" enquired Murray.

"Son," replied Bertram, "and nephew of General Walsingham."

"Not your fault, of course," observed Murray. "Best to make a clean breast of these things, though.... Had any sort of military training?" he added.

"Absolutely none whatever. Soon after war broke out I felt I was a disgrace to my family—they are all soldiers—and I thought of going home and enlisting.... Then I thought it was a pity if nearly twenty years of expensive education had fitted me for nothing more useful than what any labourer or stable–boy can do—and I realised that I'm hardly strong enough to be of much good in the trenches during a Belgian winter—I've been there—so I wrote to my father and my uncle and told them I'd like to get into the Indian Army Reserve of Officers. I thought I might soon learn enough to be able to set free a better man, and, in time, I might possibly be of some good—and perhaps go to the Frontier or something...."

"Goo' *boy*," said the merry Murray. "I could strain you to my bosom."

"Then I received some papers from the Military Secretary, filled them up, and returned them with a medical certificate. I bought some kit and ordered a uniform, and studied the drill–book night and day.... I got that wire yesterday—and here I am."

"I love you, Bertram," repeated the Adjutant.

"I feel a dreadful fraud, though," continued the boy, "and I am afraid my uncle, General Walsingham, thinks I am 'one of the Greenes' in every way, whereas I'm a most degenerate and unworthy member of the clan. Commonly called 'Cupid' and 'Blameless Bertram,' laughed at … . Really he is my father's cousin—but I've always called him 'Uncle,'" he added ingenuously.

"Well—sit you there awhile and I'll be free in a bit. Then I'll take you round the Lines and put you up to a few things…."

"I should be most grateful," replied Bertram.

Macteith entered and sat him down at the other desk, and for half an hour there was a *va et vient* of orderlies, clerks, Sepoys and messengers, with much ringing of the telephone bell.

When he had finished his work, Murray kept his promise, gave Bertram good advice and useful information, and, before tiffin, introduced him to the other officers—who treated him with cordial friendliness. The Colonel did not appear at lunch, but Bertram's satisfaction at the postponement of his interview was somewhat marred by a feeling that Lieutenant Macteith eyed him malevolently and regarded his advent with disapproval.

---

[1] Plain.

[2] Loin–cloth.

[3] Good.

[4] Make.

[5] "I want the Colonel. Where is he?"

CHAPTER II

And is Ordered to East Africa

That afternoon the Adjutant very good–naturedly devoted to assisting Bertram to remedy his utter nakedness and ashamedness in the matter of necessary campaigning kit. Taking him in his dog–cart to the great Madrutta Emporium, he showed him what to buy, and, still better, what not to buy, that he might be fully equipped, armed and well prepared, as a self–supporting and self–dependent unit, provided with all he needed and nothing he did not need, that he might go with equal mind wheresoever Fate—or the Military Secretary—might suddenly send him.

After all, it was not very much—a very collapsible camp–bed of green canvas, hardwood and steel; a collapsible canvas washstand to match; a collapsible canvas bath (which was destined to endanger the blamelessness of Blameless Bertram's language by providing more collapses than baths); a canteen of cooking utensils; a green canvas valise which contained bedding, and professed to be in itself a warm and happy home from home, even upon the cold hard ground; and a sack of similar material, provided with a padlock, and suitable as a receptacle for such odds and ends of clothing and kit as you might choose to throw in it.

"Got to remember that, if you go on active service, your stuff may have to be carried by coolies," said the Adjutant. "About forty pounds to a man. No good trying to make one big package of your kit. Say, one sack of spare clothing and things; one bundle of your bed, bath, and washing kit; and the strapped–up valise and bedding. If you had to abandon one of the three, you'd let the camp–bed, bath and wash–stand go, and hang on to the sleeping–valise and sack of underclothes, socks, boots, spare uniform and sundries," and much other good advice.

To festoon about Cupid's person, in addition to his sword, revolver, water–bottle and haversack, he selected a suitable compass, map–case, field–glasses, ammunition–pouch, whistle and lanyards, since his earnest and anxious protégé desired to be fitted out fully and properly for manœuvres, and as though for actual active service.

Assurance being received that his purchases would be forthwith dispatched to the Adjutant's bungalow, Bertram drove back to the Mess with that kindly officer, and gratefully accepted his invitation to dine with him, that night, at the famous Madrutta Club.

"What about kit, though?" enquired Bertram. "I've only got what I stand up in. I left all my—"

"That's all right," was the reply. "Everybody's in khaki, now we're mobilised—except the miserable civilians," he added with a grin, whereat Bertram, the belted man of blood, blushed and smiled.

At dinner Bertram sat respectfully silent, collecting the pearls of wisdom that fell from the lips of his seniors, fellow–guests of the Adjutant. And his demeanour was of a gravity weighty and serious even beyond his wont, for was he not now a soldier among soldiers, a uniformed, commissioned, employed officer of His Majesty the King Emperor, and attached to a famous fighting regiment? Yes—a King's Officer, and one who might conceivably be called upon to fight, and perhaps to die, for his country and for those simple Principles for which his country stood.

He was a little sorry when some of his bemedalled fellow–guests joked on solemn and sacred subjects, and spoke a little slightingly of persons and principles venerable to him; but he comforted and consoled himself with the recollection and reflection that this type of man so loathed any display, or even mention, of sentiment and feeling, that it went to the opposite extreme, and spoke lightly of things weighty, talked ribaldly of dignitaries, and gave a quite wrong impression as to its burning earnestness and enthusiasm.

After dinner, when the party broke up for bridge, billiards or the bar, he sat on, listening with all his ears to the conversation of the Adjutant and an officer, who seemed exceedingly well informed on the subject of the battle of Tanga, in German East Africa, concerning which the general public knew nothing at all.

Murray noticed his intelligent and attentive silence, and counted it for righteousness unto the boy, that he could "keep his head shut," at any rate....

And next day The Blow fell!

For poor Captain and Adjutant Murray, of the Hundred and Ninety–Ninth Infantry, it dawned like any ordinary day, and devoid of baleful omens.

There was nothing ominous about the coming of the tea, toast, and oranges that "Abdul the Damned," his bearer, brought into the big, bare and comfortless room (furnished with two camp–beds, one long chair, one *almirah* [6] and a litter on the floor) in which he and Bertram slept.

Early morning parade passed off without unusual or untoward event.

Breakfast was quite without portent, omen, or foreshadow of disaster. The Colonel's silence was no more eloquent than usual, the Major's remarks were no ruder, the Junior Subaltern's no sillier, and those of the other fellows were no more uninteresting than upon other days; and all unconscious of his fate the hapless victim strayed into his office, followed by his faithful and devoted admirer, Second–Lieutenant Bertram Greene, who desired nothing better than to sit at his feet and learn....

And then it came!

It came in the shape of a telegram from the Military Secretary, and, on the third reading of the fair–writ type, Murray had to realise that the words undoubtedly and unmistakably were:

To O.C. 199th Infantry, A.A.A.

Second–Lieutenant Greene, I.A.R., to proceed to Mombasa forthwith in charge of your draft of one hundred P.M.'s and one Native Officer, by s.s. Elymas to–morrow and report to O.C., One Hundred and Ninety–Eighth immediately. A.A.A. Military Secretary, Delhi.

He read it through once again and then laid it on his table, leant his head on his hand and felt physically faint and sick for a moment. He had not felt quite as he did then more than three or four times in the whole of his life. It was like the feeling he had when he received the news of his mother's death; when his proposal of marriage to the one–and–only girl had been rejected; when he had been bowled first ball in the Presidency Match, and when he had taken a toss from his horse at the Birthday Parade, as the beast, scared at the *feu–de–joie*, had suddenly bucked and bounced like an india–rubber ball.... He handed the telegram to Bertram without comment.

That young gentleman read it through, and again. He swallowed hard and read it once more. His hand shook. He looked at the Adjutant, who noticed that he had turned quite pale.

"Got it?" enquired Murray. "Here, sit down." He thought the boy was going to faint.

"Ye–e–s. I—er—think so," was the reply. "*I* am to take the draft from the Hundred and Ninety–Ninth to the Hundred and Ninety–Eighth in East Africa! ... Oh, Murray, I *am* sorry—for you.... And I am so utterly inadequate and incompetent.... It is cruel hard luck for you. ..."

The Adjutant, a really keen, good soldier, said nothing. There was nothing to say. He felt that his life lay about him in ruins. At the end of the war—which might come anywhen now that Russia had "got going"—he would be one of the few professional soldiers without active service experience, without a medal or decoration of any sort whatever.... Children who had gone straight from Sandhurst to the Front would join this very battalion, after the war, with their honours thick upon them—and when he, the Adjutant, tried to teach them things, they'd smile and say: "We—ah!—didn't do it like that at the Marne and Ypres...." He could go straight away and shoot himself then and there.... And this pink civilian baby! This "Cupid"! No, there was nothing to say—apart from the fact that he could not trust himself to speak.

For minutes there was complete silence in the little office. Bertram was as one in a dream—a dream which was partly sweet and partly a nightmare. *He* to go to the Front to–morrow? To go on Active Service? He whom fellows always ragged, laughed at, and called Cupid and Blameless Bertram and Innocent Ernest? To go off from here in sole charge of a hundred of these magnificent fighting–men, and then to be an officer in a regiment that had been fighting for weeks and had already lost a third of its men and a half of its officers, in battle? He, who had never fired a gun in his life; never killed so much as a pheasant, a partridge, a grouse or a rabbit; never suffered so much as a tooth–extraction—to shoot at his fellow–men, to risk being horribly mangled and torn! ... Yes—but what was that last compared with the infinitely greater horror, the unspeakable ghastliness of being *inadequate*, of being too incapable and inexperienced to do his duty to the splendid fellows who would look to him, the White Man, their Officer, for proper leadership and handling?

To fail them in their hour of need.... He tried to moisten dry lips with a dry tongue.

Oh, if only he had the knowledge and experience of the Adjutant—he would then change places with no man in the world. Why had the England that had educated him so expensively, allowed him to grow up so hopelessly ignorant of the real elemental essentials of life in the World–As–It–Is? He had been brought up as though the World were one vast Examination Hall, and nothing else. Yes—he had been prepared for examinations all his life, not prepared for the World at all. Oh, had he but Murray's knowledge and experience, or one–tenth part of it—he would find the ability, courage, enthusiasm and willingness all right.

But, as it was, who was *he*, Bertram Greene, the soft–handed sedentary, the denizen of libraries and lecture–rooms, the pale student, to dare to offer to command, control and guide trained and hardy men of war? What had he (brought up by a maiden "aunt"!) to do with arms and blood, with stratagems and ambuscades, with gory struggles in unknown holes and corners of the Dark Continent? Why, he had never shouted an order in his life; never done a long march; never administered a harsh reprimand; never fired a revolver nor made a pass with a sword. (If only he *had* had more to do with such "passes" and less with his confounded examination passes—he might feel less of an utter fraud now.) At school and at Oxford he had been too delicate for games, and in India, too busy, and too interested in more intellectual matters, for shikar, sport and hunting. He had just been "good old Blameless Bertram" and "our valued and respected Innocent Ernest," and "our pretty pink Cupid"—more at home with antiquarians, ethnologists, Orientalists and scientists than with sportsmen and soldiers....

The fact was that Civilisation led to far too much specialisation and division of labour. Why shouldn't fellows be definitely trained and taught, physically as well as mentally? Why shouldn't every man be a bit of an artisan, an agriculturalist, a doctor, and a soldier, as well as a mere wretched book–student? Life is not a thing of books....

Anyhow, in the light of this telegram, it was pretty clear that his uncle, General Sir Hugh Walsingham, K.C.S.I., had described him more optimistically than accurately when forwarding his application for admission to the Indian Army Reserve of Officers, to the Military Secretary.... Another awful thought—suppose he let Uncle Hugh down badly.... And what of his father? ...

Well—there was one thing, he would do his absolute utmost, his really ultimate best; and no one could do more. But, oh, the fathomless profundity of his ignorance and inexperience! Quite apart from any question of leading men in battle, how could he hope to avoid incurring their contempt on the parade–ground? They'd see he was an Ass, and a very ignorant one to boot, before he had been in front of them for five minutes.... One thing—he'd know that drill–book absolutely by heart before long. His wretched examination training would stand him in good stead there, at any rate....

"Must tell the Colonel," said Murray suddenly, and he arose and left the office.

A few minutes later the Quartermaster, Lieutenant Macteith, entered. Instead of going to his desk and settling down to work, he took a powerful pair of field–glasses from their case on Murray's table and carefully examined Bertram through them.

Bertram coloured, and felt quite certain that he did not like Macteith at all.

Reversing the glasses, that gentleman then examined him through the larger end.

"Oh, my God!" he ejaculated at last, and then feigned unconquerable nausea.

He had heard the news, and felt personally injured and insulted that this miserable half–baked rabbit should be going on Active Service while Lieutenant and Quartermaster Macteith was not.

An orderly entered, saluted, and spoke to him in Hindustani.

"Colonel wants you," he said, turning to Bertram, as the orderly again saluted, wheeled about, and departed. "He wants to strain you to his breast, to clasp your red right hand, to give you his photograph and beg for yours—or else to wring your neck!" And as Bertram rose to go, he added: "Here—take this pen with you."

"What for?" asked Bertram.

"To write something in his autograph–album and birthday–book—he's sure to ask you to," was the reply.

Bertram turned and departed, depressed in spirit. He hated anyone to hate him, and he had done Macteith no harm. But in spite of his depression, he was aware of a wild little devil of elation who capered madly at the back of his brain. This exuberant little devil appeared to be screaming joyous war–whoops and yelling: "*Active Service*! ... *You are going to see service and to fight*! ... *You will have a war medal and clasps*! ... *You are going to be a real war–hardened and experienced soldier*! ... *You are going to be a devil of a fellow*! ... *Whoop and dance, you Ass*! ... *Wave your arms about, and caper*! ... *Let out a loud yell, and do a fandango*! ..." But in the Presence of the Colonel, Bertram declined to entertain the little devil's suggestions, and he neither whooped nor capered. He wondered, nevertheless, what this cold monument of imperturbability would do if he suddenly did commence to whoop, to caper and to dance before him. Probably say "H'm!"—since that was generally reported to be the only thing he ever said....

Marching into the room in which the Colonel sat at his desk, Bertram halted abruptly, stood at attention stiffly, and saluted smartly. Then he blushed from head to foot as he realised that he had committed the ghastly *faux pas*, the horrible military crime, of saluting bare–headed. He could have wept with vexation. To enter so smartly, hearing himself like a trained soldier—and then to make such a Scarlet Ass of himself! ... The Colonel gazed at him as at some very repulsive and indescribable, but very novel insect.

"... And I'll make a list of the cooking–pots and other kit that they'll have to take for use on board, sir, and give it to Greene with a letter to Colonel Rock asking him to have them returned here," the Adjutant was saying, as he laid papers before the Colonel for signature.

"H'm!" said the Colonel.

"I have ordered the draft to parade at seven to–morrow, sir," he continued, "and told the Bandmaster they will be played down to the Docks.... Greene can take them over from me at seven and march them off. I have arranged for the kits to go down in bullock–carts beforehand...."

"H'm!" said the Colonel.

"I'll put Greene in the way of things as much as possible to–day," went on the Adjutant. "I'll go with him and get hold of the cooking–pots he'll take for the draft to use on board—and then I'd better run down and see the Staff Embarkation Officer with him, about his cabin and the men's quarters on the *Elymas*, and..."

"H'm!" said the Colonel, and taking up his cane and helmet, departed thence without further remark.

"... And—I hope you'll profit by every word you've heard from the Colonel, my lad," the Adjutant concluded, turning ferociously upon Bertram. "Don't stand there giggling, flippant and indifferent—a perfect picture of the Idle Apprentice, I say," and he burst into a peal of laughter at the solemn, anxious, tragic mask which was Bertram's face.

"No," he added, as they left the room. "Let the Colonel's wise and pregnant observations sink into your mind and bring forth fruit.... Such blossoming, blooming flowers of rhetoric *oughter* bring forth fruit in due season, anyhow.... Come along o' me."

Leaving the big Mess bungalow, the two crossed the *maidan*, wherein numerous small squads of white–clad recruits were receiving musketry–instruction beneath the shady spread of gigantic banyans. The quickly signalled approach of the dread Adjutant–Sahib galvanised the Havildar and Naik instructors to a fearful activity and zeal, which waned not until he had passed from sight. In one large patch of shade the Bandmaster—an ancient Pathan, whose huge iron–rimmed spectacles accorded but incongruously with his fierce hawk face, ferocious curling white moustache and beard, and bemedalled uniform—was conducting the band's tentative rendering of "My Bonnie is over the Ocean," to Bertram's wide–eyed surprise and interest. Through the Lines the two officers made a kind of Triumphal Progress, men on all sides stiffening to "attention" and saluting as they passed, to where, behind a cook–house, lay nine large smoke–blackened cooking–pots under a strong guard.

"There they are, my lad," quoth the hitherto silent Adjutant. "Regard them closely, and consider them well. Familiarise yourself with them, and ponder."

"Why?" asked Bertram.

"For in that it is likely that they, or their astral forms, will haunt your thoughts by day, your dreams by night. Your every path through life will lead to them," answered the Adjutant.

"What have I got to do with them?" enquired Bertram, with uncomfortable visions of adding the nine big black cauldrons to his kit.

"Write about them," was the succinct reply.

"To whom?" was the next query.

"Child," said the Adjutant solemnly, "you are young and ignorant, though earnest. To you, in your simplicity and innocence—

> 'A black cooking–pot by a cook–house door
> A black cooking–pot is, and nothing more,'

as dear William Wordsworth so truly says in his *Ode on the Imitations of Immorality*, is it—or is it in '*Hark how the Shylock at Heaven's gate sings*'? I forget.... But these are *much* more. Oh, very much."

"How?" asked the puzzled but earnest one.

"*How*? ... Why they are the subject–matter, from this moment, of a Correspondence which will be still going on when your children's grandchildren are doddering grey–beards, and you and I are long since swept into the gulf of well–deserved oblivion. *Babus* yet unborn will batten on that Correspondence and provide posts for their relatives unnumbered as the sands of the seashore, that it may be carried on unfailing and unflagging. As the pen drops from their senile palsied hands they will see the Correspondence take new lease of life, and they will turn their faces to the wall, smile, and die happy."

"I am afraid I don't really understand," admitted Bertram.

"*Do* you think Colonel Rock will return these pots? Believe me, he will not. He will say, '*A pot in the hand is worth two in the bush–country*,' or else '*What I have I hold*,' or '*Ils suis, ils reste*'—being a bit of a scholar like—or perhaps he'll just swear he bought 'em off a man he went to see about a dog, just round the corner, at the pub. I don't know about *that*—but return them he will not...."

"But if I say they belong to Colonel Frost and that he wants them back—and that I promised to make it clear to him that Colonel Frost desires their immediate return," protested Bertram, who visualised himself between the anvil of Colonel Rock and the hammer of Colonel Frost.

"Why then he'll probably say they now 'belong to Colonel Rock and that he *doesn't* want them to go back, and that you must promise to make it clear to Colonel Frost that he desires *his* immediate return'—to the devil," replied the Adjutant.

"Yes—every time," he continued. "He will pretend that fighting Germans is a more urgent and important matter than returning pots. He will lay aside no plans of battle and schemes of strategy to attend to the pots. He will detail no force of trusty soldiers to convoy them to the coast.... He will refuse to keep them prominently before his vision.... In short, he will hang on to the damn things.... And when the war is o'er and he returns, he'll swear he never had a single cooking–pot in Africa, and in any case they are his own private property, and always were...."

"I shall have to keep on reminding him about them," observed Bertram, endeavouring to separate the grain of truth from the literal "chaff" of the Adjutant—who seemed to be talking rapidly and with bitter humour, to keep himself from thinking of his cruel and crushing disappointment, or to hide his real feelings.

"If you go nightly to his tent, and, throwing yourself prostrate at his feet, clasp him around the knees, and say: '*Oh, sir, think of poor pot–less Colonel Frost*,' he will reply: '*To hell with Colonel Frost*! …' Yes—every time…. Until, getting impatient of your reproachful presence, he will say: '*You mention pots again and I'll fill you with despondency and alarm…*' He'll do it, too—he's quite good at it."

"Rather an awkward position for me," ventured Bertram.

"Oh, quite, quite," agreed Murray. "Colonel Frost will wire that unless you return his pots, he'll break you—and Colonel Rock will state that if you so much as hint at pots, *he'll* break you…. But that's neither here nor there—the Correspondence is the thing. It will begin when you are broke by one of the two—and it will be but waxing in volume to its grand climacteric when the war is forgotten, and the pots are but the dust of rust…. A great thought. . . Yes…"

Bertram stared at the Adjutant. Had he gone mad? Fever? A touch of the sun? It was none of these things, but a rather terrible blow, a blighting and a shattering of his almost–realised hopes—and he must either talk or throw things about, if he were not to sit down and blaspheme while he drank himself into oblivion….

For a time they regarded the pots in awed contemplative silence and felt themselves but ephemeral in their presence, as they thought of the Great Correspondence, but yet with just a tinge of that comforting and sustaining *quorum pais magna fui* feeling, to which Man, the Mighty Atom, the little devil of restless interference with the Great Forces, is ever prone.

In chastened silence they returned to the Adjutant's office, and Bertram sat by his desk and watched and wondered, while that official got through the rest of his morning's work and dealt faithfully with many—chiefly sinners.

He then asked the Native Adjutant, who had been assisting him, to send for Jemadar Hassan Ali, who was to accompany Bertram and the draft on the morrow, and on that officer's arrival he presented him to the young gentleman.

As he bowed and shook hands with the tall, handsome Native Officer, Bertram repressed a tendency to enquire after Mrs. Ali and all the little Allies, remembering in time that to allude directly to a native gentleman's wife is the grossest discourtesy and gravest immorality. All he could find to say was: "*Salaam, Jemadar Sahib*! *Sub achcha hai*?" [7] which at any rate appeared to serve, as the Native Officer gave every demonstration of cordiality and pleasure. What he said in reply, Bertram did not in the least understand, so he endeavoured to put on a look combining pleasure, comprehension, friendliness and agreement—which he found a slight strain—and remarked: "*Béshak*! *Béshak*!" [8] as he nodded his head….

The Jemadar later reported to his colleagues that the new Sahib, albeit thrust in over the heads of tried and experienced Native Officers, appeared to *be* a Sahib, a gentleman of birth, breeding, and good manners; and evidently possessed of far more than such slight perception and understanding as was necessary for proper appreciation of the worth and virtues of Jemadar Hassan Ali. Also that he was but a hairless–faced babe—but doubtless the Sircar knew what it was about, and was quite right in considering that a young boy of the Indian Army Reserve was fitter to be a Second–Lieutenant in the *pultan*, than was a Jemadar of fifteen years' approved service and three medals. One of his hearers laughed sarcastically, and another grunted approval, but the Subedar–Major remarked that certain opinions, however tenable, were, perhaps, better left unvoiced by those who had accepted service under the Sircar on perfectly clear and definite terms and conditions.

When the Jemadar had saluted and left the office, Murray turned upon Bertram suddenly, and, with a concentrated glare of cold ferocity, delivered himself.

"Young Greene," quoth he, "yesterday I said you were a Good Egg and a desirable. I called you Brother, and fell upon your neck, and I welcomed you to my hearth. I overlooked your being the son of a beknighted General. I looked upon you and found you fair and good—as a 'relief.' You were a stranger, and I took you in.... Now you have taken *me* in—and I say you are a cuckoo in the nest, a viper in the back–parlour, a worm in the bud, a microbe in the milk, and an elephant in the ointment. ... You are a—a—".

"I'm *awfully* sorry, Murray," interrupted the unhappy Bertram. "I'd do *anything*—"

"Yes—and any *body*," continued the Adjutant. "I say you are a pillar of the pot–houses of Gomorrah, a fly–blown turnip and a great mistake. Though of apparently most harmless exterior and of engaging manners, you are an orange filled with ink, an addled egg of old, and an Utter Improbability. I took you up and you have done me down. I took you out and you have done me in. I took you in and you have done me out—of my chance in life.... Your name is now as a revolting noise in my ears, and your face a repulsive sight, a thing to break plates on ... and they 'call you *Cupid*'!"

"I can't tell you how distressed I am about it, Murray," broke in the suffering youth. "If only there were anything I could do so that you could go, and not I—"

"You can do nothing," was the cold reply. "You can not even, in mere decency, die this night like a gentleman.... And if you did, they'd only send some other pale Pimple to take the bread out of a fellow's mouth.... This is a civilians' war, mark you; they don't want professional soldiers for a little job like this...."

"It wasn't *my* fault, Murray," protested Bertram, reduced almost to tears by his sense of wicked unworthiness and the injustice to his kind mentor of yesterday.

"Perhaps not," was the answer, "but why were you ever *born*, Cupid Greene, that's what I ask? You say it isn't your fault—but if you'd never been born ... Still, though I can never forget, I forgive you, and would share my last pot of rat–poison with you cheerfully.... Here—get out your note–book," and he proceeded to give the boy every "tip" and piece of useful advice and information that he could think of as likely to be beneficial to him, to the men, to the regiment, and to the Cause.

---

[6] Cupboard.

[7] "Is all well?"

[8] "Without doubt."

CHAPTER III

Preparations

That night Bertram could not sleep. The excitement of that wonderful day had been too much for his nerves, and he lay alternating between the depths of utter black despair, fear, self–distrust and anxiety on the one hand, and the heights of exultation, hope, pride, and joy on the other.

At one moment he saw himself the butt of his colleagues, the contempt of his men, the *bête noir* of his Colonel, the shame of his Service, and the disgrace of his family.

At another, he saw himself winning the approval of his brother officers by his modesty and sporting spirit, the affection and admiration of his men by his kindness and firmness, the good–will of his Colonel by his obvious desire to learn and his keen enthusiasm in his duty, the respect of his Service for winning a decoration, and the loving regard of the whole clan of Greene for his general success as a soldier.

But these latter moments were, alas, far less realistic and convincing than the others. In them he merely hoped and imagined—while in the black ones he felt and *knew*. He could not do otherwise than realise that he was utterly inexperienced, ignorant, untried and incompetent, for it was the simple fact. If *he* could be of much use, then what is the good of training men for years in colleges, in regiments, and in the field, to prepare them to take their part in war?

He knew nothing of either the art or the science of that great and terrible business. He had neither the officer's trained brain nor the private soldier's trained body; neither the theory of the one nor the practice of the other. Even if, instead of going to the Front to–morrow as an officer, he had been going in a British regiment as a private, he would have been equally useless. He had never been drilled, and he had never used a weapon of any kind. All he had got was a burning desire to be of use, a fair amount of intelligence, and, he hoped, the average endowment of courage. Even as to this last, he could not be really certain, as he had never yet been tried—but he was very strongly of opinion that the dread of showing himself a coward would always be far stronger than the dread of anything that the enemy could do to his vile body. His real fear was that he should prove incompetent, be unequal to emergency, and fail those who relied upon him or trusted in him. When he thought of that, he knew Fear, the cold terror that causes a fluttering of the heart, a dryness of the mouth, a weakness of the knees, and a sinking of the stomach.

That was the real dread, that and the fear of illness which would further decrease capacity and usefulness. What were mere bullets and bayonets, wounds and death, beside revealed incompetence and failure in duty?

Oh, that he might have luck in his job, and also keep in sufficient health to be capable of his best—such as it was.

When Hope was in the ascendant, he assured himself that the greatest work and highest duty of a British officer in a Native regiment was to encourage and enhearten his men; to set them a splendid example of courage and coolness; to hearten them up when getting depressed; to win their confidence, affection and respect, so that they would cheerfully follow him anywhere and "stick it" as long as he did, no matter what the hardship, danger, or misery. These things were obviously a thousand times more important than parade–ground knowledge and such details as correct alignment, keeping step, polishing buttons, and so forth—important as these might be in their proper place and season. And one did not learn those greater things from books, nor on parade, nor at colleges. A man as ignorant as even he of drill, internal economy, tactics and strategy, might yet be worth his rations in the trenches, on the march, yes, or in the wild, fierce bayonet–charge itself, if he had the attributes that enable him to encourage, uplift, enhearten and give confidence.

And then his soaring spirit would swiftly stoop again, as he asked himself: "And have *I* those qualities and attributes?" and sadly replied: "Probably not—but what is, at any rate, certain, is the fact that I have no knowledge, no experience, no understanding of the very alphabet of military lore, no slightest grasp of the routine details of regimental life, discipline, drill, regulations, internal economy, customs, and so forth—the things that are the elementary essentials of success to a body of armed men proceeding to fight." … And in black misery and blank despair he would groan aloud: "*I cannot go. I cannot do it.*" … He was very young, very much a product of modern civilisation, and a highly specialised victim of a system and a generation that had taken too little account of naked fact and elemental basic tendency—a system and a generation that pretended to believe that human nature had changed with human conditions. As he realised, he had, like a few million others, been educated not for Life and the World–As–It–Is, but for examinations and the world as it is not, and never will be….

He tossed and turned through the long hot night on the little hard camp–bed, listening to Murray's regular breathing and the scampering of the rats as they disported themselves on the other side of the canvas ceiling cloth and went about their unlawful occasions. . . .

He reviewed the events of that epoch–making day from the arrival of the telegram to his getting into bed…. A memorable morning, a busy afternoon and evening, a rotten night—with a beastly climax—or anti–climax…. Would he never get to sleep on this hard, narrow bed? … What would he be fit for on the dreadful morrow if he slept not at all? … What a day it had been! Rather amusing about those cooking–pots. It wouldn't be very amusing for *him* if the situation developed as Murray had prophesied…. Rather a good bit of work that he had put in between lunch and dinner with the drill–book and a box of matches. Matches made good sections, companies, and battalions for practising drill–manœuvres on a desk—but it would he a different thing to give the orders correctly and audibly to hundreds of men who watched one with inscrutable eyes…. How he wished he had declined the invitation of Bludyer to accompany him and Macteith to the theatre…. They had proceeded in a car to the Club and there picked up some other fellows. The play was *The Girl in the Taxi*, and Bertram sat ashamed, humiliated and angry, as a third–rate company of English actors and actresses performed their sorry parts in a travesty of European life and manners, before the avid eyes of hundreds of natives. There they sat, with faces contemptuous, sensual, blank, eager, gleeful or disgusted, according to their respective conditions and temperaments—the while they gathered from the play that English life is a medley of infidelity, dissipation, intrigue and vulgarity.

And, after the play, Macteith had said: "Let's go to the Home–from–Home for a 'drink–and–a–little–music—what—what'?"

Bertram had thought it a somewhat strange proceeding to go to a Home, at eleven o'clock at night, for music, and he would greatly have preferred to go to bed. However, he could not very well say that they must take him back to bed first, nor announce his intention of leaving the party and walking home….

… Macteith having given instructions to the Eurasian chauffeur, the taxi sped away and, skirting the sea–shore, turned off into a quiet avenue of giant palms, in which stood detached bungalows of retiring and unobtrusive mien. Into the compound of one of these the taxi turned, and a bell rang loudly, apparently of its own volition. As they got out of the car, a lady came out to the brilliantly lighted verandah from the drawing–room which opened on to it. Bertram did not like the look of this lady at all. Her face reminded him of that of a predatory animal or bird, with its fierce eyes, thin, hard lips and aquiline nose. Nor, in his estimation, did the obvious paint and powder, the extreme–fashioned satin gown, and the profusion of jewellery which she wore, do anything to mitigate the unfavourable impression received at first sight of her face. … Really the last person one would have expected to find in charge of a Home…. Nor was Macteith's greeting of "Hullo, Fifi, my dear! Brought some of the Boys along," calculated to allay a growing suspicion that this was not really a Home at all.

Entering the drawing–room with the rest, Bertram beheld a bevy of ladies sitting in an almost perfect circle, each with a vacant chair beside her. Some of them were young, and some of them presumably had been. All were in evening dress and in the exaggerated extreme of fashion. All seemed to be painted and powdered, and all looked tired and haggard. Another attribute common to the whole party was that they all seemed to be foreigners—judging by their accents as they welcomed Macteith and some of the others as old acquaintances.

Bertram liked the look of these ladies as little as he did that of the person addressed as "Fifi," and he hoped that the party would not remain at the house long. He was tired, and he felt thoroughly uncomfortable, as noisy horse–play and badinage began, and waxed in volume and pungency. A servant, unbidden, entered with a tray on which stood three bottles of champagne and a number of glasses. He noticed that the bottles had been opened, that the corks and gold–foil looked weary and experienced, and that the wine, when poured out, was singularly devoid of bubbles and froth. He wished he had not come. . . . He did not want to drink alleged champagne at midnight…. There was no music, and the people were of more than doubtful breeding, taste and manners…. Macteith had actually got his arm round the waist of one woman, and she was patting his cheek as she gazed into his eyes. Another pair exchanged a kiss before his astonished gaze. He decided to walk out of the house, and was about to do so when the girl nearest to him seized his hand and said: "You seet daown 'ere an' spik to me, sare," as she pulled him towards the chair that stood vacant beside her. In an agony of embarrassment born of a great desire to refuse to stay another minute, and a somewhat unnecessary horror of hurting the young lady's feelings by a refusal, he seated himself with the remark: "Merci, mam'selle—mais il se fait tard. Il est sur les une heure … " as she appeared to be a French woman.

"Laissez donc!" was the reply. "Il est l'heure du berger," a remark the point of which he missed entirely. Finding that he knew French, she rattled on gaily in that tongue, until Bertram asked her from what part of France she came. On learning that she was from Alais in Provence, he talked of Arles, Nismes, Beaucaire, Tarascon, Avignon and the neighbourhood, thinking to please her, until, to his utter amazement and horror, she turned upon him with a vile, spitting oath, bade him be silent, and then burst into tears. Feeling more shocked, unhappy and miserable than he had ever felt before, he begged the girl to accept his regrets and apologies—as well as his farewell—and to tell him if he could in any way compensate her for the unintentional hurt he had somehow inflicted.

On her sullen reply of "Argent comptant porte médecine," Bertram dropped a fifty rupee note into her lap and literally fled from the house….

… Yes—a rotten night with a beastly anti–climax to the wonderful day on which he had received … *he*, of all people in the world! … had received orders to proceed to the Front…. Bertram Greene on Active Service! How could he have the impudence—and it all began again and was revolved once more in his weary mind….

Dawn brought something of hope and a little peace to the perturbed soul of the over–anxious boy.

Chapter IV

Terra Marique Jactatus

As he arrayed himself in all his war–paint, after his sleepless and unhappy night, Bertram felt feverish, and afraid. His head throbbed violently, and he had that distressing sensation of being remorselessly urged on, fatedly fury–driven and compelled to do all things with terrible haste and hurry.

Excitement, anxiety, sleeplessness and the conflicting emotions of hope and fear, were taking their toll of the nervous energy and vitality of the over–civilised youth.

He felt alarmed at his own alarm, and anxious about his own anxiety—and feared that, at this rate, he would be worn out before he began, a physical and mental wreck, fitter for a hospital–ship than a troop–ship, before ever he started.

"The lad's over–engined for his beam," observed Murray to himself, as he lay on his camp cot, drinking his *choti hazri* tea, and watching Bertram, who, with white face and trembling fingers, stood making more haste than speed, as he fumbled with straps and buckles. "Take it easy, my son," he said kindly. "There's tons of time, and then some. I'll see you're not late…."

"Thanks, Murray," replied Bertram, "but—"

"Here—take those belts off at once," interrupted the Adjutant. "Take the lot off and lie down again—and smoke this cigarette…. *At once*, d'ye hear?" and the tone was such that Bertram complied without comment. He sank on to the camp–bed, swung up his long legs, with their heavy boots, shorts, and puttees and puffed luxuriously. He had intended to be a non–smoker as well as a teetotaller, now that he was "mobilised," but it would be as well to obey Murray now and begin his abstinence from tobacco when he got on board. He lay and smoked obediently, and soon felt, if not better, at least calmer, cooler and quieter.

"Blooming old tub won't start till to–night—you see'f she does," said Murray. "Sort of thing we always do in the Army…. *Always*…. Harry and hurry everybody on parade at seven, to catch a boat that doesn't profess to sail till two, and probably won't actually do it till midnight."

"I should die of shame if I were late for my first parade," said Bertram anxiously.

"You'd die of the Colonel, if you didn't of shame," was the reply…. "I'll see you're not late. You take things a bit easier, my son. Your King and Country want you in East Africa, not in a lunatic asylum—"

"*Pappa*! *What part did you take in the Great War*?" squeaked a falsetto voice from the door, and looking up, Bertram beheld Lieutenant Bludyer, always merry and bright, arrayed in crimson, scarlet–frogged pyjama coat, and pink pyjama trousers. On his feet were vermilion velvet slippers.

"I'll take a leading part in your dirty death," said the Adjutant, turning to the speaker, or squeaker.

"Thought this might be useful, Greene," continued Bludyer in his natural voice, as he handed Bertram a slab of thin khaki linen and a conical cap of a kind of gilded corduroy. "Make yourself a regimental *puggri* in the day of battle. Put the cap on your nut and wind the turban over it. … Bloke with a helmet and a white face hasn't an earthly, advancing with a line of Sepoys in *puggris*. The enemy give him their united attention until he is outed...."

"Oh, thanks, awfully, Bludyer," began Bertram.

"So go dirty till your face is like Murray's, grow a hoary, hairy beard, an' wear a turban on your fat head," continued Bludyer. "Your orderly could do it on for you, so that it wouldn't all come down when you waggled...."

"Thanks, most awfully. It's exceedingly kind of you, Bludyer," acknowledged Bertram, and proceeded to stuff the things into his haversack.

"Wow! Wow!" ejaculated Bludyer. "Nice–mannered lad and well brought up, ain't he, Randolph Murray?" and seating himself on that officer's bed, he proceeded to use the tea–cosy as a foot–warmer, the morning being chilly.

The Adjutant arose and proceeded to dress.

"Devil admire me!" he suddenly shouted, pointing at Bertram. "Look at that infernal lazy swine! Did you ever see anything like it, Bludyer? Lying hogging there, lolling and loafing in bed, as if he had all day to finish nothing in! ... Here, get up, you idle hound, and earn your living. Dress for parade, if you can do nothing else."

And Bertram gathered that he might now get on with his preparations.

"Yes," added Bludyer, "you really ought to get on with the war, Greene. *Isn't* he a devil–may–care fellow, Murray? He don't give a damn if it snows," and adding that it was his flute–night at the Mission, and he now must go, the young gentleman remained seated where he was.

"You aren't hurrying a bit, Greene," he remarked, after eyeing Bertram critically for a few minutes. "He won't prosper and grow rich like that, will he, Randolph Murray? That is not how the Virtuous Apprentice got on so nicely, and married his master's aunt.... No.... And Samuel Smiles was never late for parade—of that I'm quite certain. No. '*Self*–help' was *his* motto, and the devil take the other fellow.... Let me fasten that for you. This strap goes under not over...." And, with his experienced assistance, Bertram was soon ready, and feeling like a trussed fowl and a Christmas–tree combined, by the time he had festooned about him his sword, revolver, full ammunition–pouches, field–glasses, water–bottle, belt–haversack, large haversack, map–case, compass–pouch, whistle–lanyard, revolver–lanyard, rolled cape, and the various belts, straps and braces connected with these articles.

By the time the last buckle was fastened, he longed to take the whole lot off again for a few minutes, and have a really comfortable breathe. (But he *did* wish Miranda Walsingham could see him.)

* * * * *

In a corner of the parade–ground stood the Hundred, the selected draft which was to proceed to Africa to fill the gaps that war had torn in the ranks of the Hundred and Ninety–Eighth. On their flank the regimental band was drawn up in readiness to play them to the docks. The men wore khaki turbans, tunics, shorts, puttees and hob–nailed boots, and carried only haversacks, water–bottles, bandoliers, rifles and bayonets. The rest of their kit, each man's done up in a neat bundle inside his waterproof ground–sheet and striped cotton sleeping–*dhurrie*, had gone on in bullock–carts to await them at the wharf.

Around the Hundred stood or squatted the remainder of the battalion, in every kind and degree of dress and undress. Occasionally one of these would arise and go unto his pal in the ranks, fall upon his neck, embrace him once again, shake both his hands alternately, and then return to the eligible site whence, squatting on his heels, he could feast his eyes upon his *bhai*, his brother, his friend, so soon to be torn from him.... As the officers approached, these spectators fell back. Bertram's heart beat so violently that he feared the others would hear it. Was he going to have "palpitations" and faint, or throw a fit or something? He was very white, and felt very ill. Was his ignorance and incompetence to be exposed and manifested now? ...

"Look fierce and take over charge, my son," said the Adjutant, as the small party of officers came in front of the draft.

"Company!" shouted Bertram, "Shun!"

That was all right. He had hit the note nicely, and his voice had fairly boomed. He had heard that men judge a new officer by his voice, more than anything.

The Hundred sprang to attention, and Bertram, accompanied by the Adjutant and Macteith, walked slowly down the front rank and up the rear, doing his best to look as though he were critically and carefully noting certain points, and assuring himself that certain essentials were in order. He was glad that he had not suddenly to answer such a question as "*What* exactly are you peering at and looking for?" He wished he had sufficient Hindustani to ask a stern but not unkindly question here and there, or to make an occasional comment in the manner of one from whom no military thing is hid. He suddenly remembered that he knew the Hindustani for "How old are you?" so he asked this question of a man whose orange–coloured beard would obviously have been white but for henna dye. Not in the least understanding the man's reply, he remarked "H'm!" in excellent imitation of the Colonel, and passed on.

"Not the absolute pick of the regiment, I should think, are they?" he remarked to Murray, as they returned to the front of the company.

"They are not," he said.

"Pretty old, some of them," added Bertram, who was privately hoping that he did not look such a fraudulent Ass as he felt.

Major Fordinghame strolled up and returned the salutes of the group of officers.

"This experienced officer thinks the draft is not the pure cream of the regiment, Major," said Murray, indicating Bertram.

"Fancy that, now," replied Major Fordinghame, and Bertram blushed hotly.

"I thought some of them seemed rather old, sir," he said, "but—er—perhaps old soldiers are better than young ones?"

"It's a matter of taste—as the monkey said when he chewed his father's ear," murmured Bludyer.

Silence fell upon the little group.

"And both have their draw–backs—as the monkey said when she pulled her twins' tails," he added pensively.

Bertram wondered what he had better do next.

The Native Officer of the draft came hurrying up, and saluted. Another Hindustani sentence floated into Bertram's mind. "You are late, Jemadar Sahib," said he, severely.

Jemadar Hassan Ali poured forth a torrent of excuse or explanation which Bertram could not follow.

"What do you do if a Havildar or Naik or Sepoy is late for parade?" he asked, or attempted to ask, in slow and barbarous Hindustani.

Another torrent of verbiage, scarcely a word of which was intelligible to him.

He put on a hard, cold and haughty look, or attempted to do so, and kept, perforce, an eloquent but chilling silence. Murray and the Major exchanged glances.

"Greene Sahib is *very* particular and *very* strict, Jemadar Sahib," said the Major. "You had better bear it in mind, and tell the men too. He'll stand no sort of nonsense from anybody. You'll find him very kind so long as he is satisfied, but if he isn't—well!" and the Major shrugged his shoulders expressively.

Bertram looked gratefully at the Major (for he understood "Englishman's Hindustani"), and as sternly as he could at the Jemadar, who saluted again and retired.

The Colonel rode up, and the officers sprang to attention.

"Everything ready, sir," said the Adjutant. "They can march off when you like."

"H'm!" said the Colonel, and stared at Bertram as though he honestly and unaffectedly did wonder why God made such things. He then wheeled his horse towards the waiting Hundred. "Men of the Hundred and Ninety–Ninth," said he in faultless Hindustani, "you are now going across the Black Water to fight the enemies of the King Emperor, and of yourselves. They would like to conquer your country and oppress you. You go to fight for your own homes and children, as well as for your Emperor. Bring honour to your regiment and yourselves. Show the *Germanis* and their *Hubshis* [9] what Indian Sepoys can do—both in time of battle and in time of hunger, thirst, and hardship. Before God I say I would give anything to come with you, but I have to do my duty here—for the present. We may meet again in Africa. Good–bye. Good luck.... Good–bye...." The Jemadar called for three cheers for the Colonel, and the Hundred lustily cried: "*'Eep, 'Eep, 'Oorayee.*" The remainder of the regiment joined in, and then cheered the Hundred. Meanwhile, the Colonel turned to Bertram.

"Good–by, young Greene. Good luck," he said, and leaning from his horse, wrung Bertram's hand as though it had been that of his only son.

Similarly did the others, with minor differences.

"Well—it's useless to weep these unavailing tears," sobbed Bludyer. "There's an end to everything, as the monkey said when he seized the tip of his mother's nose...."

"Farewell, my blue–nosed, golden–eyed, curly–eared Mother's Darling," said Macteith.

"Good luck, sonny. Write and let me know how you get on," said Murray. "You'll do. You've got the guts all right, and you'll very soon get the hang of things...."

"March 'em off, now," he added. "Chuck a chest, and don't give a damn for anybody," and Bertram carefully collected his voice, swallowed a kind of lump in his throat, bade his wildly beating heart be still, gave thought to the drill–book, and roared:

"Company! … *'Shun*! … Slope *Arms*! … Form *fours*! … *Right*! … Quick *march*!"—the band struck up—and they were off.

Yes, he, Bertram Greene, pale clerkly person, poet and æsthete, was marching proudly, in full military attire, at the head of a hundred fighting–men—marching to the inspiring strains of the regimental band, to where the trooper waited on the tide! If his father could only see him! He was happy as he had never been before in his life, and he was proud as he never had been before… . If Miranda could only see him! He, Bertram Greene, was actually marching to war, with sword on thigh, and head held high, in sole command of a hundred trained fighting–men!

His heart beat very fast, but without pain now, and he was, for the moment, free of his crushing sense of inadequacy, inexperience and unworthiness. He was only conscious of a great pride, a great hope, and a great determination to be worthy, so far as in him lay the power, of his high fate….

No man forgets his first march at the head of his own force, if he forgets his first march in uniform. For Bertram this was both. It was his first march in uniform, and he was in whole and sole control of this party—like a Centurion of old tramping the Roman Road at the head of his hundred Legionaries—and Bertram felt he would not forget it if he lived till his years equalled the number of his men.

It was not a very long march, and it was certainly not a very picturesque one—along the cobbled Dock Road, with its almost innumerable cotton–laden bullock–carts—but Bertram trod on air through a golden dream city and was exalted, brother to the Knights of Arthur who quested for the Grail and went about to right the wrong and to succour the oppressed….

Arrived at the dock–gates, he was met and guided aright, by a brassarded myrmidon of the Embarkation Staff Officer, to where His Majesty's Transport *Elymas* lay in her basin beside a vast shed–covered wharf.

Beneath this shed, Bertram halted his men, turned them into line, and bade them pile arms, fall out, and sit them down in close proximity to their rifles.

Leaving the Jemadar in charge, he then went up the gangway of the *Elymas* in search of the said Embarkation Staff Officer, who, he had been told, would allot him and his men their quarters on the ship. As he gazed around the deserted forward well–deck, he saw an officer, who wore a lettered red band round his arm, hurrying towards him along the promenade deck, his hands full of papers, a pencil in his mouth, and a careworn, worried look upon his face.

"You Greene, by any chance?" he called, as he ran sideway down the narrow ladder from the upper deck.

"Yes, sir," replied Bertram, saluting as he perceived that the officer was a captain. "Just arrived with a draft of a hundred men from the Hundred and Ninety–Ninth," he added proudly.

"Good dog," was the reply, "keep the perishers out of it for a bit till I'm ready…. Better come with me now though, and I'll show you, *one*, where they're to put their rifles; *two*, where they're to put themselves; *three*, where they will do their beastly cooking; and *four*, where you will doss down yourself…. Don't let there be any mistakes, because there are simply millions more coming," and he led the way to a companion hatch in the after well–deck, and clattered down a ladder into the bowels of the ship, Bertram following him in his twists and turns with a growing sense of bewilderment.

He was very glad to hear that he and his merry men were not to have the ship to themselves, for there were a thousand and one points that he would be very glad to be able to refer to the decision of Authority, or the advice of Experience.

The Embarkation Officer, dripping and soaked and sodden with perspiration, as was Bertram himself, wound his devious way, along narrow passages, ladders and tunnels, to a kind of cage–like cloak–room fitted with racks.

"Your men'll come here in single file, by the way we have come," said he, "enter this armoury one by one, leave their rifles on these racks, and go up that ladder to the deck above, and round to the ladder leading out on the forward well–deck. You'll have to explain it carefully, and shepherd 'm along too, or there'll be a jam and loss of life and—worse—loss of time.... In the early days we managed badly on one occasion and got a crowd of Sikhs pushing against a crowd of Pathans...." He then led the disintegrating Bertram by devious paths to a dark oven–like and smelly place (which Bertram mentally labelled "the horizontal section of the fo'c'sle, three storeys down") in which the Hundred were to live, or to die—poor devils! There would hardly be standing room—and thence to the scene of their culinary labours. Lastly, when the bewildered youth was again feeling very ill, the Embarkation Officer retraced his steps, showed him certain water–taps for the use of his men, and led the way up and out to the blessed light of day, fresh air, and the comparative coolness of the deck. "Your cabin's along here," said he, entering a long corridor that debouched on to the well–deck. "Let's see, Number 43, I think. Yes. A two–berth cabin to yourself—and last trip we had three generals in a one–berth cabin, four colonels in a bath at once, and five common officers on top of one another in each chair at table.... Fact—I assure you.... Go in and chuck away all that upholstery—you can run about in your shirt–sleeves now, or naked if you like, so long as you wear a helmet to show you are in uniform.... Bye–bye—be a good boy," and he bustled away.

Bertram thankfully took the Embarkation Officer's advice, and cast off all impedimenta until he was clad only in khaki shirt, shorts, puttees and boots. He thought he could enter into the feelings of a butterfly as it emerges from the constricting folds of its cocoon.

He sat down for a minute on the white bed prepared for his occupation. The other was cumbered with his valise, sack, and strapped bundle, which had come down on the first of the bullock–carts and been brought on board at once. He looked round the well–appointed, spotless cabin, with its white paint and mahogany fittings, electric fans and lights. That one just beside his pillow would be jolly for reading in bed. Anyhow, he'd have a comfortable and restful voyage. What a blessing that he had a cabin to himself, and what a pity that the voyage took only about ten days.... Would life on a troop–ship be a thing of disciplined strenuousness, or would it be just a perfectly slack time for everybody? ... It should be easy for him to hide his ignorance while on board—there couldn't be very much in the way of drill.... How his head throbbed, and how seedy and tired he felt! ... He lay back on his bed and then sprang up in alarm and horror at what he had done. A pretty way to commence his Active Service!—and, putting on his heavy and uncomfortable helmet, he hurried to the wharf.

Going down the gangway, he again encountered the Embarkation Officer.

"Better let your men file on board with their rifles first, and then off again for their kits and bedding, and then back again to the quarters I showed you. Having pegged out their claims there, and each man hung his traps on the peg above his sleeping–mat, they can go up on the after well–deck and absolutely nowhere else. See? And no man to leave the ship again, on any pretence whatever. Got it?"

"Yes, sir," replied Bertram, and privately wondered if he would even find his way again to that cage–like cloak–room in the hold, and that "horizontal section of the fo'c'sle three storeys down."

But he *must* do this, his very first job, absolutely correctly, and without any bungling and footling. He must imagine that he was going in for an examination again—an examination this time in quite a new subject, "The art of getting men on board a ship, bedding them down, each with his own bundle of kit, in one place, and storing their rifles in another, without confusion or loss of time." *Quite* a new subject, and one in which previous studies, Classics, Literature, Philosophy, Art, were not going to be of any great value.

Perhaps it would be as well to take the Jemadar, Havildars and Naiks on a personally conducted tour to the armoury, quarters, cooking–places and taps, and explain the *modus operandi* to them as well as he could. One can do a good deal to eke out a scanty knowledge of the vernacular by means of signs and wonders—though sometimes one makes the signs and the other person wonders....

Returning to the oven–like shed, resonant with the piercing howls of *byle–ghari–wallas*, [10] coolies, Lascars and overseers; the racking rattle and clang and clatter of chains, cranes, derricks and donkey–engines; the crashing of iron–bound wheels over cobble–stones, and the general pandemonium of a busy wharf, he beckoned the Jemadar to him and made him understand that he wanted a couple of Havildars and four Naiks to accompany him on board.

Suddenly he had a bright idea. (Good old drill–book and retentive memory of things read, heard, or seen!) ... "Why have you set no sentry over the arms, Jemadar Sahib? It should not be necessary for me to have to give the order," he said as well as he could in his halting Hindustani.

The Jemadar looked annoyed—and distinctly felt as he looked. Half the men had heard the reproof. He, an old soldier of fifteen years' service, to be set right by a child like this! And the annoying part of it was that the amateur was right! Of course he should have put a sentry over the arms. It was probably the first time he had omitted to do so, when necessary, since he had first held authority ... and he raged inwardly. There are few things that annoy an Indian more than to be "told off" before subordinates, particularly when he is obviously in the wrong. Was this youthful Greene Sahib a person of more knowledge and experience than had been reported by the Adjutant's Office *babu*? The *babu* had certainly described him as one whom the other officers laughed at for his ignorance and inexperience. Had not the worthy Chatterji Chuckerbutti related in detail how Macteith Sahib had called upon his gods and feigned great sickness after offensively examining Greene Sahib through his field–glasses? Strange and unfathomable are the ways of Sahibs, and perhaps the true inwardness of the incident had been quite otherwise? It might have been an honorific ceremony, in fact, and Macteith Sahib might have feigned sickness at his own unworthiness, according to etiquette? ... After all, the military salute itself is only a motion simulating the shading of one's eyes from the effulgent glory of the person one salutes; and the Oriental bowing and touching the forehead is only a motion simulating taking up dust and putting it on one's head.... Yes—the *babu* may have been wrong, and Macteith Sahib may really have been acclaiming Greene Sahib his superior, and declaring his own miserable unworthiness.... One never knew with Sahibs. Their minds are unreadable, and one can never get at what they are thinking, or grasp their point of view. One could only rest assured that there is always method in their madness—that they are clever as devils, brave as lions, and—averse from giving commissions as lieutenants, captains, majors, and colonels to Indian Native Officers...

"Get a move on, Jemadar Sahib," said the voice of Greene Sahib curtly, in English, and the Jemadar bustled off to set the sentry and call the Havildars and Naiks—rage in his heart....

More easily than he had expected, Bertram found his way, at the head of the party, to the required places, and showed the Jemadar and Non–commissioned Officers how the men should come and depart, in such manner as to avoid hindering each other and to obviate the possibility of a jam.

The Jemadar began to ask questions, and Bertram began to dislike the Jemadar. He was a talker, and appeared to be what schoolboys call "tricky." He knew that Bertram had very little Hindustani, and seemed anxious to increase the obviousness of the fact.

Bertram felt unhappy and uncomfortable. He wished to be perfectly courteous to him as a Native Officer, but it would not do to let the man mistake politeness for weakness, and inexperience for inefficiency.... Was there a faint gleam of a grin on the fellow's face as he said: "I do not understand," at the end of Bertram's attempt at explanation?

"Do *you* understand?" the latter said, suddenly, turning to the senior Havildar, the man who had turned out the Guard for him on his first approach to the Lines on that recent day that seemed so long ago.

"*Han*, [11] *Sahib*," replied the man instantly and readily. "*Béshak*!" [12]

"Then you'd better explain to the Jemadar Sahib, who does not," said Bertram with a click of his jaw, as he turned to depart.

The Jemadar hastened to explain that he *fully* understood, as Bertram strode off. Apparently complete apprehension had come as soon as he realised that his dullness was to be enlightened by the explanation of the quicker–witted Havildar. He gave that innocent and unfortunate man a look of bitter hatred, and, as he followed Bertram, he ground his teeth. Havildar Afzul Khan Ishak should live to learn the extreme unwisdom of understanding things that Jemadar Hassan Ali professed not to understand. As for Second–Lieutenant Greene—perhaps he should live to learn the unwisdom of quarrelling with an experienced Native Officer who was the sole channel of communication between that stranger and the Draft at whose head he had been placed by a misguided Sircar....

Returning to the wharf, and conscious that he had a splitting head, a sticky mouth, shaking limbs, sore throat and husky voice, Bertram roared orders to the squatting Sepoys, who sprang up, fell in, unpiled arms, and marched in file up the gangway and down into the bowels of the ship, shepherded and directed by the Non–commissioned Officers whom he had posted at various strategic points. All went well, and, an hour later, his first job was successfully accomplished. His men were on board and "shaking down" in their new quarters. He was free to retire to his cabin, bathe his throbbing head, and lie down for an hour or so.

* * * * *

At about midday he arose refreshed, and went on deck, with the delightful feeling that, his own labours of the moment accomplished, he could look on at the accomplishment of those of others. Excellent! ... And for many days to come he would be free from responsibility and anxiety, he would have a time of rest, recuperation, and fruitful thought and study. ... Throughout the morning detachments of Sepoys of the Indian Army and Imperial Service Troops continued to arrive at the wharf and to embark. Bertram was much interested in a double–company of Gurkhas under a Gurkha Subedar, their yellowish Mongolian faces eloquent of determination, grit, and hardiness.

They contrasted strongly with a company of tall, hairy Sikhs, almost twice their size, man for man, but with evidences of more enthusiasm than discipline in their bearing. Another interesting unit was a band of warriors of very mixed nationality, under a huge Jemadar who looked a picture of fat contentment, his face knowing no other expression than an all–embracing smile. It was whispered later that this unit saw breech–loading rifles for the first time, on board the *Elymas*, having been more familiar, hitherto, with jezails, jingals, match–locks, flintlocks, and blunderbusses. Probably a gross exaggeration, or an invention of Lieutenant Stanner, of the Hundred and Ninety–Eighth, who gave them the name of "The Mixed Pickles."

All three of these detachments were Imperial Service Troops—that is to say, were in the service of various Indian Rajahs—but were of very different value, both the Gurkhas and the Sikhs being as good material as could be found among native troops anywhere in the world.

To Bertram, the picture of the little Gurkha Subedar, the tall Sikh Subedar, and the burly Jemadar of the Mixed Pickles, was a very interesting one, as the three stood together on the wharf, eyeing each other like three strange dogs of totally different breeds—say, a fighting terrier, a wolf–hound and a mastiff.

With a snap and a slick, and a smart "*One two*," a company of British Infantry arrived and embarked. Beside the Mixed Pickles they were as a Navy motor–launch beside a native bunderboat. At them they smiled amusedly, at the Sikhs they stared, and at the Gurkhas they grinned appreciatively.

The news having spread that the *Elymas* would not start until the morrow, various visitors came on board, in search of friends whom they knew to be sailing by her. Captain Stott, R.A.M.C., came over from the *Madras* hospital ship, in search of Colonel Haldon. Murray and Macteith came down to see Stanner, of the Hundred and Ninety–Eighth, and one Terence Brannigan, of the Baluchis....

"Who's the chap on your right, Colonel?" asked Captain Stott, of gentle and kindly old Colonel Haldon at dinner that evening. "Rather an unusual face to be 'in' khaki—or one would have said so before the war," and he indicated Bertram.

"Dunno," was the reply. "Stranger to me. Nice–lookin' boy.... Looks a wee–trifle more like a chaplain than a butcher, as you say," though Captain Stott had not said that at all.

Seeing Bertram talking to Murray and Macteith after dinner, Captain Stott asked the latter who he was, for physiognomy and character–study were a hobby of his.

Macteith told him what he knew, and added: "And they're sending *that* half–baked milksop to British East" (and implied: "While *I*, Lieutenant and Quartermaster Reginald Macteith, remain to kick my heels at the depot.")

Next day the *Elymas* began her voyage, a period of delightful *dolce far niente* that passed like a dream, until one wonderful evening, the palm–clad shores of Africa "arose from out of the azure sea," and, with a great thrill of excitement, hope, anxiety and fear Bertram gazed upon the beautiful scene, as the *Elymas* threaded the lovely Kilindini Creek which divides the Island of Mombasa from the mainland.

---

[9] Woolly ones. Negroes.

[10] Bullock–cart men.

[11] Yes.

[12] Without doubt.

CHAPTER V

Mrs. Stayne-brooker

And on those same palm–clad shores that arose from out the azure sea, an unhappy woman had been expiating, by long years of bitter suffering, in tears and shame and humiliation, the madness of a moment....

Mrs. Stayne–Brooker's life in German East Africa was, if possible less happy than her life in the British colony. The men she met in Nairobi, Mombasa, Zanzibar, Witu or Lamu, though by no means all gentlemen, all treated her as a gentlewoman; while the men she met in Dar–es–Salaam, Tanga, Tabora, Lindi or Bukoba, whether "gentlemen" or otherwise, did not. In British East Africa her husband was treated by planters, Government officials, sportsmen, and Army men, as the popular and cheery old Charlie Stayne–Brooker—a good man in the club–bar, card–room and billiard–room, on the racecourse, at the tent club, and on shooting trips. With several Assistant District Commissioners and officers of the King's African Rifles he was very intimate. In German East Africa he was treated differently—in a way difficult to define. It was as though he were a person of importance, but *déclassé* and contemptible, and this impression she gained in spite of her knowing no German (a condition of ignorance upon which her husband insisted). The average German official and officer, whether of the exiled Junker class, or of plebeian origin, she loathed—partly because they seemed to consider her "fair game," and made love to her, in more or less broken English, without shame or cessation. Nor did it make life easier for the poor lady that her husband appeared to take delight in the fact. She wondered whether this was due to pride in seeing a possession of his coveted by his "high–well–born," and other, compatriots, or to a desire to keep ever before her eyes a realisation of what her fate would be if he cast her off, or she ran away from him.

Worst of all was life in the isolated lonely house on his coffee and rubber plantation, where for months on end she would never see a white face but his, and for weeks on end, when he was away on his mysterious affairs, no white face at all.... And at the bottom of his compound were *bandas*, grass huts, in an enclosure, wherein dwelt native women. ...

One night, in the year 1914, she sat alone in the silent lonely house, thinking of her daughter Eva at Cheltenham, of her happy, if hapless, girlhood in her father's house, of her brief married life with an honourable English gentleman (oh, the contrast!), and wondering how much longer she could bear her punishment... Suddenly and noiselessly appeared in the verandah her husband's chief factotum, head house–boy, and familiar, one Murad, an Arab–Swahili, whom she feared and detested.

"*Bwana* coming," said he shortly, and as noiselessly disappeared.

Going out on to the verandah, she saw her husband and a few "boys" (gun–bearers, porters, and servants) coming through the garden. It was seven weeks since she had seen or heard anything of him.

"Pack," was his greeting, "at once. You start on *safari* to the railway as soon as possible, or sooner. You are going to Mombasa. I have cabled to Eva to come out by the next boat.... P. and O. to Aden, and thence to Mombasa.... She should be here in three weeks or so ... " and he went off to bath and change. At dinner he informed her that she was to settle at Mombasa with Eva, make as many new friends as possible, entertain, and generally be the most English of English matrons with the most English of English daughters—the latter fresh from boarding–school in England.... Dear old Charlie Stayne–Brooker, it was to be known, had gone to Bukoba, to the wonderful sleeping–sickness hospital, for diagnosis of an illness. Nothing serious, really, of course—but one couldn't be too careful when one had trouble with the glands of the neck, and certain other symptoms, after spending some time in that beastly tsetse–fly country.... She was to give the impression that he had made light of it, and quite "taken her in"—wouldn't dream of allowing his wife and daughter to go up there. People were to form the opinion that poor old Charlie might be in a worse way than his wife imagined.

And if such a thing as war broke out; *if* such a thing came to pass, mark you; her house in Mombasa was to be a perfect Home–from–Home for the officers of the British Expeditionary Force which would undoubtedly be dispatched from India. It would almost certainly be the Nth Division from Bombay—so she need not anticipate the pleasure of receiving her late husband and his friends.... Further instructions she would receive in the event of war, but meanwhile, and all the time, her business was to demonstrate the utter Englishness of the Stayne–Brooker family, and to keep her eyes and ears open. What General or Staff–Officer will not "talk" to a beautiful woman—of the right sort? Eh? Ha–Ha! That was her business in Mombasa now—*and ten times more so if war broke out*—to be a beautiful woman—of the right sort, tremendously popular with the people who know things and do things. Moreover, Eva, her daughter, was to be trained right sedulously to be a beautiful woman—of the right sort.... Staff–officers in her pocket. Eh? Ha–Ha! ... And, sick at heart, loving her daughter, loathing her husband, and loathing the unspeakable rôle he would force upon her, Mrs. Stayne–Brooker travelled to Mombasa, met her daughter with mingled joy and terror, happiness and apprehensive misery, and endeavoured to serve two masters—her conscience and her husband.

CHAPTER VI

Mombasa

"If you'd like to go ashore and have a look at Mombasa after tiffin, Mr. Greene," said the fourth officer of the *Elymas* to Bertram, the next morning, as he leant against the rail and gazed at the wonderful palm–forest of the African shore, "some of us are going for a row—to stretch our muscles. We could drop you at the Kilindini *bunder*."

"Many thanks," replied Bertram. "I shall be very much obliged," and he smiled his very attractive and pleasant smile.

This was a welcome offer, for, privately, he hated being taken ashore from a ship by natives of the harbour in which the ship lay. One never knew exactly what to pay the wretches. If one asked what the fare was, they always named some absurd amount, and if one used one's common sense and gave them what seemed a reasonable sum they were inevitably hurt, shocked, disappointed in one, indignantly broken–hearted, and invariably waxed clamorous, protestful, demanding more. It had been the same at Malta, Port Said and Aden on his way out to India. In Bombay harbour he had once gone for a morning sail in a bunderboat, and on their return, the captain of the crew of three had demanded fifteen rupees for a two–hour sail. A pound for two hours in a cranky sailing–boat!—and the scoundrels had followed him up the steps clamouring vociferously, until a native policeman had fallen upon them with blows and curses.... How he wished he was of those men who can give such people their due in such a manner that they receive it in respectful silence, with apparent contentment, if not gratitude. Something in the eye and the set of the jaw, evidently—and so was glad of the fourth officer's kind suggestion.

He would have been still more glad had he heard the fourth officer announce, at table, to his colleagues: "I offered to drop that chap, Lieutenant Greene, at Kilindini this afternoon, when we go for our grind. He can take the tiller–ropes.... I like him the best of the lot—no blooming swank and side about him."

"Yes," agreed the "wireless" operator, "he doesn't talk to you as though he owned the earth, but was really quite pleased to let you stand on it for a bit.... I reckon he'll do all right, though, when he gets–down–to–it with the Huns—if he doesn't get done in...."

And so it came to pass that Bertram was taken ashore that afternoon by some half–dozen officers and officials (including the doctor, the purser, and the Marconi operator) of the *Elymas*—worthy representatives of that ill–paid, little–considered service, that most glorious and beyond–praise, magnificent service, the British Mercantile Marine—and, landing in state upon the soil of the Dark Continent, knew "the pleasure that touches the souls of men landing on strange shores."

Arrived at the top of the stone steps of the Kilindini quay, Bertram encountered Africa in the appropriately representative person of a vast negro gentleman, who wore a red fez cap (or tarboosh), a very long white calico night–dress and an all–embracing smile.

"*Jambo*!" quoth the huge Ethiopian, and further stretched his lips an inch nearer to his ears on either side.

Not being aware that the African "*Jambo*" is equivalent to the Indian "*Salaam*," and means "Greeting and Good Health," or words to that effect, Bertram did not counter with a return "*Jambo*," but nodded pleasantly and said: "Er—good afternoon."

Whereupon the ebon one remarked: "Oh, my God, sah, ole chap, thank you," to show, in the first place, that he quite realised the situation (to wit, Bertram's excusable ignorance of Swahili–Arabic), and that he was himself, fortunately, a fluent English scholar. Bertram stared in amazement at the pleasant–faced, friendly–looking giant.

"*Bwana* will wanting servant, ole chap," continued the negro, "don't it? I am best servant for *Bwana*. Speaking English like hell, sah, please. Waiting here for *Bwana* before long time to come. Good afternoon, thank you, please, Master, by damn, ole chap. Also bringing letter for *Bwana*.... You read, thanks awfully, your mos' obedient servant by damn, oh, God, thank you, sah," and produced a filthy envelope from some inner pocket of the aforementioned night–dress, which, innocent of buttons or trimming, revealed his tremendous bare chest.

Bertram felt uncomfortable, and, for a moment, again wished that he was one of those men–with–an–eye–and–a–jaw who could give a glare, a grunt, and a jerk of the head which would cause the most importunate native to fade unobtrusively away.

On the one hand, he knew it would be folly to engage as a servant the first wandering scoundrel who accosted him and suggested that he should do so; while, on the other, he distinctly liked this man's cheery, smiling face, he realised that servants would probably be at a decided premium, and he recognised the extreme desirability of having a servant, if have one he must, who spoke English, however weird, and understood it when spoken. Should he engage the man then and there? Would he, by so doing, show himself a man of quick decision and prompt action—one of those forceful, incisive men he so admired? Or would he merely be acting foolishly and prematurely, merely exhibiting himself as a rash and unbalanced young ass? Anyhow, he would read the "chits" which the filthy envelope presumably contained. If these were satisfactory, he would tell the man that the matter was under consideration, and that he might look out for him again and hear his decision.

As Bertram surmised, the envelope contained the man's "chits," or testimonials. The first stated that Ali Sloper, the bearer, had been on *safari* with the writer, and had proved to be a good plain cook, a reliable and courageous gun–carrier, a good shot, and an honest, willing worker. The second was written by a woman whose house–boy Ali Suleiman had been for two years in Mombasa, and who stated that she had had worse ones. The third and last was written at the Nairobi Club by a globe–trotting Englishman named Stayne–Brooker, who had employed the man as personal "boy" and headman of porters, on a protracted lion–shooting trip across the Athi and Kapiti Plains and found him intelligent, keen, cheery, and staunch. (*Where had he heard the name Stayne–Brooker before—or had he dreamed it as a child?*) Certainly this fellow was well–recommended, and appeared to be just the man to take as one's personal servant on active service. But *did* one take a servant on active service? One could not stir, or exist, without one in India, and officers took syces and servants with them on frontier campaigns—but Africa is not India.... However, he could soon settle that point by asking.

"I'll think about it," he said, returning the chits. "I shall be coming ashore again to–morrow.... How much pay do you want?"

"Oh, sah! Master not mentioning it!" was the reply of this remarkable person. "Oh, nothing, nothing, sah! *Bwana* offering me forty rupees a mensem, I say 'No, sah! Too much.' ... Master not mention it."

"It might not be half a bad idea to mention it, y'know," said Bertram, smiling and turning to move on.

"Oh, God, sah, thank you, please," replied Ali Sloper, *alias* Ali Suleiman. "I do not wanting forty. I am accepting thirty rupees, sah, and am now your mos' obedient servant by damn from the beginning for ever. And when *Bwana*, loving me still more, can pay more, ole chap. God bless my thank–you soul"—and "fell in" behind Bertram as though prepared to follow him thence to the end of the world or beyond.

Bertram gazed around, and found that he was in a vast yard, two sides of which were occupied by the largest corrugated–iron sheds he had ever seen in his life. One of these appeared to be the Customs shed, and into another a railway wandered. Between two of them, great gates let a white sandy road escape into the Unknown. On the stone quay the heat, shut in and radiated by towering iron sheds, was the greatest he had ever experienced, and he gasped for breath and trickled with perspiration. He devoutly hoped that this was not a fair sample of Africa's normal temperature. Doubtless it would be cooler away from the quay, which, with the iron sheds, seemed to form a Titanic oven for the quick and thorough baking of human beings. It being Sunday afternoon, there were but few such, and those few appeared to be thoroughly enjoying the roasting process, if one might judge from their grinning faces and happy laughter. They were all Africans, and, for the most part, clad in long, clean night–dresses and fez caps. Evidently Ali Sloper or Suleiman was dressed in the height of local fashion. On a bench, by the door of the Customs shed, lounged some big negroes in dark blue tunics and shorts, with blue puttees between bare knees and bare feet. Their tall tarbooshes made them look even taller than they were, and the big brass plates on their belt–buckles shone like gold. Bertram wondered whether the Germans had just such brawny giants in their Imperial African Rifles, and tried to imagine himself defeating one of them in single combat. The effort was a failure.

At the gates was a very different type of person, smarter, quicker, more active and intelligent–looking, a Sikh Sepoy of the local military police. The man sprang to attention and saluted with a soldierly promptness and smartness that were a pleasure to behold.

Outside the dock, the heat was not quite so intense, but the white sandy road, running between high grass and palms, also ran uphill, and, as the perspiration ran down his face, Bertram wished he might discover the vilest, most ramshackle and moth–eaten *tikka–ghari* that ever disgraced the streets of Bombay. That the hope was vain he knew, and that in all the island of Mombasa there is no single beast of burden, thanks to the tsetse fly, whose sting is death to them.... And the Mombasa Club, the Fort, and European quarter were at the opposite side of the island, four miles away, according to report. Where were these trolley–trams of which he had heard? If he had to walk much farther up this hill, his uniform would look as though he had swum ashore in it.

"Master buck up like hell, ole chap, thank you," boomed a voice behind. "Trolley as nearer as be damned please. Niggers make push by Jove to Club, thank God," and turning, Bertram beheld the smiling Ali beaming down upon him as he strolled immediately behind him.

"Go away, you ass," replied the hot and irritated Bertram, only to receive an even broader smile and the assurance that his faithful old servant would never desert him—not after having been his devoted slave since so long a time ago before and for ever more after also. And a minute or two later the weary warfarer came in sight of a very narrow, single tram–line, beside the road. Where this abruptly ended stood a couple of strange vehicles, like small, low railway–trolleys, with wheels the size of dinner–plates. On each trolley was a seat of sufficient length to accommodate two people, and above the bench was a canvas roof or shade, supported by iron rods. From a neighbouring bench sprang four men, also clad in night–dresses and fez caps, who, with strange howls and gesticulations, bore down upon the approaching European.

"*Hapa*, [13] *Bwana*!" they yelled. "*Trolley hapa*," and, for a moment, Bertram thought they would actually seize him and struggle for possession of his body. He determined that if one of the shrieking fiends laid a hand upon him, he would smite him with what violence he might. The heat was certainly affecting his temper. He wondered what it would feel like to strike a man—a thing he had never done in his life. But, on reaching him, the men merely pointed to their respective trolleys and skipped back to them, still pointing, and apparently calling Heaven to witness their subtle excellences and charms.

As Bertram was about to step on to the foremost trolley, the men in charge of the other sprang forward with yelps of anguish, only to receive cause for louder yelps of deeper anguish at the hands of Ali, who, with blows and buffets, drove them before him. Bertram wondered why the pair of them, each as big as their assailant, should flee before him thus. Was it by reason of Ali's greater moral force, juster cause, superior social standing as the follower of a white man, or merely the fact that he took it upon him to be the aggressor. Probably the last. Anyhow—thank Heaven for the gloriously cool and refreshing breeze, caused by the rapid rush of the trolley through the heavy air, as the trolley–"boys" ran it down the decline from the hill–top whence they had started.

As soon as the trolley had gained sufficient momentum, they leapt on to the back of the vehicle, and there clung until it began to slow down again. Up–hill they slowly pushed with terrific grunts, on the level they maintained a good speed, and down–hill the thing rattled, bumped and bounded at a terrific pace, the while Bertram wondered how long it would keep the rails, and precisely what would happen if it jumped them. Had he but known it, there was a foot–brake beneath the seat, which he should have used when going down–hill. 'Twas not for the two specimens of Afric's ebon sons, who perched and clung behind him, to draw his attention to it. Was he not a *Bwana*, a white man, and therefore one who knew all things? And if he wanted to break his neck had he not a right so to do? And if they, too, should be involved in the mighty smash, would not that fact prove quite conclusively that it was their *kismet* to be involved in the smash, and therefore inevitable? Who shall avoid his fate? ... And so, in blissful ignorance, Bertram swooped down–hill in joyous, mad career. He wished the pace were slower at times, for everything was new and strange and most interesting. Native huts, such as he had seen in pictures (labelled "kaffir–kraals") in his early geography book, alternated with official–looking buildings, patches of jungle; gardens of custard–apple, mango, paw–paw, banana, and papai trees; neat and clean police–posts, bungalows, cultivated fields, dense woods and occasional mosques, Arab houses, go–downs, [14] temples, and native infantry "lines."

On the dazzlingly white road (which is made of coral and nothing else) were few people. An occasional Indian Sepoy, a British soldier, an *askari* of the King's African Rifles, an official *peon* with a belt–plate as big as a saucer (and bearing some such legend as *Harbour Police* or *Civil Hospital*), a tall Swahili in the inevitable long night–dress and tarboosh, or a beautifully worked skull cap, a file of native women clad each in a single garment of figured cotton which extended from arm–pit to ankle, leaving the arms and shoulders bare. The hairdressing of these ladies interested Bertram, for each head displayed not one, but a dozen, partings, running from the forehead to the neck, and suggesting the seams on a football. At the end of each parting was a brief pigtail bound with wire. Bertram wondered why these women always walked one behind the other in single file, and decided that it was an inherited and unconscious instinct implanted by a few thousand years of use of narrow jungle–paths from which they dared not stray as the armed men–folk did....

After half an hour or so of travelling this thrillingly interesting road, Bertram perceived that they were drawing near to the busy haunts of men. From a church, a congregation of Goanese or else African–Portuguese was pouring. The scene was a very Indian one—the women, with their dusky faces and long muslin veils worn *sari*–fashion over their European dresses of cotton or satin; the men, with their rusty black suits or cotton coats and trousers and European hats or solar *topis*. One very venerable gentleman, whose ancestors certainly numbered more Africans than Portuguese, wore a golfing suit (complete, except for the stockings), huge hob–nailed boots, and an over–small straw–yard with a gay ribbon. A fine upstanding specimen of the race, obviously the idol of his young wife, who walked beside him with her adoring gaze fixed upon his shining face, began well with an authentic silk hat, continued excellently with a swallow–tailed morning–coat, white waistcoat, high collar and black satin tie, but fell away from these high achievements with a pair of tight short flannel tennis–trousers, grey Army socks, and white canvas shoes.

"An idol with feet of pipe–clay," smiled Bertram to himself, as his chariot drove heavily through the throng, and his charioteers howled "*Semeele*! *Semeele*!" at the tops of their voices.

Soon the tram–line branched and bifurcated, and tributary lines joined it from garden–enclosed bungalows and side turnings. Later he discovered that every private house has its own private tram–line running from its front door down its drive out to the main line in the street, and that, in Mombasa, one keeps one's own trolley for use on the public line, as elsewhere one keeps one's own carriage or motor–car.

On, past the Grand Hotel, a stucco building of two storeys, went the rumbling, rattling vehicle, past a fine public garden and blindingly white stucco houses that lined the blindingly white coral road, across a public square adorned with flowering shrubs and trees, to where arose a vast grey pile, the ancient blood–drenched Portuguese fort, and a narrow–streeted, whitewashed town of tall houses and low shops began.

Here the trolley–boys halted, and Bertram found himself at the entrance of the garden of the Mombasa Club, which nestles in the shadow of its mighty neighbour, the Fort—where once resided the Portuguese Governor and the garrison that defied the Arab and kept "the Island of Blood" for Portugal, and where now reside the Prison Governor and the convicts that include the Arab, and keep the public gardens for the public.

Boldly entering the Club, Bertram left his card on the Secretary and Members (otherwise stuck it on a green–baize board devoted to that purpose), and commenced a tour of inspection of the almost empty building. Evidently Society did not focus itself until the cool of the evening, in Africa as in India, and evidently this club very closely resembled a thousand others across the Indian Ocean from Bombay to Hong Kong, where the Briton congregates in exile. The only difference between this and any "station" club in India appeared to be in the facts that the servants were negroes and the trophies on the walls were different and finer. Magnificent horns, such as India does not produce, alternated with heads of lion and other feral beasts. Later Bertram discovered another difference in that the cheery and hospitable denizens of the Mombasa Club were, on the whole, a thirstier race than those of the average Indian club, and prone to expect and desire an equal thirst in one their guest. He decided that it was merely a matter of climate—a question of greater humidity.

Emerging from an airy and spacious upstairs bar–room on to a vast verandah, his breath was taken away by the beauty of the scene that met his eye, a scene whose charm lay chiefly in its colouring, in the wonderful sapphire blue of the strip of sea that lay between the low cliff, on which the club was built, and the bold headland of the opposite shore of the mainland, the vivid emerald green of the cocoa–palms that clothed that same headland, the golden clouds, the snowy white–horses into which the wind (which is always found in this spot and nowhere else in Mombasa) whipped the wavelets of the tide–rip, the mauve–grey distances of the Indian Ocean, with its wine–dark cloud–shadows, the brown–grey of the hoary fort (built entirely of coral), the rich red of tiled roofs, the vivid splashes of red, orange, yellow and purple from flowering vine and tree and shrub—a wonderful colour–scheme enhanced and intensified by the dazzling brightness of the sun and the crystal clearness of the limpid, humid air.... And in such surroundings Man had earned the title of "The Island of Blood" for the beautiful place—and, once again, as in those barbarous far–off days of Arab and Portuguese, the shedding of blood was the burden of his song and the high end and aim of his existence.... Bertram sank into a long chair, put his feet up on the mahogany leg–rests, and slaked the colour–thirst of his æsthetic soul with quiet, joyous thankfulness.... Beautiful! ...

What would his father say when he knew that his son was at the Front? …

What was Miranda doing? Nursing, probably…. What would *she* say when she knew that he was at the Front? … Dear old Miranda….

Where had he heard the name, *Stayne–Brooker*, before? *Had* he dreamed it in a nightmare as a child—or had he heard it mentioned in hushed accents of grief and horror by the "grown–ups" at Leighcombe Priory? … Some newspaper case perhaps…. He had certainly heard it before. … He closed his eyes….

A woman strolled by with a selection of magazines in her hand, and took a chair that commanded a view of his. Presently she noticed him…. A new–comer evidently, or she would have seen him before…. What an exceedingly nice face he had—refined, delicate…. Involuntarily she contrasted it with the face of the evil and sensual satyr to whom she was married…. She would like to talk to him….

Bertram opened his eyes, and Mrs. Stayne–Brooker became absorbed in the pages of her magazine….

What a beautiful face she had, and *how* sad and weary she looked … drawn and worried and anxious…. Had she perhaps a beloved husband in the fighting–line somewhere? He would like to talk to her—she looked so kind and so unhappy…. A girl, whose face he did not see, came and called her away…

---

[13] Here.

[14] Store–sheds.

Chapter VII

The Mombasa Club

As Bertram lay drinking in the beauty of the scene, the Club began to fill, and more particularly that part of it devoted to the dispensation and consumption of assorted alcoholic beverages. Almost everybody was in uniform, the majority in that of the Indian Army (as there was a large base camp of the Indian Expeditionary Force at Kilindini), and the remainder in those of British regiments, the Navy, the Royal Indian Marine, the Royal Engineers, the Royal Army Medical Corps, Artillery, local Volunteer Corps, and the "Legion of Frontiersmen." A few ladies adorned the lawn and verandahs. Two large and weather–beaten but unascetic–looking men of middle age sat them down in chairs which stood near to that of Bertram. They were clad in khaki tunics, shorts and puttees, and bore the legend "C.C." in letters of brass on each shoulder–strap.

"Hullo!" said the taller of them to Bertram, who was wondering what "C.C." might mean. "Just come ashore from the *Elymas*? Have a drink?"

"Yes," replied he; "just landed.... Thanks—may I have a lime–squash?"

"What the devil's that?" asked the other, and both men regarded him seriously and with a kind of shocked interest. "Never heard of it."

"Don't think they keep it here," put in the shorter of the two men. "How d'you make it?"

"Lemon–juice, soda–water, and sugar," replied Bertram, and felt that he was blushing in a childish and absurd manner.

Both men shook their heads, more in sorrow than in anger. They looked at each other, as might two physicians at the bedside of one whose folly has brought him to a parlous pass.

"Quite new to Africa?" enquired the taller.

"Yes. Quite," confessed Bertram.

"Ah! Well, let me give you a word of advice then," continued the man. "*Don't touch dangerous drinks*. Avoid all harmful liquor as you would poison. It is poison, in this climate. Drink is the curse of Africa. It makes the place the White Man's Grave. You can't be too careful.... Can you, Piggy?" he added, turning to his friend.

"Quite right, Bill," replied "Piggy," as he rang a little bell that stood on a neighbouring table. "Let's have a 'Devil's Own' cocktail and then some beer for a start, shall we? ... No—can't be too careful.... Look at me f'r example. Been in the country quarter of a century, an' never exceeded once! Never *tasted* it, in fact."

"What—alcohol?" enquired Bertram.

"No.... I was talking about harmful liquor," replied Piggy patiently. "Things like—*what* did you call it? ... Chalk–squash?"

"Lime–squash," admitted Bertram with another glowing blush.

"Give it up, Sonny, give it up," put in Bill. "Turn over a new leaf and start afresh. Make up your mind that, Heaven helping you, you'll never touch a drop of the accursed poison again, but forswear slops and live cleanly; totally abstaining from—what is it?—soda–crunch?—fruit–juice, ginger–beer, lemonade, toast water, barley water, dirty water, raspberryade, and all such filthy decoctions and inventions…."

"Yes—give the country a chance," interrupted Piggy. "Climate's all right if you'll take reasonable care and live moderately," and he impatiently rang the little bell again. "'Course, if you *want* to be ill and come to an early and dishonourable grave, drink all the rot–gut you can lay hands on—and break your mother's heart…."

Piggy lay back in his chair and gazed pensively at the ceiling. So did Bill. Bertram felt uncomfortable. "Dear, dear, dear!" murmured Bill, between a sigh and a grunt. "Chalk–powder and lemonade! … what a nerve! … Patient, unrecognised, unrewarded heroism. . . ."

"Merciful Heaven," whispered Piggy, "slaked–lime and ginger–beer! . . What rash, waste courage and futile bravery…." And suddenly leapt to his feet, swung the bell like a railway porter announcing the advent of a train, and roared "*Boy*!" until a white–clad, white–capped Swahili servant came running.

"*N'jo*, Boy!" he shouted. "Come here! … Lot of lazy, fat *n'gombe*. [15] … Three 'Devil's Own' cocktails, *late hapa*," [16] and as, with a humble "*Verna, Bwana*," the servant hurried to the bar, grumbling.

"And now he'll sit and have a *shauri* [17] with his pals, while we die of thirst in this accursed land of sin and sorrow…. Beastly *shenzis*. [18] … "

"You don't like Africa?" said Bertram, for the sake of something to say.

"Finest country on God's earth…. The *only* country," was the prompt reply.

"I suppose the negro doesn't make a very good servant?" Bertram continued, as Piggy rumbled on in denunciation.

"Finest servants in the world," answered that gentleman. "The *only* servants, in fact…."

"Should I take one with me on active service?" asked Bertram, suddenly remembering Ali Suleiman, *alias* Sloper.

"If you can get one," was the reply. "You'll be lucky if you can…. All snapped up by the officers of the Expeditionary Force, long ago."

"Yes," agreed Bill. "Make all the difference to your comfort if you can get one. Don't take any but a Swahili, though…. You can depend on 'em, in a tight place. The good ones, that is…."

A big, fat, clean–shaven man, dressed in white drill, strolled up to the little group. He reminded Bertram of the portraits of Mr. William Jennings Bryan who had recently visited India, and in three days unhesitatingly given his verdict on the situation, his solution of all political difficulties, and his opinion of the effete Britisher—uttering the final condemnation of that decadent.

"Hello! Hiram Silas P. Pocahantas of Pah," remarked Piggy, with delicate pleasantry, and the big man nodded, smiled, and drew up a chair.

"The drinks are on me, boys," quoth he. "Set 'em up," and bursting into song, more or less tunefully, announced—

"I didn't raise my boy to be a soldier,"

whereat Bill hazarded the opinion that the day might unexpectedly and ruddily dawn when he'd blooming well wish he bally well *had*, and that he could join them in a cocktail if he liked—or he could bung off if he didn't. Apparently William disapproved of the American's attitude, and that of his Government, toward the War and the Allies' part therein; for, on the American's "allowing he would *con*sume a highball" and the liquor arriving, he drank a health to those who are not too proud to fight, to those who do not give themselves airs as the Champions of Freedom, and then stand idly by when Freedom is trampled in the dust, and to those whose Almighty God is not the Almighty Dollar!

Expecting trouble, Bertram was surprised to find that the American was apparently amused, merely murmured "Shucks," and, in the midst of a violent political dissertation from Bill, ably supported by Piggy, went to sleep with a long thin cigar in the corner of his long thin mouth. He had heard it all before.

Bertram found his Devil's Own cocktail an exceedingly potent and unpleasant concoction. He decided that his first meeting with this beverage of the Evil One should be his last, and when Piggy, suddenly sitting up, remarked: "What's wrong with the drinks?" and tinkled the bell, he arose, said a hurried farewell in some confusion, and fled.

"'Tain't right to send a half–baked lad like that to fight the Colonial German," observed Bill, idly watching his retreating form.

"Nope," agreed the American, waking up. "I *was* going to say it's adding insult to injury—but you ain't injured Fritz any, yet, I guess," and went to sleep again before either of the glaring Englishmen could think of a retort.

Ere Bertram left the Club, he heard two pieces of "inside" military information divulged quite openly, and by the Staff itself. As he reached the porch, a lady of fluffy appearance and kittenish demeanour was delaying a red–tabbed captain who appeared to be endeavouring to escape.

"And, oh, Captain, *do* tell me what 'A.S.C.' and 'C.C.' mean," said the lady. "I saw a man with 'A.S.C.' on his shoulders, and there are two officers with 'C.C.,' in the Club.... *Do* you know what it means? I am *so* interested in military matters. Or is it a secret?"

"Oh, no!" replied the staff–officer, as he turned to flee. "'A.S.C.' stands for Ally Sloper's Cavalry, of course, and 'C.C.' for Coolie Catchers.... They are slave–traders, really, with a Government contract for the supply of porters. They get twenty rupees for each slave caught and delivered alive, and ten for a dead one, or one who dies within a week."

"What do they want the *dead* ones for?" she whispered.

"*That* I dare not tell you," replied the officer darkly, and with a rapid salute, departed.

Emerging from the Club garden on to the white road, Bertram gazed around for his trolley–boys and beheld them not.

"All right, ole chap," boomed the voice of Ali, who suddenly appeared beside him. "I looking after *Bwana*. Master going back along shippy? I fetch trolley now and see *Bwana* at Kilindini, thank you, please sah, good God," and he disappeared in the direction of the town, returning a couple of minutes later with the trolley.

"Master not pay these dam' thieves too much, ole chap," he remarked. "Two journey and one hour wait, they ask five rupees. Master give two–an'–a–puck."

"How much is a 'puck'?" enquired Bertram, ever anxious to learn.

"Sah?" returned the puzzled Ali.

"What's a puck?" repeated Bertram, and a smile of bright intelligence engulfed the countenance of the big Swahili.

"Oh, yessah!" he rumbled. "Give two rupee and what *Bwana* call 'puck–in–the–neck.' All the same, biff–on–the–napper, dig in the ribs, smack in the eye, kick–up–the—"

"*Oh*, yes, I see," interrupted Bertram, smiling—but at the back of his amusement was the sad realisation that he was not of the class of *bwanas* who can gracefully, firmly and finally present two–and–a–puck to extortionate and importunate trolley–boys.

He stepped on to the trolley and sat down, as Ali, saluting and salaaming respectfully, again bade him be of good cheer and high heart, as he would see him at Kilindini.

"How will you get there? Would you like to ride?" asked the kind–hearted and considerate Bertram (far too kind–hearted and considerate for the successful handling of black or brown subordinates and inferiors).

"Oh, God, sah, no, please," replied the smiling Ali. "This Swahili slave cannot sit with *Bwana*, and cannot run with damn low trolley–boys. Can running by self though like gentleman, thank you, please," and as the trolley started, added: "So long, ole chap. See Master at Kilindini by running like hell. Ta–ta by damn!" When the trolley had disappeared round a bend of the road, he generously kilted up his flowing night–dress and started off at the long loping trot which the African can maintain over incredible distances.

Arrived at Kilindini, Bertram paid the trolley–boys and discovered that, while they absorbed rupees with the greatest avidity, they looked askance at such fractions thereof as the eight–anna, four–anna, and two–anna piece, poking them over in their palms and finally tendering them back to him with many grunts and shakes of the head as he said:

"Well, you'll *have* to take them, you silly asses," to the uncomprehending coolies. "*That* lot makes a rupee—one half–a–rupee and two quarters, and that lot makes a rupee—four two–anna bits and two four–annas, doesn't it?"

But the men waxed clamorous, and one of them threw his money on the ground with an impudent and offensive gesture. Bertram coloured hotly, and his fist clenched. He hesitated; ought he.... *Smack*! *Thud*! and the man rolled in the dust as Ali Sloper, *alias* Suleiman, sprang upon him, smote him again, and stood over him, pouring forth a terrific torrent of violent vituperation.

As the victim of his swift assault obediently picked up the rejected coins, he turned to Bertram.

“These dam’ niggers not knowing *annas*, sah,” he said, “only *cents*. This not like East Indiaman’s country. Hundred cents making one rupee here. All shopkeepers saying, ‘No damn good’ if master offering annas, please God, sah.”

“Well—I haven’t enough money with me, then—” began Bertram.

“I pay trolley–boys, sah,” interrupted Ali quickly, “and Master can paying me to–morrow—or on pay–day at end of mensem.”

“But, look here,” expostulated Bertram, as this new–found guide, philosopher and friend sent the apparently satisfied coolies about their business. “I might not see you to–morrow. You’d better come with me to the ship and—”

“Oh, sah, sah!” cried the seemingly hurt and offended Ali, “am I not *Bwana’s* faithful ole servant?” and turning from the subject as closed, said he would produce a boat to convey his cherished employer to his ship.

“Master bucking up like hell now, please,” he advised. “No boat allowed to move in harbour after six pip emma, sah, thank God, please.”

“Who on earth’s Pip Emma?” enquired the bewildered Bertram, as they hurried down the hill to the quay.

“What British soldier–mans and officer–*bwanas* in Signal Corps call ‘p.m.,’ sah,” was the reply. “Master saying ‘six p.m.,’ but Signal *Bwana* always saying ‘six pip emma’—all same meaning but different language, please God, sah. P’r’aps German talk, sah? I do’n’ know, sah.”

And Bertram then remembered being puzzled by a remark of Maxton (to the effect that he had endeavoured to go down to his cabin at “three ack emma” and being full of “beer,” had fallen “ack over tock” down the companion), and saw light on the subject. Truly these brigade signaller people talked in a weird tongue that might seem a foreign language to an uninitiated listener.

At the pier he saw Commander Finnis, of the Royal Indian Marine, and gratefully accepted an offer of a joy–ride in his launch to the good ship *Elymas*, to which that officer was proceeding.

“We’re disembarking you blokes to–morrow morning,” said he to Bertram, as they seated themselves in the stern of the smart little boat. “Indian troops going under canvas here, and British entraining for Nairobi. Two British officers of Indian Army to proceed by tug at once to M’paga, a few hours down the coast, in German East. Scrap going on there. Poor devils will travel on deck, packed tight with fifty sheep and a gang of nigger coolies.... *Some* whiff!” and he chuckled callously.

“D’you know who are going?” asked Bertram eagerly. Suppose he should be one of them—and in a “scrap” by this time to–morrow! How would he comport himself in his first fight?

“No,” yawned the Commander. “O.C. troops on board will settle that.”

And Bertram held his peace, visualising himself as collecting his kit, hurrying on to a dirty little tug to sit in the middle of a flock of sheep while the boat puffed and panted through the night along the mysterious African shore, landing on some white coral beach beneath the palms at dawn, hurrying to join the little force fighting with its back to the sea and its face to the foe, leaping into a trench, seizing the rifle of a dying man whose limp fingers unwillingly relaxed their grip, firing rapidly but accurately into the—

"Up you go," quoth Commander Finnis, and Bertram arose and stepped on to the platform at the bottom of the ladder that hospitably climbed the side of His Majesty's Troop–ship *Elymas*.

---

[15] Oxen.

[16] Bring here.

[17] Talk, palaver.

[18] Savages.

Chapter VIII

Military and Naval Manœuvres

However nonchalant in demeanour, it was an eager and excited crowd of officers that stood around the foot of the boat–deck ladder awaiting the result of the conference held in the Captain's cabin, to which meeting–place its proprietor had taken Commander Finnis before requesting the presence of Colonel Haldon, the First Officer, and the Ship's Adjutant, to learn the decision and orders of the powers–that–be concerning all and sundry, from the ship's Captain to the Sepoys' cook.

Who would Colonel Haldon send forthwith to M'paga, where the scrap was even then in progress (according to Lieutenant Greene, quoting Commander Finnis)? What orders did the papers in the fateful little dispatch–case, borne by the latter gentleman, contain for the various officers not already instructed to join their respective corps? Who would be sent to healthy, cheery Nairobi? Who to the vile desert at Voi? Who to interesting, far–distant Uganda? Who to the ghastly mangrove–swamps down the coast by the border of German East? Who to places where there was real active service, fighting, wounds, distinction and honourable death? Who to dreary holes where they would "sit down" and sit tight, rotting with fever and dysentery, eating out their hearts, without seeing a single German till the end of the war....

Bertram thought of a certain "lucky–dip bran–tub," that loomed large in memories of childhood, whence, at a Christmas party, he had seen three or four predecessors draw most attractive and delectable toys and he had drawn a mysterious and much–tied parcel which had proved to contain a selection of first–class coke. What was he about to draw from Fate's bran–tub to–day?

When the Ship's Adjutant, bearing sheets of foolscap, eventually emerged from the Captain's cabin, ran sidling down the boat–deck ladder and proceeded to the notice–board in the saloon–companion, followed by the nonchalantly eager and excited crowd, as is the frog–capturing duck by all the other ducks of the farm–yard, Bertram, with beating heart, read down the list until he came to his own name—only to discover that Fate had hedged.

The die was not yet cast, and Second–Lieutenant B. Greene would disembark with detachments, Indian troops, and, at Mombasa, await further orders.

Captain Brandone and Lieutenant Stanner would proceed immediately to M'paga, and with wild cries of "Yoicks! Tally Ho!" and "Gone away!" those two officers fled to their respective cabins to collect their kit.

Dinner that night was a noisy meal, and talk turned largely upon the merits or demerits of the places from Mombasa to Uganda to which the speakers had been respectively posted.

"Where are you going, Brannigan?" asked Bertram of that cheery Hibernian, as he seated himself beside him.

"Where am Oi goin', is ut, me bhoy?" was the reply. "Faith, where the loin–eating man—Oi mane the man–eating loins reside, bedad. Ye've heard o' the man–eaters of Tsavo? That's where Oi'm goin', me bucko—to the man–eaters of Tsavo."

Terence had evidently poured a libation of usquebagh before dining, for he appeared wound up to talk.

"Begorra—if ut's loin–eaters they are, it's Terry Brannigan'll gird up *his* loins an' be found there missing entoirely.... Oi'd misloike to be 'aten by a loin, Greene ... " and he frowned over the idea and grew momentarily despondent.

"'Tis not phwat I wint for a sojer for, at all, at all," he complained, and added a lament to the effect that he was not as tough as O'Toole's pig. But the mention of this animal appeared to have a cheering effect, for he burst into song.

> "Ye've heard of Larry O'Toole,
> O' the beautiful town o' Drumgool?
> Faith, he had but wan eye
> To ogle ye by,
> But, begorra, that wan was a jool...."

After dinner, Bertram sought out Colonel Haldon for further orders, information and advice.

"Everybody clears off to–morrow morning, my boy," said he, "and in twenty–four hours we shall be scattered over a country as big as Europe. You'll be in command, till further orders, of all native troops landed at Mombasa. I don't suppose you'll be there long, though. You may get orders to bung off with the Hundred and Ninety–Ninth draft of the Hundred and Ninety–Eighth, or you may have to see them off under a Native Officer and go in the opposite direction yourself.... Don't worry, anyway. You'll be all right...."

That night Bertram again slept but little, and had a bad relapse into the old state of self–distrust, depression and anxiety. This sense of inadequacy, inexperience and unworth was overwhelming. What did he know about Sepoys that he should, for a time, be in sole command and charge of a mixed force of Regular troops and Imperial Service troops which comprised Gurkhas, Sikhs, Pathans, Punjabi Mahommedans, Deccani Marathas, Rajputs, and representatives of almost every other fighting race in India? It would be bad enough if he could thoroughly understand the language of any one of them. As it was, he had a few words of cook–house Hindustani, and a man whom he disliked and distrusted as his sole representative and medium of intercourse with the men. Suppose the fellow was rather his *mis–*representative? Suppose he fomented trouble, as only a native can? What if there were a sudden row and quarrel between some of the naturally inimical races—a sort of inter–tribal shindy between the Sikhs and the Pathans, for example? Who was wretched little "Blameless Bertram," to think he could impose his authority upon such people and quell the riot with a word? What if they defied him and the Jemadar did not support him? What sort of powers and authority had he? ... He did not know.... Suppose there *were* a row, and there was real fighting and bloodshed? It would get into the papers, and his name would be held up to the contempt of the whole British Empire. It would get into the American papers too. Then an exaggerated account of it would be published in the Press of the Central Powers and their wretched allies, to show the rotten condition of the Indian Army. The neutral papers would copy it. Soon there would not be a corner of the civilised world where people had not heard the name of Greene, the name of the wretched creature who could not maintain order and discipline among a few native troops, but allowed some petty quarrel between two soldiers to develop into an "incident." Yes—that's what would happen, a "regrettable incident." ... And the weary old round of self–distrust, depreciation and contempt went its sorry cycle once again....

Going on deck in the morning, Bertram discovered that supplementary orders had been published, and that all native troops would be disembarked under his command at twelve noon, and that he would report, upon landing, to the Military Landing Officer, from whom he would receive further orders.... Troops would carry no ammunition, nor cooked rations. All kits would go ashore with the men....

Bertram at once proceeded to the companion leading down to the well–deck, called a Sepoy of the Hundred and Ninety–Ninth, and "sent his salaams" to the Jemadar of that regiment, to the Subedar of the Gurkhas, the Subedar of the Sherepur Sikhs and the Jemadar of the Very Mixed Contingent.

To these officers he endeavoured to make it clear that every man of their respective commands, and every article of those men's kit, bedding, and accoutrements, and all stores, rations and ammunition, must be ready for disembarkation at midday.

The little Gurkha Subedar smiled brightly, saluted, and said he quite understood—which was rather clever of him, as his Hindustani was almost as limited as was Bertram's. However, he had grasped, from Bertram's barbarous and laborious "*Sub admi ... sub saman ... sub chiz ...tyar ... bara badji ... ither se jainga ...* " that "all men ... all baggage ... all things ... at twelve o'clock ... will go from here"—and that was good enough for him.

"Any chance of fighting to–morrow, Sahib?" he asked, but Bertram, unfortunately, did not understand him.

The tall, bearded Sikh Subedar saluted correctly, said nothing but "*Bahut achcha, Sahib,*" [19] and stood with a cold sneer frozen upon his hard and haughty countenance.

The burly Jemadar of the Very Mixed Contingent, or Mixed Pickles, smiled cheerily, laughed merrily at nothing in particular, and appeared mildly shocked at Bertram's enquiry as to whether he understood. Of *course,* he understood! Was not the Sahib a most fluent speaker of most faultless Urdu, or Hindi, or Sindhi, or Tamil or something? Anyhow, he had clearly caught the words "all men ready at twelve o'clock"—and who could require more than a nice clear *hookum* like that.

Jemadar Hassan Ali looked pained and doubtful. So far as his considerable histrionic powers permitted, he gave his rendering of an honest and intelligent man befogged by perfectly incomprehensible orders and contradictory directions which he may not question and on which he may not beg further enlightenment. His air and look of "*Faithful to the last I will go forth and strive to obey orders which I cannot understand, and to carry out instructions given so incomprehensibly and in so strange a tongue that Allah alone knows what is required of me*" annoyed Bertram exceedingly, and having smiled upon the cheery little Subedar and the cheery big Jemadar, and looked coldly upon the unpleasant Sikh and the difficult Hassan Ali, he informed the quartette that it had his permission to depart.

As they saluted and turned to go, he caught a gleam of ferocious hatred upon the face of the Gurkha officer whom the Sikh jostled, with every appearance of intentional rudeness and the desire to insult. Bertram's sympathy was with the Gurkha and he wished that it was with him and his sturdy little followers that he was to proceed to the front. He felt that they would follow him to the last inch of the way and the last drop of their blood, and would fight for sheer love of fighting, as soon as they were shown an enemy.

After a somewhat depressing breakfast, at which he found himself almost alone, Bertram arrayed himself in full war paint, packed his kit, said farewell to the ship's officers and then inspected the troops, drawn up ready for disembarkation on the well–decks. He was struck by the apparent cheerfulness of the Gurkhas and the clumsy heaviness of their kit which included a great horse–collar roll of cape, overcoat or ground–sheet strapped like a colossal cross–belt across one shoulder and under the other arm; by the apparent depression of the men of the Very Mixed Contingent and their slovenliness; by what seemed to him the critical and unfriendly stare of the Sherepur Sikhs as he passed along their ranks; and by the elderliness of the Hundred and Ninety–Ninth draft. Had these latter been perceptibly aged by their sea–faring experiences and were they feeling terribly *terra marique jactati*, or was it that the impossibility of procuring henna or other dye had caused the lapse of brown, orange, pink and red beards and moustaches to their natural greyness? Anyhow, they looked distinctly old, and on the whole, fitter for the ease and light duty of "employed pensioner" than for active service under very difficult conditions against a ferocious foe upon his native heath. His gentle nature and kindly heart led Bertram to feel very sorry indeed for one bemedalled old gentleman who had evidently had a very bad crossing, still had a very bad cough, and looked likely to have another go of fever before very long.

As he watched the piling–up of square–sided boxes of rations, oblong boxes of ammunition, sacks, tins, bags and jars, bundles of kit and bedding, cooking paraphernalia, entrenching tools, mule harness, huge zinc vessels for the transport of water, leather *chhagals* and canvas *pakhals* or waterbags, and wished that his own tight–strapped impedimenta were less uncomfortable and heavy, a cloud of choking smoke from the top of the funnel of some boat just below him, apprised him of the fact that his transport was ready. Looking over the side he saw a large barge, long, broad, and very deep, with upper decks at stem and stern, which a fussy little tug had just brought into position below an open door in the middle of the port side of the *Elymas*. It was a long way below it too, and he realised that unless a ladder were provided every man would have to drop from the threshold of the door to the very narrow edge of the barge about six feet below, make his way along it to the stern deck, and down a plank on to the "floor" of the barge itself. When his turn came he'd make an ass of himself—he'd fall—he knew he would!

He tried to make Jemadar Hassan Ali understand that two Havildars were to stand on the edge of the barge, one each side of the doorway and guide the errant tentative feet of each man as he lowered himself and clung to the bottom of the doorway. He also had the sacks thrown where anyone who missed his footing and fell from the side of the barge to the bottom would fall upon them and roll, instead of taking the eight feet drop and hurting himself. When this did happen, the Sepoys roared with laughter and appeared to be immensely diverted. It occurred several times, for it is no easy matter to lower oneself some six feet, from one edge to another, when heavily accoutred and carrying a rifle. When every man and package was on board, Bertram cast one last look around the *Elymas*, took a deep breath, crawled painfully out backwards through the port, clung to the sharp iron edge, felt about wildly with his feet which were apparently too sacred and superior for the Havildars to grab and guide, felt his clutching fingers weaken and slip, and then with a pang of miserable despair fell—and landed on the side of the barge a whole inch below where his feet had been when he fell. A minute later he had made his way to the prow, and, with a regal gesture, had signified to the captain of the tug that he might carry on.

And then he sat him down upon the little piece of deck and gazed upon the sea of upturned faces, black, brown, wheat–coloured, and yellow, that spread out at his feet from end to end and side to side of the great barge.

Of what were they thinking, these men from every corner of India and Nepal, as they stood shoulder to shoulder, or squatted on the boxes and bales that covered half the floor of the barge? What did they think of him? Did they really despise and dislike him as he feared, or did they admire and like and trust him—simply because he was a white man and a Sahib? He had a suspicion that the Sikhs disliked him, the Mixed Contingent took him on trust as an Englishman, the Hundred and Ninety–Ninth kept an open mind, and the Gurkhas liked him—all reflecting really the attitude of their respective Native Officers....

In a few minutes the barge was run alongside the Kilindini quay, and Bertram was, for the second time, climbing its stone stairs, in search of the Military Landing Officer, the arbiter of his immediate destiny.

As he reached the top of the steps he was, as it were, engulfed and embraced in a smile that he already knew—and he realised that it was with a distinct sense of pleasure and a feeling of lessened loneliness and unshared friendless responsibility that he beheld the beaming face of his "since–long–time–to–come" faithful old retainer Ali Suleiman.

"God bless myself please, thank you, *Bwana*," quoth that gentleman, saluting repeatedly. "*Bwana* will now wanting Military Embarkation Officer by golly. I got him, sah," and turning about added, "*Bwana* come along me, sah, I got him all right," as though he had, with much skill and good luck, tracked down, ensnared, and encaged some wary and wily animal....

At the end of the little stone pier was a rough table or desk, by which stood a burly officer clad in slacks, and a vast spine–pad of quilted khaki. On the tables were writing–materials and a mass of papers.

"Mornin'," remarked this gentleman, turning a crimson and perspiring face to Bertram. "I'm the M.L.O. You'll fall your men in here and they'll stack their kits with the rations and ammunition over there. Then you must tell off working–parties to cart the lot up to the camp. I've only got two trucks and your fatigue–parties'll have to man–handle 'em. You'll have to ginger 'em up or you'll be here all day. I don't want you to march off till all your stuff's up to the camp.... Don't bung off yourself, y'know.... Right O. Carry on...." Bertram saluted.

Another job which he must accomplish without hitch or error. The more jobs he *could* do, the better. What he dreaded was the job for the successful tackling of which he had not the knowledge, ability or experience.

"Very good, sir," he replied. "Er—where *are* the trolleys?" for there was no sign of any vehicle about the quay.

"Oh, they'll roll up by and by, I expect," was the reply. Bertram again saluted and returned to the barge. Calling to the Native Officers he told them that the men would fall in on the bunder and await further orders, each detachment furnishing a fatigue–party for the unloading of the impedimenta. Before very long, the men were standing at ease in the shade of a great shed, and their kits, rations and ammunition were piled in a great mound at the wharf edge.

And thus, having nothing to do until the promised trucks arrived, Bertram realised that it was terribly hot; suffocatingly, oppressively, dangerously hot; and that he felt very giddy, shaky and faint.

The sun seemed to beat upward from the stone of the quay and sideways from the iron of the sheds as fiercely and painfully as it did downward from the sky. And there was absolutely nowhere to sit down. He couldn't very well squat down in the dirt.... No—but the men could—so he approached the little knot of Native Officers and told them to allow the men to pile arms, fall out, and sit against the wall of the shed—no man to leave the line without permission.

Jemadar Hassan Ali did not forget to post a sentry over the arms on this occasion. For an hour Bertram strolled up and down. It was less tiring to do that than to stand still. His eyes ached most painfully by reason of the blinding glare, his head ached from the pressure on his brows of his thin, but hard and heavy, helmet (the regulation pattern, apparently designed with an eye to the maximum of danger and discomfort) and his body ached by reason of the weight and tightness of his accoutrements. It was nearly two o'clock and he had breakfasted early. Suppose he got sunstroke, or collapsed from heat, hunger, and weariness? What an exhibition! When would the men get their next meal? Where were those trolleys? It was two hours since the Military Landing Officer had said they'd "roll up by and by." He'd go and remind him.

The Military Landing Officer was just off to his lunch and well–earned rest at the Club. He had been on the beastly bunder since six in the morning—and anybody who wanted him now could come and find him, what?

"Excuse me, sir," said Bertram as Captain Angus flung his portfolio of papers to his orderly, "those trucks haven't come yet."

"*Wha'* trucks?" snapped the Landing Officer. He had just told himself he had *done* for to–day—and he had had nothing since half–past five that morning. People must be reasonable—he'd been hard at it for eight solid hours damitall y'know.

"The trucks for my baggage and ammunition and stuff."

"Well, *I* haven't got 'em, have I?" replied Captain Angus. "Be reasonable about it... I can't *make* trucks... Anybody'd think I'd stolen your trucks.... You must be *patient*, y'know, and *do* be reasonable.... *I* haven't got 'em. Search me."

The Military Landing Officer had been on his job for months and had unconsciously evolved two formulæ, which he used for his seniors and juniors respectively, without variation of a word. Bertram had just heard the form of prayer to be used with Captains and unfortunates of lower rank, who showed yearnings for things unavoidable. To Majors and those senior thereunto the crystallised ritual was:

"Can't understand it, sir, at all. I issued the necessary orders all right—but there's a terrible shortage. One must make allowances in these times of stress. It'll turn up all right. *I*'ll see to it ... " etc., and this applied equally well to missing trains, mules, regiments, horses, trucks, orders, motor–cars or anything else belonging to the large class of Things That Can Go Astray.

"You told me to wait, sir," said Bertram.

"Then why the devil *don't you*?" said Captain Angus.

"I am, sir," replied Bertram.

"Then what's all this infernal row about?" replied Captain Angus.

Bertram felt that he understood exactly how children feel when, unjustly treated, they cannot refrain from tears. It was *too* bad. He had stood in this smiting sun for over two hours awaiting the promised trucks—and now he was accused of making an infernal row because he had mentioned that they had not turned up! If the man had told him where they were, surely he and his three hundred men could have gone and got them long ago.

"By the way," continued Captain Angus, "I'd better give you your route—for when you *do* get away—and you mustn't sit here all day like this, y'know. You must ginger 'em up a bit" (more formula this) "or you'll all take root. Well, look here, you go up the hill and keep straight on to where a railway–bridge crosses the road. Turn to the left before you go under the bridge, and keep along the railway line till you see some tents on the left again. Strike inland towards these, and you'll find your way all right. Take what empty tents you want, but don't spread yourself *too* much—though there's only some details there now. You'll be in command of that camp for the present.... Better not bung off to the Club either—you may be wanted in a hurry.... I'll see if those trucks are on the way as I go up. Don't hop off till you've shifted all your stuff... So long! ... " and the Military Landing Officer bustled off to where at the Dock gates a motor–car awaited him....

Before long, Bertram found that he must either sit down or fall down, so terrific was the stifling heat, so heavy had his accoutrements become, and so faint, empty and giddy did he feel.

Through the open door of a corrugated–iron shed he could see a huge, burly, red–faced European, sitting at a little rough table in a big bare room. In this barn–like place was nothing else but a telephone–box and a chair. Could he go in and sit on it? That dark and shady interior looked like a glimpse of heaven from this hell of crashing glare and gasping heat.... Perhaps confidential military communications were made through that telephone though, and the big man, arrayed in a singlet and white trousers, was there for the very purpose of receiving them secretly and of preventing the intrusion of any stranger? Anyhow—it would be a minute's blessed escape from the blinding inferno, merely to go inside and ask the man if he could sit down while he awaited the trucks. He could place the chair in a position from which he could see his men.... He entered the hut, and the large man raised a clean–shaven crimson face, ornamented with a pair of piercing blue eyes, and stared hard at him as he folded a pinkish newspaper and said nothing at all, rather disconcertingly.

"May I come in and sit down for a bit, please?" said Bertram. "I think I've got a touch of the sun."

"Put your wacant faice in that wacant chair," was the prompt reply.

"Thanks—may I put it where I can see my men?" said Bertram.

"Putt it where you can cock yer feet on this 'ere table an' lean back agin that pertition, more sense," replied the large red man, scratching his large red head. "*You* don' want to see yore men, you don't," he added. "They're a 'orrid sight.... All natives is.... You putt it where you kin get a good voo o' *me*.... Shed a few paounds o' the hup'olstery and maike yerself atome.... Wisht I got somethink to orfer yer—but I ain't.... Can't be 'osspitable on a basin o' water wot's bin washed in—can yer?"

Bertram admitted the difficulty, and, with a sigh of intense relief, removed his belt and cross–belts and all that unto them pertained. And, as he sank into the chair with a grateful heart, entered Ali Suleiman, whom he had not seen for an hour, bearing in one huge paw a great mug of steaming tea, and in the other a thick plate of thicker biscuits.

Bertram could have wrung the hand that fed him. Never before in the history of tea had a cup of tea been so welcome.

"Heaven reward you as I never can," quoth Bertram, as he drank. "Where on earth did you raise it?"

"Oh, sah!" beamed Ali. "Master not mentioning it. I am knowing cook–fellow at R.E. Sergeants' Mess, and saying my frien' Sergeant Jones, R.E., wanting cup of tea and biscuits at bunder P.D.Q."

"P.D.Q.?" enquired Bertram.

"Yessah, all 'e same 'pretty dam quick'—and bringing it to *Bwana* by mistake," replied Ali, the son of Suleiman.

"But *isn't* there some mistake?" asked the puzzled youth. "I don't want to . . ."

"Lookere," interrupted the large red man, "*you* don' wanter discover no mistakes, not until you drunk that tea, you don't. ... You push that daown yore neck and then give that nigger a cent an' tell 'im to be less careful nex' time. You don' wanter *dis*courage a good lad like that, you don't. Not 'arf, you do."

"But—Sergeant Jones's tea" began Bertram, looking unhappily at the half–emptied cup.

"*Sergeant Jones's tea*!" mimicked the rude red man, in a high falsetto. "*If* ole Shifter Jones drunk a cup o' tea it'd be in all the paipers nex' mornin', it would. Not arf it wouldn't. Don' believe 'e ever tasted tea, I don't, an' if he *did*—"

But at this moment a white–clad naval officer of exalted rank strode into the room, and the large red man sprang to his feet with every sign of respect and regard. Picking up a Navy straw hat from the floor, the latter gentleman stood at attention with it in his hand. Bertram decided that he was a naval petty officer on some shore–job or other, perhaps retired and now a coast–guard or Customs official of some kind. Evidently he knew the exalted naval officer and held him, or his Office, in high regard.

"Get my message, William Hankey?" he snapped.

"Yessir," replied William Hankey.

"Did you telephone for the car at once?"

"Nossir," admitted Hankey, with a fluttering glance of piteous appeal.

The naval officer's face became a ferocious and menacing mask of wrath and hate, lit up by a terrible glare. Up to that moment he had been rather curiously like Hankey. Now he was even more like a very infuriated lion. He took a step nearer the table, fixed his burning, baleful eye upon the wilting William, and withered him with the most extraordinary blast of scorching invective that Bertram had ever heard, or was ever likely to hear, unless he met Captain Sir Thaddeus Bellingham ffinch Beffroye again.

"You blundering bullock," quoth he; "you whimpering weasel; you bleating blup; you miserable dog–potter; you horny–eyed, bleary–nosed, bat–eared, lop–sided, longshore loafer; you perishing shrimp–peddler; you Young Helper; you Mother's Little Pet; you dear Ministering Child; you blistering bug–house body–snatcher; you bloated bumboat–woman; you hopping hermaphrodite—what d'ye mean by it? Eh? … *What d'ye mean by it*, you anæmic Aggie; you ape–faced anthropoid; you adenoid; you blood–stained buzzard; you abject abortion; you abstainer; you sickly, one–lunged, half–baked, under–fed alligator; you scrofulous scorbutic; you peripatetic pimple; you perambulating pimp–faced poodle; what about it? Eh? *What about it*?"

Mr. William Hankey stood silent and motionless, but in his face was the expression of one who, with critical approval, listens and enjoys. Such a look may be seen upon the face of a musician the while he listens to the performance of a greater musician.

Having taken breath, the Captain continued: "What have you got to say for yourself, you frig–faced farthing freak, you? Nothing! You purple poultice–puncher; you hopeless, helpless, herring–gutted hound; you dropsical drink–water; you drunken, drivelling dope–dodger; you mouldy, mossy–toothed, mealy–mouthed maggot; you squinny–faced, squittering, squint–eyed squab, you—what have you got to say for yourself? Eh? … *Answer me*, you mole; you mump; you measle; you knob; you nit; you noun; you part; you piece; you portion; you bald–headed, slab–sided, jelly–bellied jumble; you mistake; you accident; you imperial stinker; you poor, pale pudding; you populous, pork–faced parrot—why don't you speak, you doddering, dumb–eared, deaf–mouthed dust–hole; you jabbering, jawing, jumping Jezebel, why don't you answer me? Eh? *D'ye hear* me, you fighting gold–fish; you whistling water–rat; you Leaning Tower of Pisa–pudding; you beer–belching ration–robber; you pink–eyed, perishing pension–cheater; you flat–footed, frog–faced fragment; you trumpeting tripe–hound? Hold your tongue and listen to me, you barge–

bottom barnacle; you nestling gin–lapper; you barmaid–biting bun–bolter; you tuberculous tub; you mouldy manure–merchant; you moulting mop–chewer; you kagging, corybantic cockroach; you lollipop–looting lighterman; you naval know–all. *Why didn't you telephone for the car*?"

"'Cos it were 'ere all the time, sir," replied Mr. William Hankey, perceiving that his superior officer had run down and required rest.

"*That's* all right, then," replied Captain Sir Thaddeus Bellingham ffinch Beffroye pleasantly, and strode to the door. There he turned, and again addressed Mr. Hankey.

"Why couldn't you say so, instead of chattering and jabbering and mouthing and mopping and mowing and yapping and yiyiking for an hour, Mr. Woozy, Woolly–witted, Wandering William Hankey?" he enquired.

The large red man looked penitent.

"Hankey," the officer added, "you are a land–lubber. You are a pier–head yachtsman. You are a beach pleasure–boat pilot. You are a canal bargee."

Mr. Hankey looked hurt, *touché*, broken.

"Oh, *sir*!" said he, stricken at last.

"William Hankey, you are a *volunteer*," continued his remorseless judge.

Mr. Hankey fell heavily into his chair, and fetched a deep groan.

"William Hankey–Pankey—you are a *conscientious objector*," said the Captain in a quiet, cold and cruel voice.

A little gasping cry escaped Mr. Hankey. He closed his eyes, swayed a moment, and then dropped fainting on the table, the which his large red head smote with a dull and heavy thud, as the heartless officer strode away.

A moment later Mr. Hankey revived, winked at the astonished Bertram, and remarked:

"I'd swim in blood fer 'im, I would, any day. I'd swim in beer wi' me mouf shut, if 'e ast me, I would.... 'E's the pleasant–manneredest, kindest, nicest bloke I was ever shipmates wiv, 'e is..."

"His bark is worse than his bite, I suppose?" hazarded Bertram.

"Bark!" replied Mr. Hankey. "'E wouldn' bark at a blind beggar's deaf dog, 'e wouldn't.... The ship's a 'Appy Ship wot's got *'im* fer Ole Man.... Why—the matlows do's liddle things jest to git brought up before 'im to listen to 'is voice.... Yes.... Their Master's Voice.... Wouldn' part brass–rags wiv 'im for a nogs'ead o' rum...."

Feeling a different man for the tea and biscuits, Bertram thanked Mr. Hankey for his hospitality, and stepped out on to the quay, thinking, as the heat–blast struck him, that one would experience very similar sensations by putting his head into an oven and then stepping on to the stove. In the shade of the sheds the Sepoys sprawled, even the cheery Gurkhas seemed unhappy and uncomfortable in that fiery furnace.

Bertram's heart smote him. Had it been the act of a good officer to go and sit down in that shed, to drink tea and eat biscuits, while his men …? Yes, surely that was all right. He was far less acclimatised to heat and glare than they, and it would be no service to them for him to get heat–stroke and apoplexy or "a touch of the sun." They had their water–bottles and their grain–and–sugar ration and their cold *chupattis*. They were under conditions far more closely approximating to normal than he was. Of course it is boring to spend hours in the same place with full equipment on, but, after all, it was much worse for a European, whose thoughts run on a cool club luncheon–room; a bath and change; and a long chair, a cold drink and a novel, under a punkah on the club verandah thereafter.... Would those infernal trucks *never* come? Suppose they never did? Was he to stay there all night? He had certainly received definite orders from the "competent military authority" to stay there until all his baggage had been sent off. Was that to relieve the competent military authority of responsibility in the event of any of it being stolen? … Probably the competent military authority was now having his tea, miles away at the Club. What should he do if no trucks had materialised by nightfall? How about consulting the Native Officers? … Perish the thought! … They'd have to stick it, the same as he would. The orders were quite clear, and all he had got to do was to sit tight and await trucks—if he grew grey in the process.

Some six hours from the time at which he had landed, a couple of small four–wheeled trucks were pushed on to the wharf by a fatigue–party of Sepoys from the camp; the Naik in charge of them saluted and fled, lest he and his men be impounded for further service; and Bertram instructed the Gurkha Subedar to get a fatigue–party of men to work at loading the two trucks to their utmost capacity, with baggage, kit, and ration–boxes. It was evident that the arrival of the trucks did not mean the early departure of the force, for several journeys would he necessary for the complete evacuation of the mound of material to be shifted. Having loaded the trucks, the fatigue–party pushed off, and it was only as the two unwieldy erections of baggage were being propelled through the gates by the willing little men, that it occurred to Bertram to enquire whether they had any idea as to where they were going.

Not the slightest, and they grinned cheerily. Another problem! Should he now abandon the force and lead the fatigue–party in the light of the Military Landing Officer's description of the route, or should he endeavour to give the Gurkha Subedar an idea of the way, and send him off with the trucks? And suppose he lost his way and barged ahead straight across the Island of Mombasa? That would mean that the rest of them would have to sit on the wharf all night—if he obeyed the Military Landing Officer's orders.... Which he *must* do, of course.... Bertram was of a mild, inoffensive and quite unvindictive nature, but he found himself wishing that the Military Landing Officer's dinner might thoroughly disagree with him.... His own did not appear likely to get the opportunity.... He then and there determined that he would never again be caught, while on Active Service, without food of some kind on his person, if he could help it—chocolate, biscuits, something in a tablet or a tin.... Should he go and leave the Native Officer in command, or should he send forth the two precious trucks into the gathering gloom and hope that, dove–like, they would return? …

And again the voice of Ali fell like balm of Gilead, as it boomed, welcome, opportune and cheering.

"Sah, I will show the Chinamans the way to camp and bring them back P.D.Q.," quoth he.

"Oh! Good man!" said Bertram. "Right O! But they're not Chinamen—they are Gurkha soldiers.... Don't you hit one, or chivvy them about...."

"Sah, I am knowing all things," was the modest reply, and the black giant strode off, followed by the empiled wobbling waggons.

More weary waiting, but, as the day waned, the decrease of heat and sultriness failed to keep pace with the increasing hunger, faintness and sickness which made at least one of the prisoners of the quay wish that either he or the Emperor of Germany had never been born….

Journey after journey having been made, each by a fresh party of Gurkhas (for Bertram, as is customary, used the willing horse, when he saw that the little hill–men apparently liked work for its own sake, as much as the other Sepoys disliked work for any sake), the moment at last arrived when the ammunition–boxes could be loaded on to the trucks and the whole force could be marched off as escort thereunto, leaving nothing behind them upon the accursed stones of that oven, which had been their gaol for ten weary hours.

Never was the order, "Fall in!" obeyed with more alacrity, and it was with a swinging stride that the troops marched out through the gates in the rear of their British officer, who strode along with high–held head and soldierly bearing, as he thanked God there was a good moon in the heavens, and prayed that there might soon be a good meal in his stomach.

Up the little hill and past the trolley "terminus" the party tramped, and the hot, heavy night seemed comparatively cool after the terrible day on the shut–in, stone and iron heat–trap of the quay…. As he glanced at the diamond–studded velvet of the African sky, Bertram thought how long ago seemed that morning when he had made his first march at the head of his company. It seemed to have taken place, not only in another continent, but in another age. Already he seemed an older, wiser, more resourceful man….

"*Bwana* turning feet to left hands here," said Ali Suleiman from where, abreast of Bertram, he strode along at the edge of the road. "If *Bwana* will following me in front, I am leading him behind"—with which clear and comprehensible offer, he struck off to the left, his long, clean night–shirt looming ahead in the darkness as a pillar of cloud by night. …

Again Bertram blessed him, and thanked the lucky stars that had brought him across his path. He had seen no railway–bridge nor railway–line; he could see no tents, and he was exceedingly thankful that it was not his duty to find, by night, the way which had seemed somewhat vaguely and insufficiently indicated for one who sought to follow it by day. Half an hour later he saw a huge black mass which, upon closer experience, proved to be a great palm grove, in the shadow of which stood a number of tents.

* * * * *

In a remarkably short space of time, the Sepoys had occupied four rows of the empty tents, lighted hurricane lamps, unpacked bedding and kit bundles, removed turbans, belts and accoutrements, and, set about the business of cooking, distributing, and devouring their rations.

The grove of palms that had looked so very inviolable and sacredly remote as it stood untenanted and silent in the brilliant moonlight, now looked and smelt (thanks to wood fires and burning ghee) like an Indian bazaar, as Sikhs, Gurkhas, Rajputs, Punjabis, Marathas, Pathans and "down–country" Carnatics swarmed in and out of tents, around cooking–fires, at the taps of the big railway water–tank, or the kit–and–ration dump—the men of each different race yet keeping themselves separate from those of other races….

As the unutterably weary Bertram stood and watched and wondered as to what military and disciplinary conundrums his motley force would provide for him on the morrow, his ancient and faithful family retainer came and asked him for his keys. That worthy had already, in the name of his *Bwana*, demanded the instant provision of a fatigue–party, and directed the removal of a tent from the lines to a spot where there would be more privacy and shade for its occupant, and had then unstrapped the bundles containing his master's bed, bedding and washhand–stand, and now desired further to furnish forth the tent with the suitable contents of the sack. …

And so Bertram "settled in," as did his little force, save that he went to bed supperless and they did not. Far from it for a goat actually strayed bleating into the line and met with an accident—getting its silly neck in the way of a *kukri* just as its owner was, so he said, fanning himself with it (with the *kukri*, not the goat). So some fed full, and others fuller.

Next day, Bertram ate what Ali, far–foraging, brought him; and rested beneath the shade of the palms and let his men rest also, to recover from their sea–voyage and generally to find themselves…. For one whole day he would do nothing and order nothing to be done; receive no reports, issue no instructions, harry nobody and be harried by none. Then, on the morrow, he would arise, go on the warpath in the camp, and grapple bravely with every problem that might arise, from shortage of turmeric to excess of covert criticism of his knowledge and ability.

But the morrow never came in that camp, for the Base Commandant sent for him in urgent haste at eventide, and bade him strain every nerve to get his men and their baggage, lock, stock and barrel, on board the *Barjordan*, just as quickly as it could be done (and a dam' sight quicker), for reinforcements were urgently needed at M'paga, down the coast.

Followed a sleepless nightmare night, throughout which he worked by moonlight in the camp, on the quay, and on the *Barjordan's* deck, reversing the labours of the previous day, and re–embarking his men, their kit, ammunition, rations and impedimenta—and in addition, two barge–loads of commissariat and ordnance requisites for the M'paga Brigade.

At dawn the last man, box, and bale was on board and Bertram endeavoured to speak a word of praise, in halting Hindustani, to the Gurkha Subedar, who, with his men, had shown an alacrity and gluttony for work, beyond all praise. All the other Sepoys had worked properly in their different shifts—but the Gurkhas had revelled in work, and when their second shift came at midnight, the first shift remained and worked with them!

Having gratefully accepted coffee from Mr. Wigger, the First Officer, Bertram, feeling "beat to the world," went down to his cabin, turned in, and slept till evening. When he awoke, a gazelle was gazing affectionately into his face.

He shut his eyes and shivered…. Was this sunstroke, fever, or madness? He felt horribly frightened, his nerves being in the state natural to a person of his temperament and constitution when overworked, underfed, affected by the sun, touched by fever, and overwrought to the breaking–point by anxiety and worry.

He opened his eyes again, determined to be cool, wise and brave, in face of this threatened breakdown, this hallucination of insanity.

The gazelle was still there—there in a carpeted, comfortable cabin, on board a ship, in the Indian Ocean….

He rubbed his eyes.

Then he put out his hand to pass it through the spectral Thing and confirm his worst fears.

The gazelle licked his hand, and he sat up and said: "Oh, damn!" and laughed weakly.

The animal left the cabin, and he heard its hoofs pattering on the linoleum.

Later he found it to be a pet of the captain of the *Barjordan*, Captain O'Connor.

Next morning the ship anchored a mile or so from a mangrove swamp, and the business of disembarkation began again, this time into the ship's boats and some sailing dhows that had met the *Barjordan* at this spot.

When all the Sepoys and stores were in the boats and dhows, he put on the *puggri* which Bludyer had given him, with the assistance of Ali Suleiman and the Gurkha Subedar, looked at himself in the glass, and wished he felt as fine and fierce a fellow as he looked.... He then said "Farewell" to kindly Captain O'Connor and burly, energetic Mr. Wigger—both of whom he liked exceedingly—received their hearty good wishes and exhortations to slay and spare not, and went down on the motor–launch that was to tow the laden boats to the low gloomy shore—if a mangrove swamp can be called a shore....

One more "beginning"—or one more stage on the road to War! Here was *he*, Bertram Greene, armed to the teeth, with a turban on his head, about to be landed—and left—on the shores of the mainland of this truly Dark Continent. He was about to invade Africa! ...

If only his father and Miranda could see him *now*!

---

[19] "Very good, sir."

Chapter IX

Bertram Invades Africa

Bertram waded ashore and looked around.

Through a rank jungle of high grass, scrub, palms, trees and creepers, a narrow mud path wound past the charred remnants of a native village to where stood the shell–scarred ruins of a whitewashed *adobe* building which had probably been a Customs–post, treasury, post–office and Government Offices in general.... He was on the mainland of the African Continent, and he was on enemy territory in the war area! How far away was the nearest German force? What should he do if he were attacked while disembarking? How was he to find the main body of his own brigade? What should he do if there were an enemy force between him and them? And what was the good of asking himself conundrums, instead of concentrating every faculty upon a speedy and orderly disembarkation?

Turning his back upon the unutterably dreary and depressing scene, as well as upon all doubts and fears and questions, he gave orders that the Gurkhas should land first. His only object in this was to have what he considered the best fighting men ashore first, and to form them up as a covering force, ready for action, in the event of any attack being made while the main body was still in the confusion, muddle and disadvantage of the act of disembarkation. And no bad idea either—but the Subedar of the Sherepur Sikhs saw, or affected to see, in this Gurkha priority of landing, an intentional and studied insult to himself, his contingent, and the whole Sikh race. He said as much to his men, and then, standing up in the bows of the boat, called out:

"Sahib! Would it not be better to let the Sherepur Sikh Contingent land first, to ensure the safety of—er—those beloved of the Sahib? There might be an attack...."

Not understanding in the least what the man was saying, Bertram ignored him altogether, though he disliked the sound of the laughter in the Sikh boat, and gathered from the face of the Gurkha Subedar that something which he greatly resented had been said.

"*Khabadar* ... *tum*!" [20] the Gurkha hissed, as he stepped ashore, and, with soldierly skill and promptness, got his men formed up, in and around the ruined building and native village, in readiness to cover the disembarkation of the rest. Five minutes after he had landed, Bertram found it difficult to believe that a hundred Gurkha Sepoys were within a hundred yards of him, for not one was visible. At the end of a couple of hours the untowed dhows had arrived, all troops, ammunition, supplies and baggage were ashore, the boats had all departed, and Bertram again found himself the only white man and sole authority in this mixed force, and felt the burden of responsibility heavy upon him.

The men having been formed up in their respective units, with the rations, ammunition, and kit dump in their rear, Bertram began to consider the advisability of leaving a strong guard over the latter, and moving off in search of the brigade camp. Would this be the right thing to do? Certainly his force was of no earthly use to the main body so long as it squatted in the mud where it had landed. Perhaps it was urgently wanted at that very moment, and the General was praying for its arrival and swearing at its non–arrival—every minute being precious, and the fate of the campaign hanging upon its immediate appearance. It might well be that an attack in their rear by four hundred fresh troops would put to flight an enemy who, up to that moment, had been winning. He would not know the strength of this new assailant, nor whether it was to be measured in hundreds or in thousands. Suppose the General was, at that very moment, listening for his rifles, as Wellington listened for the guns of his allies at Waterloo! And here he was, doing nothing—wasting time.... Yes, but suppose this dense bush were full of scouts and spies, as it well might be, and probably was, and supposing that the ration and ammunition dump was captured as soon as he had marched off with his main body? A pretty start for his military career—to lose the ammunition and food supply for the whole force within an hour or two of getting it ashore! His name would be better known than admired by the British Expeditionary Force in East Africa.... What would Murray have done in such a case? ... Suppose he "split the difference" and neither left the stores behind him nor stuck in the mud with them? Suppose he moved forward in the direction of the Base Camp, taking everything with him? But that would mean that every soldier in the force would be burdened like a coolie–porter—and, moreover, they'd have to move in single file along the mud path that ran through the impenetrable jungle. Suppose they were attacked? ...

Bertram came to the conclusion that it may be a very fine thing to have an independent command of one's own, but that personally he would give a great deal to find himself under the command of somebody else—be he never so arrogant, unsympathetic and harsh. Had Colonel Frost suddenly appeared he would (metaphorically) have cast himself upon that cold, stern man's hard bosom in transports of relief and joy.... He was going to do his very best, of course, and would never shirk nor evade any duty that lay before him—but—he felt a very lonely, anxious, undecided lad, and anxiety was fast becoming nervousness and fear—fear of doing the wrong thing, or of doing the right thing in the wrong way.... Should he leave a strong guard over the stores and advance? Should he remain where he was, and protect the stores to the last? Or should he advance with every man and every article the force possessed? ...

Could the remainder carry all that stuff if he told off a strong advance–guard and rear–guard? And, if so, what could a strong advance–guard or rear–guard do in single file if the column were attacked in front or rear? How could he avoid an ambush on either flank by discovering it in time—in country which rendered the use of flank guards utterly impossible? A man could only make his way through that jungle of thorn, scrub, trees, creepers and undergrowth by the patient and strenuous use of a broad axe and a saw. A strong, determined man might do a mile of it in a day.... Probably no human foot had trodden this soil in a thousand years, save along the little narrow path of black beaten mud that wound tortuously through it. Should he send on a party of Gurkhas with a note to the General, asking whether he should leave the stores or attempt to bring them with him? The Gurkhas were splendid jungle–fighters and splendidly willing.... But that would weaken his force seriously, in the event of his being attacked.... And suppose the party were ambushed, and he stuck there waiting and waiting, for an answer that could never come....

With a heavy sigh, he ran his eye over the scene—the sullen, oily water, the ugly mangrove swamp of muddy, writhing roots and twisted, slimy trunks, the dense, brooding jungle, the grey, dull sky—all so unfriendly and uncomfortable, giving one such a homeless, helpless feeling. The Gurkhas were invisible. The Sherepur Sikhs sat in a tight–packed group around their piled arms and listened to the words of their Subedar, the men of the Hundred and Ninety–Ninth squatted in a double row along the front of the *adobe* building, and the Very Mixed Contingent was just a mob near the ration–dump, beside which Ali Suleiman stood on guard over his master's kit.... Suppose there were a sudden attack? But there couldn't be? An enemy could only approach down that narrow path in single file. The impenetrable jungle was his friend until he moved. Directly he marched off it would be his terrible foe, the host and concealer of a thousand ambushes.

He felt that he had discovered a military maxim on his own account. *Impenetrable jungle is the friend of a force in position, and the enemy of a force on the march*.... Anyhow, the Gurkhas were out in front as a line of sentry groups, and nothing could happen to the force until they had come into action.... Should he—

"*Sahib*! *Ek Sahib ata hai…. Bahut hubshi log ata hain*," said a voice, and he sprang round, to see the Gurkha Subedar saluting.

What was that? "*A sahib is coming…. Many African natives are coming*!" … Then they *were* attacked after all! A German officer was leading a force of *askaris* of the Imperial African Rifles against them—those terrible Yaos and Swahilis whom the Germans had disciplined into a splendid army, and whom they permitted to loot and to slaughter after a successful fight….

His mouth went dry and the backs of his knees felt loose and weak. He was conscious of a rush of blood to the heart and a painful, sinking sensation of the stomach…. It had come…. The hour of his first battle was upon him….

He swallowed hard.

"*Achcha*, [21] *Subedar Sahib*," he said with seeming nonchalance, "*shaitan–log ko maro. Achcha kam karo*,"[22] and turning to the Sherepur Sikhs, the Hundred and Ninety–Ninth and the Very Mixed Contingent bawled: "*Fall in*!" in a voice that made those worthies perform the order as quickly as ever they had done it in their lives.

"*Dushman nahin hai*, [23] *Sahib*," said the Gurkha Subedar—as he realised that Bertram had ordered him "to kill the devils"—and explained that the people who approached bore no weapons.

Hurrying forward with the Subedar to a bend in the path beyond the burnt–out native village, Bertram saw a white man clad in khaki shirt, shorts and puttees, with a large, thick "pig–sticker" solar–topi of pith and quilted khaki on his head, and a revolver and hunting–knife in his belt. Behind him followed an apparently endless column of unarmed negroes. Evidently these were friends—but there would be no harm in taking all precautions in case of a ruse.

"Be ready," he said to the Subedar.

That officer smiled and pointed right and left to where, behind logs, mounds, bushes, and other cover, both natural and hastily prepared, lay his men, rifles cuddled lovingly to shoulder, fingers curled affectionately round triggers, eyes fixed unswervingly upon the approaching column, and faces grimly expectant. So still and so well hidden were they, that Bertram had not noticed the fact of their presence. He wondered whether the Subedar had personally strewn grass, leaves and brushwood over them after they had taken up their positions. He thought of the Babes in the Wood, and visualised the fierce little Gurkha as a novel kind of robin for the work of burying with dead leaves. …

He stopped in the path and awaited the arrival of the white man.

"Good morning, Mr. Greene," said that individual, as he approached. "Sorry if I've kept you waiting, but I had another job to finish first."

Bertram stared in amazement at this person who rolled up from the wilds of the Dark Continent with an unarmed party, addressed him by name, and apologised for being late! He was a saturnine and pessimistic–looking individual, wore the South African War ribbons on his breast, and the letters C.C. on his shoulders, and a lieutenant's stars.

"Good morning," replied Bertram, shaking hands. "I'm awfully glad to see you. I was wondering whether I ought to push off or stay here…."

“No attractions much here,” said the new–comer. “I should bung off. ... Straight along this path. Can’t miss the way.”

“Is there much danger of attack?” asked Bertram.

“Insects,” replied the other.

“Why not by Germans?” enquired Bertram.

“River on your left flank,” was the brief answer of the saturnine and pessimistic one.

“Can’t they cross it by bridges?”

“No; owing to the absence of bridges. I’m the only Bridges here,” sighed Mr. Bridges, of the Coolie Corps.

“Why not in boats then?”

“Owing to the absence of boats.”

“Might not the Germans open fire on us from the opposite bank then?” pursued the anxious Bertram, determined not to begin his career in Africa with a “regrettable incident,” due to his own carelessness.

“No; owing to the absence of Germans,” replied Mr. Bridges. “Where’s your stuff? I’ve brought a thousand of my blackbirds, so we’ll shift the lot in one journey. If you like to shove off at once, I’ll see nothing’s left behind....” And then, suddenly realising that there was not the least likelihood of attack nor cause for anxiety, and that all he had to do was to stroll along a path to the camp, where all responsibility for the safety of men and materials would be taken from him, Bertram relaxed, and realised that the heat was appalling and that he felt very faint and ill. His kit had suddenly grown insupportably heavy and unsufferably tight about his chest; his turban gave no shade to his eyes nor protection to his temples and neck, and its weight seemed to increase by pounds per minute. He felt very giddy, blue lights appeared before his eyes, and there was a surging and booming in his ears. He sat down, to avoid falling.

“Hullo! Seedy?” ejaculated Bridges, and turned to a big negro who stood behind him, and appeared to be a person of quality, inasmuch as he wore the ruins of a helmet, a khaki shooting–jacket much too small for him, and a whistle on a string. (“Only that and nothing more.”)

“Here, MacGinty–my–lad,” said Bridges to this gentleman, “*m’dafu late hapa*,” and with a few whistling clicks and high–pitched squeals, the latter sped another negro up a palm tree. Climbing it like a monkey, the negro tore a huge yellow coco–nut from the bunch that clustered beneath the spreading palm leaves, and flung it down. This, Mr. MacGinty–my–lad retrieved and, with one skilful blow of a *panga*, a kind of *machete* or butchers’ axe, decapitated.

“Have a swig at this,” said Bridges, handing the nut to Bertram, who discovered it to contain about a quart of deliciously cool, sweet “milk,” as clear as distilled water.

“Thanks awfully, Bridges,” said he. “I think I had a touch of the sun. ...”

“Had a touch of breakfast?” enquired the other.

“No,” replied Bertram.

"Hence the milk in the coco–nut," said Bridges, and added, "If you want to live long and die happy in Africa, you *must* do yourself well. It's the secret of success. You treat your tummy well—and often—and it'll do the same for you.... If you don't, well, you'll be no good to yourself nor anyone else."

"Thanks," said the ever–grateful Bertram, and arose feeling much better.

"Fall in, Subedar Sahib," said he to the Gurkha officer, and the latter quickly assembled his men as a company in line.

The Subedar of the Sherepur Sikhs approached and saluted. "We want to be the advance–guard, Sahib," he said.

"Certainly," replied Bertram, and added innocently, "There is no enemy between here and the camp."

The Sikh flashed a glance of swift suspicion at him.... Was this an intentional *riposte*? Was the young Sahib more subtle than he looked? Had he meant "The Sikhs may form the advance–guard *because* there is no fear of attack," with the implication that the Gurkhas would again have held the post of honour and danger if there had been any danger?

"I don't like the look of that bloke," observed Bridges, as the Sikh turned away, and added: "Well—I'll handle your stuff now, if you'll bung off," and continued his way to the dump, followed by Mr. MacGinty and a seemingly endless file of very tall, very weedy, Kavirondo negroes, of an unpleasant, scaly, greyish–black colour and more unpleasant, indescribable, but fishlike odour. These worthies were variously dressed, some in a *panga* or *machete*, some in a tin pot, others in a gourd, a snuff–box, a tea–cup, a saucepan or a jam–jar. Every man, however, without exception, possessed a red blanket, and every man, without exception, wore it, for modesty's sake, folded small upon his head—where it also served the purpose of a porter's pad, intervening between his head and the load which it was his life's work to bear thereupon.... When these people conversed, it was in the high, piping voices of little children, and when Bridges, Mr. MacGinty–my–lad, or any less *neapara* (head man), made a threatening movement towards one of them, the culprit would forthwith put his hands to his ears, draw up one foot to the other knee, close his eyes, cringe, and emit an incredibly thin, small squeal, a sound infinitely ridiculous in the mouth of a man six feet or more in stature.... When the last of these quaint creatures had passed, Bertram strode to where the Sherepur Sikhs had formed up in line, ready to march off at the head of the force. The Subedar gave an order, the ranks opened, the front rank turned about, and the rifles, with bayonet already fixed, came down to the "ready," and Bertram found himself between the two rows of flickering points.

"*Charge magazhinge*," shouted the Subedar, and Bertram found an odd dozen of rifles waving in the direction of his stomach, chest, face, neck and back, as their owners gaily loaded them.... Was there going to be an "accident"? ... Were there covert smiles on any of the fierce bearded faces of the big men? ... Should he make a dash from between the ranks? ... No—he would stand his ground and look displeased at this truly "native" method of charging magazines. It seemed a long time before the Subedar gave the orders, "Front rank—about turn.... Form fours.... Right," and the company was ready to march off.

"All is ready, Sahib," said the Subedar, approaching Bertram. "Shall I lead on?"

"Yes, Subedar Sahib," replied Bertram, "but why do your men face each other and point their rifles at each other's stomachs when they load them?"

His Hindustani was shockingly faulty, but evidently the Subedar understood.

"They are not afraid of being shot, Sahib," said he, smiling superiorly.

"Then it is a pity they are not afraid of being called slovenly, clumsy, jungly recruits," replied Bertram—and before the scowling officer could reply, added: "March on—and halt when I whistle," in sharp voice and peremptory manner.

Before long the little force was on its way, the Gurkhas coming last—as the trusty rear–guard, Bertram explained—and, after half an hour's uneventful march through the stinking swamp, reached the Base Camp of the M'paga Field Force—surely one of the ugliest, dreariest and most depressing spots in which ever a British force sat down and acquired assorted diseases.

---

[20] "Be careful—*you*!"

[21] "Good!"

[22] "Kill the devils. Do well."

[23] "It is not the enemy."

CHAPTER X

M'paga

Halting his column, closing it up, and calling it to attention, Bertram marched past the guard of King's African Rifles and entered the Camp. This consisted of a huge square, enclosed by low earthen walls and shallow trenches, in which were the "lines" of the Indian and African infantry, composing the inadequate little force which was invading German East Africa, rather with the idea of protecting British East than achieving conquest. The "lines" of the Sepoys and *askaris* consisted of rows of tiny low tents, while along the High Street of the Camp stood hospital tents, officers' messes, the General's tent, and that of his Brigade Major, and various other tents connected with the mysteries of the field telegraph and telephone, the Army Service Corps' supply and transport, and various offices of Brigade and Regimental Headquarters. As he passed the General's tent (indicated by a flagstaff and Union Jack), a tall lean officer, with a white–moustached, keen–eyed face, emerged and held up his hand. Seeing the crossed swords of a General on his shoulder–straps, Bertram endeavoured to rise to the occasion, roared: "*Eyes right*," "*Eyes front*," and then "*Halt*," saluted and stepped forward.

The General shook hands with him, and said: "Glad to see you. Hope you're ready for plenty of hard work, for there's plenty for you… Glad to see your men looking so businesslike and marching so smartly…. All right—carry on…."

Bertram would gladly have died for that General on the spot, and it was positively with a lump (of gratitude, so to speak) in his throat that he gave the order "*Quick march*," and proceeded, watched by hundreds of native soldiers, who crawled out of their low tents or rose up from where they lay or squatted to clean accoutrements, gossip, eat, or contemplate Infinity.

Arrived at the opposite entrance of the Camp, Bertram felt foolish, but concealed the fact by pretending that he had chosen this as a suitable halting place, bawled: "*Halt*," "*Into line—left turn*," "*Stand at ease*," "*Stand easy*," and determined to wait events. He had carried out his orders and brought the troops to the Camp as per instructions. Somebody else could come and take them if they wanted them….

As he stood, trying to look unconcerned, a small knot of British officers strolled up, headed by a tall and important–looking person arrayed in helmet, open shirt, shorts, grey stockings and khaki canvas shoes.

"Greene?" said he.

"Yes, sir," said Bertram, saluting.

"Brigade Major," continued the officer, apparently introducing himself. "March the Hundred and Ninety–Ninth on and report to Colonel Rock. The Hundred and Ninety–Eighth are outside the perimeter," and he pointed to where, a quarter of a mile away, were some grass huts and rows of tiny tents. "The remainder will be taken over by their units here, and your responsibility for them ceases."

Bertram, very thankful to be rid of them, marched on with the Hundred, and halted them in front of the low tents, from which, with whoops of joy, poured forth the warriors of the Hundred and Ninety–Eighth in search of any *bhai*, pal, townee, bucky, or aunt's cousin's husband's sister's son—(who, as such, would have a strong claim upon his good offices)—in the ranks of this thrice–welcome reinforcement.

Leaving the Hundred in charge of Jemadar Hassan Ali to await orders, Bertram strode to a large grass *banda*, or hut, consisting of three walls and a roof, through the open end of which he could see a group of British officers sitting on boxes and stools, about a long and most uneven, undulating table of box–sides nailed on sticks and supported by four upright logs.

At the head of this table, on which were maps and papers, sat a small thick–set man, who looked the personification of vigour, force and restless activity. Seeing that this officer wore a crown and star on his shoulder–strap, Bertram went up to him, saluted, and said:

"Second–Lieutenant Greene, I.A.R., sir. I have brought a hundred men from the Hundred and Ninety–Ninth, and nine cooking–pots—which Colonel Frost wishes to have returned at once…."

"The men or the cooking–pots, or both?" enquired Colonel Rock, whose habit of sarcastic and savage banter made him feared by all who came in contact with him, and served to conceal a very kindly and sympathetic nature.

"The cooking–pots, sir," replied Bertram, blushing as the other officers eyed him critically and with half–smiles at the Colonel's humour. Bertram felt, a little cynically, that such wit from an officer of their own rank would not have seemed so pleasingly humorous to some of these gentlemen, and that, moreover, he had again discovered a Military Maxim on his own account. *The value and humorousness of any witty remark made by any person in military uniform is in inverse ratio to the rank and seniority of the individual to whom it is made.* In other words, a Colonel must smile at a General's joke, a Major must grin broadly, a Captain laugh appreciatively, a Subaltern giggle right heartily, a Warrant Officer or N.C.O. explode into roars of laughter, and a private soldier roll helpless upon the ground in spasms and convulsions of helpless mirth.

Hearing a distinct snigger from the end of the table, Bertram glanced in that direction, said to himself, "You're a second–lieutenant, by your appreciative giggle," and encountered the sneering stare of a vacant–faced youth whom he heartily disliked on sight.

"Wants the cooking–pots back, but not the men, eh?" observed the Colonel, and, turning to the officer who sat at his left hand, a tall, handsome man with a well–bred, pleasant, dark face, who was Adjutant of the Hundred and Ninety–Ninth, added:

"Better go and see if there's good reason for his not wanting them back, Hall…. Colonel Frost's a good man at selling a horse—perhaps he's sold us a pup…."

More giggles from the vacant faced youth as Captain Hall arose and went out of the shed of grass and sticks, thatched on a framework of posts, which was the Officers' Mess of the Hundred and Ninety–Eighth Regiment.

Feeling shy and nervous, albeit most thankful to be among senior officers who would henceforth relieve him of the lonely responsibility he had found so trying and burdensome, Bertram seized the opportunity of the Adjutant's departure to escape, and followed that officer to where the Hundred awaited the order to dismiss.

"Brought a tent?" asked Captain Hall, as they went along.

"No," replied Bertram. "Ought I to have done so?"

"If you value your comfort on these picnics," was the answer. "You'll find it a bit damp o' nights when it rains, in one of these grass huts.... You can pig in with me to–night, and we'll set a party of Kavirondo to build you a *banda* to–morrow if you're staying on here."

"Thanks awfully," acknowledged Bertram. "Am I likely to go on somewhere else, though?"

"I did hear something about your taking a provision convoy up to Butindi the day after to–morrow," was the reply. "One of our Majors is up there with a mixed force of Ours and the Arab Company, with some odds and ends of King's African Rifles and things.... Pity you haven't a tent."

After looking over the Hundred and committing them to the charge of the Subedar–Major of the Hundred and Ninety–Eighth, Captain Hall invited Bertram "to make himself at home" in his hut, and led the way to where a row of green tents and grass huts stood near the Officers' Mess. On a Roorkee chair, at the door of one of these, sat none other than the Lieutenant Stanner whom Bertram had last seen on the deck of *Elymas*. With him was another subaltern, one of the Hundred and Ninety–Eighth.

"Hullo, Greene–bird!" cried Stanner. "Welcome home. Allow me to present you to my friend Best.... He is Very Best to–day, because he has got a bottle of whisky in his bed. He'll only be Second Best to–morrow, because he won't have any by then.... Not if he's a gentleman, that is," he added, eyeing Best anxiously.

That officer grinned, arose, and entering the hut, produced the whisky, a box of "sparklets," a kind of siphon, and a jug of dirty water.

"You already know Hall?" continued Stanner, the loquacious. "I was at school with his father. He's a good lad. Address him as Baronial Hall when you want something, Music Hall when you're feeling girlish, Town Hall when he's coming the pompous Adjutant over you, and Mission Hall when you're tired of him."

"Don't associate with him, Greene. Come away," said Captain Hall. "He'll teach you to play shove–ha'penny, to smoke, and to use bad language," but as Best handed him a whisky–and–dirty–water, feebly aerated by a sparklet, he tipped Stanner from his chair, seated himself in it, murmured, "When sinners entice thee, consent thou some," and drank.

"Why are you dressed like that? Is it your birthday, or aren't you very well?" enquired Stanner suddenly, eyeing Bertram's lethal weapons and Sepoy's turban. Bertram blushed, pleaded that he had nowhere to "undress," and had only just arrived. Whereupon the Adjutant, remarking that he must be weary, arose and took him to his hut.

"Get out of everything but your shirt and shorts, my son," said he, "and chuck that silly *puggri* away before you get sunstroke. All very well if you're going into a scrap, but it's as safe as Piccadilly round here." Bertram, as he sank into the Adjutant's chair, suddenly realised that he was more tired than ever he had been in his life before.

"Where *Bwana* sleeping to–night, sah, thank you, please?" boomed a familiar voice, and before the tent stood the faithful Ali, bowing and saluting—behind him three tall Kavirondo carrying Bertram's kit. Ali had commandeered these men from Bridges' party, and had hurried them off far in advance of the porters who were bringing in the general kit, rations, and ammunition. By means best known to himself he had galvanised the "low niggers" into agility and activity that surprised none more than themselves.

"Oh—it's my servant," said Bertram to the Adjutant. "May he put my bed in here, then?"

"That's the idea," replied Captain Hall, and, in a few minutes, Bertram's camp–bed was erected and furnished with bedding and mosquito net, his washhand–stand was set up, and his canvas bucket filled with water. Not until everything possible had been done for his master's comfort did Ali disappear to that mysterious spot whereunto native servants repair beyond the ken of the master–folk, when in need of food, leisure and relaxation.

Having washed, eaten and slept, Bertram declared himself "a better and wiser man," and asked Hall if he might explore the Camp, its wonders to admire. "Oh, yes," said Hall, "but don't go into the gambling dens, boozing–kens, dancing–saloons and faro tents, to squander your money, time and health."

"*Are* there any?" asked Bertram, in wide–eyed astonishment.

"No," replied Hall.

Bertram wished people would not be so fond of exercising their humour at his expense. He wondered why it was that he was always something of a butt. It could not be that he was an absolute fool, or he would not have been a Scholar of Balliol. He sighed. *Could* one be a Scholar of Balliol and a fool? …

"You might look in on the General, though," continued Hall, "and be chatty…. It's a very lonely life, y'know, a General's. I'm always sorry for the poor old beggars. Yes—he'd be awfully glad to see you…. Ask you to call him Willie before you'd been there a couple of hours, I expect."

"D'you mean I ought to call on the General formally?" asked Bertram, who knew that Hall was "ragging" again, as soon as he introduced the "Willie" touch.

"Oh, don't be too formal," was the reply. "Be matey and cosy with him…. I don't suppose he's had a really heart–to–heart chat with a subaltern about the things that *really* matter—the Empire (the Leicester Square one, I mean); Ciro's; the girls; George Robey, George Graves, Mr. Bottomley, Mrs. Pankhurst and the other great comedians—since I dunno–when. He'd *love* to buck about what's doing in town, with *you*, y'know…."

Bertram sighed again. It was no good. *Everybody* pulled his leg and seemed to sum him up in two minutes as the sort of green ass who'd believe anything he was told, and do anything that was suggested.

"I say, Hall," he said suddenly, "I'm a civilian, y'know, and a bit of a fool, too, no doubt. I am absolutely ignorant of all military matters, particularly those of etiquette. I am going to ask you things, since you are Adjutant of the corps I'm with. If you score off me, I think it'll be rather a cheap triumph and an inglorious victory, don't you? … I'm not a bumptious and conceited ass, mind—only an ignorant one, who fully admits it, and asks for help…."

As the poet says, it is a long lane that has no public–house, and a long worm that has no turning.

Hall stared.

"Well said, Greene," quoth he, and never jested at Bertram's expense again.

"Seriously—should I leave a card on the General?" continued Bertram.

"You should not," was the reply. "Avoid Generals as you would your creditors. They're dangerous animals in peace–time. On manœuvres they're ferocious. On active service they're rapid…."

“Any harm in my strolling round the Camp?” pursued Bertram. “I’m awfully interested, and might get some ideas of the useful kind.”

“None whatever,” said Hall. “No reason why you shouldn’t prowl around like the hosts of Midian till dinner–time. There’s nothing doing in the Hundred and Ninety–Eighth till four a.m. to–morrow, and you’re not in that, either.”

“What is it?” asked Bertram.

“Oh, a double–company of Ours is going out to mop up a little post the Germans have established across the river. We’re going to learn ’em not to do such,” said Hall.

“D’you think I might go?” asked Bertram, wondering, even as he spoke, whether it was his voice that was suggesting so foolish a thing as that Bertram Greene should arise at three–thirty in the morning to go, wantonly and without reason, where bullets were flying, bayonets were stabbing, and death and disablement were abroad.

“Dunno,” yawned Hall. “Better ask the Colonel. What’s the matter with bed at four ack emma? That’s where I’d be if I weren’t in orders for this silly show.”

As Bertram left the tent on his tour of exploration he decided that he would ask the Colonel if he might go with the expedition, and then he decided that he would do nothing so utterly foolish.... No, of course he wouldn’t....

Yes, he would....

Chapter XI

Food and Feeders

Rightly or wrongly, Bertram gathered the impression, as he strolled about the Camp, that this was not a confident and high–spirited army, drunk with the heady fumes of a debauch of victory. The demeanour of the Indian Sepoys led him to the conclusion, just or unjust, that they had "got their tails down." They appeared weary, apprehensive, even despondent, when not merely apathetic, and seemed to him to be distinctly what they themselves would call *mugra*—pessimistic and depressed.

The place alone was sufficient to depress anybody, he freely admitted, as he gazed around at the dreary grey environs of this little British *pied–à–terre*—grey thorn bush; grey grass; grey baobab trees (like hideous grey carrots with whiskerish roots, pulled up from the ground and stood on end); grey shell–strewn mud; grey bushwood; grey mangroves; grey sky. Yes, an inimical minatory landscape; a brooding, unwholesome, sinister landscape; the home of fever, dysentery, disease and sudden death. And over all hung a horrible sickening stench of decay, an evil smell that seemed to settle at the pit of the stomach as a heavy weight.

No wonder if Indians from the hills, deserts, plains and towns of the Deccan, the Punjab, Rajputana, and Nepal, found this terrible place of most terrific heat, foul odour, bad water and worse mud, enervating and depressing.... Poor beggars—it wasn't *their* war either.... The faces of the negroes of the King's African Rifles were inscrutable, and, being entirely ignorant of their ways, manners, and customs, he could not tell whether they were exhibiting signs of discouragement and depression, or whether their bearing and demeanour were entirely normal. Certainly they seemed a stolid and reserved folk, with a kind of dignity and self–respecting aloofness that he had somehow not expected. In their tall tarbooshes, jerseys, shorts and puttees, they looked most workman–like and competent soldiers.... Certainly they did not tally with his preconceived idea of them as a merry, care–free, irresponsible folk who grinned all over their faces for sheer light–heartedness, and spent their leisure time in twanging the banjo, clacking the bones, singing rag–time songs and doing the cake–walk. On duty, they stood like ebon statues and opened not their mouths. Off duty they squatted like ebon statuettes and shut them. Perhaps they did not know that England expects every nigger to do his duty as a sort of born music–hall, musical minstrel—or perhaps they *were* depressed, like the Sepoys, and had laid aside their banjoes, bones, coon–songs and double–shuffle–flap–dancing boots until brighter days? ... Anyhow, decided Bertram, he would much rather be with these stalwarts than against them, when they charged with their triangular bayonets on their Martini rifles; and if the German *askaris* were of similar type, he cared not how long his first personal encounter with them might be postponed.... Nor did the Englishmen of the Army Service Corps, the Royal Engineers, the Signallers and other details, strike him as light–hearted and bubbling with the *joie de vivre*. Frankly they looked ill, and they looked anxious....

Strolling past the brushwood–and–grass hut which was the R.A.M.C. Officers' Mess, he heard the remark:

"They've only got to leave us here in peace a little while for us all to die natural deaths of malaria or dysentery. The wily Hun knows *that* all right.... No fear—we shan't be attacked here. No such luck."

"Not unless we make ourselves too much of a nuisance to him," said another voice. "'Course, if we go barging about and capturing his trading posts and 'factories,' and raiding his *shambas*, he'll come down on us all right...."

"I dunno what we're doing here at all," put in a third speaker. "You can't invade a blooming *continent* like German East with a weak brigade of sick Sepoys.... Sort of bloomin' Jameson's Raid.... Why—they could come down the railway from Tabora or Kilimanjaro way with enough European troops alone to eat us alive. What are we here, irritating 'em at all for, *I* want to know? ... "

"Why, to maintain Britain's glorious traditions—of sending far too weak a force in the first place," put in the first speaker. "They'll send an adequate army later on, all right, and do the job in style. We've got to demonstrate the necessity for the adequate army first, though...."

"Sort of bait, like," said another, and yawned. "Well, we've all fished, I expect.... Know how the worm feels now...."

"I've only fished with flies," observed a languid and euphuistic voice.

"*What* an honour for the 'appy fly!" replied the worm–fisherman, and there was a guffaw of laughter.

Bertram realised that he was loitering to the point of eavesdropping, and strolled on, pondering many things in his heart....

In one corner of the great square of mud which was the Camp, Bertram came upon a battery consisting of four tiny guns. Grouped about them stood their Sepoy gunners, evidently at drill of some kind, for, at a sudden word from a British officer standing near, they leapt upon them, laboured frantically for five seconds, stood clear again, and, behold, each gun lay dismembered and prone upon the ground—the wheels off, the trail detached, the barrel of the gun itself in two parts, so that the breech half was separate from the muzzle half. At another word from the officer the statuesque Sepoys again sprang to life, seized each man a piece of the dismembered gun, lifted it above his head, raised it up and down, replaced it on the ground and once more stood at attention. Another order, and, in five seconds, the guns were reassembled and ready to fire.

"A mountain–battery of screw guns, so called because they screw and unscrew in the middle of the barrel," said Bertram to himself, and concluded that the drill he had just witnessed was that required for putting the dissected guns on the backs of mules for mountain transport, and rebuilding them for use. Certainly they were wonderfully nippy, these Sepoys, and seemed, perhaps, rather more cheery than the others. One old gentleman who had a chestful of medal–ribbons raised and lowered a gun–wheel above his head as though it had been of cardboard, in spite of his long grey beard and pensioner–like appearance.

Bertram envied the subaltern in command of this battery. How splendid it must be to know exactly what to do and to be able to do it; to be conscious that you are adequate and competent, equal to any demand that can be made upon you. Probably this youth was enjoying this campaign in the mud and stench and heat as much as he had ever enjoyed a picnic or tramping or boating holiday in England.... Lucky dog....

At about seven o'clock that evening, Bertram "dined" in the Officers' Mess of the Hundred and Ninety–Eighth. The rickety hut, through the walls of which the fires of the Camp could be seen, and through the roof of which the great stars were visible, was lighted, or left in darkness, by a hurricane–lamp which dangled from the ridge–pole. The officers of the corps sat on boxes, cane–stools, shooting–seats, or patent "weight–less" contrivances of aluminium and canvas. The vacant–faced youth, whose name was Grayne, had a bicycle–saddle which could be raised and lowered on a metal rod. He was very proud of it and fell over backwards twice during dinner. Bertram would have had nothing whatever to sit on had not the excellent and foresighted Ali discovered the fact in time to nail the two sides of a box in the shape of the letter T by means of a stone and the nails still adhering to the derelict wood. On this Bertram balanced himself with less danger and discomfort than might have been expected, the while he viewed with mixed feelings Ali's apologies and promise that he would steal a really nice stool or chair by the morrow.

On the mosaic of box–sides that formed the undulating, uneven, and fissured table–top, the Mess servant places tin plates containing a thin and nasty soup, tasting, Bertram thought, of cooking–pot, dish–cloth, wood–smoke, tin plate and the thumb of the gentleman who had borne it from the cook–house, or rather the cook–hole–in–the–ground, to the Mess hut. The flourish with which Ali placed it before his "beloved ole marstah" as he ejaculated "Soop, sah, thick an' clear thank–you please" went some way to make it interesting, but failed to make it palatable.

Although sick and faint for want of food, Bertram was not hungry or in a condition to appreciate disgraceful cooking disgustingly served.

As he sat awaiting the next course, after rejecting the thick–an'–clear "soup," Bertram took stock of the gentlemen whom, in his heart, he proudly, if shyly, called his brother–officers.

At the head of the table sat the Colonel, looking gloomy and distrait. Bertram wondered if he were thinking of the friends and comrades–in–arms he had left in the vile jungle round Tanga—his second–in–command and half a dozen more of his officers—and a third of his men. Was he thinking of his School—and Sandhurst—and life–long friend and trusted colleague, Major Brett–Boyce, slain by the German *askaris* as he lay wounded, propped against a tree by the brave and faithful dresser of the subordinate medical service, who was murdered with him in the very midst of his noble work, by those savage and brutal disciples of a more savage and brutal *kultur*?

Behind him stood his servant, a tall Mussulman in fairly clean white garments, and a big white turban round which was fastened a broad ribbon of the regimental colours adorned with the regimental crest in silver.

"Tell the cook that he and I will have a quiet chat in the morning, if he'll be good enough to come to my tent after breakfast—and then the provost–marshal shall show him a new game, perhaps," said the Colonel to this man as he finished his soup.

With the ghost of a smile the servant bowed, removed the Colonel's plate and departed to gloat over the cook, who, as a Goanese, despised "natives" heartily and without concealment, albeit himself as black as a negro.

Returning, the Colonel's servant bore a huge metal dish on which reposed a mound of most repulsive–looking meat in lumps, rags, shreds, strings, tendrils and fibres, surrounded by a brownish clear water. This was a seven–pound tin of bully–beef heated and turned out in all its native ugliness, naked and unadorned, on to the dish. Like everyone else, Bertram took a portion on his plate, and, like everyone else, left it on his plate, and, like everyone else, left it after tasting a morsel—or attempting to taste, for bully–beef under such conditions has no taste whatever. To chew it is merely as though one dipped a ball of rag and string into dirty water, warmed it, put it in one's mouth, and attempted to masticate it. To swallow it is moreover to attain the same results—nutrient, metabolic and sensational—as would follow upon the swallowing of the said ball of rags and string.

The morsel of bully–beef that Bertram put in his mouth abode with him. Though of the West it was like the unchanging East, for it changed not. He chewed and chewed, rested from his labours, and chewed again, in an honest and earnest endeavour to take nourishment and work out his own insalivation, but was at last forced to acknowledge himself defeated by the stout and tough resistance of the indomitable lump.

It did not know when it was beaten and it did not know when it was eaten; nor, had he been able to swallow it, would the "juices" of his interior have succeeded where those of his mouth, aided by his excellent teeth, had failed. In course of time it became a problem—another of those small but numerous and worrying problems that were fast bringing wrinkles to his forehead, hollows to his cheeks, a look of care and anxiety to his eyes, and nightmares to his sleep. He could not reduce it, he could not swallow it, he could not publicly reject it. What *could* he do? ... A bright idea.... Tactics.... He dropped his handkerchief—and when he arose from stooping to retrieve it, he was a free man again. A few minutes later a lump of bully–beef undiminished, unaffected and unfrayed, travelled across the mud floor of the hut in the mandibles of an army of big black ants, to provide them also with a disappointment and a problem, and, perchance, with a bombproof shelter for their young in a subterranean dug–out of the ant–hill....

Bertram again looked around at his fellow–officers. Not one of them appeared to have reduced the evil–looking mass of fibrous tissue and gristle that lay upon his plate—nor, indeed, did Bertram, throughout the campaign, ever see anyone actually eat and swallow the disgusting and repulsive muck served out to the officers and European units of the Expeditionary Force—hungry as they often were.

To his foolish civilian mind it seemed that if the money which this foul filth cost (for even bully–beef costs money—ask the contractors) had been spent on a half or a quarter or a tithe of the quantity of *edible* meat—such as tinned ox–tongue—sick and weary soldiers labouring and suffering for their country in a terrible climate, might have had a sufficiency of food which they could have eaten with pleasure and digested with benefit, without costing their grateful country a penny more.... Which is an absurd and ridiculous notion expressed in a long and involved sentence....

Next, to the Colonel, eyeing his plate of bully–beef through his monocle and with patent disgust, sat Major Manton, a tall, aristocratic person who looked extraordinarily smart and dapper. Hair, moustache, finger–nails and hands showed signs of obvious care, and he wore tunic, tie and, in fact, complete uniform, in an assembly wherein open shirts, bare arms, white tennis shoes, slacks, shorts, and even flannel trousers were not unknown. Evidently the Major put correctness before comfort—or, perhaps, found his chief comfort in being correct. He spoke to no one, but replied suavely when addressed. He looked to Bertram like a man who loathed a rough and rude environment having the honour or pleasure or satisfaction of knowing that he noticed its existence, much less that he troubled to loathe it. Bertram imagined that in the rough and tumble of hand–to–hand fighting, the Major's weapon would be the revolver, his aim quick and clean, his demeanour unhurried and unflurried, the expression of his face cold and unemotional.

Beside him sat a Captain Tollward in strong contrast, a great burly man with the physiognomy and bull–neck of a prize–fighter, the hands and arms of a navvy, and the figure of a brewer's dray–man. Frankly, he looked rather a brute, and Bertram pictured him in a fight—using a fixed bayonet or clubbed rifle with tremendous vigour and effect. He would be purple of face and wild of eye, would grunt like a bull with every blow, roar to his men like a charging lion, and swear like a bargee between whiles.... "Thank God for all England's Captain Tollwards this day," thought Bertram as he watched the powerful–looking man, and thought of the gladiators of ancient Rome.

Stanner was keeping him in roars of Homeric laughter with his jests and stories, no word of any one of which brought the shadow of a smile to the expressionless strong face of Major Manton, who could hear every one of the jokes that convulsed Tollward and threatened him with apoplexy. Next to Stanner sat Hall, who gave Bertram, his left–hand neighbour, such information and advice as he could, anent his taking of the convoy to Butindi, should such be his fate.

"You'll see some fighting up there, if you ever get there," said he. "They're always having little 'affairs of out–posts' and patrol scraps. You may be cut up on the way, of course.... If the Germans lay for you they're bound to get you, s' far as I can see.... How *can* you defend a convoy of a thousand porters going in single file through impenetrable jungle along a narrow path that it's practically impossible to leave? ... You can have an advance–guard and a rear–guard, of course, and much good may they do you when your *safari* covers anything from a couple of miles to three or four.... What are you going to do if it's attacked in the middle, a mile or so away from where you are yourself? ... What are you going to do if they ambush your advance–guard and mop the lot up, as they perfectly easily could do, at any point on the track, if they know you're coming—as of course they will do, as soon as we know it ourselves...."

"You fill me with despondency and alarm," said Bertram, with a lightness that he was far from feeling, and a sinking sensation that was not wholly due to emptiness of stomach.

Suddenly he was aware that a new stench was contending with the familiar one of decaying vegetation, rotting shell–fish, and the slime that was neither land nor water, but seemed a foul grease formed by the decomposition of leaves, grasses, trees, fish, molluscs and animals in an inky, oily fluid that the tides but churned up for the freer exhalation of poisonous miasma, and had not washed away since the rest of the world arose out of chaos and darkness, that man might breathe and thrive.... The new smell was akin to the old one but more penetrating, more subtly vile, more *vulgar*, than that ancient essence of decay and death and dissolution, and—awaking from a brown study in which he saw visions of himself writhing beneath the bayonets of a dozen gigantic savages, as he fell at the head of his convoy—he perceived that the new and conquering odour proceeded from the cheese. On a piece of tin, that had been the lid of a box, it lay and defied competition, while, with the unfaltering step of a strong man doing right, because it is his duty, Ali Suleiman bore it from *bwana* to *bwana* with the booming murmur: "Cheese, please God, sah, thank you." To the observant and thoughtful Bertram its reception by each member of the Mess was interesting and instructive, as indicative of his character, breeding, and personality.

The Colonel eyed it with a cold smile.

"Yes. Please God it *is* only cheese," he remarked, "but take it away—quick."

Major Manton glanced at it and heaved a very gentle sigh. "No, thank you, Boy," he said.

Captain Tollward sniffed hard, turned to Stanner, and roared with laughter.

"What ho, the High Explosive!" he shouted, and "What ho, the Forty Rod Gorgonzola—so called because it put the battery–mules out of action at that distance.... Who unchained it, I say? Boy, where's its muzzle?" and he cut himself a generous slice.

Stanner buried his nose in his handkerchief and waved Ali away as he thrust the nutritious if over–prevalent delicacy upon his notice.

"Take it to Bascombe *Bwana* and ask him to fire it from his guns," said he. "Serve the Germans right for using poison–gas and liquid fire.... Teach 'em a lesson, what, Tollward?"

"Don't be dev'lish–minded," replied that officer when laughter permitted him to speak. "You're as bad as the bally Huns yourself to suggest such an atrocity...."

"Seems kinder radio–active," said Hall, eyeing it with curiosity. "Menacing ... " and he also drove it from him.

Bertram, as one who, being at war, faces the horrors of war as they come, took a piece of the cheese and found that its bite, though it skinned the roof of his mouth, was not as bad as its bark. Grayne affected to faint when the cheese reached him, and the others did according to their kind.

Following in the tracks of Ali came another servant, bearing a wooden box, which he tendered to each diner, but as one who goeth through an empty ritual, and without hope that his offering will be accepted. In the box Bertram saw large thick biscuits exceedingly reminiscent of the dog–biscuit of commerce, but paler in hue and less attractive of appearance. He took one, and the well–trained servant only dropped the box in his surprise.

"What are you going to do with *that*?" enquired Hall.

"Why!—eat it, I suppose," said Bertram.

"People don't eat *those*," replied Hall.

"Why not?" asked Bertram.

"Try it and see," was the response.

Bertram did, and desisted not until his teeth ached and he feared to break them. There was certainly no fear of breaking the biscuit. Was it a sort of practical joke biscuit—a rather clever imitation of a biscuit in concrete, hardwood, or pottery–ware of some kind?

"I understand why people do not eat them," he admitted.

"Can't be done," said Hall. "Why, even the Kavirondo who eat live slugs, dead snakes, uncooked rice, raw flesh or rotten flesh and any part of any animal there is, do not regard those things as food.... They make ornaments of them, tools, weapons, missiles, all sorts of things...."

"I suppose if one were really starving one could live on them for a time," said the honest and serious–minded Bertram, ever a seeker after truth.

"Not unless one could get them into one's stomach, I suppose," was the reply; "and I don't see how one would do it.... I was reduced to trying once, and I tried hard. I put one in a basin and poured boiling water on it.... No result whatever.... I left it to soak for an hour while I chewed and chewed a piece of bully–beef.... Result? ... It was slightly darker in colour, but I could no more bite into it than I could into a tile or a book...."

"Suppose you boiled one," suggested Bertram.

"Precisely what I did," said Hall, "for my blood was up, apart from the fact that I was starving. It was a case of Hall *versus* a Biscuit. I boiled it—or rather watched the cook boil it in a *chattie*.... I gave it an hour. At the end of the hour it was of a slightly still darker colour—and showed signs of splitting through the middle. But never a bit could I get off it.... 'Boil the dam' thing all day and all night, and give it me hot for breakfast,' said I to the cook.... As one who patiently humours the headstrong, wilful White Man, he went away to carry on the foolish struggle...."

"What was it like in the morning?" enquired Bertram, as Hall paused reminiscent, and chewed the cud of bitter memory.

"Have you seen a long–sodden boot–sole that is resolving itself into its original layers and laminæ?" asked Hall. "Where there should be one solid sole, you see a dozen, and the thing gapes, as it were, showing serried rows of teeth in the shape of rusty nails and little protuberances of leather and thread?"

"Yes," smiled Bertram.

"That was my biscuit," continued Hall. "At the corners it gasped and split. Between the layers little lumps and points stood up, where the original biscuit holes had been made when the dreadful thing was without form, and void, in the process of evolution from cement–like dough to brick–like biscuit...."

"Could you eat it?" asked Bertram.

"Could *you* eat a boiled boot–sole?" was the reply. "The thing had turned from dry concrete to wet leather.... It had exchanged the extreme of brittle durability for that of pliant toughness.... *Eat* it!" and Hall laughed sardonically.

"What becomes of them all, then, if no one eats them?" asked Bertram.

"Oh—they have their uses, y' know. Boxes of them make a jolly good breastwork... The Army Service Corps are provided with work—taking them by the ton from place to place and fetching them back again.... I reveted a trench with biscuits once.... Looked very neat.... Lonely soldiers, in lonely outposts, do *GOD BLESS OUR HOME* and other devices with them—and you can make really attractive little photo–frames for 'midgets' and miniature with them if you have a centre–bit and carving tools... The handy–men of the R.E. make awf'ly nice boxes of children's toy–building–bricks with them, besides carved *plaques* and all sorts of little models.... I heard of a prisoner who made a complete steam–engine out of biscuits, but I never saw it myself.... Oh, yes, the Army would miss its biscuits—but I certainly never saw anybody eat one...."

Nor did Bertram, throughout the campaign. And here again it occurred to his foolish civilian mind that if the thousands of pounds spent on wholly and utterly inedible dog–biscuit had been spent on the ordinary biscuits of civilisation and the grocer's shop, sick and weary soldiers, working and suffering for their country in a terrible climate, might have had a sufficiency of food that they could have eaten with pleasure and digested with benefit, without costing their grateful country a penny more.

"Which would be the better," asked Bertram of himself—"to send an army ten tons of 'biscuit' that it cannot eat, or one ton of real biscuit that it can eat and enjoy?"

But, as an ignorant, simple, and silly civilian, he must be excused....

Dessert followed, in the shape of unripe bananas, and Bertram left the table with a cupful of thin soup, a small piece of cheese, and half a crisp, but pithy and acidulous banana beneath his belt. As the Colonel left the hut he hurried after him.

"If you please, sir," said he, "may I go out with the force that is to attack the German post to–morrow?"

Having acted on impulse and uttered the fatal words, he regretted the fact. Why should he be such a silly fool as to seek sorrow like this? Wasn't there danger and risk and hardship enough—without going out to look for it?

"In what capacity?" asked Colonel Rock, and added: "Hall is in command, and Stanner is his subaltern."

“As a spectator, sir,” said Bertram, “and I might—er—be useful perhaps—er—if—”

“Spectator!” mused the Colonel. “Bright idea! We might *all* go, of course.... Two hundred men go out on the job, and a couple of thousand go with ’em to whoop ’em on and clap, what? Excellent notion.... Wonder if we could arrange a ‘gate,’ and give the gate–money to the Red Cross, or start a Goose Club or something...” and he turned to go into his tent.

Bertram was not certain as to whether this reply was in the nature of a refusal of his request. He hoped it was.

“May I go, sir?” he said.

“You may not,” replied the Colonel, and Bertram felt very disappointed.

CHAPTER XII

Reflections

That night Bertram was again unable to sleep. Lying awake on his hard and narrow bed, faint for want of food, and sick with the horrible stench of the swamp, his mind revolved continually round the problem of how to "personally conduct" a convoy of a thousand porters through twenty miles of enemy country in such a way that it might have a chance if attacked. After tossing and turning for hours and vainly wooing sleep, he lay considering the details of a scheme by which the armed escort should, as it were, circulate round and round from head to tail of the convoy by a process which left ten of the advance–guard to occupy every tributary turning that joined the path and to wait at the junction of the two paths until the whole convoy had passed and the rear–guard had arrived. The ten would then join the rear–guard and march on with them. By the time this had been repeated sufficiently often to deplete the advance–guard, the convoy should halt while the bulk of the rear–guard marched up to the head of the column again and so *da capo*. It would want a lot of explaining to whoever was in command of the rear–guard, for it would be impossible for him, himself, to struggle up and down a line miles long—a line to which anything might happen, at any point, at any moment.... He could make it clear that at any turning he would detail ten men from the advance–guard, and then, when fifty had been withdrawn for this flanking work, he would halt the column so that the officer commanding the rear–guard could send fifty back.... Ten to one the fool would bungle it, and he might sit and await the return of the fifty until the crack of doom, or until he went back and fetched them up himself. And as soon as he had quitted the head of the column there would be an attack on it! ... Yes—or perhaps the ass in command of the ten placed to guard the side–turnings would omit to join the rear–guard as it passed—and he'd roll up at his destination, with a few score men short.... What would be done to him if he—

Bang! ...

Bertram's heart seemed to leap out of his body and then to stand still. His bones seemed to turn to water, and his tongue to leather. Had a shell burst beneath his bed? ... Was he soaring in the air? ... Had a great mine exploded beneath the Camp, and was the M'paga Field Force annihilated? ... Captain Hall sat up, yawned, put his hand out from beneath the mosquito curtain of his camp–bed and flashed his electric torch at a small alarm–clock that stood on a box within reach.

"What was that explosion?" said Bertram as soon as he could speak.

"Three–thirty," yawned Hall. "Might as well get up, I s'pose.... Wha'? ... 'Splosion? ... Some fool popped his rifle off at nothing, I sh'd say.... Blast him! Woke me up..."

"It's not an attack, then?" said Bertram, mightily relieved. "It sounded as though it were right close outside the hut...."

"Well—you don't attack with *one* rifle shot—nor beat off an attack with *none*. I don't, at least," replied Hall... "Just outside, was it?" he added as he arose. "Funny! There's no picket or sentry there. You must have been dreaming, my lad."

"I was wide awake before it happened," said Bertram. "I've been awake all night.... It was so close, I—I thought I was blown to bits...."

"'Oo wouldn' sell 'is liddle farm an' go ter War," remarked Hall in Tommy vein. "It's a wearin' life, being blowed outer yer bed at ar' pars free of a mornin', ain't it, guv'nor?"

A deep and hollow groan, apparently from beneath Bertram's bed, almost froze that young gentleman's blood.

Pulling on his slippers and turning on his electric torch, Hall dashed out of the hut. Bertram heard him exclaim, swear, and ask questions in Hindustani. He was joined by others, and the group moved away....

"Bright lad nearly blown his hand off," said Hall, re–entering the hut and lighting a candle–lamp. "Says he was cleaning his rifle...."

"Do you clean a rifle while it is loaded, and also put one hand over the muzzle and the other on the trigger while you do it?" asked Bertram.

"*I* don't, personally," replied Captain Hall, shortly. He was loath to admit that this disgrace to the regiment had intentionally incapacitated himself from active service, though it was fairly obvious.

"I wish he'd gone somewhere else to clean his rifle," said Bertram. "I believe the thing was pointed straight at my ear. I tell you—I felt as though a shell had burst in the hut."

"Bullet probably came through here," observed Hall nonchalantly as he laced his boots. (Later Bertram discovered that it had actually cut one of the four sticks that supported his mosquito curtain, and had torn the muslin thereof.)

Sleep being out of the question, Bertram decided that he might as well arise and watch the setting–forth of the little expedition.

"Going to get up and see you off the premises," said he.

"Stout fella," replied Hall. "I love enthusiasm—but it'll wear off.... The day'll come, and before long, when you wouldn't get out of bed to see your father shot at dawn.... Not unless you were in orders to command the firing–party, of course," he added...

Bertram dressed, feeling weak, ill and unhappy....

"Am I coming in, sah, thank you?" said a well–known voice at the doorless doorway of the hut.

"Hope so," replied Bertram, "if that's tea you've got."

It was. In a large enamel "tumbler" was a pint of glorious hot tea, strong, sweet and scalding.

"Useful bird, that," observed Hall, after declining to share the tea, as he was having breakfast at four o'clock over in the Mess. "I s'pose you hadn't ordered tea at three forty–five, had you?"

Bertram admitted that he had not, and concealed the horrid doubt that arose in his mind—born of memories of Sergeant Jones's tea at Kilindini—as to whether he was not drinking, under Hall's very nose, the tea that should have graced Hall's breakfast, due to be on the table in the Mess at that moment....

If Captain Hall found his tea unduly dilute he did not mention the fact when Bertram came over to the Mess *banda*, and sat yawning and watching him—the man who could nonchalantly sit and shovel horrid–

looking porridge into his mouth at four a.m., and talk idly on indifferent subjects, a few minutes before setting out to make a march in the darkness to an attack at dawn....

Ill and miserable as he felt, Bertram forgot everything in the thrilling interest of watching the assembly and departure of the little force. Out of the black darkness little detachments appeared, sometimes silhouetted against the red background of cooking fires, and marched along the main thoroughfare of the Camp to the place of assembly at the quarter–guard. Punctual to the minute, the column was ready to march off, as Captain Hall strolled up, apparently as unconcerned as if he were in some boring peace manœuvres, or about to ride to a meet, instead of to make a cross–country night march, by compass, through an African jungle–swamp to an attack at dawn, with the responsibility of the lives of a couple of hundred men upon his shoulders, as well as that of making a successful move on the chess–board of the campaign....

At the head of the column were a hundred Sepoys of the Hundred and Ninety–Eighth, under Stanner. In the light of the candle–lantern which he had brought from the *banda*, Bertram scrutinised their faces. They were Mussulmans, and looked determined, hardy men and fine soldiers. Some few looked happily excited, some ferocious, but the prevailing expression was one of weary depression and patient misery. Very many looked ill, and here and there he saw a sullen and resentful face. On the whole, he gathered the impression of a force that would march where it was led and would fight bravely, venting on the foe its anger and resentment at his being the cause of their sojourning in a stinking swamp to rot of malaria and dysentery.

How was Stanner feeling, Bertram wondered. He was evidently feeling extremely nervous, and made no secret of it when Bertram approached and addressed him. He was anything but afraid, but he was highly excited. His teeth chattered as he spoke, and his hand shook when he lit a cigarette.

"Gad! I should hate to get one of their beastly expanding bullets in my stomach," said he. "They fire a brute of a big–bore slug with a flat nose. Bad as an explosive bullet, the swine," and he shuddered violently. "Stomach's the only part I worry about, and I don't give a damn for bayonets.... But a bullet through your stomach! You live for weeks...."

Bertram felt distinctly glad to discover that a trained regular officer, like Stanner, could entertain these sensations of nervous excitement, and that he himself had no monopoly of them. He even thought, with a thrill of hope and confidence, that when his turn came he would be less nervous than Stanner. He knew that Stanner was not frightened, and that he did not wish he was snug in bed as his brother–officers were, but he also knew that Bertram Greene would not be frightened, and hoped and believed he would not be so palpably excited and nervous....

Behind the detachment of the Hundred and Ninety–Eighth came a machine–gun team of *askaris* of the King's African Rifles, in charge of a gigantic Sergeant. The dismounted gun and the ammunition–boxes were on the heads of Swahili porters.

Bertram liked the look of the Sergeant. He was a picture of quiet competence, reliability and determination. Although a full–blooded Swahili, his face was not unhandsome in a fierce, bold, and vigorously purposeful way, and though he had the flattened, wide–nostrilled nose of the negro, his mouth was Arab, thin–lipped and clear cut as Bertram's own. There was nothing bovine, childish nor wandering in his regard, but a look of frowning thoughtfulness, intentness and concentration.

And Sergeant Simba was what he looked, every inch a soldier, and a fine honourable fighting–man, brave as the lion he was named after; a subordinate who would obey and follow his white officer to certain death, without question or wavering; a leader who would carry his men with him by force of his personality, courage and leadership, while he could move and they could follow.... Beside Sergeant Simba, the average German soldier is a cur, a barbarian, and a filthy brute, for never in all the twenty years of his "savage" warfare has Sergeant Simba butchered a child, tortured a woman, murdered wounded enemies, abused (nor used) the white flag, fired on the Red Cross, turned captured dwelling–places into pig–styes and latrines in demonstration of his *kultur*—nor, when caught and cornered, has he waggled dirty hands about cunning, cowardly head with squeal of *Kamerad*! *Kamerad*! ... Could William the Kultured but have officered his armies with a hundred thousand of Sergeant Simba, instead of with his high–well–born Junkers, the Great War might have been a gentleman's war, a clean war, and the word *German* might not have become an epithet for all time, nor the "noble and knightly" sons of ancient houses have received commissions as Second Nozzle–Holder in the Poison–Gas Grenadiers, Sub Tap–Turner in a Fire–Squirting Squadron, or Ober Left–behind to Poison Wells in the Prussic (Acid) Guard....

As Bertram watched this sturdy–looking Maxim–gun section, with their imperturbable, inscrutable faces, an officer of the King's African Rifles emerged from the circumambient gloom and spoke with Sergeant Simba in Swahili. As he departed, after giving his orders and a few words of advice to Sergeant Simba, he raised his lantern to the face of the man in charge of the porters who carried the gun and ammunition. The man's face was instantly wreathed in smiles, and he giggled like a little girl. The officer dug him affectionately in the ribs, as one smacks a horse on dismounting after a long run and a clean kill, and the giggle became a cackle of elfin laughter most incongruous. Evidently the man was the officer's pet butt and prize fool.

"*Cartouchie n'gapi*?" asked the officer.

"Hundrem millium, *Bwana*," replied the man, and as the officer turned away with a laugh, Bertram correctly surmised that on being asked how many cartridges he had got, the man had replied that he possessed a hundred million.

Probably he spoke in round numbers, and used the only English words he knew.... The African does not deal in larger quantities than ten–at–a–time, and his estimates are vague, and still more vague is his expression of them. He will tell you that a place is "several nights distant," or perhaps that it is "a few rivers away." It is only just, however, to state that he will cheerfully accept an equal vagueness in return, and will go to your tent with the alacrity of clear understanding and definite purpose, if you say to him: "Run quickly to my tent and bring me the thing I want. You will easily distinguish it, as it is of about the colour of a flower, the size of a piece of wood, the shape of elephant's breath, and the weight of water. *You* know—it's as long as some string and exactly the height of some stones. You'll find it about as heavy as a dead bird or a load on the conscience. That thing that looks like a smell and feels like a sound...." He may bring your gun, your tobacco–pouch, your pyjamas, your toothbrush, or one slipper, but he will bring *something*, and that without hesitation or delay, for he immediately and clearly grasped that that particular thing, and none other, was what you wanted. He recognised it from your clear and careful description. It was not as though you had idly and carelessly said: "Bring me my hat" (or my knife or the matches or some other article that he handled daily), and left him to make up his mind, unaided, as to whether you did not really mean trousers, a book, washhand–stand, or the pens, ink, and paper of the gardener's aunt....

Behind the Swahili was a half–company of Gurkhas of the Kashmir Imperial Service Troops. As they stood at ease and chatted to each other, they reminded Bertram of a class of schoolboys waiting to be taken upon some highly pleasurable outing. There was an air of cheerful excitement and joyous expectancy.

"*Salaam, Subedar Sahib*," said Bertram, as the fierce hard face of his little friend came within the radius of the beams of his lantern.

"*Salaam, Sahib*," replied the Gurkha officer, "*Sahib ata hai*?" he asked.

"*Nahin*," replied Bertram. "*Hamara Colonel Sahib hamko hookum dea ki* '*Mut jao*,'" and the Subedar gathered that Bertram's Colonel had forbidden him to go. He commiserated with the young Sahib, said it was bad luck, but doubtless the Colonel Sahib in his wisdom had reserved him for far greater things.

As he strolled along their flank, Bertram received many a cheery grin of recognition and many a "Salaam, Sahib," from the friendly and lovable little hill–men.

In their rear, Bertram saw, with a momentary feeling that was something like the touch of a chill hand upon his heart, a party of Swahili stretcher–bearers, under an Indian of the Subordinate Medical Department, who bore, slung by a crossbelt across his body, a large satchel of dressings and simple surgical appliances.... Would these stretcher–bearers come back laden—sodden and dripping with the life–blood of men now standing near them in full health and strength and vigour of lusty life? Perhaps this fine Sergeant, perhaps the Subedar–Major of the Gurkhas? Stanner? Hall? ...

Suddenly the column was in motion and passing through the entrance by which Bertram had come into the Camp—was it a month ago or only yesterday?

Without disobeying the Colonel, he might perhaps go with the column as far as the river? There was a water–picket there permanently. If he did not go beyond the picket–line, it could not be held that he had "gone out" with the force in face of the C.O.'s prohibition.

Along the narrow lane or tunnel which wound through the impenetrable jungle of elephant–grass, acacia scrub, live oak, baobab, palm, thorn, creeper, and undergrowth, the column marched to the torrential little river, thirty or forty yards wide, that swirled brown, oily, and ugly, between its reed–beds of sucking mud. Here the column halted while Hall and Stanner, lantern in hand, felt their slow and stumbling way from log to log of the rough and unrailed bridge that spanned the stream. On the far side Hall waited with raised lantern, and in the middle stayed Stanner and bade the men cross in single file, the while he vainly endeavoured to illuminate each log and the treacherous gap beside it. Before long the little force had crossed without loss—(and to fall through into that deep, swift stream in the darkness with accoutrements and a hundred rounds of ammunition was to be lost for ever)—and in a minute had disappeared into the darkness, swallowed up and lost to sight and hearing, as though it had never passed that way....

Bertram turned back to Camp and came face to face with Major Manton.

"Morning, Greene," said he. "Been to see 'em off? Stout fella." And Bertram felt as pleased and proud as if he had won a decoration....

The day dawned grey, cheerless and threatening over a landscape as grey, cheerless and threatening as the day. The silent, menacing jungle, the loathsome stench of the surrounding swamp, the heavy, louring sky, the moist, suffocating heat; the sense of lurking, threatening danger from savage man, beast and reptile, insect and microbe; the feeling of utter homelessness and rough discomfort, combined to oppress, discourage and disturb....

Breakfast, eaten in silence in the Mess *banda*, consisted of porridge that required long and careful mastication by any who valued his digestion; pieces of meat of dull black surface and bright pink interior, also requiring long and careful mastication by all who were not too wearied by the porridge drill; and bread.

The bread was of interest—equally to the geologist, the zoologist, the physiologist, the chemist, and the merely curious. To the dispassionate eye, viewing it without prejudice or partiality, the loaf looked like an oblate spheroid of sandstone—say the Old Red Sandstone in which the curious may pick up a mammoth, aurochs, sabre–toothed tiger, or similar ornament of their little world and fleeting day—and to the passionate hand hacking *with* prejudice and partiality (for crumb, perhaps), it also felt like it. It was Army Bread, and quite probably made since the outbreak of the war. The geologist, wise in Eras—*Paleolithic, Pliocene, Eocene, May–have–been*—felt its challenge at once. To the zoologist there was immediate appeal when, by means of some sharp or heavy tool, the outer crust had been broken. For that interior was honey–combed with large, shiny–walled cells, and every cell was filled with a strange web–like kind of cocoon of finest filaments, now grey, now green, to which adhered tiny black specks. Were these, asked the zoologist, the eggs of insects, and, if so, of what insects? Were they laid before the loaf petrified, or after? If before, had the burning process in the kiln affected them? If after, how did the insect get inside? Or were they possibly of vegetable origin—something of a fungoid nature—or even on that strange borderland 'twixt animal and vegetable where roam the yeasty microbe and boisterous bacillus? Perhaps, after all, it was neither animal nor vegetable, but mineral? ... So ponders the geologist who incurs Army Bread in the wilds of the earth.

The physiologist merely wonders once again at the marvels of the human organism, that man can swallow such things and live; while the chemist secretes a splinter or two, that he may make a qualitative and quantitative analysis of this new, compound, if haply he survive to return to his laboratory.

To the merely curious it is merely curious—until he essays to eat it—and then his utterance may not be merely precious....

After this merry meal, Bertram approached the Colonel, saluted, and said:

"Colonel Frost, of the Hundred and Ninety–Ninth, ordered me to be sure to request you to return his nine cooking–pots at your very earliest convenience, sir, if you please."

Colonel Rock smiled brightly upon Bertram.

"He always was a man who liked his little joke," said he.... "Remind me to send him—"

"Yes, sir," interrupted Bertram, involuntarily, so pleased was he to think that the Pots of Contention were to be returned after all.

"...A Christmas–card—will you?" finished Colonel Rock.

Bertram's face fell. He thought he could hear, afar off, the ominous sound of the grinding of the mill–stones, between the upper and the nether of which he would be ground exceeding small.... Would Colonel Frost send him a telegram? What would Colonel Rock say if he took it to him? Could he pretend that he had never received it. Base thought! If he received one every day? ...

Suppose he were wounded. Could he pretend that his mind and memory were affected—loss of memory, loss of identity, loss of cooking–pots? ...

"By the way," said the Colonel, as Bertram saluted to depart, "you'll leave here to–morrow morning with a thousand porters, taking rations and ammunition to Butindi. You will take the draft from the Hundred and Ninety–Ninth as escort, and report to Major Mallery there. Don't go and get scuppered, or it'll be bad for them up at Butindi.... Start about five. Lieutenant Bridges, of the Coolie Corps, will give you a guide. He's been up there.... Better see Captain Brent about it to–night. He'll hand over the thousand porters in good condition in the morning.... The A.S.C. people will make a separate dump of the stuff you are to take.... Make sure about it, so that you don't pinch the wrong stuff, and turn up at Butindi with ten tons of Number Nine pills and other medical comforts...."

Bertram's heart sank within him, but he strove to achieve a look that blent pleasure, firmness, comprehension, and wide experience of convoy–work into one attractive whole. Wending his way to his *banda*, Bertram found Ali Suleiman making work for himself and doing it.

"I am going to Butindi at five to–morrow morning," he announced. "Have you ever been that way?"

"Oh, yes, sah, please God, thank you," replied Ali. "I was gun–bearer to a *bwana*, one 'Mericani gentlyman wanting to shoot sable antelope—very rare inseck—but a lion running up and bite him instead, and shocking climate cause him great loss of life."

"Then you could be guide," interrupted Bertram, "and show me the way to Butindi?"

"Yes, sah," replied Ali, "can show *Bwana* everythings.... *Bwana* taking much quinine and other *n'dawa* [24] there though. Shocking climate causing *Bwana* bad *homa*, bad fever, and perhaps great loss of life also...."

"D'you get fever ever?" asked Bertram.

"Sometimes, sah, but have never had loss of life," was the reassuring answer....

That morning and afternoon Bertram spent in watching the work of the Camp, as he had no duties of his own, and towards evening learnt of the approach of the expedition of the morning....

The column marched along with a swing, evidently pleased with itself, particularly the Swahili detachment, who chanted a song consisting of one verse which contained but one line. "*Macouba Simba na piga mazungo*," [25] they sang with wearying but unwearied regularity and monotony. At their head marched Sergeant Simba, looking as fresh as when he started, and more like a blackened European than a negro.

The Subedar and his Gurkhas had been left to garrison the outpost, but a few had returned on the stretchers of the medical detachment.

Bertram, with sinking heart and sick feelings of horror, watched these blood–stained biers, with their apparently lifeless burdens, file over the bridge, and held his breath whenever a stretcher–bearer stumbled on the greasy logs.

As the last couple safely crossed the bridge and laid their dripping stretcher down for a moment, the occupant, a Gurkha rifleman, suddenly sat up and looked round. His face was corpse–like, and his uniform looked as though it had just been dipped in a bath of blood. Painfully he rose to his feet, while the Swahili bearers gaped in amazement, and tottered slowly forward. Reeling like a drunken man, he followed in the wake of the disappearing procession, until he fell. Picking up the empty stretcher, the bearers hurried to where he lay—only to be waved away by the wounded man, who again arose and reeled, staggering, along the path.

Bertram met him and caught his arm as he collapsed once more.

"*Subr karo*," said Bertram, summoning up some Hindustani of a sort. "*Stretcher men baitho*." [26]

"*Nahin, Sahib,*" whispered the Gurkha; "*kuch nahin hai.*" [27]He evidently understood and spoke a little of the same kind. No. It was nothing. Only seven holes from Maxim–gun fire, that had riddled him as the German N.C.O. sprayed the charging line until a *kukri* halved his skull.... It was nothing.... No—it would take more than a *Germani* and his woolly–haired *askaris* to put Rifleman Thappa Sannu on a stretcher....

Bertram's hand seemed as though it were holding a wet sponge. He felt sick, and dreaded the moment when he must look at it and see it reeking red.

"*Mirhbani, Sahib,*" whispered the man again. "*Kuch nahin hai. Hamko mut pukkaro.*" [28]

He lurched free, stumbled forward a dozen yards, and fell again.

There was no difficulty about placing him upon the stretcher this time, and he made no remonstrance, as he was dead.

Bertram went to his *banda*, sat on the edge of his bed, and wrestled manfully with himself.

By the time Hall had made his report to the Colonel and come to the hut for a wash and rest, Bertram had conquered his desire to be very sick, swallowed the lump in his throat, relieved the stinging in his eyes, and contrived to look and behave as though he had not just had one of the most poignant and disturbing experiences of his life....

"Ripping little show," said Captain Hall, as he prepared for a bath and change. "The Gurkhas did in their pickets without a sound. Gad! They can handle those *kukris* of theirs to some purpose. Sentry on a mound in the outpost pooped off for some reason. They must just have been doing their morning Stand–to.... All four sides of the post opened fire, and we were only attacking on one.... They'd got a Maxim at each corner.... Too late, though. One hurroosh of a rush before they knew anything, and we were in the *boma* with the bayonet. Most of them bunked over the other side.... Got three white men, though. A Gurkha laid one out—on the Maxim, he was—and the Sergeant of the Swahilis fairly spitted another with his bayonet.... Third one got in the way of my revolver... I don't s'pose the whole thing lasted five minutes from the time their sentry fired.... The Hundred and Ninety–Eighth were fine. Lost our best Havildar, though. He'd have been Jemadar if he'd lived. He was leading a rush of his section in fine style, when he 'copped a packet.' Stopped one badly. Clean through the neck. One o' those beastly soft–nosed slugs the swine give their *askaris* for 'savage' warfare.... As if a German knew of any other kind...."

"Many casualties?" asked Bertram, trying to speak lightly.

"No—very few. Only eleven killed and seven wounded. Wasn't time for more. Shouldn't have had that much, only the blighter with the Maxim was nippy enough to get going with it while we charged over about forty yards from cover. The Gurkhas jumped the ditch like greyhounds and over the parapet of the inner trench like birds.... You *should* ha' been there.... They never had a chance...."

"Yes," said Bertram, and tried to visualise that rush at the belching Maxim.

"Didn't think much of their *bundobust,*" continued Hall. "Their pickets were pretty well asleep and the place hadn't got a yard of barbed wire nor even a row of stakes. They hadn't a field of fire of more than fifty yards anywhere.... Bit provincial, what? ... "

While Hall bathed, Bertram went in search of Captain Brent of the Coolie Corps.

Dinner that night was a vain repetition of yesterday's, save that there was more soup and cold bully–beef gravy available, owing to the rain.

The roof of the *banda* consisting of lightly thatched grass, reeds, twigs, and leaves, was as a sieve beneath the tropical downpour. There was nothing to do but to bear it, with or without grinning. Heavy drops in rapid succession pattered on bare heads, resounded on the tin plates, splashed into food, and, by constant dropping, wore away tempers. By comparison with the great heat of the weather, the rain seemed cold, and the little streams that cascaded down from pendent twig or reed were unwelcome as they invaded the back of the neck of some depressed diner below.

A most unpleasant looking snake, dislodged or disturbed by the rain, fell with sudden thud upon the table from his lodging in the roof. Barely had it done so when it was skewered to the boards by the fork of Captain Tollward. "Good man," said Major Manton, and decapitated the reptile with his knife.

"Just as well to put him out of pain," said he coolly; "it's a *mamba*. Beastly poisonous," and the still–writhing snake was removed with the knife and fork that had carved him. "Lucky I got him in the neck," observed Tollward, and the matter dropped.

Bertram wondered what he would have done had a small and highly poisonous serpent suddenly flopped down with a thump in front of his plate. Squealed like a girl perhaps?

Before long he was sitting huddled up beneath a perfect shower–bath of cold drops, with his feet in an oozy bog which soon became a pool and then a stream, and by the end of "dinner" was a torrent that gurgled in at one end of the Mess *banda*, and foamed out at the other. In this filthy water the Mess servants paddled to and fro, becoming more and more suggestive of drowned birds, while the yellowish khaki–drill of their masters turned almost black as it grew more sodden. One by one the lamps used by the cook and servants went out. That in the *banda* went out too, and the Colonel, who owned a tent, followed its example. Those officers who had only huts saw no advantage in retiring to them, and sat on in stolid misery, endeavouring to keep cigarettes alight by holding them under the table between hasty puffs.

Having sat—as usual—eagerly listening to the conversation of his seniors—until the damp and depressed party broke up, Bertram splashed across to his *banda* to find that the excellent Ali had completely covered his bed with his water–proof ground–sheet, had put his pyjamas and a change of underclothing into the bed and the rest of his kit under it. He had also dug a small trench and drain round the hut, so that the interior was merely a bog instead of a pool....

Bertram then faced the problem of how to undress while standing in mud beneath a shower–bath, in such a manner as to be able to get into bed reasonably dry and with the minimum of mud upon the feet....

As he lay sick and hungry, cold and miserable, with apparently high promise of fever and colic, listening to the pattering of heavy drops of water within the hut, and the beating of rain upon the sea of mud and water without, and realised that on the morrow he was to undertake his first really dangerous and responsible military duty, his heart sank.... Who was *he* to be in sole charge of a convoy upon whose safe arrival the existence of an outpost depended? What a *fool* he had been to come! Why should *he* be lying there half starving in that bestial swamp, shivering with fever, and feeling as though he had a very dead cat and a very live one in his stomach? . . . Raising his head from the pillow, he said aloud: "I would not be elsewhere for anything in the world...."

[24] Medicine.

[25] “Great Simba has killed a white man.”

[26] “Wait. Lie on the stretcher.”

[27] “It is nothing.”

[28] “Thanks. It is nothing. Do not hold me.”

Chapter XIII

Baking

When Bertram was awakened by Ali at four o'clock the next morning, he feared he would be unable to get up. Had he been at home, he would have remained in bed and sent for the doctor. His head felt like lead, every bone in his body ached, and he had that horrible sense of internal *malaise*, than which few feelings are more discouraging, distressing and enervating.

The morning smelt horrible, and, by the light of the candle–lamp, the floor was seen to have resigned in favour of the flood. Another problem: Could a fair–sized man dress himself on a tiny camp–bed beneath a small mosquito curtain? If not, he must get out of bed into the water, and paddle around in that slimy ooze which it hid from the eye but not from the nose. Subsidiary problem: Could a man step straight into a pair of wet boots, so as to avoid putting bare feet into the mud, and then withdraw alternate feet from them, for the removal of pyjamas and the putting–on of shorts and socks, while the booted foot remained firmly planted in the slush for his support?

Or again: Sitting precariously on the edge of a canvas bed, could an agile person, with bare feet coyly withdrawn from contact with the foulness beneath, garb his nether limbs to the extent that permitted the pulling–on of boots? …

He could try anyhow…. After much groping and fumbling, Bertram pulled on his socks and shorts, and then, still lying on his bed, reached for his boots. These he had left standing on a dry patch beneath his bed, and now saw standing, with the rest of his kit, in a couple of inches of filthy water. Balancing himself on the sagging edge of the strip of canvas that served as bed–laths, palliasse and mattress, he struggled into the resisting and reluctant boots, and then boldly entered the water, pleased with the tactics that had saved him from touching it before he was shod…. It was not until he had retrieved his sodden puttees and commenced to put them on, that he realised that he was still wearing the trousers of his pyjamas!

And then it was that Bertram, for the first time in his life, furiously swore—long and loud and heartily. Let those who say in defence of War that it rouses man's nobler instincts and brings out all that is best in him, note this deplorable fact.

Could he keep them on, or must he remove those clinging, squelching boots and partially undress again?

Striped blue and green pyjamas, showing for six inches between his shorts and his puttees, would add a distinctly novel touch to the uniform of a British officer…. No. It could not be done. Ill as he felt, and deeply as he loathed the idea of wrestling with the knots in the sodden boot–laces of those awful boots, he must do it—in spite of trembling hands, swimming head, and an almost unconquerable desire to lie down again.

And then—alas! for the moral maxims of the copy–books, the wise saws and modern instances of the didactic virtuous—sheer bad temper came to his assistance. With ferocious condemnations of everything, he cut his boot–laces, flung his boots into the water, splashed about violently in his socks, as he tore off the offending garments and hurled them after the boots, and then completed his dressing with as little regard to water, mud, slime, filth, and clay as though he were standing on the carpet of his dressing–room in England.

"*I'm fed up*!" quoth he, and barged out of the *banda* in a frame of mind that put the Fear of God and Second–Lieutenant Bertram Greene into all who crossed his path.... (*Cupid* forsooth!)

The first was Ali Suleiman, who stood waiting in the rain, until he could go in and pack his master's kit.

"Here you pack my kit sharp, and don't stand there gaping like a fish in a frying–pan. Stir yourself before I stir *you*," he shouted.

The faithful Ali dived into the *banda* like a rabbit into its hole. Excellent! This was the sort of *bwana* he could reverence. Almost had he been persuaded that this new master was not a real gentleman—he was so gentle....

Bertram turned back again, but not to apologise for his harsh words, as his better nature prompted him to do.

"Where's my breakfast, you lazy rascal?" he shouted.

"On the table in Mess *banda*, please God, thank you, sah," replied Ali Suleiman humbly, as one who prays that his grievous trespasses may be forgotten.

"Then why couldn't you say so, you—you—you—" and here memories of the Naval Officer stole across his subconsciousness, "you blundering burden, you posthumous porridge–punter, you myopic megalomaniac, you pernicious, piebald pacifist...."

Ali Suleiman rolled his eyes and nodded his head with every epithet.

"Oh, my God, sah," said he, as Bertram paused for breath, "I am a dam man mos' blasted sinful"—and, so ridiculous a thing is temper, that Bertram neither laughed nor saw cause for laughter.

Splashing across to the Mess *banda*, he discovered a battered metal teapot, an enamelled tumbler, an almost empty tin of condensed milk, and a tin plate of very sad–looking porridge. By the light of a lamp that appealed more to the olfactory and auditory senses than to the optic, he removed from the stodgy mess the well–developed leg of some insect unknown, and then tasted it—(the porridge, not the leg).

"*Filthy muck*," he remarked aloud.

"Sahib calling me, sir?" said a voice that made him jump, and the Cook's Understudy, a Goanese youth, stepped into the circle of light—or of lesser gloom.

"Very natural you should have thought so," answered Bertram. "I said *Filthy Muck*."

"Yessir," replied the acting deputy assistant adjutant cooklet, proudly, "I am cooking breakfast for the Sahib."

"*You* cooked this?" growled Bertram, and half rose, with so menacing an expression and wild an eye that the guilty fled, making a note that this was a Sahib to be properly served in future, and not, as he had foolishly thought him, a poor polite soul for whom anything was good enough....

Pushing the burnt and nauseating horror from him, Bertram essayed to pour out tea, only to find that the fluid was readily procurable from anywhere but the spout. A teapot that will not "pour out" freely is an annoyance at the best of times, and to the most placid of souls. (The fact that tea through the lid is as good as tea through the spout is more than counter–balanced by the fact that tea in the cup is better than tea on the table–cloth. And it is a very difficult art, only to be acquired by patient practice, to pour tea into the cup and the cup alone, from the top of a spout–bunged teapot. Try it.)

Bertram's had temper waxed and deepened.

"*Curse the thing*!" he swore, and banged the offending pot on the table, and, forgetting his nice table–manners, blew violently down the spout. This sent a wave of tea over his head and scalded him, and there the didactic virtuous, and the copy–book maxims, scored.

Sorely tempted to call to the cooklet in honeyed tones, decoy him near with fair–seeming smiles, with friendly gestures, and then to fling the thing at his head, he essayed to pour again.

A trickle, a gurgle, a spurt, a round gush of tea—and the pale wan skeletal remnants of a once lusty cockroach, sodden and soft, leapt into the cup. Swirling round and round, it seemed giddily to explore its new unresting–place, triumphant, as though chanting, with the Ancient Mariner, some such pæan as

> "I was the first that ever burst
> Into this silent tea...."

Heaven alone knew to how many cups of tea that disintegrating corpse had contributed of its best before the gusts of Bertram's temper had contributed to its dislodgment.

(Temper seems to have scored a point here, it must be reluctantly confessed.)

Bertram arose and plunged forth into the darkness, not daring to trust himself to call the cook.

Raising his clenched hands in speechless wrath, he drew in his breath through his clenched teeth—and then slipped with catastrophic suddenness on a patch of slimy clay and sat down heavily in very cold water.

He arose a distinctly dangerous person....

Near the ration–dump squatted a solid square of naked black men, not precisely savages, raw *shenzis* of the jungle, but something between these and the Swahilis who work as personal servants, gun–bearers, and the better class of *safari* porters. They were big men and looked strong. They smelt stronger. It was a perfectly indescribable odour, like nothing on earth, and to be encountered nowhere else on earth—save in the vicinity of another mass of negroes.

In the light of a big fire and several lanterns, Bertram saw that the men were in rough lines, and that each line appeared to be in charge of a headman, distinguished by some badge of rank, such as a bowler hat, a tobacco tin worn as an ear–ring, a pair of pink socks, or a frock coat. These men walked up and down their respective lines and occasionally smote one of their squatting followers, hitting the chosen one without fear or favour, without rhyme or reason, and apparently without doing much damage. For the smitten one, without change of expression or position, emitted an incredibly thin piping squeal, as though in acknowledgment of an attention, rather than as if giving natural vent to anguish....

Every porter had a red blanket, and practically every one wore a *panga*. The verbs are selected. They *had* blankets and they *wore* pangas. The blankets they either sat upon or folded into pads for insertion beneath the loads they were to carry upon their heads. The *pangas* were attached to strings worn over the shoulder. This useful implement serves the African as toothpick, spade, axe, knife, club, toasting–fork, hammer, weapon, hoe, cleaver, spoon, skinning–knife, and every other kind of tool, as well as being correct jungle wear for men for all occasions, and in all weathers. He builds a house with it; slays, skins and dismembers a bullock; fells a tree, makes a boat, digs a pit; fashions a club, spear, bow or arrow; hews his way through jungle, enheartens his wife, disheartens his enemy, mows his lawn, and makes his bed....

Not far away, a double company of the Hundred and Ninety–Eighth "stood easy." The fact that they were soaked to the skin did nothing to give them an air of devil–may–care gaiety.

The Jemadar in command approached and saluted Bertram, who recognised the features of Hassan Ali.

"It's *you*, is it!" he grunted, and proceeded to explain that the Jemadar would command the rear–guard of one hundred men, and that by the time it was augmented to a hundred and fifty by the process of picking up flankers left to guard side–turnings, the column would be halted while fifty men made their way up to the advance–guard again, and so on.

"D'you understand?" concluded Bertram.

"*Nahin, Sahib,*" replied the Jemadar.

"*Then fall out,*" snapped Bertram. "I'll put an intelligent private in command, and you can watch him until you do," and then he broke into English: "I've had about enough of you, my lad, and if you give me any of your damned nonsense, I'll twist your tail till you howl. Call yourself an *officer*! ... " and here the Jemadar, saluting repeatedly, like an automaton, declared that light had just dawned upon his mind and that he clearly understood.

"And so you'd better," answered Bertram harshly, staring with a hard scowl into the Jemadar's eyes until they wavered and sank. "So you'd *better*, if you want to keep your rank.... March one hundred men down the path past the Officers' Mess, and halt them a thousand yards from here.... The coolies will follow. You will return and fall in behind the coolies with the other hundred as rear–guard. See that the coolies do not straggle. March behind your men—so that you are the very last man of the whole convoy. D'you understand?"

Jemadar Hassan Ali did understand, and he also understood that he'd made a bad mistake about Second–Lieutenant Greene. He was evidently one of those subtle and clever people who give the impression that they are not *hushyar*, [29] that they are foolish and incompetent, and then suddenly destroy you when they see you have thoroughly gained that impression.

Respect and fear awoke in the breast of the worthy Jemadar, for he admired cunning, subtlety and cleverness beyond all things.... He marched a half of his little force off into the darkness, halted them some half–mile down the path (or rivulet) that led into the jungle, put them in charge of the senior Havildar and returned.

Meanwhile, Lieutenant Bridges, in a cloak and pyjamas, had arrived, yawning and shivering, to superintend the loading up of the porters. At an order, given in Swahili, the first line of squatting Kavirondo arose and rushed to the dump.

"Extraordinary zeal!" remarked Bertram to Bridges.

"Yes—to collar the lightest loads," was the illuminating reply.

The zeal faded as rapidly as it had glowed when he coldly pointed with the *kiboko*, which was his badge of office and constant companion, to the heavy ammunition–boxes.

"I should keep that near the advance–guard and under a special guard of its own," said he.

"I'm going to—naturally," replied Bertram shortly, and added: "Hurry them along, please. I want to get off to–day."

Bridges stared. This was a much more assured and autocratic person than the mild youth he had met at the water's edge a day or two ago.

"Well—if you like to push off with the advance–guard, I'll see that a constant stream of porters files off from here, and that your rear–guard follows them," said he.

"Thanks—I'll not start till I've seen the whole convoy ready," replied Bertram.

Yesterday he'd have been glad of advice from anybody. Now he'd take it from no one. Orders he would obey, of course—but "a poor thing but mine own" should be his motto with regard to his method of carrying out whatever he was left to do. They'd told him to take their beastly convoy; they'd left him to do it; and he'd do it as he thought fit.... Curse the rain, the mud, the stench, the hunger, sickness and the beastly pain that nearly doubled him up and made him feel faint....

Grayne strolled over.

"Time you bunged off, my lad," quoth he, loftily.

"If you'll mind your own business, I shall have the better chance to mind mine," replied Bertram, eyeing him coldly—and wondering at himself.

Grayne stared open–mouthed, and before he could speak Bertram was hounding on a lingering knot of porters who had not hurried off to the line as soon as their boxes of biscuit were balanced on their heads, but stood shrilly wrangling about something or nothing.

"*Kalele*! *Kalele*!" shouted Bertram, and sprang at them with raised fist and furious countenance, whereat they emitted shrill squeals and fled to their places in the long column.

He had no idea what "*Kalele*!" meant, but had heard Bridges and the headman say it. Later he learnt that it meant "Silence!" and was a very useful word....

Ali Suleiman approached, seized three men, and herded them before him to fetch Bertram's kit. Having loaded them with it, he drove them to the head of the column and stationed them in rear of the advance–guard.

Returning, he presented Bertram with a good, useful–looking cane.

"*Bwana* wanting a *kiboko*," said he. "*Shenzis* not knowing anything without *kiboko* and not feeling happy in mind. Not thinking *Bwana* is a real master."

Yesterday Bertram would have chidden Ali gently, and explained that kind hearts are more than coronets and gentle words than cruel whips. To–day he took the cane, gave it a vicious swish, and wished that it were indeed a *kiboko*, one of those terrible instruments of hippopotamus hide, four feet in length, as thick as a man's wrist at one end, tapering until it was of the thinness of his little finger at the other. . . .

A big Kavirondo seized a rum jar. His bigger neighbour dropped a heavy box and tried to snatch it from him. He who had the lighter jar clung to it, bounded away, and put it on his head. The box–wallah, following, gave him a sudden violent blow in the back, jerking the jar from his head.

Raising his cane, Bertram brought it down with all his strength on the starboard quarter of the box–wallah as he stooped to grab the jar. With a wild yelp, he leapt for his box and galloped to his place in the column.

"Excellent!" said Bridges, "you'll have no trouble with the *safari* people, at any rate."

"I'll have no trouble with anybody," replied Bertram with a quiet truculence that surprised himself, "not even with a *Balliol* negro."

Bridges decided that he had formed his estimate of Lieutenant Greene too hastily and quite wrongly. He was evidently a bit of a tough lad when he got down to it. Hot stuff....

At last the dump had disappeared completely, and its original components now swayed and turned upon the heads of a thousand human beasts of burden—human in that they walked erect and used fire for cooking food; beasts in that they were beastly and beast–like in all other ways. Among them, and distinguished by being feebler of physique, and, if possible, feebler of mind, was a party of those despised savages, the Kikuyu, rendered interesting as providing the great question that shook the Church of England to its foundations, and caused Lord Bishops to forget the wise councils of good Doctor Watts' hymn. (It is to be feared that among the even mightier problems of the Great War, the problem of the spiritual position and ecclesiastical condition of the Communicating Kikuyu has been temporarily lost sight of. Those who know the gentleman, with his blubber–lipped, foreheadless face, his teeth filed to sharp points, his skin a mass of scar patterns, done with a knife, and his soulless, brainless animalism and bestiality, would hate to think he was one short on the Thirty–Nine Articles or anything of that sort.)

Bertram gave a last injunction to Jemadar Hassan Ali, said farewell to Bridges, and strode to the head of the column. Thence he sent out a "point" of a Havildar and three men, and waited to give the word to advance, and plunge into the jungle, the one white man among some fifteen hundred people, all of whom looked to him, as to a Superior Being, for guidance and that competent command which should be their safeguard.

As the point disappeared he turned and looked along the apparently endless line, cried "*Quick March*," and set off at a smart pace, the first man of the column.

He was too proud and excited to realise how very ill he felt, or to be ashamed of the naughty temper that he had so clearly and freely exhibited.

---

[29] Clever and competent.

CHAPTER XIV

The Convoy

Bertram never forgot this plunge into the primeval jungle with its mingled suggestions of a Kew hot–house, a Turkish bath, a shower bath, a mud bath and a nightmare.

His mind was too blunted with probing into new things, his brain too dulled by the incessant battering of new ideas, too drunk with draughts of strange mingled novelty, too covered with recent new impressions for him to be sensitive to fresh ones.

Had an elephant emerged from the dripping jungle, wagged its tail and sat up and begged, he would have experienced no great shock of surprise. He, a town–bred, town–dwelling, pillar of the Respectable, the Normal and the Established, was marching through virgin forest at the head of a thousand African porters and two hundred Indian soldiers and their camp–followers, surrounded by enemies—varying from an *ex*–Prussian Guard armed with a machine–gun to a Wadego savage armed with a poisoned arrow—to the relief of hungry men in a stockaded outpost! ... What further room was there for marvels, wonders, and surprises? As he tramped, splashed, slipped and stumbled along the path, and the gloom of early morning, black sky, mist, and heavy rain slowly gave way to dawn and daylight, his fit of savage temper induced by "liver," hunger, headache and disgust, slowly gave way, also, to the mental inertia, calm, and peace, induced by monotonous exercise. The steady dogged tramp, tramp, tramp, was an anodyne, a sedative, a narcotic that drugged the mind, rendering it insensitive to the pains and sickness of the body as well as to its own worries, anxieties and problems....

Bertram felt that he could go on for a very long time; go on until he fell; but he knew that when he fell it would be quite impossible for him to get up again. Once his legs stopped moving, the spell would be broken, the automaton would have "run down," and motion would cease quite finally....

As daylight grew, he idly and almost subconsciously observed the details of his environment.

This was better than the mangrove–thicket of the swamp, in a clearing of which the base camp lay. It was the densest of dense jungle through which the track ran, like a stream through a cañon, but it was a jungle of infinite variety. Above the green impenetrable mat of elephant grass and nameless tangle of undergrowth, scrub, shrub, liana, bush, creeper, and young trees, stood, in solid serried array, great trees by the million, palm, mango, baobab, acacia, live oak, and a hundred other kinds, with bamboo and banana where they could, in defiance of probability, squeeze themselves in. Some of the trees looked like the handiwork of prentice gods, so crude and formless were they, their fat trunks tapering rapidly from a huge ground–girth to a fine point, and putting forth little abortive leafless branches suggestive of straggly hairs. Some such produced brilliant red blossoms, apparently on the trunk itself, but dispensed with the banality of leaves and branches. Some great knotted creepers seemed to have threaded themselves with beads as big as a man's head, and the fruit of one arboreal freak was vast sausages.

Through the aerial roadways of the forest, fifty feet above the heads of the *safari*, tribes of monkeys galloped and gambolled as they spied upon it and shrieked their comment.

Apparently the varied and numerous birds held views upon the subject of *safaris* also, and saw no reason to conceal them.

One accompanied the advance–guard, piping and fluting: “*Poli–Poli*! *Poli–Poli*!” which, as Ali Suleiman informed Bertram, is Swahili for “Slowly! *Slowly*!”

Another bird appeared to have fitted up his home with a chime of at least eight bells, for, every now and then, a sweet and sonorous tolling rang through the jungle. One bird, sitting on a branch a few feet from Bertram’s head, emitted two notes that for depth of timbre and rich sonorous sweetness could be excelled by no musical instrument or bell on earth. He had but the two notes apparently, but those two were marvellous. They even roused Bertram to the reception of a new impression and a fresh sensation akin to wonder.

From many of the overhanging trees depended the beautifully woven bottle–like nests of the weaver–bird. Brilliant parrots flashed through the tree–tops, incredible horn–bills carried their beaks about, the hypocritical widower–bird flaunted his new mourning, the blue starling, the sun–bird, and the crow–pheasant, with a score of other species, failed to give the gloomy, menacing jungle an air of brightness and life, seemed rather to emphasise its note of gloom, its insistence upon itself as the home of death where Nature, red in tooth and claw, pursued her cycle of destruction with fierce avidity and wanton masterfulness….

Suddenly a whistle rang out—sharp, clear, imperative. Its incisive blow upon the silence of the deadly jungle startled Bertram from his apathy. His tired wits sprang to life and activity, urged on his weary flagging muscles. He wheeled round and faced the Sepoys just behind him, even as the blast of the whistle ceased.

“*Halt*! *Baitho*!” [30] he shouted—gave the drill–book sign to lie down—and waited, for a second that seemed like a year, to feel the withering blast of fire that should tear through them at point–blank range…. Why did it not come? … Why did no guttural German voice shout an order to fire? … . He remained standing upright, while the Sepoys, crouching low, worked the bolts of their rifles to load the latter from their magazines. He was glad to see that they made ready thus, without awaiting an order, even as they sank to the ground. Would it not be better to march in future with a cartridge in the chamber and the cut–off of the magazine open? … Accidents? … Not if he made them march with rifles at the “slope.” … Better the risk of an accident than the risk of being caught napping…. Why did not the accursed German give the order to fire? … Was it because Bertram had got his men crouching down so quickly? … Would the crashing volley thunder out, the moment they arose? … They could not stay squatting, kneeling and lying in the mud for ever…. Where was the ambush? … Had they Maxims in trees, commanding this path? … Were the enemy massed in a clearing a foot or two from the road, and separated from it only by a thin screen of foliage? … . What should he do if there were a sudden bayonet–charge down the path, by huge ferocious *askaris*? … You can’t meet a charge with efficient rifle–fire when you are in single file and your utmost effort at deployment would get two, or possibly three crowded and hampered men abreast…. On the other hand, the enemy would not be charging under ideal conditions either…. More likely a machine–gun would suddenly nip out, from concealment beside the path, and wither the column away with a blast of fire at six hundred rounds a minute…. Perhaps the “point” marching on ahead would have the sense and the courage and the time to get into the gun–team with their bayonets before it got the gun going? … *Why did not the enemy fire*? … He would go mad if they didn’t do so soon…. Were they playing with him, as a cat plays with a mouse? …

The whistle rang out again, harsh, peremptory, fateful and then Ali Suleiman laughed, and pointed at a small bird. As he did so, the bird whistled again, with precisely the note of a police–whistle blown under the stress of fear, excitement or anger, a clamant, bodeful, and insistent signal.

Bertram would have welcomed warmly an opportunity to wring little birdie's neck, in the gust of anger that followed the fright.

Giving the signal to rise and advance, Bertram strode on, and, still under the stimulus of alarm, forgot that he was tired.

He analysed his feelings.... Was he frightened and afraid? Not at all. The whistle had "made him jump," and given him a "start," of course. The waiting for the blast of fire, that he knew would follow the signal, had been terribly trying—a torture to the nerves. The problem of what to do, in response to the enemy's first move, had been an agonising anxiety—but he would certainly have done something—given clear orders as to object and distance if there had been anything to fire at; used his revolver coolly and set a good example if there had been a charge down the path; headed a fierce rush at the Maxim if one had come out of cover and prepared to open fire.... No—he decidedly was not frightened and afraid... He was glad that he had remained erect, and, with his hand on his revolver, had, with seeming coolness, scanned the surrounding trees and jungle for signs of an ambushed enemy....

The road forked, and he turned to Ali Suleiman, who had marched near him from the start, in the proud capacity of guide.

"Which of these paths?" said he.

"The left hands, sah, please God," was the reply; "the right is closed also."

"What d'you mean?" asked Bertram, staring down the open track that branched to the right.

"See, *Bwana*," replied Ali, pointing to a small branch that lay in the middle of the path, with its broken end towards them and its leaves away from them. "Road closed. I 'spec *askari* patrol from Butani putting it there, when they know *Bwana* coming, thank God, please."

Apparently this twig, to the experienced eye, was precisely equivalent to a notice–board bearing the legend, *No Thoroughfare*. Bertram signalled a halt and turned to the Havildar at the head of the advance–guard.

"Take ten men and patrol down that path for a thousand yards," said he. "Then march back, wait for the rear–guard, and report to the Jemadar Sahib."

The man saluted, and Bertram saw him and his patrol move off, before he gave the order for the column to advance again.... That should secure the *safari* from attack down *that* path, anyhow. Ten determined men could hold up any number for any length of time, if they did the right thing.... These beastly bush fighting conditions cut both ways.... Yes—then suppose a small patrol of enemy *askaris* were on this track in front of him, and decided to hold the convoy up, what could he do?

To advance upon them, practically in single file, would be like approaching a long stick of sealing–wax to the door of a furnace—the point would melt and melt until the whole stick had disappeared without reaching the fire.... Of course, if there was a possibility of getting into the jungle, he would send out parties to take them in flank as he charged down the path. But that was just the point—you *couldn't* get more than a few yards into the jungle in the likeliest places, and, when you'd done that, you'd be utterly out of touch with your right and left–hand man in no time—not to mention the fact that you'd have no sense of direction or distance....

No.... He'd just head a charge straight for them, and if it were a really determined one and the distance not too great, enough of the advance–guard might survive to reach them with the bayonet.... Evidently, if there were any rules at all in this jungle warfare, one would be that the smaller of the two forces should dispose itself to bring every rifle to bear with magazine fire, and the larger should make the swiftest charge it possibly could. If it didn't—a dozen men would be as good as a thousand—while their ammunition held out.... What an advantage over the Indian Sepoy, with his open order *maidan* [31] training, the *askari*, bred and born and trained to this bush–fighting, would have! The German *ought* to win this campaign with his very big army of indigenous soldiers and his "salted" Colonials. What chance had the Sepoy or the British Regular in these utterly strange and unthought–of conditions? ... As well train aviators and then put them in submarines as train the Indian Army for the frontier and the plains and then put them in these swamps and jungles where your enemy is invisible and your sole "formation" is single file. What about the sacred and Medean Law: *Never fire until you can see something to fire at*? They'd never fire at all, at that rate, with an enemy who habitually used machine–guns from tree–tops and fired from dense cover—and small blame to him....

A sound of rushing water, and a few minutes later the path became the edge of a river–bank beneath which the torrent swirled. It looked as though its swift erosion would soon bring the crumbling and beetling bank down, and the path would lead straight into the river. He must mention the fact at Butindi.

He stared at the jungle of the opposite bank, apparently lifeless and deserted, though menacing, secretive and uncanny. An ugly place.... Suppose the Germans bridged the river just here.... He found that he had come to a halt and was yearning to sit down.... He must not do that. He must keep moving. But he did not like that gap in the path where, for some yards, it ran along the edge of the bank. It was a gap in the wall, an open door in the house, a rent in the veil of protection. The jungle seemed a friend instead of a blinding and crippling hindrance, impediment, and obstacle, now that the path lay open and exposed along that flank. Suppose there were an ambush in the jungle on the other side of the narrow rushing river, and a heavy fire was opened upon his men as they passed? He could not get at an enemy so placed, nor return their fire for long, from an open place, while they were in densest cover. They could simply prohibit the passing of the *safari*.... Anyhow, he'd leave a force there to blaze like fury into the jungle across the river if a shot were fired from there.

"Naik," said he, to a corporal, "halt here with twenty men and line the edge of the bank. If you are fired at from across the river, pour in magazine fire as hard as you can go—and make the porters *run* like the devil across this gap." He then translated, as well as he could, and marched on. He had done his best, anyhow.

For another hour he doggedly tramped on. The rain ceased, and the heat grew suffocating, stifling, terrible to bear. He felt that he was breathing pure steam, and that he must climb a tree in search of air—do *something* to relieve his panting lungs.... He tore his tunic open at the throat.... *Help*! he was going to faint and fall.... With a great effort he swung about and raised his hand for the "halt" and lowered it with palm horizontal downward for the "lie down." ... If the men were down themselves they would not realise that he had fallen.... It would not do to fall while marching at their head, to fall and lie there for the next man to stumble over him, to set an example of weakness.... The officer should be the last man to succumb to anything—but wounds—in front....

He sank to the ground, and feeling that he was going to faint away, put his head well down between his knees, and, after a while, felt better.

"*Bwana* taking off tunic and belts," said Ali Suleiman, "and I carry them. *Bwana* keep only revolver, by damn, please God, sah."

A bright idea! Why not? Where was the sense in marching through these foul swamps and jungles as though it were along the Queen's Road at Bombay? And Ali, who would rather die than carry a load upon his head, like a low *shenzi* of a porter, would be proud to carry his master's sword and personal kit.

In his shirt–sleeves, with exposed chest, Bertram felt another man, gave the signal to advance, and proceeded free of all impedimenta save his revolver….

Suddenly the narrow, walled–in path debouched into a most beautiful open glade of trees like live oaks. These were not massed together; there was no undergrowth of bush; the grass was short and fine; the ground sloping slightly upward was gravelly and dry—the whole spot one of Africa's freakish contrasts.

Bertram determined to halt the whole *safari* here, get it "closed up" into something like fours, and see every man, including the rear–guard, into the place before starting off again.

With the help of Ali, who interpreted to the headmen, he achieved his object, and, when he had satisfied himself that it was a case of "all present and correct," he returned to the head of the column and sat him down upon the trunk of a fallen tree….

Everybody, save the sentries, whom he had posted about the glade, squatted or lay upon the ground, each man beside his load….

Though free now of the horrible sense of suffocation, he felt sick and faint, and very weary. Although he had not had a proper meal since he left the *Barjordan*, he was not hungry—or thought he was not…. Would it be his luck to be killed in the first fight that he took part in? His *good* luck? When one is ill and half starved, weary beyond words, and bearing a nightmare burden of responsibility in conditions as comfortless and rough as they can well be, Death seems less a grisly terror than a friend, bearing an Order of Release in his bony hand….

Ali stood before him unbuckling his haversack.

"Please God, sah, I am buying *Bwana* this chocolates in Mombasa when finding master got no grubs for emergency rasher," said he, producing a big blue packet of chocolate.

"Good man!" replied Bertram. "I meant to get a stock of that myself…."

He ate some chocolate, drank of the cold tea with which the excellent Ali had filled his water–bottle, and felt better.

After an hour's rest he gave the order to fall in, the headmen of the porters got their respective gangs loaded up again, and the *safari* wound snake–like from the glade along the narrow path once more, Bertram at its head. He felt he was becoming a tactical soldier as he sent a lance–naik to go the round of the sentries and bid them stand fast until the rear–guard had disappeared into the jungle, when they were to rejoin it.

On tramped the *safari*, hour after hour, with occasional halts where the track widened, or the jungle, for a brief space, gave way to forest or *dambo*. Suddenly the head of the column emerged from the denser jungle into an undulating country of thicket, glade, scrub, and forest. Bertram saw the smoke of campfires far away to the left; and with one accord the porters commenced to beat their loads, drum–wise, with their *safari* sticks as they burst into some tribal chant or pæan of rejoicing. The convoy had reached Butindi in safety.

[30] Sit down.

[31] Open plain.

Chapter XV

Butindi

Half a mile beyond a village of the tiniest huts—built for themselves by the Kavirondo porters, and suggesting beehives rather than human habitations—Bertram beheld the entrenched and stockaded *boma*, zariba, or fort, that was to be his home for some months.

At that distance, it looked like a solid square of grass huts and tents, surrounded by a high wall. He guessed each side to be about two hundred yards in length. It stood in a clearing which gave a field of fire of some three hundred yards in every direction.

Halting the advance–guard, he formed it up from single file into fours; and, taking his kit from Ali, resumed it. Giving the order to march at "attention," he approached the *boma*, above the entrance to which an officer was watching him through field–glasses.

Halting his men at the plank which crossed the trench, he bade them "stand easy," and, leaving them in charge of a Havildar, crossed the little bridge and approached the gateway which faced sideways instead of outwards, and was so narrow that only one person at a time could pass through it.

Between the trench and the wall of the *boma* was a space some ten yards in width, wherein a number of small men in blue uniform, who resembled neither Indians nor Africans, were employed upon the off–duty duties of the soldier—cleaning rifles and accoutrements, chopping wood, rolling puttees, preparing food, washing clothing, and pursuing trains of thought or insects.

Against the wall stood the long lean–to shelters, consisting of a roof of plaited palm–leaf, supported by poles, in which they lived. By the entrance was a guard–house, which suggested a rabbit–hutch; and a sentry, who, seeing the approach of an armed party, turned out the guard. The Sergeant of the Guard was an enormous man with a skin like fine black satin, a skin than which no satin could be blacker nor more shiny. He was an obvious negro, Nubian or Soudanese, but the men of the guard were small and fair, and wore blue turbans, of which the ornamental end hung tail–wise down their backs. Beneath their blue tunics were unpleated kilts or skirts, of a kind of blue tartan, reaching to their knees. They had blue puttees and bare feet.

Saluting the guard, Bertram entered the *boma* and found himself in the High Street of a close–packed village of huts and tents, which were the dwelling–places of the officers, the hospital and sick–lines, the commissariat store, the Officers' Mess, the cook–house, orderly–room, and offices.

In the middle of the High Street stood four poles which supported a roof. A "table" of posts and packing–case boards, surrounded by native bedsteads of wood and string—by way of seats—constituted this, the Officers' Mess, Club, Common Room and Bar. A bunch of despondent–looking bananas hanging from the ridge–pole suggested food, and a bath containing a foot of water and an inch of mud suggested drink and cholera.

About the table sat several British officers in ragged shirts and shorts, drinking tea and eating native *chupatties*. They looked ill and weary. The mosaic of scraps of stencilled packing–case wood, the tin plates, the biscuit–box "sugar–basin," the condensed milk tin "milk–jug," the battered metal teapot and the pile of sodden–looking *chupatties* made as uninviting an afternoon tea ménage as could be imagined, particularly in that setting of muddy clay floor, rough and dirty *angarebs*, and roof–and–wall thatch of withered leaves and grass. A typical scene of modern glorious war with its dirt, discomfort and privation, its disease, misery and weary boredom….

Bertram approached the rickety grass hut and saluted.

A very tall man, with the face and moustache of a Viking, rose and extended his hand.

"How do, Greene?" said he. "Glad to see you…. Hope you brought the rum ration safe…. Take your bonnet off and undo your furs…. Hope that pistol's not loaded…. Nor that sword sharp…. Oughtn't to go about with nasty, dangerous things like that…. Hope the rum ration's safe…. Have some tea and a bloater…. Berners, go and do Quartermaster, like a good lad…. Have some rum and a bloater, Greene…."

"Thank you, sir," said Bertram, noting that the big man had a crown on one shoulder of his shirt and a safety–pin spanning a huge hole on the other. His great arms and chest were bare, and a pair of corduroy riding–breeches, quite unfastened at the knee and calf, left an expanse of bare leg between their termination and the beginning of grey, sagging socks. Hob–nailed boots, fastened with string, completed his attire. He looked like a tramp, a scarecrow, and a strong leader of men.

"'Fraid you'll have to drink out of a condensed milk tin, until your kit turns up…" said a pale and very handsome youth. "You get a flavour of milk, though," he added with an air of impartiality, "as well as of tin and solder…. They burn your fingers so damnably, though, when you go to pick 'em up…. Or why not drink out of the teapot, if everyone has finished? … Yes—I'll drop in a spot of condensed milk."

"No—damn it all, Vereker," put in the Major, "let's do him well and create an impression. Nothing like beginning as you don't mean to go on—or can't possibly go on…. He can have The Glass this evening. And some fresh tea. And his own tin of condensed…. And a bloater. Hasn't he brought us rum and hope? … "

The pale and handsome Vereker sighed.

"You create a *false* impression, sir," he said, and, taking a key from his neck, arose and unlocked a big chop–box that stood in a corner of the *banda*. Thence he produced a glass tumbler and set it before Bertram.

"There's The Glass," said he. "It's now in your charge, present and correct. I'll receive it from you and return the receipt at 'Stand–to.' …"

Bertram gathered that the tumbler was precious in the Major's sight, and that honour was being shown him. He had a faint sense of having reached Home. He was disappointed when a servant brought fresh tea, a newly–opened tin of milk, and the lid of a biscuit–box for a plate, to discover that the banana which reposed upon it was the "bloater" of his hopes and the Major's promise.

"For God's sake use plenty of condensed milk," said that gentleman, as Bertram put some into the glass, preparatory to pouring out his tea. Bertram thought it very kind and attentive of him—until he added: "And pour the tea *on* to it, and not down the side of the glass…. That's how the other tumbler got done in…."

As he gratefully sipped the hot tea and doubtfully munched a *chapatti*, Bertram took stock of the other members of the Mess. Beside Major Mallery sat a very hard–looking person, a typical fighting–man with the rather low forehead, rather protruding ears, rather high cheek–bones, heavy jaw and jutting chin of his kind. He spoke little, and that somewhat truculently, wore a big heavy knife in his belt, looked like a refined prize–fighter, and answered to the name of Captain Macke.

Beside him, and in strong contrast, sat a young man of the Filbert genus. He wore a monocle, his nails were manicured, he spoke with the euphuism and euphemism of a certain Oxford type, he had an air of languor, boredom and acute refinement, was addressed as Cecil Clarence, when not as Gussie Augustus Gus, and seemed to be one of the very best.

On the same string bed, and in even stronger contrast, sat a dark–faced Indian youth. On his shoulder–straps were the letters I.M.S. and two stars. A lieutenant of the Indian Medical Service, and, as such, a member of this British Officers' Mess. Bertram wondered why the fact that he had been to England and read certain books should have this result; and whether the society of the Subedar–Major of the regiment would have been preferred by the British officers. The young man talked a lot, and appeared anxious to show his freedom from anxiety, and his knowledge of English idiom and slang. When he addressed anyone by the nickname which intimate pals bestowed upon him, Bertram felt sorry for this youth with the hard staccato voice and raucous, mirthless laugh. Cecil Clarence said of him that "if one gave him an inch he took an 'ell of a lot for granted." His name was Bupendranath Chatterji, and his papa sat cross–legged and bare–footed in the doorway of a little shop in a Calcutta bazaar, and lent moneys to the poor, needy and oppressed, for a considerable consideration.

"'Bout time for Stand–to, isn't it?" said the Major, consulting his wrist–watch. "Hop it, young Clarence.... You might come round with me to–night, Greene, if you've finished tea.... Can't offer you another bloater, I'm afraid...."

The other officers faded away. A few minutes later a long blast was blown on a whistle, there were near and distant cries of "Stand–to," and Cecil Clarence returned to the Mess *banda*. He was wearing tunic and cross–belt. On his cheerful young face was a look of portentous solemnity as he approached the Major, halted, saluted, stared at him as at a perfect stranger, and said: "Stand–to, sir. All present and correct."

Over the Major's face stole a similar expression. He looked as one who has received sudden, interesting and important but anxious news.

"Thank you," said he. "I'll—ah—go round. Yes. Come with me, will you? ..." Cecil Clarence again saluted, and fell in behind the Major as he left the *banda*. Bertram followed. The Major went to his tent and put on his tunic and cross–belt. These did little to improve the unfastenable riding–breeches, bare calves and grey socks, but were evidently part of the rite.

Proceeding thence to the entrance to the *boma*, the Major squeezed through, was saluted by the guard, and there met by an English officer in the dress of the small men whom Bertram had noticed on his arrival. His white face looked incongruous with the blue turban and tartan petticoat. "All present and correct, sir," said he. Half his men were down in the trench, their rifles resting in the loop–holes of the parapet. These loop–holes were of wicker–work, like bottomless waste–paper baskets, and were built into the earthwork of the parapet so that a man, looking through one, had a foot of earth and logs above his head. The other half of his blue–clad force was inside the *boma* and lining the wall. This wall, some eight feet in height, had been built by erecting two walls of stout wattle and posts, two feet apart, and then filling the space between these two with earth. Along the bottom of the wall ran a continuous fire–step, some two feet in height, and a line of wicker–work loop–holes pierced it near the top. In the angle, where this side of the *boma* met the other, was a tower of posts, wattle and earth, some twelve feet in height, and on it, within an earth–and–wattle wall, and beneath a thatched roof, was a machine–gun and its team of King's African

Rifles *askaris*, in charge of an English N.C.O. On the roof squatted a sentry, who stared at the sky with a look of rapt attention to duty.

"How are those two men, Black?" asked the Major, as the N.C.O. saluted.

"Very bad, sir," was the reply. "They'll die to night. I'm quite sure the Germans had poisoned that honey and left it for our *askari* patrols to find. I wondered at the time that they 'adn't skoffed it themselves. ... And it so near their *boma* and plain to see, an' all.... I never thought about poison till it was too late...."

"Foul swine!" said the Major. "I suppose it's a trick they learnt from the *shenzis*, this poisoning wild honey? ... "

"More like they taught it 'em, sir," was the reply. "There ain't no savage as low as a German, sir.... I lived in German East, I did, afore the war.... I *know* 'em...."

The next face of the *boma* was held by the Hundred and Ninety–Eighth. Captain Macke met the Major and saluted him as a revered stranger. He, too, wore tunic and cross–belt and a look of portentous solemnity, such as that on the faces of the Major, Cecil Clarence, and, indeed, everybody else. Bertram, later, labelled it the Stand–to face and practised to acquire it.

"How many sick, Captain Macke?" enquired the Major.

"Twenty–seven, sir," was the reply. Bertram wondered whether they were "present" in the spirit and "correct" in form.

"All fever or dysentery—or both, I suppose?" said the Major.

"Yes—except one with a poisoned foot and one who seems to be going blind," was the reply.

As they passed along, the Major glanced at each man, looked into the canvas water–tanks, scrutinised the residential sheds beneath the wall—and, in one of them discovered a scrap of paper! As the ground was covered with leaves, twigs, and bits of grass, as well as being thick with mud, Bertram did not see that this piece of paper mattered much. This only shows his ignorance. The Major pointed at it, speechless. Captain Macke paled—with horror, wrath or grief. Gussie Augustus Gus stooped and stared at it, screwing his monocle in the tighter, that he might see the better and not be deceived. Vereker turned it over with his stick, and only then believed the evidence of three of his senses. The Jemadar shook his head with incredulous but pained expression. He called for the Havildar, whose mouth fell open. The two men were very alike, being relatives, but while the senior wore a look of incredulous pain, the junior, it seemed to Bertram, rather wore one of pained incredulity. That is to say, the Jemadar looked stricken but unable to believe his eyes, whereas the Havildar looked as though he could not believe his eyes but was stricken nevertheless.

All stared hard at the piece of paper.... It was a poignant moment.... No one moved and no one seemed to breathe. Suddenly the Havildar touched a Naik who stood behind his men, with his back to the group of officers, and stared fixedly at Nothing. He turned, beheld the paper at which the Havildar's accusing finger pointed, rigid but tremulous.... What next? The Naik pocketed the paper, and the incident was closed.

Bertram was glad that he had witnessed it. He knew, thenceforth, the proper procedure for an officer who, wearing the Stand–to face, sees a piece of paper.

The third wall of the *boma* was occupied by a company of Dogras of an Imperial Service Corps, under a Subedar, a fine–looking Rajput, and a company of Marathas of the Hundred and Ninety–Eighth, under the Subedar–Major of that regiment. Bertram was strongly attracted to this latter officer, and thought that never before had he seen an Indian whose face combined so much of patient strength, gentle firmness, simple honesty, and noble pride.

He was introduced to Bertram, and, as they shook hands and saluted, the fine old face was lit up with a smile of genuine pleasure and friendly respectfulness. A man of the old school who recognised duties as well as "rights"—and in whose sight "*false to his salt*" was the last and lowest epithet of uttermost degradation.

"You'll have charge of this face of the fort to–morrow, Greene," said the Major, as they passed on. "Subedar–Major Luxman Atmaram is a priceless old bird. He'll see you have no trouble…. Don't be in a hurry to tell him off for anything, because it's a hundred to one you'll find he's right."

Bertram smiled to himself at the thought of his being the sort to "tell off" anybody without due cause and was secretly pleased to find that Major Mallery had thought such a thing possible….

The remaining side of the fort was held by Gurkhas, and Bertram noted the fact with pleasure. He had taken a great fancy to these cheery, steady people. Another machine–gun, with its team of *askaris* of the King's African Rifles, occupied the middle of this wall.

"Don't cough or sneeze near the gun," murmured Vereker to Bertram, "or it may fall to pieces again. The copper–wire is all right, but the boot–lace was not new to begin with."

"What kind of gun is it?" he asked.

"It was a Hotchkiss once. It's a Hot–potch now," was the reply. "Don't touch it as you pass," and the puzzled Bertram observed that it was actually bound with copper–wire at one point and tied with some kind of cord or string at another.

By the hospital—a horrible pit with a tent over it—stood the Indian youth and a party of Swahili stretcher–bearers.

Bertram wondered whether it would ever be his fate to be carried on one of those blood–stained stretchers by a couple of those negroes, laid on the mud at the bottom of that pit, and operated on by that young native of India. He shuddered. Fancy one's life–blood ebbing away into that mud. Fancy dying, mangled, in that hole with no one but a Bupendranath Chatterji to soothe one's last agonies….

Having completed his tour of inspection, Major Mallery removed the Stand–to face and resumed his ordinary one, said: "They can dismiss," to Captain Macke and the group of officers, and tore off his cross–belt and tunic.

All his hearers relaxed their faces likewise, blew their whistles, cried "Dismiss!" in the direction of their respective Native Officers, and removed their belts and tunics almost as quickly as they had removed their Stand–to faces.

They then proceeded to the Bristol Bar.

CHAPTER XVI

The Bristol Bar

"Come along to the Bristol Bar and have a drink, Greene," said Cecil Clarence, *alias* Gussie Augustus Gus, emerging from his *banda*, into which he had cast his tunic and Sam Browne belt.

"Thanks," replied Bertram, wondering if there were a Jungle Hotel within easy reach of the *boma*, or whether the outpost had its own Place, "licensed for the sale of beer, wine, spirits, and tobacco, to be consumed on the premises...."

In the High Street, next door to the Officers' Mess, were two green tents, outside one of which stood a rough camp–table of the "folding" variety, a native string bed, and a circle of Roorkee chairs, boxes and stools. On an erection of sticks and withes, resembling an umbrella stand, stood an orderly array of fresh coco–nuts, the tops of which had been sliced off to display the white interior with its pint or so of sweet, limpid milk.

Emerging from the tent, an Arab "boy" in a blue turban, blue jacket buttoning up to the chin, blue petticoat and puttees, placed bottles of various kinds on the table, together with a "sparklet" apparatus and a pannikin of water. The Bristol Bar was open.... From the other tent emerged an officer in the blue uniform of the little fair men.

He eyed the muddy ground, the ugly grey *bandas* of withered grass and leaves, the muddy, naked Kavirondo—piling their loads on the commissariat dump, and the general dreary, cheerless scene, with the cold eye of extreme distaste and disfavour.

"*Yah*!" said he. He eyed the bottles on the table.

"*Ah*!" said he, and seated himself behind the Bristol Bar.

"Start with a Ver–Gin, I think, as I've been such a good boy to–day," he murmured, and, pouring a measure of Italian vermuth into an enamelled mug, he added a smaller allowance of gin.

"Wish some fool'd roll up so that I can get a drink," he grumbled, holding the mug in his hand.

It did not occur to him to "*faire Suisse*," as the French say—to drink alone. He must at least say "Chin–chin" or "Here's how" to somebody else with a drink in his hand. Had it been cocoa, now, or something of that sort, one might drink gallons of it without a word to a soul. One could lie in bed and wallow and soak, lap it up like a cat or take it in through the pores—but this little drop of alcohol must not be drunk without a witness and a formula. So Lieutenant Forbes possessed his soul in impatience.

A minute later, from every *banda* and tent, from the Officers' Mess and from all directions, came British officers, bearing each man in his hands something to drink or something from which to drink.

The Major bore The Glass, and, behind him, the Mess butler carried a square bottle of ration whisky. He was followed by a Swahili clasping to his bosom a huge jar of ration rum, newly arrived. "Leesey" Lindsay, of the Intelligence Department, brought a collapsible silver cup, which, as he said, only wanted knowing. It leaked and it collapsed at inappropriate moments, but, on the other hand, it *did* collapse, and you could put it in your pocket—where it collected tobacco dust, crumbs, fluff, and grit. Vereker carried a fresh coco–nut and half a coco–nut shell. This latter he was going to carve and polish. He said that coco–nut shells carved beautifully and took a wonderful polish.... His uncle, an admiral, had one which he brought from the South Sea Islands. It was beautifully carved and had taken a high polish—from someone or other. A cannibal chief had drunk human blood from it for years.... Vereker was going to drink whisky from his for years, and keep it all his life—carving and polishing it between whiles.... "Yes. I used that as a drinking–cup all through my first campaign. It nearly fell on my head in the first battle I ever fought. Cut off the tree by a bullet. Carved and polished it myself," he would be able to say, in years to come. Meanwhile it looked a very ordinary half–shell of the common coco–nut of commerce as known to those who upon Saints' Days and Festivals do roll, bowl, or pitch....

Captain Macke brought a prepared siphon of "sparklet" water and his ration whisky. Gussie Augustus Gus walked delicately, bearing a brimming condensed milk tin, and singing softly—

"Dear, sweet Mother,
Kind and true;
She's a boozer,
Through and through ....
But roll your tail,
And roll it high,
And you'll be an angel
By and by...."

Lieutenant Bupendranath Chatterji brought a harsh laugh and an uncultivated taste, but a strong liking, for assorted liquors, preferably sweet. The officer who had been in command of the side of the fort occupied by the men in blue entered the tent and, having removed his belt, seated himself beside Lieutenant Forbes, behind the bar.

"Good evening, Major," said he; "won't you come and have a drink? ... Do!"

Regarding The Glass with a look of surprise, and as though wondering how the devil it came to be there, the Major considered the invitation.

"Thanks!" said he. "Don't mind if I *do* sit down for a moment." And he placed The Glass upon the table. Strangely enough, his own Roorkee chair was already in the centre of the circle facing the said table, as it had been any evening at this time for the last fifty nights. The Mess butler put the rum and whisky beneath his chair. "Let me introduce Lieutenant Greene, attached to Ours. Wavell ... " said he.... "Captain Wavell of Wavell's Arabs, Greene," and Bertram shook hands with a remarkable and romantic soldier of fortune, explorer and adventurous knight–errant, whom he came to like, respect, and admire with the greatest warmth. The others drifted up and dropped in, accidentally and casually, as it were, until almost all were there, and the Bristol Bar was full; the hour of the evening star and the evening drink had arrived; *l'heure d'absinthe*, *l'heure verte* had struck; the sun was below the yard–arm; now the day was over, night was drawing nigh, shadows of the evening stole across the sky; and, war or no war, hunger, mud, disease and misery, or no hunger, mud, disease and misery, the British officer was going to have his evening cocktail, his evening cheroot, and his evening "buck" at the club bar—and to the devil with all Huns who'd interfere with his sacred rights and their sacred rites.

"Here's the best, Major," said Forbes, and drank his ver–gin with gusto and appreciation. His very fine long–lashed eyes beneath faultlessly curving eyebrows—eyes which many a woman had enviously and regretfully considered to be criminally wasted on a mere man—viewed the grey prospect with less disgust.

The first drink of the day provided the best minute of the day to this exile from the cream of the joys of Europe; and he eyed the array of bottles with something approaching optimism as he considered the question of what should be his drink for the evening.

"Cheerioh!" responded the Major, and took a pull at the whisky and slightly–aerated water in The Glass. "Here's to Good Count Zeppelin our finest recruiting agent, and Grandpa Tirpitz who'll bring America in on our side…."

"What'll you drink, Greene?" asked Wavell. "Vermuth? Whisky? Rum? Gin? Try an absinthe? Or can I mix you a Risky—rum and whisky, you know—or a Whum—whisky and rum, of course?"

"They're both helpful and cheering," added Forbes.

"Let me make you a cock–eye," put in Gussie Augustus Gus. "Thing of my own. Much better than a mere cocktail. Thought of it in bed last night while I was sayin' my prayers. This is one," and he raised his condensed milk tin. "Cross between milk–punch, cocktail, high–ball, gin–sling, rum–shrub, and a bitters…. Go down to posterity as a 'Gussie'—along with the John Collins and Elsie May…. Great thought…. Let us pause before it…."

"What's in it?" asked Captain Macke.

"Condensed milk," replied Augustus, "ration lime–juice, ration rum, ration whisky, medical–comfort brandy, vermuth, coco–nut milk, angostura, absinthe, glycerine…."

"And a damn great flying caterpillar," added the Major as a hideous insect, with a fat, soft body, splashed into the pleasing compound.

"Dirty dog!" grumbled Augustus, fishing for the creature. "Here, don't play submarines in the mud, Eustace—be a sport and swim…. I can drink down to him, anyhow," he added, failing to secure the enterprising little animal with a finger and thumb that groped short of the bottom stratum of his concoction. "Got his head stuck in the toffee–milk at the bottom." Bertram declined a "Gussie," feeling unworthy, also unable.

"Have you tried rum and coco–nut milk?" asked Wavell. "It's a kind of local industry since we've been here. The Intelligence Department keeps a Friendly Tribe at work bringing in fresh coco–nuts, and our numerous different detachments provide fatigue–parties in rotation to open them…. Many a worse drink than half a tumbler of ration rum poured into the coco–nut…."

"Point of fact—I'm a teetotaller just at present," replied Bertram, sadly but firmly. "May I substitute lime–juice for rum? … "

Vereker screwed in his monocle and regarded him. Not with astonishment or interest, of course, for nothing astonished or interested him any more. He was too young and wise for those emotions. But he regarded him.

"What a dreadful habit to contract at your age, Greene," observed Augustus, slightly shocked. "Y'ought to pull yourself together, y'know. … Give it up…. Bad…. Bad…" and he shook his head.

"What's it feel like?" asked Captain Macke.

"You've been getting into bad company, my lad," said Major Mallery.

"Oah! Maan, maan! You must not do thatt!" said Mr. Chatterji.

"I've got some ration lime–juice here," said Wavell, "but I really don't advise it as a drink in this country. It's useful stuff to have about when you can't get vegetables of any sort—but I believe it thins your blood, gives you boils, and upsets your tummy.... Drop of rum or whisky in the evening ... do you more good."

Bertram's heart warmed to the kindly friendliness of his voice and manner—the more because he felt that, like himself, this famous traveller and explorer was of a shy and diffident nature.

"Thanks. I'll take your advice then," he said, and reflected that what was good enough for Wavell was good enough for him, in view of the former's unique experience of African and Asiatic travel. "I'll try the rum and coco–nut milk if I may," he added.

"Three loud cheers!" remarked Augustus. "Won't mother be pleased! ... I'm going to write a book about it, Greene, if you don't mind.... 'The Redemption of Lieutenant Greene' or somethin'.... *You* know—how on the Eve of Battle, in a blinding flash of self–illuminating introspection, he saw his soul for the Thing it was, saw just where he stood—on the brink of an Abyss.... And repented in time.... Poignant.... Repented and drank rum.... Searching."

"Probably Greene's pulling our legs the whole time, my good ass," put in Vereker. "Dare say he's really a frightful drunkard. Riotous reveller and wallowing wassailer.... He's got rather a wild eye...."

Bertram laughed with the rest. It was impossible to take offence, for there was nothing in the slightest degree offensive about these pleasant, friendly people.

Berners joined the group and saluted the Major. "Ammunition and ration indents all present and correct, sir," said he.

"Rum ration all right?" asked the Major. "How do you know the jars aren't full of water?"

"P'raps he'd better select one at random as a sample and bring it over here, Major," suggested Macke. And it was so....

Another officer drifted in and was introduced to Bertram as Lieutenant Halke of the Coolie Corps, in charge of the Kavirondo, Wakamba, and Monumwezi labourers and porters attached to the Butindi garrison.

He was an interesting man, a big, burly planter, who had been in the colony for twenty years. "I want your birds to dig another trench to–morrow, Halke," said the Major. "Down by the water–picket."

"Very good, sir," replied Halke. "I'm glad that convoy rolled up safely to–day. Their *posho* [32] was running rather low ... " and the conversation became technical.

Bertram felt distinctly better for his rum and milk. His weariness fell from him like a garment, and life took on brighter hues. He was not a wretched, weary lad, caught up in the maelstrom of war and flung from pleasant city streets into deadly primeval jungles, where lurked Death in the form of bacillus, savage beast, and more savage and more beastly Man. Not at all. He was one of a band of Britain's soldiers in an outpost of Empire on her far–flung battle–line.... One of a group of cheery comrades, laughing and jesting in the face of danger and discomfort.... He had Answered His Country's Call, and was of the great freemasonry of arms, sword on thigh, marching, marching.... Camp–fire and bivouac... . The Long Trail.... Beyond the Ranges.... Men who have Done Things.... A sun–burnt, weather–beaten man from the Back of Beyond.... Strong, silent man with a Square Jaw.... Romance.... Adventure.... Life. He drank some more of his rum and felt very happy. He nodded, drooped, snored—and nearly fell off his stool. Wavell smiled as he jerked upright again, and tried to look as though he had never slept in his life.

"So Pappa behaved nasty," Gussie Augustus Gus was saying to a deeply interested audience. "He'd just been turned down himself by a gay and wealthy widowette whom he'd marked down for his Number 2. When I said, 'Pappa, I'm going to be married on Monday, please,' he spake pompous platitudes, finishing up with: '*A young man married is a young man marred.*' ... 'Yes, Pappa,' says I thoughtlessly, '*and an old man jilted is an old man jarred.*' ... Caused quite a coolness. So I went to sea." Augustus sighed and drank—and then almost choked with violent spluttering and coughing.

"That blasted Eustace!" he said, as he suddenly and vehemently expelled something.

"Did you marry her?" asked Vereker, showing no sympathy in the matter of the unexpected recovery of the body of Eustace.

"No," said Augustus. "Pappa did." ...

"That's what I went to see," he added.

"Don't believe you ever had a father," said Vereker.

"I didn't," said Gussie Augustus Gus. "I was an orphan.... Am still. ... Poignant.... Searching...."

Lieutenant Bupendranath Chatterji listened to this sort of thing with an owlish expression on his fat face. When anybody laughed he laughed also, loudly and raucously.

It was borne in upon Bertram that it took more than fever, hunger, boredom, mud, rain and misery to depress the spirits of the officers of the garrison of Butindi....

"*Khana tyar hai*, [33] *Sahib*," announced the Major's butler, salaaming.

"Come and gnaw ropes and nibble bricks, Greene," said the officer addressed, and with adieux to Wavell and Forbes, who ran a mess of their own, the guests departed from the Bristol Bar and entered the Officers' Mess. Here Bertram learnt the twin delights of a native bedstead when used as a seat. You can either sit on the narrow wooden edge until you feel as though you have been sitting on a hot wire for a week, or you can slide back on to the string part and slowly, slowly disappear from sight, and from dinner.

"This water drawn from the river and been standing in the bath all day, boy?"

"*Han*, [34] *Sahib*," replied that worthy.

"Alum in the water?"

"*Han, Sahib.*"

"Water then filtered?"

"*Han, Sahib.*"

"Water then boiled?"

"*Han, Sahib.*"

"*Pukka* boiled?"

"*Han, Sahib*, all bubbling."

"Filtered again? You saw it all done yourself?"

"*Han, Sahib.*"

"That's all right, then," concluded the Major.

This catechism was the invariable prelude to the Major's use of water for drinking purposes, whether in the form of *aqua pura*, whisky and water, or tea. For the only foe that Major Mallery feared was the disease–germ. To bullet and bayonet, shrapnel and shell–splinter, he gave no thought. To cholera, enteric and dysentery he gave much, and if care with his drinking water would do it, he intended to avoid those accursed scourges of the tropics. Holding up the glass to the light of the hurricane lamp which adorned the clothless table of packing–case boards, he gazed through it—as one may do when caressing a glass of crusted ruby port—and mused upon the wisdom that had moved him to make it the sole and special work of one special man to see that he had a plentiful supply of pure fair water.

He gazed.... And slowly his idle abstracted gaze became a stare and a glare. His eyes protruded from his head, and he gave a yell of gasping horror and raging wrath that drew the swift attention of all—

While round and round in the alum–ised, filtered, boiled and re–filtered water, there slowly swam—a little fish.

* * * * *

Dinner was painfully similar to that at M'paga, save that the party, being smaller, was more of a Happy Family. It began with what Vereker called "Chatty" soup (because it was "made from talkative meat, in a chattie"), proceeded to inedible bully–beef, and terminated with dog–biscuit and coco–nut—unless you chose to eat your daily banana then.

During dinner, another officer, who had been out all day on a reconnaissance–patrol, joined the party, drank a pint of rum–and–coco–nut milk and fell asleep on the bedstead whereon he sat. He looked terribly thin and ill.

Macke punched him in the ribs, sat him up, and banged the tin plate of cold soup with his knife till the idea of "dinner" had penetrated the sleepy brain of the new–corner. "Feed yer face, Murie," he shouted in his ear.

"Thanks awf'ly," said that gentleman, took up his spoon, and toppled over backwards on to the bed with a loud snore.

"Disgustin' manners," said Gussie Augustus Gus.

"I wish we had a siphon of soda–water. I'd wake him all right."

"Set him on fire," suggested Vereker.

"He's too beastly wet, the sneak," complained Gussie.

"Oah, he iss sleepee," observed Lieutenant Bupendranath Chatterji.

Vereker regarded him almost with interest.

"What makes you think so?" he asked politely. In the laugh that followed, the sleeper was forgotten and remained where he was until Stand–to the following morning. He was living on quinine and his nerves—which form an insufficient diet in tropical Africa.

"Where *Bwana* sleeping to–night, sah, please Mister?" whispered Ali, as, dinner finished, Bertram sat listening with deep interest to the conversation.

Pipes alight, and glasses, mugs and condensed milk tins charged, the Mess was talking of all things most distant and different from jungle swamps and dirty, weary war....

"Quite most 'sclusive Society in Oxford, I tell you," Gussie was saying. "Called ourselves *The Astronomers*...."

"What the devil for? Because you were generally out at night?" asked Macke.

"No—because we studied the Stars—of the Stage," was the reply....

"Rotten," said Vereker, with a shiver. "You sh'd have called yourselves *The Botanists*," he added a minute later.

"Why?"

"Because you culled Peroxide Daisies and Lilies of the Ballet."

"Ghastly," observed Gussie, with a shudder. "And *cull* is a beastly word. One who culls is a cully.... How'd you like to be called *Cully*, Murie?" he shouted in that officer's ear. Receiving no reply, he pounded upon the sleeper's stomach with one hand while violently rolling his head from side to side with the other.

Murie awoke.

"Whassup?" he jerked out nervously.

"How'd you like to be called *Cully*?" shouted Gussie again.

Murie fixed a glassy eye on him. His face was chalky white and his black hair lay dank across his forehead.

"Eh?" said he.

Gussie repeated his enquiry.

"Call me anything—but don't call me early," was the reply, as he realised who and where he was, and closed his eyes again.

"*You're* an ornament to the Mess. *You* add to the gaiety of nations. *You* ought to be on the halls," shouted the tormentor. "You're a refined Society Entertainer…."

"Eh?" grunted Murie.

"Come for a walk in the garden I said," shouted Augustus. "Oh, you give me trypanosomiasis to look at you," he added.

"You go to Hell," replied Murie, and snored as he finished speaking.

Bertram felt a little indignant.

"Wouldn't it be kinder to let him sleep?" he said.

"No, it wouldn't," was the reply. "He'll sleep there for an hour, and then go over to his hut and be awake all night because he's had no dinner."

"I beg your pardon," said Bertram—and asked the Major where he was to sleep that night.

"On your right side, with your mouth shut," was the reply; to which Augustus added:

"Toe of the right foot in line with the mouth; thumb in rear of the seam of the pyjamas; heel of the left foot in the hollow of the back; and weight of the body on the chin–strap—as laid down in the drill–book."

"Haven't you a tent?" asked the Major, and, in learning that Bertram had not, said that a *banda* should be built for him on the morrow, and that he could sleep on or under the Mess table that night….

When the Major had returned to his tent with the remark "All lights out in fifteen minutes," Ali set up Bertram's bed in the Mess *banda*, and in a few minutes the latter was alone…. As he sat removing his boots, Bertram was surprised to see Gussie Augustus Gus return to the Mess, carrying a native spear and a bundle of white material. Going to where Murie lay, he raised the spear and drove it with all his force—apparently into Murie's body! Springing to his feet, Bertram saw that the spear was stuck into the clay and that the shaft, protruding through the meshes of the bed string, stood up beside Murie. Throwing the mosquito–net over the top of it, Gussie enveloped the sleeper in its folds, as well as he could, and vanished.

---

[32] Food.

[33] "Dinner is ready."

[34]Yes.

Chapter XVII

More Baking

Bertram was awakened at dawn by the bustle and stir of Stand–to. He arose and dressed, by the simple process of putting on his boots and helmet, which, by reason of rain, wind, mud and publicity, were the only garments he had removed. Proceeding to that face of the fort which was to be his special charge, he found that one half of its defenders were lining its water–logged trench, and the other half, its wall. It was a depressing hour and place. Depressing even to one who had not slept in his wet clothes and arisen with throbbing head, horrible mouth, aching limbs and with the sense of a great sinking void within.

Around the fort was a sea of withering brushwood, felled trees, scrub and thorn, grey and ugly: inside the fort, a lake of mud. Burly Subedar–Major Luxman Atmaram seemed cheery and bright, so Bertram endeavoured to emulate him.

The Major, accompanied by Vereker (who called himself Station Staff Officer, Aide–de–camp to the O.C. Troops, Assistant Provost Marshal, and other sonorous names), passed on his tour of inspection. Bertram saluted.

"Good morning, sir," said he.

"Think so?" said the Major, and splashed upon his way.

"Good morning, Vereker," said Bertram, as that gentleman passed.

"Nothing of the sort. Wrong again," replied Vereker, and splashed upon *his* way.

Both were wearing the Stand–to face, and looked coldly upon Bertram, who was not.

After "Dismiss," Bertram returned to the Mess *banda*.

"Good morning, Greene," said the Major, and:

"Good morning, Greene," echoed Vereker.

Bertram decided that his not being properly dressed in the matter of the Stand–to face, was overlooked or condoned, in view of his youth and inexperience.... The vast metal teapot and a tray of dog–biscuits made their appearance.

"I'm going to have my bloater now," said Berners, plucking a banana from the weary–looking bunch. "Will someone remind me that I have had it, if I go to take another?"

"I will," volunteered Augustus. "Any time you pluck a bloater and I hit you on the head three times with the tent–peg mallet, that means 'Nay, Pauline.' See?" ...

"What's the Programme of Sports for to–day, sir?" asked Berners of the Major, as he cleansed his fingers of over–ripe banana upon Augustus's silky hair.

"Macke takes a strong Officer's Patrol towards Muru," replied the Major. "Halke starts getting the trenches deepened a bit. You can wrestle with commissariat and ammunition returns, and the others might do a bit of parade and physical jerks or something this morning. I'm going to sneak round and catch the pickets on the hop. You'd better come with me, Greene, and see where they're posted. Tell the Subedar–Major what you want your men to do. Wavell's taking his people for a march. Murie will be in charge of the fort...."

"Murie has temperature of one hundred and five," put in Lieutenant Bupendranath Chatterji. "He has fever probably."

"Shouldn't be at all surprised," observed the Major dryly. "What are you giving him?"

"Oah, he will be all right," was the reply.

"I've got three fresh limes I pinched from that *shamba*," [35] said Augustus. "If he had those with a quart of boiling water and half a tin of condensed milk, he might be able to do a good sweat and browse a handful of quinine."

"No more condensed milk," said Berners. "Greene had the last tin last night, and the hog didn't bring any with him."

"I shall be delighted to contribute the remainder of it," said Bertram, looking into his tin. "There's quite three–quarters of it left."

"Good egg," applauded Augustus. "If you drink your tea from the tin, you'll get the flavour of milk for ever so long," and Ali having been despatched to the cook–house for a kettle of boiling water, Augustus fetched his limes and the two concocted the brew with their condensed milk and lime–juice in an empty rum–jar.

"What about a spot of whisky in it?" suggested Vereker.

"Better without it when fever is violent," opined the medical attendant, and Augustus, albeit doubtfully, accepted the *obiter dicta*, as from one who should know.

"Shall I shove it into him through the oil–funnel if he is woozy?" he asked, and added: "Better not, p'r'aps. Might waste half of it down his lungs and things ... " and he departed, in search of his victim.

As Bertram left the *boma* in company of the Major, he found it difficult to realise that, only a few hours earlier he had not set eyes on the place. He seemed to have been immured within its walls of mud and wattle for days, rather than hours.

About the large clearing that lay on that side of the fort, Sepoys, servants, porters and *askaris* came and went upon their occasions; the stretcher–bearers, gun–teams, and a company of Gurkhas were at drill; and in the trenches, the long, weedy bodies of the Kavirondo rose and fell as they dug in the mud and clay. Near the gate a doleful company of sick and sorry porters squatted and watched a dresser of the Indian Subordinate Medical Department, as he sprinkled iodoform from a pepperbox on to the hideous sores and wounds of a separate squad requiring such treatment. The sight of an intensely black back, with a huge wound of a glowing red, upon which fell a rain of brilliant yellow iodoform, held Bertram's spell–bound gaze, while it made him feel exceedingly sick. Those patients suffering from ghastly sores and horrible festering wounds seemed gay and lighthearted and utterly indifferent, while the remainder, suffering from *tumbo*, [36] fever, cold in the head, or world–weariness, appeared to consider themselves at the last gasp, and each, like the Dying Gladiator, did lean his head upon his hand while his manly brow consented to Death, but conquered agony.

"The reason why the African will regard a gaping wound, or great festering sore, with no more than mild interest, while he will wilt away and proceed to perish if he has a stomach–ache is an interestin' exemplification of *omne ignotum pro magnifico*," remarked the Major.

Bertram stared at his superior officer in amazement. The tone and language were utterly different from those hitherto connected, in Bertram's experience, with that gentleman. Was this a subtle mockery of Bertram as a civilian Intellectual? Or was it that the Major liked to be "all things to all men" and considered this the style of conversation likely to be suitable to the occasion?

"Yes, sir?" said Bertram, a trifle shortly.

"Yes," continued Major Mallery. "He believes that all internal complaints are due to Devils. A stomach–ache is, to him, painful and irrefragible proof that he hath a Devil. One has entered into him and abideth. It's no good telling him anything to the contrary—because he can *feel* It there, and surely he's the best judge of what he can feel? So any internal complaint terrifies him to such an extent that he dies of fright—whereas he'll think nothing of a wound that would kill you or me. ..."

Here, apparently, the Major's mocking fancy tired, or else his effort to talk "high–brow" to an Intellectual could be no further sustained, for he fell to lower levels with the remark:

"Rum blokes... Dam' funny..." and fell silent.

A well–trodden mud path led down to the river, on the far side of which was the water–picket commanding the approach, not to a ford, but to the only spot where impenetrable jungle did not prevent access to the river. ...

"Blighters nearly copped us badly down here before we built the fort," said the Major. "Look in here ... " and he parted some bushes beside the path and disappeared. Following him, Bertram found himself in a long, narrow clearing cut out of the solid jungle and parallel with the path.

"They had a hundred men at least, in here," said Major Mallery, "and you might have come along the path a hundred times without spotting them. There was a machine–gun up that tree, to deal with the force behind the point of ambush, and a big staked pit farther down the path to catch those in front who ran straight on.... Lovely trap.... They used to occupy it from dawn to sunset every day, poor fellers...."

"What happened?" asked Bertram.

"Our Intelligence Department learnt all about it from the local *shenzis*, and we forestalled them one merry morn. They were ambushed in their own ambush.... The *shenzi* doesn't love his Uncle Fritz a bit. No appreciation of *Kultur*–by–*kiboko*. He calls the Germans '*the Twenty–Five Lashes People*,' because the first thing the German does when he goes to a village is to give everybody twenty–five of the best, by way of introducing himself and starting with a proper understanding. Puts things on a proper footing from the beginning...."

"Their *askaris* are staunch enough, aren't they?" asked Bertram.

"Absolutely. They are well paid and well fed, and they are allowed to do absolutely as they like in the way of loot, rape, arson and murder, once the fighting is over.... They flog them most unmercifully for disciplinary offences—and the nigger understands that. Also they leave the defeated foe—his village, crops, property, women, children and wounded—to their mercy—and the nigger understands *that* too.... Our *askaris* are not nearly so contented with our milder punishments, cumbrous judicial system, and absolute prohibition of loot, rape, arson and the murder of the wounded. Yes—the German *askari* will stick to the German so long as he gets the conqueror's rights whenever he conquers—as is the immemorial law and custom of Africa.... 'What's the good of fighting a cove if you're going to cosset and coddle him directly you've won, and give him something out of the poor–box—instead of dismembering him?' says he.... You might say the *askari*–class is to the Native what the Junker–class is to the peasant, in Germany."

And conversing thus, the two officers visited the pickets and the sentries, who sat on *machans* in the tops of high trees and, in theory at any rate, scoured the adjacent country with tireless all–seeing eye.

Returning to the fort, Bertram saw the materials for his own private freehold residence being carried to the eligible site selected for its erection by the united wisdom of the Station Staff Officer and the Quartermaster. It was built and furnished in less than an hour by a party of Kavirondo, who used no other tools than their *pangas*, and it consisted of a framework of stout saplings firmly planted in the ground, wattle, and thatched leaves, twigs and grass. It had a window–frame and a doorway, and it kept out the sun and the first few drops of a shower of rain. If a *banda* does little else, it provides one's own peculiar place apart, where one can be private and alone.... On the table and shelf—of sticks bound together with strips of bark—Ali set forth his master's impedimenta, and took a pride in the Home....

Finding that the spine–pad of quilted red flannel—which Murray had advised him to get and to wear buttoned on to the inner side of his shirt, as a protection against the sun's actinic rays—was soaked with perspiration, Bertram gave it to Ali that it might be dried. What he did not foresee was that his faithful retainer would tie a long strip of bark from the new *banda* to the opposite one across the "street," and pin the red flannel article to flap in the breeze and the face of the passer–by. ...

"Oh, I say, you fellers, look here!" sang out the voice of Gussie Augustus Gus, as Bertram was finishing his shave, a few minutes later. "Here's that careless fellow, Greene, been and left his chest–protector off! ... It's on the line to air, and I *don't* know what he's doing without it." The voice broke with anguish and trouble as it continued: "Perhaps running about with nothing on at all.... On his chest, I mean...."

There was a laugh from neighbouring *bandas* and tents where Vereker, Berners, Halke and "Leesey" Lindsay were washing by their cottage doors, preparatory to breakfast.

Bertram blushed hotly in the privacy of his hut. *Chest–protector*! Confound the fellow's impudence—and those giggling' idiots. He had half a mind to put his head out and remark; "The laughter of fools is as the crackling of thorns beneath a pot," and in the same moment wiser counsels prevailed.

Thrusting a soapy face out of the window, he said, in a tone expressive more of sorrow than of anger:

"I am surprised at *you*, Clarence! ... To laugh at the infirmities of your elders! ... Is it *my* fault I have housemaid's knee?"

To which Augustus, with tears in his eyes and voice, replied:

"Forgive me, Pappa. I have known trouble too. *I* had an Aunt with a corn.... *She* wore one.... Pink, like yours.... Poignant.... Searching...."

This cheerful and indefatigable young gentleman had, in his rôle of Mess President, found time, after parade and kit–inspection that morning, to prepare a breakfast *menu*. Consulting it, Bertram discovered promise of

1. *Good Works*. Taken out of some animal, or animals, unknown.
Perhaps Liver. Perhaps not. Looks rather poignant.
2. *Shepherd's Bush* (or is it Plaid or Pie?) or Toed–in–the–Hole.
Same as above, bedded down in manioc. Looks very poignant.

3. There were *Sausages on Toast*, but they are in bad odour, uppish, and peevish to the eye, and there is no bread.

4. *Curried Bully–beef*. God help us. And Dog–biscuit.

5. *Arm of monkey*. No 'arm in that? *But*—One rupee reward is offered for a missing Kavirondo baby. Answers to the name of Horatio, and cries if bitten in the stomach.... Searching.

"Great news," quoth the author of this document, seating himself on the bed–frame beside Bertram and eyeing a plate of Good Works without enthusiasm. "There's to be a General Court–Martial after breakfast. You and I and Berners. Leesey Lindsay is prosecuting a bloke for spying and acting as guide to German raiding parties—him bein' a British subjick an' all... Splendid! ... Shall we hang him or shoot him? ... "

"*I* am Provost–Marshal," put in Vereker, "and *I* shall hang him. I know exactly how to hang, and am a recognised good hanger. Anyhow, no one has complained.... Wish we had some butter...."

"Whaffor?" asked Augustus.

"Grease the rope," was the reply. "They like it. Butter is awfully good."

"Put the knot under the left ear, don't you?" asked Augustus.

"*I* do," answered Vereker. "Some put it under the right.... I have seen it at the back. Looks bad, though. Depressin'. Bloke hangs his head. Mournful sight...."

"Got any rope?" enquired Augustus.

"No! ... How thoughtless of me! ... Never mind—make up something with strips of bark.... Might let the bloke make his own—only himself to blame, then, if it broke and he met with an accident."

"I *have* heard of suicides—and—people hanging themselves with their braces," observed Augustus.

"Wadego *shenzis* don't have braces," replied Vereker.

"No, but Greene does. I'm perfectly sure he'd be delighted to lend you his. He's kindness itself. Or would you rather he were shot, Greene? We must remember there's no blood about a hanging, whereas there's lots the other way—'specially if it's done by *askaris* with Martinis.... On the other hand, hanging lasts longer. I dunno *what* to advise for the best...."

"Suppose we try him first," suggested Bertram.

"Of course!" was the somewhat indignant reply. "I'm surprised at *you*, Greene. You wouldn't put him to the edge of the sword without a trial, would you?"

"No, Greene," added Vereker. "Not goin' to waste a good *shenzi* like that. We're goin' to have a jolly good Court–Martial out of him before we do him in.... And I shall hang him, Clarence—rope or no rope."

"May I swing on his feet, Vereker?" begged Augustus. "*Do* let me! ... Be a sport...."

"Everything will be done properly and nicely," was the reply, "and in the best style. There will be no swinging on the prisoner's legs while *I*'m M.C.... Not unless the prisoner himself suggests it," he added.

"How'll we tell him of his many blessin's, and so on?" enquired Berners.

"There's an Arab blighter of Lindsay's who professes to know a tongue spoken by a porter who knows Wadego. The bloke talks to the porter in Wadego, the porter talks to the Arab in the Tongue, the Arab talks to Wavell in Arabic, and Wavell talks to us in any language we like—French, German, Swahili, Hindustani, Latin, Greek, American, Turkish, Portuguese, Taal or even English. He knows all those...."

"Let's ask him to talk them all at once, while we smoke and quaff beakers of rum," suggested Augustus. "And I *say*—couldn't we torture the prisoner? I know lots of ripping tortures."

"Well, I'm not going to have him ripped," vetoed Vereker. "You gotter hand him over to the Provost–Marshal in good condition... Fair wear and tear of trial and incarceration allowed for, of course.... Bound to be *some* depreciation, I know."

"What's 'to incarcerate' mean, exactly?" enquired Augustus.

"Same as 'incinerate.'"

"Can we do it to him by law?" asked Augustus.

"You read the Orders, my lad," replied Vereker. "On the notice–board in the Orderly Room. That post's the Orderly Room. Written and signed by the Station Staff Officer. And look up Field and General Court–Martials in the King's Regulations and you'll know what your Powers are."

"I say, Berners. Let me find you the least contrary of those turned sausages, and have it nicely fried for you," begged Augustus. "You'd hardly taste anything awkward about it if you had some lemon–peel done with it. Plenty of lemon–peel and some coco–nut. I'll find the peel I threw away this morning.... *Do*."

"This is very kind and thoughtful of you, Gussie. What's the idea?" replied Berners.

"I want to propitiate you, Berners. You'll be President of the Court–Martial."

"And?"

"I want you to promise you won't have the prisoner found Guilty unless Vereker promises to let me swing on his feet.... I've *never* once had the chance.... And now my chance has come.... And Vereker feels thwartful.... It's due to his having a boil—and no cushion with him.... Be a good soul, Berners..."

"Let's see the sausages," said the President–elect.

"That's done it," admitted Augustus, and dropped the subject with a heavy sigh.

Bertram noticed that, in spite of his flow of cheery nonsense, Augustus ate nothing at all and looked very ill indeed. He remembered a sentence he had read in a book on board the *Elymas*:

"Comedy lies lightly upon all things, like foam upon the dark waters. Beneath are tragedy and the tears of time."

---

[35] Cultivation, garden.

[36] Over–eating.

CHAPTER XVIII

Trial

After breakfast Bertram attended Court, which was a table under a tree, and took his seat on the Bench, an inverted pail, as a Ruler and a Judge, for the first and last time in his life. He felt that it was a strange and terrible thing that he should thus be suddenly called upon to try a man for his life.

Suppose that his two fellow–judges, Berners and Clarence, disagreed as to the death–sentence, and he had to give his verdict, knowing that a man's life depended on it! …

A couple of *askaris* of the King's African Rifles, police–orderlies of "Leesey" Lindsay's, brought in the prisoner. He was a powerful and decidedly evil–looking negro, clad in a striped petticoat. He had more of the appearance of furtive intelligence than is usual with *shenzis* of his tribe. Bertram decided that he carried his guilt in his face and had trickster and traitor written all over it. He then rebuked himself for pre–judging the case and entertaining prejudice against an untried, and possibly innocent, man.

"Guilty," said Augustus Gus. "Who's coming for a walk?"

"I'm President of this Court," replied Berners. "Who asked you to open your head? If I'm not sure as to his guilt, I may consult you later. Or I may not."

"Look here, Berners—let's do the thing properly," was the reply. "There's a Maxim—or is it a Hotchkiss—of English Law which says that a man is to be considered Guilty until he is proved to be Innocent. Therefore we start fair. He is Guilty, I say. Now we've got to prove him Innocent. Do be a sport, and give the poor blighter a show."

"I b'lieve it's the other way about," said Berners.

"Oh, indeed!" commented Augustus. "You'd say the feller's innocent and then start in to prove him guilty, would you? … Dirty trick, I call it. Filthy habit."

Wavell appeared at the entrance to his tent, holding a green, silk–covered book in his hand. The cover was richly embroidered and had a flap, like that of an envelope, provided with strings for tying it down. It was a copy of the Koran, and on it all witnesses were sworn, repeating an oath administered by Wavell in Arabic….

"Ready?" asked he of the President, and proceeded with great patience, skill and knowledge of languages and dialects, to interpret the statements of Wadegos, Swahilis, Arabs, and assorted Africans. Occasionally it was beyond his power, or that of any human being, to convey the meaning of some simple question to a savage mind, and to get a rational answer.

For the prosecution, Lindsay, who was down with dysentery, had produced fellow–villagers of the accused, from each of whom Wavell obtained the same story.

Prisoner was enamoured of a daughter of the headman of the village, and, because his suit was dismissed by this gentleman, he had led a German raiding–party to the place, and, moreover, had shown them where hidden treasures were *cached*, and where fowls, goats, and cattle had been penned in the jungle, and where grain was stored. Also, he had "smelt out" enemies of the *Germanis* among his former neighbours, wicked men who, he said, had led English raiding–parties into the country of the *Germanis*, and had otherwise injured them. These enemies of the *Germanis* were all, as it happened, enemies of his own.... When this raiding–party of *askaris*, led by half a dozen *Germanis*, had burnt the village, killed all the villagers who had not escaped in time, and carried off all they wanted in the way of livestock, women, grain and gear, they had rewarded accused with a share of the loot....

"Do they all tell the same tale in the same way, as though they had concocted it and learnt it by heart?" asked Bertram.

"No," replied Wavell. "I didn't get that impression."

"Let's question them one by one," said Berners.

A very, very old man, a sort of "witch–doctor" or priest, by his ornaments, entered the witness–box—otherwise arose from the group of witnesses and stood before the Court—to leeward by request.

"Hullo, Granpa! How's things?" said Augustus.

The ancient ruin mumbled something in Swahili, and peered with horny eyes beneath rheumy, shrivelled lids at the Court, as he stood trembling, his palsied head ashake.

"Don't waggle your head at *me*, Rudolph," said Augustus severely, as the old man fixed him with a wild and glassy eye. "*I*'m not going to uphold you.... Pooh! *What* an odour of sanctity! You're a *high* priest, y'know," and murmured as he sought his handkerchief, "Poignant! ... Searching...."

The old man repeated his former mumble.

"He says he did not mean to steal the tobacco," interpreted Wavell.

"Sort of accident that might happen to anybody, what?" observed Augustus. "Ask him if he knows the prisoner."

The question was put to him in his own tongue, and unfalteringly he replied that he had not meant to steal the tobacco—had not *really* stolen it, in fact.

Patiently Wavell asked, and patiently he was answered. "Do you know the prisoner?"

"I never steal."

"Do you know this man?"

"Tobacco I would never steal."

"What is this man's name?"

"Tobacco."

"Have you ever seen that man before?"

"What man?"

"This one."

"Yes. He is the prisoner."

"When have you seen him before?"

"Last night."

"When, before that?"

"He ate rice with us last night. He is the prisoner."

"Do you know him well?"

"Yes, I know he is the prisoner. *He* stole the tobacco."

"Have you known him long?"

"No. He is only a young man. He steals tobacco."

"Does he come from your village?"

"Yes."

"Have you known him all his life?"

"No, because he went and spent some time in the *Germanis'* country. I think he went to steal tobacco."

"Did he come back alone from the *Germanis'* country?"

"No. He brought *askaris* and *muzangos*. [37] They killed my people and burnt my village."

"You are sure it was this man who brought them?"

"Is he not a prisoner?"

Suddenly an ancient hag arose from the group of witnesses and bounded into Court. At the feet of Wavell she poured forth a torrent of impassioned speech.

"Cheer up, Auntie!" quoth Augustus, and as the woman ceased, added: "Ask her if she'd come to Paris for the week–end."

"What does she say?" enquired the President of the Court.

"In effect—that she will be security for *witness's* good behaviour, as he is her only child and never steals tobacco. He only took the tobacco because he wanted a smoke. He is ninety years of age, and a good obedient son to her. It is her fault for not looking after him better. She hopes he will not be hung, as she is already an orphan, and would then be a childless orphan.... She undertakes to beat him with a *runga*." [38]

"Does she identify prisoner as the man who led the German raiding–party?" asked Bertram, after Augustus had called for three loud cheers for the witness, had been himself called to order by the President, and had threatened that he would not play if further annoyed by that official.

Again, in careful Swahili, Wavell endeavoured to find traces of evidence for or against the accused.

"Do you know this man?"

"Yes, *Bwana*."

"Who is he?"

"The prisoner, *Bwana Macouba* (Great Master)."

"Why is he a prisoner?"

"Because he brought the *Germanis* to Pongwa, oh, *Bwana Macouba Sana* (Very Great Master)."

"How do you know he brought the *Germanis* to Pongwa?"

"Because he has been made prisoner for doing so, oh, *Bwana Macouba Kabeesa Sana* (Very Greatest Master)."

"Do you know anything about him?"

"He is the man who stole the tobacco which my little boy took."

All being translated and laid before the Court, it was decided that, so far, prisoner was scarcely proven guilty.

"Let's ask him whether he would like to say anything as to the evidence of the last two witnesses," suggested Bertram.

"He doesn't understand Swahili," objected Berners.

"I feel sure he does," replied Bertram. "I have been watching his face. He half grinned when they talked about tobacco, and looked venomous when they talked about him."

"Do you understand Swahili?" asked Wavell, suddenly, of the prisoner.

"No, not a word," replied that individual in the same tongue.

"Can you speak it?"

"No, not a word," he reaffirmed in Swahili.

"Well—did the last two witnesses tell the truth about you?"

"They did not. I have never seen them before. They have never seen me before. I do not know where Pongwa is. I think this is a very fine trial. I like it."

Other witnesses swore that the accused had indeed done the treacherous deed. One swore with such emphasis and certainty that he carried conviction to the minds of the Court—until it was discovered that witness was swearing that prisoner had stolen a bundle of leaf–tobacco from the son of the woman who was an orphan….

The Court soon found that it could tell when a point was scored against the defendant, without waiting for translation, inasmuch as he always seized his stomach with both hands, groaned, rolled his eyes, and cried that he was suffering horribly from *tumbo*, when evidence was going unfavourably.

At length all witnesses had been examined, even unto the last, who swore he was the prisoner's brother, and that he saw the prisoner leading the *Germanis* and, lo, it wasn't his brother at all, and concluded with: "Yes—this is true evidence. I have spoken well. I can prove it, for I can produce the *sufuria* [39] which prisoner gave me to say that I am his brother, and to speak these truths. He is my innocent brother, and was elsewhere when he led the *Germanis* to Pongwa."

"Let's give him something out of the poor–box," suggested Augustus when this speech was interpreted, and then marred this intimation of kindly feelings by adding: "and then hang the lot of them."

"Has the prisoner anything to say?" asked the President.

The prisoner had.

"This is a good trial," quoth he, in Swahili. "I am now an important man. All the witnesses are liars. I have never seen any of them before. I do not associate with such. I have never seen Pongwa, and I have never seen a *Germani*. I will tell … "

Wavell looked at him suddenly, but made no movement.

"*Noch nichte*!" said he in German, very quietly.

The man stopped talking at once.

"You understand German. You speak German!" said Wavell, in that language, and pointing at him accusingly. "Answer quickly. You speak German."

"*Ganz klein wenig*—just a very little," replied the prisoner, adding in English: "I am a very clever man"—and then, in German: "*Ich hab kein Englisch*."

"Prisoner has never seen a *Germani*—but he understands German!" wrote Bertram in his notes of the trial. "Also Swahili and English."

"Please ask him if he hasn't had enough trial now, and wouldn't he like to be hanged to save further trouble," said Augustus.

"*Tiffin tyar hai*, [40] *Sahib*," said the Mess butler, approaching the President, and the Court adjourned.

The afternoon session of the Court proved dull up to the moment when the lady who was an orphan and the mother of the ninety–year–old, bounded into Court with a scream of:

"Ask him where he got his petticoat!"

Apparently this was very distressful to the defendant, for he was instantly seized with violent stomachic pains.

"Poignant! ... Searching! ... " murmured Augustus.

"Where did you get that *'Mericani*?" asked Wavell of the prisoner, pointing to his only garment.

"He got it from the *Germanis*. It was part of his share of the loot," screamed the old lady. "It is from my own shop. I know it by that mark," and she pointed to a trade–mark and number stencilled in white paint upon the selvedge of the loin–cloth.

Terrible agonies racked the prisoner as he replied: "She is a liar."

"Trade–mark don't prove much," remarked the President. "My pants and vest might have same trade–mark as the Kaiser's—but that wouldn't prove he stole them from me."

The sense of this remark was conveyed to the witness.

"Then see if a mark like *this* is not in the corner of that piece of *'Mericani*," said the old lady, and plucking up her own wardrobe, showed where a small design was crudely stitched.

The *askaris* in charge of the prisoner quickly demonstrated that an identical "laundry–mark" ornamented his also. Presumably the worthy woman's secret price–mark, or else her monogram.

Terrific agonies seized the prisoner, and with a groan of "*Tumbo*," he sank to the ground.

A kick from each of the *askaris* revived him, and he arose promptly and took a bright interest in the subsequent proceedings, which consisted largely in the swearing by several of the villagers that they had seen the *Germanis* loot the old lady's store and throw some pieces of the *'Mericani* to the accused. Two of the witnesses were wearing petticoats which they had bought from the female witness, and which bore her private mark....

"Gentlemen," said the President at length, "I should like your written findings by six o'clock this evening, together with the sentence you would impose if you were sole judge in this case. The Court is deeply indebted to Captain Wavell for his courteous and most valuable assistance as interpreter. The witnesses may be discharged, and the prisoner removed to custody.... Clear the blasted Court, in fact, and come to the Bristol Bar...."

"Oh, hang it all, Berners," objected Augustus, "let's hang him *now*. We can watch him dangle while we have tea...." But the Court had risen, and the President was asking where the devil some bally, fat–headed fool had put his helmet, eh? ...

For an hour Bertram sat in his *banda* with throbbing, aching head, considering his verdict. He believed the man to be a spy and a treacherous, murderous scoundrel—but what was really *proven*, save that he knew German and wore a garment marked similarly to those of three inhabitants of Pongwa? Were these facts sufficient to warrant the passing of the death sentence and to justify Bertram Greene, who, till a few days ago, was the mildest of lay civilians, to take the responsibility of a hanging judge and imbrue his hands with the blood of this man? If all that was suspected of him were true, what, after all, was he but a savage, a barbarous product of barbaric uncivilisation? . . . What right had anyone to apply the standards of a cultured white man from London to a savage black man from Pongwa? ... A savage who had been degraded and contaminated by contact with Germans moreover....

After many unsatisfactory efforts, he finally wrote out his judgment on leaves torn from his military pocket–book, and proposed, as verdict, that the prisoner be confined for the duration of the war as a spy, and receive twenty–five strokes of the *kiboko* for perjury....

On repairing to Berners' hut at the appointed time, he found that Clarence had written a longer and better judgment than his own, and had proposed as sentence that the accused be detained during the King's pleasure at Mombasa Gaol, since it was evident that he had dealings with Germans and had recently been in German East Africa. He found the charge of leading a German raiding–party Not Proven.

The sentence of the President was that prisoner should receive twenty lashes and two years' imprisonment, for receiving stolen goods, well knowing them to be stolen, and for committing perjury.

"And that ought to dish the lad till the end of the war," observed he, "whereafter he'll have precious small use for his German linguistic lore—unless he goes to Berlin for the Iron Cross or a Commission in the Potsdammer Poison–Gas Guards, or somethin', what?"

---

[37] White men.

[38] Club.

[39] Cooking–pot.

[40] "Lunch is ready."

Chapter XIX

Of a Pudding

There was a sound of revelry by night, at the Bristol Bar. A Plum Pudding had arrived. Into that lonely outpost, where men languished and yearned for potatoes, cabbage, milk, cake, onions, beer, steaks, chocolate, eggs, cigarettes, bacon, fruit, coffee, bread, fish, jam, sausages, honey, sugar, ham, tobacco, pastry, toast, cheese, wine and other things of which they had almost forgotten the taste, a Plum Pudding had drifted. When it had begun to seem that food began and ended with coco–nut, maize, bully–beef and dog–biscuit—a Plum Pudding rose up to rebuke error.

At least, it was going to do so. At present it lay, encased in a stout wooden box and a soldered sarcophagus of tin, at the feet of the habitués of the Bristol Bar, what time they looked upon the box and found it good in their sight....

"You'll dine with us and sample it, I hope, Wavell?" said the Major, eyeing the box ecstatically.

"Thanks," was the reply. "Delighted.... May I bring over some brandy to burn round it?"

"Stout fella," said the Major warmly.

"Do we eat it as it is—or fry it, or something, or what?" he added. "I fancy you bake 'em...."

"I believe puddings are boiled, sir," remarked Bertram.

"Yes—I b'lieve you're right, Greene," agreed Major Mallery.... "I seem to know the expression, 'boiled plum–pudding.' ... Yes—boiled plum–pudding...."

"Better tell the cook to boil the bird at once, hadn't we?" suggested Captain Macke.

"Yes," agreed Vereker. "I fancy I've heard our housekeeper at home talk about boiling 'em for *hours*. Hours and hours.... Sure of it."

"But s'pose the beastly thing's *bin* boiled already—what then?" asked Augustus. "Bally thing'd *dissolve*, I tell you.... Have to drink it...."

"Very nice, too," declared Halke.

"I'd sooner eat pudding and drink brandy, than drink pudding and burn brandy," stated Augustus firmly. "What would we boil it in, anyhow?" he added. "It wouldn't go in a kettle, an' if you let it loose in a dam' great *dekchi* or something, it'd all go to bits...."

"Tie it up in a shirt or something," said Forbes.... "What's your idea, Greene—as a man of intellect and education?"

"I'd say boil it," replied Bertram. "I don't believe they *can* be boiled too much.... I fancy it ought to be tied up, though, as Clarence suggests, or it might disintegrate, I suppose."

“Who’s got a clean shirt or vest or pants or something?” asked the Major. “Or could we ram it into a helmet and tie it down?”

It appeared that no one had a *very* clean shirt, and it happened that nobody spoke up with military promptitude and smart alacrity when Lieutenant Bupendranath Chatterji offered to lend his pillow–case.

“I know,” said the Major, in a tone of decision and finality. “I’ll send for the cook, tell him there’s a plum–pudding, an’ he can dam’ well serve it hot for dinner as a plum–pudding *ought* to be served—or God have mercy on him, for we will have none....”

And so it was. Although at first the cook protested that the hour being seven and dinner due at seven–thirty, there was not time for the just and proper cooking of a big plum–pudding. But, “To hell with that for a Tale,” said the Major, and waved pudding and cook away, with instructions to serve the pudding steaming hot, in half an hour, with a blaze of brandy round it, a sprig of holly stuck in it, and a bunch of mistletoe hung above it.

“And write ‘*God Bless Our Home*’ on the *banda* wall,” he added, as a happy after–thought. The cook grinned. He was a Goanese, and a good Christian cheat and liar.

The Bristol Bar settled down again to talk of Home, hunting, theatres, clubs, bars, sport, hotels, and everything else—except religion, women and war....

“Heard about the new lad, Major?” asked Forbes. “Real fuzzy–wuzzy dervish Soudanese. Lord knows how he comes to be in these parts. Smelt war like a camel smells water, I suppose.... Got confused ideas about medals though.... Tell the tale, Wavell.”

“Why—old Isa ibn Yakub, my Sergeant–Major—you know Isa, six–feet–six and nine medals, face like black satin”—began Wavell, “brought me a stout lad—with grey hair—who looked like his twin brother. Wanted to join my Arab Company. He’d come from Berbera to Mombasa in a dhow, and then strolled down here through the jungle.... Conversation ran somewhat thus:

“‘You want to enlist in my Arab Company, do you? Why?’

“‘I want to fight.’

“‘Against the *Germanis*?’

“‘Anybody.’

“‘You know what the pay is?’

“‘Yes. It is enough. But I also want my Omdurman medal—like that worn by Isa ibn Yakub.’

“‘Oh—you have fought before? And at Omdurman.’

“‘Yes. And I want my medal.’

“‘You are sure you fought at Omdurman?’

“‘Yes. Was I not wounded there and left for dead? Look at this hole through my side, below my arm. I want my medal—like that of Isa ibn Yakub.’

"'How is it that you have not got it, if you fought there as you say?'

"'They would not give it to me. I want you to get it for me.'

"'I do not believe you fought at Omdurman at all.'

"'I did. Was I not shot there?'

"'Were you in a Soudanese Regiment?'

"'No.'

"'What then?'

"'In the army of Our Lord the Mahdi. And I was shot in front of the line of British soldiers who wear petticoats! … '"

"Did you take him?" asked the Major, as the laugh subsided.

"Rather!" was the reply. "A lad who fought against us and expects us to give him a medal for it, evidently thinks we are sportsmen, and probably is one himself. I fancy he's done a lot of mixed fighting at different times…. Says he knew Gordon…."

The cook, Mess butler, and a deputation of servants approached, salaamed as one man, and held their peace.

"What's up?" asked the Major. "Anyone dead?"

"The Pudding, sah," said the cook, and all the congregation said, "The Pudding."

A painful brooding silence settled upon the Bristol Bar.

"If you've let pi–dogs or *shenzis* or kites eat that pudding, they shall eat you—alive," promised the Major—and he had the air of one whose word is his bond.

"Nossir," replied the cook. "Pudding all gone to damn. Sahib come and see. I am knowing nothing. It is bad."

"*What*?" roared the Major, and rose to his feet.

"Sah, I am a poor man. You are my father and my mother," said the cook humbly, and all the congregation said that they were poor men and that the Major was their father and their mother.

The Major said that the congregation were liars.

"*Bad*?" stammered Forbes. "Puddings can't go *bad*…."

"Oh, Mother, Mother!" said Augustus, and cried, his head upon his knees.

"Life in epitome," murmured Vereker. "*Tout lasse*; *tout passe*; *tout casse*."

"Strike me blind!" said Halke.

“Feller’s a purple liar…. Must be,” opined Berners.

“Beat the lot of them,” suggested Macke. “Puddings keep for ever if you handle ’em properly.”

“Yes—the brutes haven’t treated it kindly,” said Augustus, wiping his eyes. “Here, Vereker, you’re Provost–Marshal. Serve them so that *they* go bad—and see how they like it.”

“It may just have a superficial coating of mould or mildew that can be taken off,” said Bertram.

“Let’s go an’ interview the dam’ thing,” suggested Augustus. “We can then take measures—or rum.”

The Bristol Bar was deserted in the twinkling of an eye as, headed by the Major, the dozen or so of British officers sought out the Pudding, that they might hold an inquest upon it….

Near the cooking–fire in the straw shed behind the Officers’ Mess *banda*, upon some boards beside a tin sarcophagus, lay a large green ball, suggestive of a moon made of green cheese.

In silent sorrow the party gazed upon it, stricken and stunned. And the congregation of servants stood afar off and watched.

Suddenly the Major snatched up the gleaming *panga* that had been used for prising open the case and for cutting open the tin box in which the green horror had arrived.

Raising the weapon above his head, the Major smote with all his might. Right in the centre of the Pudding the heavy, sharp–edged blade struck and sank…. The Pudding fell in halves, revealing an interior even greener and more horrible than the outside, as a cloud of greenish, smoke–like dust went up to the offended heavens….

“Bury the damned Thing,” said the Major, and in his wake the officers of the Butindi garrison filed out, their hearts too full, their stomachs too empty for words.

And the servants buried the Pudding, obeying the words of the Major.

But in the night the Sweeper arose and exhumed the Pudding and ate of it right heartily. And through the night of sorrow he groaned. And at dawn he died. This is the truth.

* * * * *

Dinner that night was a silent meal, if meal it could be called. No man dared speak to his neighbour for fear of what his neighbour might reply. The only reference to the Pudding was made by Augustus, who remarked, as a servant brought in a dish of roasted maize–cobs, where the Pudding should have come—chicken–feed where should have been Food of the Gods—“I am almost glad poor Murie and Lindsay are so ill that they couldn’t possibly have eaten any Pudding in any case…. Seems some small compensation to ’em, don’t it, poor devils….”

“I do not think Murie will get better,” observed Lieutenant Bupendranath Chatterji. “Fever and dysentery, both violent, and I have not proper things….”

The silence seemed to deepen as everybody thought of the two sick men, lying in their dirty clothes, on dirty camp–beds, in leaky grass huts, with a choice of bully–beef, dog–biscuit, coco–nut and maize as a dysentery diet.

Whose turn next? And what sort of a fight could the force put up if attacked by Africans when all the Indians and Europeans were ill with fever and dysentery? Heaven bless the Wise Man who had kept the African Army of British East Africa so small and had disbanded battalions of the King's African Rifles just before the war. What chance would Indians and white men, who had lived for months in the most pestilential swamp in Africa, have against salted Africans led by Germans especially brought down from the upland health–resorts where they lived? …

"Can you give me a little quinine, Chatterji?" asked Augustus. "Got any calomel? I b'lieve my liver's as big as my head to–day. I feel a corner of it right up between my lungs. Stops my breathing sometimes…."

"Oah, yees. Ha! Ha!" said the medical gentleman. "I have a few tablets. I will presently send you some also…."

Next morning Augustus came in last to breakfast.

"Thanks for the quinine tablets, Chatterji," said he. "The hospital orderly brought them in his bare palm. I swallowed all ten, however. What was it—twenty grains?"

"Oah! That was calomel!" replied the worthy doctor, and Augustus arose forthwith and retired, murmuring: "Poignant! *Searching*!"

He had once taken a quarter of a grain of calomel, and it had tied him in knots.

When Bertram visited Murie, Lindsay and Augustus in their respective huts, Augustus seemed the worst of the three. With white face, set teeth, and closed eyes, he lay bunched up, and, from time to time, groaned, "Oh, poignant! *Searching*! … "

It being impossible for him to march, it fell to Bertram to take his duty that day, and lead an officers' patrol to reconnoitre a distant village to which, according to information received by the Intelligence Department, a German patrol had just paid a visit. For some reason the place had been sacked and burnt.

It was Bertram's business to discover whether there were any signs of a *boma* having been established by this patrol; to learn anything he could about its movements; whence it had come and whither it had gone; whether the massacre were a punishment for some offence, or just the result of high animal (German) spirits; whether there were many *shambas*, of no further use to slaughtered people, in which the raiders had left any limes, bananas, papai or other fruits, vegetables, or crops; whether any odd chicken or goat had been overlooked, and was wanting a good home; and, in short, to find out anything that could be found out, see all that was to be seen, do anything that might be done…. As he marched out of the Fort at the head of a hundred Gurkhas, with a local guide and interpreter, he felt proud and happy, quite reckless, and absolutely indifferent to his fate. He would do his best in any emergency that might arise, and he could do no more. He'd leave it at that.

He'd march straight ahead with a "point" in front of him, and if he was ambushed, he was ambushed.

When they reached the village, he'd deploy into line and send scouts into the place. If he was shot dead—a jolly good job. If he were wounded and left lying for the German *askaris* to find—or the wild beasts at night … he turned from the thought.

Anyhow, he'd got good cheery, sturdy Gurkhas with him, and it was a pleasure and an honour to serve with them.

One jungle march is precisely like another—and in three or four hours the little column reached the village, deployed, and skirmished into it, to find it a deserted, burnt–out ruin. *Kultur* had passed that way, leaving its inevitable and unmistakable sign–manual. The houses were only blackened skeletons; the gardens, wildernesses; the byres, cinder–heaps; the fruit–trees, withering wreckage. What had been pools of blood lay here and there, with clumps of feathers, burnt and broken utensils, remains of slaughtered domestic animals and chickens.

Kultur had indeed passed that way. To Bertram it seemed, in a manner, sadder that this poor barbarous little African village should be so treated than that a walled city of supermen should suffer… "Is there not more cruelty and villainy in violently robbing a crying child of its twopence than in snatching his gold watch from a portly stockbroker?" thought he, as he gazed around on the scene of ruin, desolation and destruction.

To think of Europeans finding time, energy, and occasion to effect *this* in such a spot, so incredibly remote from their marts and ways and busy haunts! Christians! …

Having posted sentries and chosen a spot for rally and defence, he sent out tiny patrols along the few jungle paths that led to the village, and proceeded to see what he could, as there was absolutely no living soul from whom he could learn anything. There was little that the ablest scoutmaster could deduce, save that the place had been visited by a large party of mischievously destructive and brutal ruffians, who wore boots. There was nothing of use or of value that had not been either destroyed or taken. Even papai trees that bore no fruit had been hacked down, and the *panga* had been laid to the root of tree and shrub and sugar–cane. Not a plantain, lime, mango, or papai was to be seen.

Bertram entered one of the least burnt of the well–made huts of thatch and wattle. There was what had been blood on the earthen floor, blackened walls, charred stools, bed–frames and domestic utensils. He felt sick…. In a corner was a child's bed of woven string plaited over a carved frame. It would make a useful stool or a resting–place for things which should not lie on the muddy floor of his *banda*. He picked it up. Underneath it was a tiny black hand with pinkish finger–tips. He dropped the bed and was violently sick. *Kultur* had indeed passed that way….

Hurrying out into the sunlight, as soon as he was able to do so, he completed his tour of inspection. There was little of interest and nothing of importance.

Apparently the hamlet had boasted an artist, a sculptor, some village Rodin, before the Germans came to freeze the genial current of his soul. … As Bertram studied the handiwork of the absent one, his admiration diminished, however, and he withdrew the "Rodin." The man was an arrant, shameless plagiarist, a scoundrelly pick–brain imitator, a mere copying ape, for, seen from the proper end, as it lay on its back, the clay statue of a woman, without form and void, boneless, wiggly, semi–deliquescent, was an absolutely faithful and shameless reproduction of the justly world–famous Eppstein Venus.

"The man ought to be prosecuted for infringement of copyright," thought Bertram, "if there is any copyright in statues…."

The patrols having returned with nothing to report, Bertram marched back to Butindi and reported it.

CHAPTER XX

Stein-brücker Meets Bertram Greene—and Death

And so passed the days at Butindi, with a wearisome monotony of Stand–to, visiting the pickets, going out on patrol, improving the defences of the *boma*, foraging, gathering information, reconnoitring, trying to waylay and scupper enemy patrols, communicating with the other British outposts, surveying and map–making, beating off half–hearted attacks by strong raiding–patrols—all to the accompaniment of fever, dysentery, and growing weakness due to malnutrition and the terrible climate.

To Bertram it all soon became so familiar and normal that it seemed strange to think that he had ever known any other kind of life. His chief pleasure was to talk to Wavell, that most uncommon type of soldier, who was also philosopher, linguist, student, traveller, explorer and ethnologist.

From the others, Bertram learnt that Wavell was, among other things, a second Burton, having penetrated into Mecca and Medina in the disguise of a *haji*, a religious pilgrim, at the very greatest peril of his life. He had also fought, as a soldier of fortune, for the Arabs against the Turks, whom he loathed as only those who have lived under their rule can loathe them. He could have told our Foreign Office many interesting things about the Turk. (When, after he had been imprisoned and brutally treated by them at Sanaa, in the Yemen, he had appealed to our Foreign Office, it had sided rather with the Turk indeed, confirming the Unspeakable One's strong impression that the English were a no–account race, even as the Germans said.) So Wavell had fought against them, helping the Arabs, whom he liked. And when the Great War broke out, he had raised a double company of these fierce, brave, and blood–thirsty little men in Arabia, and had drilled them into fine soldiers. Probably no other Englishman—or European of any sort—could have done this; but then Wavell spoke Arabic like an Arab, knew the Koran almost by heart, and knew his Arabs quite by heart.

That he showed a liking for Bertram was, to Bertram, a very great source of pride and pleasure. When Wavell went out on a reconnoitring–patrol, he went with him if he could get Major Mallery's permission, and the two marched through the African jungle discussing art, poetry, travel, religion, and the ethnological problems of Arabia—followed by a hundred or so Arabs—Arabs who were killing Africans and being killed by Africans, often of their own religion and blood, because a gang of greedy materialists, a few thousand miles away, was suffering from megalomania. …

Indeed to Bertram it was food for much thought that in that tiny *boma* in a tropical African swamp, Anglo–Indians, Englishmen, Colonials, Arabs, Yaos, Swahilis, Gurkhas, Rajputs, Sikhs, Marathas, Punjabis, Pathans, Soudanese, Nubians, Bengalis, Goanese, and a mob of assorted *shenzis* of the primeval jungle, should be laying down their lives because, in distant Berlin, a hare–brained Kaiser could not control a crowd of greedy and swollen–headed military aristocrats.

* * * * *

"Your month's tobacco ration, Greene," said Berners one morning, as he entered Bertram's hut, "and *don't* leave your boots on the floor to attract jigger–fleas—unless you *want* blood–poisoning and guinea–worm—or is it guinea–fowl? Hang them on the wall.... And look between your toes every time you take 'em off. Jigger–fleas are, hell, once they get under the skin and lay their eggs..." and he handed Bertram some cakes of perfectly black tobacco.

“But, my dear chap, I couldn’t smoke *that*,” said Bertram, eyeing the horrible stuff askance.

“Of course you can’t *smoke* it,” replied Berners.

“What can I do with it, then?” he asked.

“Anything you like.... I don’t care.... It’s your tobacco ration, and I’ve issued it to you, and there the matter ends. .. . You can revet your trench parapet with it if you like—or give it to the Wadegos to poison their arrows with.... Jolly useful stuff, really.... Sole your boots, tile the roof of your *banda*, make a parquet floor round your bed, put it in Chatterji’s tea, make a chair seat, lay down a pathway to the Mess, make your mother a teapot–stand, feed the chickens—oh, lots of things. But you can’t *smoke* it, of course.... You expect too much, my lad....”

“Why do they issue it, then?” asked Bertram.

“Same reason that they issue inedible bully–beef and unbreakable biscuits, I s’pose—contractors must *live*, mustn’t they? ... Be reasonable....”

And again it seemed to the foolish civilian mind of this young man that, since tons of this black cake tobacco (which no British officer ever has smoked or could smoke) cost money, however little—there would be more sense in spending the money on a small quantity of Turkish and Virginian cigarettes that *could* be smoked, by men accustomed to such things, and suffering cruelly for lack of them. Throughout the campaign he saw a great deal of this strong, black cake issued (to men accustomed to good cigarettes, cigars or pipe–mixture), but he never saw any of it smoked. He presented his portion to Ali, who traded it to people of palate and stomach less delicate than those the British Government expects the British officer to possess....

“You look seedy, Greene,” observed the Major that same evening, as Bertram dragged himself across the black mud from his *banda* to the Bristol Bar—wondering if he would ever get there.

“Touch of fever, sir. I’m all right,” replied he, wishing that everyone and everything were not so nebulous and rotatory.

He did not mention that he had been up all night with dysentery, and had been unable to swallow solid food for three days. (Nor that his temperature was one hundred and four—because he was unaware of the fact.) But he knew that the moment was not far off when all his will–power and uttermost effort would be unable to get him off his camp–bed. He had done his best—but the worst climate in the world, a diet of indigestible and non–nutritious food, taken in hopelessly inadequate quantities; bad water; constant fever; dysentery; long patrol marches; night alarms; high nerve–tension (when a sudden bang followed by a fusillade might mean a desultory attention, a containing action while a more important place was being seriously attacked, or that final and annihilating assault of a big force which was daily expected); and the monotonous, dirty, dreary life in that evil spot, had completely undermined his strength. He was “living on his nerves,” and they were nearly gone. “You look like an old hen whose neck has been half–wrung for to–morrow’s dinner before she was found to be the wrong one, and reprieved,” said Augustus. “You let me make you a real, rousing cock–eye, and then we’ll have an *n’goma* [41]—all the lot of us....”

But finding Bertram quite unequal to dealing with a cock–eye or sustaining his part in a tribal dance that should “astonish the natives,” he helped Bertram over to his *banda*, took off his boots and got him a hot drink of condensed milk and water laced with ration rum.

In the morning Bertram took his place at Stand–to and professed himself equal to performing his duty, which was that of making a reconnoitring–patrol as far as Paso, where there was another outpost....

Here he arrived in time for tea, and had some with real fresh cow's milk in it; and had a cheery buck with Major Bidwell, Captains Tucker and Bremner, and Lieutenants Innes (another Filbert), Richardson, Stirling, Carroll, and Jones—stout fellows all, and very kind to him. He was very sorry indeed when it was time for him to march back again with his patrol.

He started on the homeward journey, feeling fairly well, for him; but he could never remember how he completed it....

The darkness gathered so rapidly that he had a suspicion that the darkness was within him. Then he found that he was continually running into trees or being brought up short by impenetrable bush that somehow sprang up before him.... Also he was talking aloud, and rather surprised at his eloquence.... Then he was lying on the ground—being put on his feet again—falling again ... trying to fight a bothering swarm of *askaris* with a quill pen, while he addressed the House of Commons on the iniquity of allowing Bupendranath Chatterji to be in medical charge of four hundred men with insufficient material to deal with a street accident.... Marching again, falling again, being put on his feet again....

* * * * *

After two days on his camp–bed he was somewhat better, and on the next day he found himself in sole command of the Butindi outpost and a man of responsibility and pride. Urgent messages had taken Major Mallery with half the force in one direction, and Captain Wavell with half the remainder in another.

Suppose there should be an attack while he was in command! He half hoped there would be....

Towards evening an alarm from a sentry and the turning out of the guard brought him running to the main gate, shouting "Stand–to!" as he ran.

Through his glasses he saw that a European and a small party of natives were approaching the *boma*....

The new–comer was an Englishman of the name of Desmont, in the Intelligence Department, who had just made a long and dangerous tour through the neighbouring parts of German East in search of information. Apparently Butindi was the first British outpost that he had struck, as he asked endless questions about others—apparently with a view to visiting them *en route* to the Base Camp. Bertram extended to him such hospitality as Butindi could afford, and gave him all the help and information in his power. He had a very strong conviction that the man was disguised (whether his huge beard was false or not), but he supposed that it was very natural in the case of an Intelligence Department spy, scout, or secret agent. Anyhow, he was most obviously English....

While he sat in the Officers' Mess and talked with the man—a most interesting conversation—Ali Suleiman entered with coco–nuts and a rum–jar. Seeing the stranger, he instantly wheeled about and retired, sending another servant in with the drinks....

After a high–tea of coco–nut, biscuit, bully–beef, and roasted mealie–cobs, Desmont, who looked worn out, asked if he might lie down for a few hours before he "moved off" again. Bertram at once took him to his own *banda* and bade him make himself at home. Five minutes later came Ali with an air of mystery to where Bertram paced up and down the "High Street," and asked if he might speak with him.

"That man a *Germani*, sah!" quoth he. "Spy–man he is. Debbil–man. His own name *not* Desmont *Bwana*, and he is big man in Dar–es–Salaam and Tabora, and knowing all the big *Germani bwanas*. I was his gun–boy and I go with him to *Germani* East.... *Bwana* go and shoot him for dead, sah, by damn!"

Bertram sat down heavily on a chop–box.

"*What*?" gasped he.

"Yessah, thank you please. One of those porters not a *shenzi* at all. He Desmont *Bwana's* head boy Murad. Very bad man, sah. Master look in this spy–man's chop–boxes. *Germani* uniform in one—under rice and posho. Master see...."

"You're a fool, Ali," said Bertram.

"Yessah," said Ali, "and Desmont *Bwana* a *Germani* spy–man. Master go an' shoot him for dead while asleep—or tie him to tree till Mallery *Bwana* coming...."

Now what was to be done? Here was a case for swift action by the "strong silent man" type of person who thought like lightning and acted like some more lightning.

If he did nothing and let the man go when he had rested, would his conduct be that of a fool and a weakling who could not act promptly and efficiently on information received—conduct deserving the strongest censure? ...

And if he arrested and detained one of their own Intelligence Officers, on the word of a native servant, would he ever hear the last of it?

"*Bwana* come and catch this bad man Murad," suggested Ali. "*Bwana* say, '*Jambo, Murad ibn Mustapha*! *How much rupees Desmont Bwana paying you for spy–work*?' and *Bwana* see him jump! By damn, sah! *Bwana* hold revolver ready." ...

"Does the man know English then?" asked the perturbed and undecided Bertram.

"Yessah—all the same better as I do," was the reply. "And he pretending to be poor *shenzi* porter. He knowing *Germani* too...."

At any rate, he might look into *this*, and if anything suspicious transpired, he could at least prevent Desmont from leaving before Mallery returned.

"Has he seen you?" asked Bertram.

"No, sah, nor has Desmont *Bwana*," was the reply—and Bertram bade Ali show him where the porters were.

They were outside the *boma*, squatting round a cooking–fire near the "lines" of the Kavirondo porters.

Approaching the little group, Bertram drew his revolver and held it behind him. He did not know why he did this. Possibly subconscious memory of Ali's advice, perhaps with the expectation that the men might attack him or attempt to escape; or perhaps a little pleasant touch of melodrama....

"*Jambo, Murad ibn Mustapha*!" he said suddenly. "*Desmont Bwana wants you at once. Go quickly*."

A man arose immediately and approached him. "Go back and sit down," said Bertram, covering the man with his revolver and speaking in German. He returned and sat down. Evidently he understood English and German and answered to the name of Murad ibn Mustapha! …

Ali had spoken the truth and it was now up to Bertram Greene to act wisely, promptly and firmly. This lot should be kept under arrest anyhow. But might not all this be part of Desmont's game as a scout, spy and secret service agent of the British Intelligence Department. Yes, *or* of the German Intelligence Department.

If there was a German uniform in one of the chop–boxes, it might well be a disguise for him to wear in German East. Or it might be his real dress. Anyhow—he shouldn't leave the outpost until Major Mallery returned. .

. . And that was a weak shelving of responsibility. He was in command of the post, and Major Mallery and the other officers with him might be scuppered. It was quite possible that neither the Major's party nor Captain Wavell's might ever get back to Butindi. He strolled over to his *banda* and looked in.

Desmont was evidently suffering from digestive troubles or a bad conscience, for his face was contorted, he moved restlessly and ground his teeth.

Suddenly he screamed like a woman and cried:

"*Ach*! *Gott in Himmel*! *Nein, Nein*! *Ich …* "

Bertram drew his revolver. The man was a German. Englishmen don't talk German in their sleep.

The alleged Desmont moaned.

"*Zu müde*," he said. "*Zu müde*." …

Bertram sat down on his camp–stool and watched the man.

* * * * *

The Herr Doktor Karl Stein–Brücker had made a name for himself in German East, as one who knew how to manage the native. This in a country where they all pride themselves on knowing how to manage the native—how to put the fear of Frightfulness and *Kultur* into his heart. He had once given a great increase to a growing reputation by flogging a woman to death, on suspicion of unfaithfulness. He had wielded the *kiboko* with his own (literally) red right hand until he was aweary, and had then passed the job on to Murad ibn Mustapha, who was very slow to tire. But even he had had to be kept to it at last….

"*Noch nichte*!" had the Herr Doktor said, "*Not yet*!" as Murad wished to stop, and

"*Ganz klein wenig*!" as the brawny arm dropped. "*Just a little more*." …

It had been a notable and memorable punishment—but the devil of it was that whenever the Herr Doktor got run down or over–ate himself, he had a most terrible nightmare, wherein Marayam, streaming with blood, pursued him, caught him, and flogged him. And when she tired, he was doomed to urge her on to further efforts. After screaming with agony, he must moan "*Zu müde*! *Zu müde*!" and then—when she would have stopped—"*Noch nichte*!" and "*Ganz klein wenig*!" so that she began afresh. Then he must struggle, break free, leap at her—and find himself sweating, weeping and trembling beside his bed.

Presently the moaning sleeper cried "*Noch nichte*!" and a little later "*Ganz klein wenig*!"—and then with a scream and a struggle, leapt from the camp cot and sprang at Bertram, whose revolver straightway went off. With a cough and a gurgle the *soi–disant* Desmont collapsed with a ·450 service bullet through his heart.

When Major Mallery returned at dawn he found a delirious Second–Lieutenant Greene (and a dead European, and a wonderful tale from one Ali Suleiman....)

With a temperature of 105·8 he did not seem likely to live....

Whether Bertram Greene lived or died, however, he had, albeit ignorantly, avenged the cruel wrong done to his father.... He—the despised and rejected one—had avenged Major Hugh Walsingham Greene. Fate plays some queer tricks and Time's whirligig performs some quaint gyrations!

---

[41] Tribal dance.

Part III: The Baking of Bertram by Love

CHAPTER I

Mrs. Stayne-brooker Again

Luckily for himself, Second–Lieutenant Bertram Greene was quite unconscious when he was lifted from his camp–bed into a stretcher by the myrmidons of Mr. Chatterji and dispatched, carriage paid, to M'paga. What might happen to him there was no concern of Mr. Chatterji's—which was the important point so far as that gentleman was concerned.

Unconscious he remained as the four Kavirondo porters, the stretcher on their heads, jogged along the jungle path in the wake of Ali and the three other porters who bore his baggage. Behind the stretcher–bearers trotted four more of their brethren who would relieve them of their burden at regular intervals.

Ali was in command, and was also in a hurry, for various reasons, including prowling enemy patrols and his master's dire need of help. He accordingly set a good pace and kept the "low niggers" of his party to it by fabulous promises, hideous threats, and even more by the charm of song—part song in fact. Lifting up his powerful voice he delivered in deep diapason a mighty

"*Ah–Nah–Nee–Nee*! *Ah–Nah–Nee–Nee*!"

to which all the congregation responded

"*Umba Jo–eel*! *Umba Jo–eel*!"

as is meet and right to do.

And when, after a few hundred thousand repetitions of this, in strophe and antistrophe, there seemed a possibility that restless and volatile minds desiring change might seek some new thing, Ali sang

"*Hay–Ah–Mon–Nee*! *Hay–Ah–Mon–Nee*!"

which is quite different, and the jogging, sweating congregation, with deep earnestness and conviction, took up the response:

"*Tunk–Tunk–Tunk–Tunk*!"

and all fear of the boredom of monotony was gone—especially as, after a couple of hours of this, you could go back to the former soulful and heartsome Threnody, and begin again. But if they got no forrader with the concert they steadily got forrader with the journey, as their loping jog–trot ate up the miles.

And, in time to their regular foot–fall and chanting, the insensible head of the white man rolled from side to side unceasingly....

Unconscious he still was when the little party entered the Base Camp, and Private Henry Hall remarked to Private John Jones:

"That there bloke's gone West all right but 'e ain't gone long.... You can see 'e's dead becos 'is 'ead's a waggling and you can see 'e ain't bin dead *long* becos 'is 'ead's a waggling...."

And Private John Jones, addressing the speaker as Mister Bloomin'–Well Sherlock 'Olmes, desired that he would cease to chew the fat.

Steering his little convoy to the tent over which the Red Cross flew, Ali handed over his master and the cleft stick holding Major Mallery's letter, to Captain Merstyn, R.A.M.C., and then stood by for orders.

It appeared that the *Barjordan* was off M'paga, that a consignment of sick and wounded was just going on board, and that Second–Lieutenant Greene could go with them....

That night Bertram was conveyed out to sea in a dhow (towed by a petrol–launch from the *Barjordan*), taken on board that ship, and put comfortably to bed. The next night he was in hospital at Mombasa and had met Mrs. Stayne–Brooker.

* * * * *

As, thanks to excellent nursing, he very slowly returned to health and strength, Bertram began to take an increasing interest in the very charming and very beautiful woman whom he had once seen and admired at the Club, who daily took his temperature, brought his meals, administered his medicine, kept his official chart, shook up his pillows, put cooling hands upon his forehead, found him books to read, talked to him at times, attended the doctor on his daily visits, and superintended the brief labours of the Swahili youth who was ward–boy and house–maid on that floor of the hospital.

Before long, the events of the day were this lady's visits, and, on waking, he would calculate the number of hours until she would enter his room and brighten it with her presence. He had never seen so sweet, kind, and gentle a face. It was beautiful too, even apart from its sweetness, kindness and gentleness. He was very thankful when he found himself no longer too weak to turn his head and follow her with his eyes, as she moved about the room. It was indescribably delightful to have a woman, and such a woman, about one's sick bed—after negro servants, Indian orderlies, *shenzi* stretcher–bearers, and Bengali doctors. How his heart swelled with gratitude as she laid her cool hand on his forehead, or raised his head and gave him a cooling drink.... But how sad she looked! ... He hated to see her putting up the mosquito–curtains that covered the big frame–work, like the skeleton of a room, in which his bed stood, and which, at night, formed a mosquito–proof room–within–a–room, and provided space for his bedside chair, table and electric–lamp, as well as for the doctor and nurse, if necessary.

One morning he sat up and said:

"*Please* let me do that, Sister—I hate to see you working for me—though I love to see *you* ... " and then had been gently pushed back on to his pillow as, with a laugh, Mrs. Stayne–Brooker said:

"That's what I'm here for—to work I mean," and patted his wasted hand. (He *was* such a dear boy, and so appreciative of what one could do for him. It made one's heart ache to see him such a wasted skeleton.)

The time came when he could sit in a long chair with leg–rest arms, and read a book; but he found that most of his time was spent in thinking of the Sister and in the joys of retrospection and anticipation. He had to put aside, quite resolutely, all thought of the day when he would be declared fit for duty and be "returned to store." Think of a *banda* at Butindi and of this white room with its beautiful outlook across the strait to the palm–feathered shore; think of Ali as one's cup–bearer and of this sweet angelic Englishwoman.... Better not think of it at all. ...

It was quite a little shock to him, one day, to notice that she wore a wedding–ring.... He had never thought of that.... He felt something quite like a little twinge of jealousy.... He was sure the man must be a splendid fellow though, or she would never have married him.... How old would she be? It was no business of his, and it was not quite gentlemanly to speculate on such a subject—but somehow he had not thought of her as "an old married woman." Not that married women are necessarily older than unmarried women.... A silly expression—"old" married women. He had imagined her to be about his own generation so to speak. Possibly a *little* older than himself—in years—but years don't make age really.... Fancy her being married! Well, well, well! ... But what did that matter—she was just as much the charming and beautiful woman for whom he would have laid down his life in sheer gratitude....

* * * * *

A man gets like this after fever. He is off his balance, weak, neurasthenic, and devoid of the sense of proportion. He waxes sentimental, and is to be forgiven.

* * * * *

But there is not even this excuse for Mrs. Stayne–Brooker.

* * * * *

She began by rather boring her daughter, Eva, about her new patient—his extreme gratitude, his charming ways and thoughts, his true gentleness of nature, his delightful views, the *niceness* of his mind, the likeableness of him.... She wondered aloud as to whether he had a mother—she must be a very nice woman. She wondered in silence as to whether he had a wife—she must be a very happy woman.... How old was he? ... It was so hard to tell with these poor fellows, brought in so wasted with fever and dysentery; and rank wasn't much guide to age nowadays. He *might* be.... Well—he'd be up and gone before long, and she'd never see him again, so what was the good of wondering.... And she continued to wonder.... And then, from rather boring Miss Stayne–Brooker with talk about Lieutenant Greene she went to the extreme, and never mentioned him at all.

For, one day, with an actual gasp of horrified amazement, she found that she had suddenly realised that possibly the poets and novelists were not so wrong as she had believed, and that there *might* be such a thing as the Love—they hymned and described—and that Peace and Happiness might be its inseparable companions.... She would read her Browning, Herrick, Swinburne, Rosetti again, her Dante, her Mistral, and some of those plays and poems of Love that the world called wonderful, beautiful, true, for she had an idea that she might see glimmerings of wonder, beauty and truth in them—*now*....

But then—how absurd!—at *her* age. Of course she would not read them again! At *her* age! ...

And proceeded to do so at *her* Dangerous Age....

Strange that *his* name should be Green or Greene—he was the fifth person of that name whom she had met since she left Major Walsingham Greene, eighteen years ago....

Chapter II

Love

All too soon for two people concerned, Doctor Mowbray, the excellent Civil Surgeon of Mombasa, in whose hospital Bertram was, decided that that young gentleman might forthwith be let loose on ticket–of–leave between the hours of ten and ten for a week or two, preparatory to his discharge from hospital for a short spell of convalescence–leave before rejoining his regiment….

"I'll call for you and take you for a drive after lunch," said Mrs. Stayne–Brooker, "and then you shall have tea with me, and we'll go over to the Club and sit on the verandah. You mustn't walk much, your first day out."

"I'm going to run miles," said Bertram, smiling up into her face and taking her hand as she stood beside his chair—a thing no other patient had dared to do or would have been permitted to do. ("He was such a dear boy—one would never dream of snubbing him or snatching away a hand he gratefully stroked—it would be like hitting a baby or a nice friendly dog….")

"Then you'll be ill again at once," rejoined Mrs. Stayne–Brooker, giving the hand that had crept into hers a little chiding shake.

"Exactly … and prolong my stay here…" said Bertram, and his eyes were very full of kindness and gratitude as they met eyes that were also very full.

("What a sweet, kind, good woman she was! And what a cruel wrench it would be to go away and perhaps never see her again….")

He went for his drive with Mrs. Stayne–Brooker in a car put at her disposal, for the purpose, by the Civil Surgeon; and found he was still very weak and that it was nevertheless good to be alive.

At tea he met Miss Stayne–Brooker, and, for a moment, his breath was taken away by her beauty and her extraordinary likeness to her mother.

He thought of an opened rose and an opening rose–bud (exactly alike save for the "open" and "opening" difference), on the same stalk…. It was wonderful how alike they were, and how young Mrs. Stayne–Brooker looked—away from her daughter…. The drive–and–tea programme was repeated almost daily, with variations, such as a stroll round the golf–course, as the patient grew stronger…. And daily Bertram saw the very beautiful and fascinating Miss Stayne–Brooker and daily grew more and more grateful to Mrs. Stayne–Brooker. He was grateful to her for so many things—for her nursing, her hospitality, her generous giving of her time; her kindness in the matter of lending him books (the books she liked best, prose works *and* others); her kind interest in him and his career, ambitions, tastes, views, hopes and fears; for her being the woman she was and for brightening his life as she had, not to mention saving it; and, above all, he was grateful to her for having such a daughter…. He told her that he admired Miss Stayne–Brooker exceedingly, and she did not tell him that Miss Stayne–Brooker did not admire him to the same extent…. She was a little sorry that her daughter did not seem as enthusiastic about him as she herself was, for we love those whom we admire to be admired. But she realised that a chit of a girl, fresh from a Cheltenham school, was not to be expected to appreciate a man like this one, a scholar, an artist to his finger–tips, a poet, a musician, a man who had read everything and could talk interestingly of anything—a man whose mind was a sweet and pleasant storehouse—a *kind* man, a gentleman, a man who, thank God, *needed* one, and yet to whom one's ideas were of as much interest as one's face and form. Of course, the average "Cheerioh" subaltern, whose talk was of dances and racing and sport, would, very naturally, be of more interest to a callow girl than this man whose mind (to Mrs. Stayne–Brooker) a kingdom was, and who had devoted to the study of music, art, literature, science, and the drama, the time that the other man had given to the pursuit of various hard and soft balls, inoffensive quadrupeds, and less inoffensive bipeds.

Thus Mrs. Stayne–Brooker, addressing, in imagination, a foolishly unappreciative Eva Stayne–Brooker.

* * * * *

As she and her daughter sat at dinner on the verandah which looked down on to Vasco da Gama Street, one evening, a month later, her Swahili house–boy brought Mrs. Stayne–Brooker a message.... A *shenzi* was without, and he had a *chit* which he would give into no hands save those of Mrs. Stayne–Brooker herself.

It was the escaped Murad ibn Mustapha, in disguise.

On hearing his news, she did what she had believed people only did in books. She fell down in a faint and lay as one dead.

* * * * *

Miss Stayne–Brooker tried to feel as strongly as her mother evidently did, but signally failed, her father having been an almost complete stranger to her. She was a little surprised that the blow should have been so great as to strike her mother senseless, for there had certainly been nothing demonstrative about her attitude to her husband—to say the least of it. She supposed that married folk got like that ... loved each other all right but never showed it at all... Nor had what she had seen of her father honestly impressed her with the feeling that he was a *very* lovable person. Neither before dinner nor after it—when he was quite a different man....

Still—here was her mother, knocked flat by the news of his death, and now lying on her bed in a condition which seemed to vary between coma and hysteria....

Knocked flat—(and yet, from time to time, she murmured, "Thank God! Oh, thank God!"). Queer!

* * * * *

When Mr. Greene called next day, Miss Eva received him in the morning–sitting–drawing–room and told him the sad news. Her father had died.... He was genuinely shocked.

"Oh, your poor, *poor* mother!" said he. "I am grieved for her"—and sat silent, his face looking quite sad. Obviously there was no need for sympathy with Miss Eva as she frankly confessed that she scarcely knew her father and felt for him only as one does for a most distant relation, whom one has scarcely ever seen.

With a request that she would convey his most heart–felt condolence and deepest sympathy to her mother, he withdrew and returned to the Mombasa Hotel, where he was now staying, an ex–convalescent awaiting orders... He had hoped for an evening with Eva. That evening the *Elymas* steamed into Kilindini harbour and Bertram, strolling down to the pier, met Captain Murray, late Adjutant of the One Hundred and Ninety–Ninth, and Lieutenant Reginald Macteith, both of whom had just come ashore from her.

He wrung Murray's hand, delighted to see him, and congratulated him on his escape from regimental duty, and shook hands with Macteith.

"By Jove, Cupid, you look ten years older than when I saw you last," said Murray, laying his hand on Bertram's shoulder and studying his face. "I should hardly have known you...."

"Quite a little man now," remarked Macteith, and proceeded to enquire as to where was the nearest and best Home–from–Home in Mombasa, where one could have A–Drink–and–a–Little–Music–what–what?

"I am staying at the Mombasa Hotel," said Bertram coldly, to which Macteith replied that he hoped it appreciated its privilege.

Bertram felt that he hated Macteith, but also had a curious sense that that young gentleman had either lost in stature or that he, Bertram, had gained.... Anyhow he had seen War, and, so far, Macteith had not. He had no sort of fear of anything Macteith could say or do—and he'd welcome any opportunity of demonstrating the fact.... Dirty little worm! Chatting gaily with Murray, he took them to the Mombasa Club and there found a note from Mrs. Stayne–Brooker asking him to come to tea on the morrow.

* * * * *

"I won't attempt to offer condolence nor express my absolute sympathy, Mrs. Stayne–Brooker," said Bertram as he took her hand and led her to her favourite settee.

"Don't," said she.

"My heart aches for you, though," he added.

"It need not," replied Mrs. Stayne–Brooker, and, as Bertram looked his wonder at her enigmatic reply and manner, she continued:

"I will not pretend to *you*. I will be honest. Your heart need not ache for me at all—because mine sings with relief and gratitude and joy. ..."

Bertram's jaw fell in amazement. He felt inexpressibly shocked.

Or was it that grief had unhinged the poor lady's mind?

"I am going to say to you what I have never said to a living soul, and will never say again.... I have never even said it to myself.... *I hated him most utterly and most bitterly....*"

Bertram was more shocked than he had ever been in his life... This was terrible! ... He wanted to say, "Oh, hush!" and get up and go away.

"I could not *tell* you how I hated him," continued Mrs. Stayne–Brooker, "for he spoilt my whole life.... I am not going into details nor am I going to say one word against him beyond that. I repeat that he *made* me loathe him—from my very wedding–day ... and I leave you to judge. . . ."

Bertram judged.

He was very young—much younger than his years—and he judged as the young do, ignorantly, harshly, cruelly....

What manner of woman, after all, was this, who spoke of her dead husband? Of her own husband—scarcely cold in his grave. Of her *husband* of all people in the world! ... He could have wept with the shame and misery of it, the disillusionment, the shattering blow which she herself had dealt at the image and idol that he had set up in his heart and gratefully worshipped.

He looked up miserably as he heard the sound of a sob in the heavy silence of the room. She was weeping bitterly, shaken from head to foot with the violence of her—her—what could it be? not grief for her husband of course. Did she weep for the life that he had "spoilt" as she expressed it? Was it because of her wasted opportunities for happiness, the years that the locust had eaten, the never–to–return days of her youth, when joy and gaiety should have been hers?

What could he say to her?—save a banal "Don't cry"? There was nothing to say. He did not know when he had felt so miserable and uncomfortable....

"It is over," she said suddenly, and dried her tears; but whether she alluded to the unhappiness of her life with her husband, or to her brief tempest of tears, he did not know.

What could he say to her? ... It was horrible to see a woman cry. And she had been *so* good to him. She had revived his interest in life when through the miasma of fever he had seen it as a thing horrible and menacing, a thing to flee from. How could he comfort her? She had made no secret of the fact that she liked him exceedingly, and that to talk to him of the things that matter in Life, Art, Literature, Music, History, was a pleasure akin to that of a desert traveller who comes upon an inexhaustible well of pure water. Perhaps she liked him so well that he could offer, acceptably, that Silent Sympathy that is said to be so much finer and more efficacious than words.... Could he? . . Could he? ...

Conquering his sense of repulsion at her attitude toward her newly dead husband, and remembering all he owed to her sweet kindness, he crossed to her settee, knelt on one knee beside her, took her hand, and put it to his lips without a word. She would understand—and he would go.

With a little sobbing cry, Mrs. Stayne–Brooker snatched her hand from him, and, throwing her arms about his neck, pressed her lips to his—her face was transfigured as with a great light—the light of the knowledge that the poets had told the great and wondrous truth when they sang of Love as the Greatest Thing—and sung but half the truth. All that she longed for, dreamed of, yearned over—and disbelieved—was true and had come to pass....

She looked no older than her own daughter—and forgot that she was a woman of thirty–seven years, and that the man who knelt in homage (the moment that she was free to receive his homage!) *might* be but little over thirty.

She did not understand—but perhaps, in that moment, received full compensation for her years of misery, and her marred, thwarted, wasted womanhood.

Oh, thank God; thank God, that he loved her ... she could not have borne it if ...

* * * * *

Glad that he had succeeded in comforting her, slightly puzzled and vaguely stirred, he arose and went out, still without a word.

* * * * *

Returning to his hotel, he found a telegram ordering him to proceed "forthwith" to a place called Soko Nassai *via* Voi and Taveta, and as "forthwith" means the next train, and the next train to Voi on the Uganda Railway went in two hours, he yelled for Ali, collected his kit, paid his Club bill and got him to the railway station without having time or opportunity to make any visits of farewell. That he had to go without seeing Miss Eva again troubled him sorely, much more so than he would have thought possible.

In fact he thought of her all night as he lay on the long bed–seat of his carriage in a fog of fine red dust, instead of sleeping or thinking of what lay before him at Taveta, whence, if all or any of the Club gossip were true, he would be embarking upon a very hard campaign, and one of "open" fighting, too. This would be infinitely more interesting than the sit–in–the–mud trench warfare, but it was not of this that he found himself thinking so much as of the length and silkiness of Miss Eva's eyelashes, the tendrils of hair at her neck, the perfection of her lips, and similar important matters. He was exceedingly glad that he was going to be attached to a Kashmiri regiment, because it was composed of Dogras and Gurkhas, and he liked Gurkhas exceedingly, but he was ten thousand times more glad that there was a Miss Eva Stayne–Brooker in the world, that she was in Mombasa, that he could think of her there, and, best of all, that he could return and see her there when the war was o'er—and he sang aloud:

> "When the war is o'er,
> We'll part no more."

No—damn it all—one couldn't sing "at Ehren on the Rhine," after the German had shown his country to be the home of the most ruffianly, degraded, treacherous and despicable brute the world has yet produced; and, turning over with an impatient jerk, he tipped a little mound of drifted red dust and sand into his mouth and his song turned to dust and ashes and angry spluttering. *Absit omen.*

At Taveta, a name on a map and a locality beneath wooded hills, Bertram found a detachment of his regiment, and was accepted by his brother–officers as a useful–looking and very welcome addition to their small Mess. He was delighted to renew acquaintance with Augustus and with the Gurkha Subedar—whom he had last seen at M'paga. Here he also found the 29th Punjabis, the 130th Baluchis, and the 2nd Rhodesians. In the intervals of thinking of Miss Eva, he thought what splendid troops they looked, and what a grand and fortunate man he was to be one of their glorious Brigade.

When he smelt the horrible fever smell of the pestilential Lumi swamp, he hoped Miss Eva would not get fever in Mombasa.

When he feasted his delighted eyes on Kilimanjaro, on the rose–flushed snows and glaciers of Kibo and Mawenzi, their amazing beauty was as the beauty of her face, and he walked uplifted and entranced.

When the daily growing Brigade was complete, and marched west through alternating dense bush and open prairie of moving grass, across dry sandy nullahs or roughly bridged torrents, he marched with light heart and untiring body, neither knowing nor caring whether the march were long or short.

When Gussie Augustus Gus said it was dam' hot and very thoughtless conduct of Jan Smuts to make innocent and harmless folk walk on their feet at midday, Bertram perceived that it *was* hot, though he hadn't noticed it. His spirit had been in Mombasa, and his body had been unable to draw its attention to such minor and sordid details as dust, heat, thirst, weariness and weakness.

The ice–cold waters of the Himo River, which flows from the Kilimanjaro snows to the Pangani, reminded him of the coolness of her firm young hands.

As the Brigade camped on the ridge of a green and flower–decked hill looking across the Pangani Valley, to the Pare Hills, a scene of fertile beauty, English in its wooded rolling richness, he thought of her with him in England; and as the rancid smell of a frying *ghee*, mingled with the acrid smell of wood smoke, was wafted from where Gurkha, Punjabi, Pathan and Baluchi cooked their *chapattis* of *atta*, he thought of her in India with him....

Day after day the Brigade marched on, and whether it marched between impenetrable walls of living green that formed a tunnel in which the red dust floated always, thick, blinding and choking, or whether it marched across great deserts of dried black peat over which the black dust hung always, thicker, more blinding and more choking—it was the same to Second–Lieutenant Bertram Greene, as he marched beside the sturdy little warriors of his regiment. His spirit marched through the realms of Love's wonderland rather than through deserts and jungles, and the things of the spirit are more real, and greater than those of the flesh.

For preference he marched alone, alone with his men that is, and not with a brother officer, that he might be spared the necessity of conversation and the annoyance of distraction of his thoughts. For miles he would trudge beside the Subedar in companionly silence. He grew very fond of the staunch little man to whom duty was a god....

When the Brigade reached Soko Nassai it joined the Division which (co–operating with Van Deventer's South African Division, then threatening Tabora and the Central Railway from Kondoa Irangi) in three months conquered German East Africa—an almost adequate force having been dispatched at last. It consisted of the 2nd Kashmir Rifles, 28th Punjabis, 130th Baluchis, the 2nd Rhodesians, a squadron of the 17th Cavalry, the 5th and 6th Batteries of the S.A. Field Artillery, a section of the 27th Mountain Battery, and a company of the 61st Pioneers, forming the First East African Brigade. There were also the 25th Royal Fusiliers, the M.I. and machine–guns of the Loyal North Lancashire Regiment, the East African Mounted Rifles, a Howitzer Battery of Cornwall Territorials, "Z" Signalling Company, a "wireless" section, and a fleet of armoured cars. In reserve were the 5th and 6th South Africans.

Few divisions have ever done more than this one did—under the greatest hardships in one of the worst districts in the world.

Its immediate task was to clear the Germans from their strong positions in the Pare and Usambara Mountains, and to seize the railway to Tanga on the coast, a task of all but superhuman difficulty, as it could only be accomplished by the help of a strong force making a flanking march through unexplored roadless virgin jungle, down the Pangani valley, the very home of fever, where everything would depend upon efficient transport—and any transport appeared impossible. How could motor transport go through densest trackless bush, or horse and bullock transport where horse–sickness and tsetse fly forbade?

The First Brigade made the Pangani march and turning movement, performing the impossible, and with it went Second–Lieutenant Bertram Greene, head in air and soul among the stars, his heart full of a mortal tenderness and caught up in a great divine uplifting,

CHAPTER III

Love and War

As he marched on, day after day, his thoughts moving to the dogged tramp of feet, the groan of laden bullock–carts, the creak of mule packs, the faint rhythmic tap of tin cup on a bayonet hilt, the clank of a swinging chain end, through mimosa thorn and dwarf scrub, dense forest, mephitic swamp or smitten desert, ever following the river whose waters gave life and sudden death, the river to leave which was to die of thirst, and to stay by which was to die of fever, this march which would have been a nightmare of suffering, was merely a dream—a dream from which he would awake to arise and go to Mombasa….

"I always thought you had guts, Greene," said Augustus coarsely, one night, as they laid their weary bones beneath a tarpaulin stretched between two carts. "I always thought you had 'em beneath your gentle–seeming surface, so to speak—but dammy, you're *all* guts…. You're a blooming whale, to march…. Why the devil don't you growl and grumble like a Christian gentleman, eh? … I hate you 'strong silent men.' … Dammitall—you march along with a smug smile on your silly face! … You're a perfect tiger, you know…. Don't like it. . . . Colonel will be saying your 'conduct under trying circumstances is an example and inspiration to all ranks.' … Will when you're dead anyhow…. Horrid habit…. You go setting an example to *me*, and I'll bite you in the stomach, my lad…."

Bertram laughed and looked out at the great stars—blue diamonds sprinkled on black velvet—and was very happy.

Was he tired? Everybody else was, so he supposed he must be.

Was he hungry? Yes—for the sight of a face…. Oh, the joy of shutting his eyes and calling it to memory's eye, and of living over again every moment spent in her presence!

He realised, with something like amazement, that Love grows and waxes without the food and sustenance of the loved one's real presence. He loved her more than he had done at Mombasa. Had he really *loved* her at Mombasa at all? Certainly not as he did now—when he thought of nothing else, and performed all his duties and functions mechanically and was only here present in the mere dull and unfeeling flesh….

As the column halted where, across an open glade, the menacing sinister jungle might at any moment burst into crackling life, as machine–gun and rifle–fire crashed out to mow men down, he felt but mild interest, little curiosity and no vestige of fear. He would do his duty to the utmost, of course, but—how sweet to get a wound that would send him back to where she was!

As the column crossed the baked mud of former floods, and his eye noted the foot–prints, preserved in it, of elephant, lion, large and small antelope, rhinoceros and leopard, these wonders moved him to but faint interest, for he had something a thousand times more interesting to think of. Things that would have thrilled him before this great event, this greatest event, of his life—such as the first complete assembling of the Brigade in the first sufficient open space it had yet encountered—by the great spare rock, Njumba–ya–Mawe, the House of Stone, on which General Jan Smuts himself climbed to see them pass, the sight of his own Kashmiris cutting a way straight through the bush with their *kukris*; the glimpses of animals he had hitherto only seen in zoological gardens; the faint sound of far–distant explosions where the retiring Germans were blowing up their railway culverts and bridges; the sight of deserted German positions with their trenches littered with coco–nut shells, husks, and mealie–cobs, their cunning machine–gun positions, and their officers' *bandas* littered with empty tins and bottles; the infernal hullabaloo when a lion got within the perimeter one night and stampeded the mules; the sudden meeting with a little band of ragged emaciated prisoners, some German patrol captured by the Pathan *sowars* of the 17th or the Mounted Infantry of the Lancashires; the passing, high in air, of a humming yellow aeroplane; the distant rattle of machine–guns, like the crackling of a forest fire, as the advance–guard came in sight of some retiring party of Kraut's force; the hollow far–off boom of some big gun brought from the *Konigsberg*—dismantled and deserted in the Rufigi river—as it fired from Sams upon the frontal feint of the 2nd Brigade's advance down the railway or at the column of King's African Rifles from M'buyini—these things which would have so thrilled him once, now left him cold—mere trifles that impinged but lightly on his outer consciousness....

"You're a blasé old bloke, aren't you, Greene?" said the puzzled Augustus. "Hardened old warrior like you can't be expected to take much interest in a dull game like war, unless they let you charge guns and squares with cavalry, what? Sport without danger's no good to you, what? You wait till you find a dam' great Yao *askari* looking for your liver with a bayonet, my lad.... See you sit up and take notice then, what? Garn! You patient, grinning Griselda ... " and so forth.

But, one evening, as the column approached the South Pare Mountains, near Mikocheni, Bertram "sat up and took notice," very considerable notice, as with a rush and a roar and a terrific explosion, a column of black smoke and dust shot up to the sky when a shell burst a few score yards away—the first of a well–placed series of four–point–one high explosive shells.

The column halted and lay low in the bush. Further progress would be more wholesome in the dark.

"Naval guns: over seven miles away: dam' good shootin'," quoth Augustus coolly, and with the air of a connoisseur, adding, "and we've got nothing that could carry half–way to 'em. I'm goin' 'ome...."

Bertram, everything driven from his mind but the thought that he was under fire, was rejoiced to find himself as cool as Augustus, who suddenly remarked, "I'm not as 'appy as you look, and I don't b'lieve you are either"—as the column hurriedly betook itself from the position–betraying dust of the open to the shelter of the scrub that lay between it and the river, the river so beautiful in the rose–glow and gold of evening, and so deadly to all who could not crawl beneath the sheltering mosquito curtains as the light faded from the sinister–lovely scene.

* * * * *

Next day the column found one of the enemy's prepared positions in the dense bush, and it was not, as hitherto, a deserted one. The first intimation was, as usual in the blind, fumbling fighting of East Africa, a withering blast of Maxim fire, and terribly heavy casualties for a couple of minutes.

At one moment, nothing at all—just a weary, plodding line of hot, weary and dusty men, crossing a *dambo*, all hypnotised from thought of danger by fatigue, familiarity and normal immunity; at the next moment, slaughter, groans, brief confusion, burst upon burst of withering fire, a line of still or writhing forms.

It is an inevitable concomitant of such warfare, wherein one feels for one's enemy rather than looks for him, and a hundred–mile march is a hundred–mile ambush.

This particular nest of machine–guns and large force of *askaris* was utterly invisible at a few yards' range, and, at a few yards' range, it blasted the head and flank of the column.

Instinctively the war–hardened Sepoys who survived dropped to earth and opened fire at the section of bush whence came the hail of death—a few scattered rifles against massed machine–guns and a battalion of highly trained *askaris*, masters of jungle–craft. As, still firing, they crawled backward to the cover of the scrub on the side of the glade opposite to the German position, the companies who had been marching behind them deployed and painfully skirmished toward the concealed enemy, halting to fire volleys into the dense bush in the probable direction, striving to keep touch with their flanking companies, to keep something like a line, to keep direction, to keep moving forward, and to keep a sharp look–out for the enemy who, having effected their surprise and caught the leading company in the open, had vanished silently, machine–guns and all, from the position which had served their purpose....

A few feet in advance of his men as they skirmished forward, extended to one pace interval, Bertram, followed by the Subedar, crossed the line of dead and wounded caught by the first blast of fire. He saw two men he knew, lieutenants of the 130th Baluchis, who had evidently been made a special target by the concealed riflemen and machine–gunners. He saw another with his leg bent in the middle at right–angles—and realised with horror that it was bent *forward.* Also that the wounded man was Terence Brannigan....

He feared he was going to be sick, and shame himself before his Gurkhas as his eye took in the face of a Baluchi whose lower jaw had been removed as though by a surgeon's knife. He noted subconsciously how raven–blue the long oiled hair of these Pathans and Baluchis shone in the sun, their *puggris* having fallen off or been shot away. The machine–guns must have over–sighted and then lowered, instead of the reverse, as everybody seemed to be hit in the head, neck or chest except Brannigan, whose knee was so shattered that his leg bent forward until his boot touched his belt—with an effect as of that of a sprawled rag doll. Probably he had been hit by one of the great soft–nosed slugs with which the swine armed their *askaris*. The hot, heavy air reeked with blood. Some of the wounded lay groaning; some sat and smiled patiently as they held up shattered arms or pressed thumbs on bleeding legs; some rose and staggered and fell, rose and staggered and fell, blindly going nowhere. One big, grey–eyed Pathan lustily sang his almost national song, "*Zakhmi Dil*"—"The Wounded Heart," but whether in bravado, delirium, sheer *berserk* joy of battle, or quiet content at getting a wound that would give him a rest, change and privileges, Bertram did not know.

"*Stretcher–bearer log ainga bhai*," [42] said Bertram, as he passed him sitting there singing in a pool of blood.

"*Béshak Huzoor*," replied the man with a grin, "*ham baitha hai*," [43] and resumed his falsetto nasal dirge. Another, crouching on all fours with his face to the ground, suddenly raised that grey–green, dripping face, and crawled towards him. Bertram saw that he was trailing his entrails as he moved. To avoid halting and being sick at this shocking sight, he rushed forward to the edge of the scrub whence all this havoc had been wrought, his left hand pressed over his mouth, all his will–power concentrated upon conquering the revolt of his stomach.

Thinking he was charging an enemy, his men dashed forward after him, only to find the place deserted. Little piles of empty cartridge–cases marked the places where the machine–guns had stood behind natural and artificial screens. One tripod had been fixed on an ant–hill screened by bushes, and must have had a fine field of fire across the glade. How far back had they gone—and then, in which direction? How long would it be before the column would again expose a few hundred yards of its flank to the sudden blast of the machine–guns of this force and the withering short–range volleys of its rifles? Would they get away now and go on ahead of the column and wait for it again, or, that being the obvious thing, would they move down toward the tail of the column, and attack there? Or was it just a rear–guard holding the Brigade up while Kraut evacuated Mikocheni? ... Near and distant rifle and machine–gun fire, rising to a fierce crescendo and dying away to a desultory popping, seemed to indicate that this ambush was one of many, or that the Brigade was fighting a regular battle.... Probably a delaying action by a strong rear–guard.... Anyhow, his business was to see that his men kept direction, kept touch, kept moving forward slowly, and kept a sharp look–out.... Firing came nearer on the right flank. That part of the line had seen something—or been fired on, evidently—and suddenly he came to the edge of the patch or belt of jungle and, looking across another glassy glade, he saw a white man striking, with a whip or stick, at some *askaris* who were carrying off a machine–gun. Apparently he was hurrying their retirement. Quickly Bertram turned to the grim little Subedar and got a section of his men to fire volleys at the spot, but there was no sign of life where, a minute earlier, he had certainly seen a German machine–gun team....

He felt very cool and very strong, but knew that this great strength might fail him at any moment and leave him shaking and trembling, weak and helpless....

He must line this edge of the jungle and examine every bush and tree of the opposite edge, across the glade, before adventuring out into its naked openness.

Suppose a dozen machine–guns were concealed a few yards within that sinister sullen wall. He bade the Subedar halt the whole line and open rapid fire upon it with a couple of sections. If he watched through his glasses carefully, he might see some movement in those menacing depths and shadows, movement induced by well–directed fire—possibly he might provoke concealed machine–gunners or *askaris* to open fire and betray their positions. If so, should he lead his men in one wild charge across the glade, in the hope that enough might survive to reach them? If only the Gurkhas could get there with their *kukris*, the guns would change hands pretty speedily.... It would be rather a fine thing to be "the chap who led the charge that got the Maxims." ...

"*Gya, Sahib*," said the Subedar as he stared across the glade. "*Kuch nahin hai.*" [44]

Should he move on? And if he led the line out into a deathtrap? ... He could see nothing of the companies on the left and right flank, even though this was thin and penetrable bush. How would he feel if he gave the order to advance and, as soon as the line was clear of cover, it was mown down like grass?

Bidding the Subedar wait, he stepped out and, with beating heart, advanced across the open.... He couldn't talk to the Gurkhas, but he could show them that a British officer considered their safety before his own. He entered the opposite scrub, his heart in his mouth, his revolver shaking wildly in his trembling hand, but an exhilarating excitement thrilling him with a kind of wild joy.... He rather hoped he would be fired at. He wished to God they would break the horrible stillness and open fire.... He felt that, if they did not soon do so, he would scream and blaspheme or run away....

Nothing there. No trenches. No suspicious broken branches or withering bushes placed *en camouflage*. He wheeled about, re–entered the glade, and gave the signal for his men to advance. They crossed the glade. Again they felt their way, tore, pushed, writhed, forced their way, through a belt of thin jungle, and again came upon a narrow glade and, as the line of jungle–bred, jungle–trained Gurkhas halted at its edge, a horde of *askaris* in a rough double line dashed out from the opposite side and, as the Gurkhas instinctively opened independent magazine fire, charged yelling across, with the greatest *élan* and ferocity. Evidently they thought they were swooping down upon the scattered remnants of the company that had headed the column, or else were in great strength, and didn't care what they "bumped into," knowing that their enemy had no prepared positions and death–traps for them to be caught in....

As he stood behind a tree, steadily firing his revolver at the charging, yelling *askaris* now some forty yards distant, Bertram was aware of another line, or extended mob, breaking like a second wave from the jungle, and saw a couple of machine–gun teams hastily fling down their boxes and set up their tripods. He knew that a highly trained German gunner would sit behind each one and fire single shots or solid streams of bullets, according to his targets and opportunities. Absolute artists, these German machine–gunners and, ruffianly brutal bullies or not, very cool, brave men.

So was he cool and brave, for the moment—but how soon he would collapse, he did not know. He had emptied his revolver, and he realised that he had sworn violently with every shot.... He reloaded with trembling fingers, and, looking up, saw that the fight was about to become a hand–to–hand struggle. Firing rapidly, as the *askaris* charged, the Gurkhas had thinned their line, and the glade was dotted with dozens of their dead and wounded—but the survivors, far outnumbering the Gurkhas, were upon them—and, with shrill yells, the little men rose and rushed at their big enemies *kukri* in hand.

The Subedar dashed at a huge non–commissioned officer who raised his fixed bayonet to drive downward in a kind of two–handed spear–thrust at the little man. Bertram thought the Gurkha was killed but, as he raised his revolver, he saw the Subedar duck low and slash with incredible swiftness at the negro's thigh and again at his stomach. In the very act of springing sideways he then struck at the *askari's* wrist and again at his neck. The little man was using his national weapon (the *kukri*, the Gurkha's terrible carved knife, heavy, broad and razor–edged, wherewith he can decapitate an ox) when it came to fighting—no sword nor revolver for him—and the negro fell, with four horrible wounds, within four seconds of raising his rifle to stab, his head and hand almost severed, his thigh cut to the bone and his abdomen laid open.

"Sha–bas!" [45] yelled Bertram, seeing red, and going mad with battle lust, and shouting "Maro! Maro!" [46] at the top of his voice, rushed into the hacking, hewing, stabbing throng that, with howls, grunts, and screams, swayed to and fro, but gradually approached the direction whence the Gurkhas had advanced....

And the two artists behind the machine–guns, the two merry manipulators of Death's brass band, sat cool and calm, playing delicate airs upon their staccato–voiced instruments—here a single note and there a single note, now an arpeggio and now a run as they got their opportunity at a single man or a group, a charging section or a firing–line. Where a whirling knot of clubbing, thrusting, slashing men was seen to be more foe than friend they treated it as foe and gave it a whole *rondo*—these heralds and trumpeters of Death.

And, as Bertram rushed out into the open, each said "Offizier!" and gave him their undivided attention.

"Shah–bas! Subedar Sahib," he yelled; "Maro! Maro!" and the Gurkhas who saw and heard him grinned and grunted, slashing and hacking, and thoroughly enjoying life.... (This was worth all the marching and sweating, starving and working.... *This* was something like! A *kukri* in your hand and an enemy to go for!)

Firing his revolver into the face of an *askari* who swung up his clubbed rifle, and again into the chest of one who drove at him with his bayonet, he shouted and swore, wondering at himself as he did so.

And then he received a blow on his elbow and his revolver was jerked from his open, powerless hand. Glancing at his arm he saw it was covered with blood, and, at the same moment, a gigantic *askari* aimed a blow at his skull—a blow that he felt would crush it like an egg ... and all he could do was to put his left arm across his face ... and wait ... for a fraction of a second.... He saw the man's knees crumple.... Why had he fallen instead of delivering that awful blow?

The nearer machine–gunner cursed the fallen man and played a trill of five notes as he got a clear glimpse of the white man....

Someone had kicked his legs from under Bertram—or had they thrown a stone—or what? He was on the ground. He felt as though a swift cricket–ball had hit his shin, and another his knee, and his right arm dropped and waggled aimlessly—and when it waggled there was a grating feeling (which was partly a grating sound) horrible to be heard.... And he couldn't get up....

He felt very faint and could see nothing, by reason of a blue light which burnt dully, but obscured his vision, destroying the sunlight. Darkness, and a loud booming and rushing sound in his ears....

Then he felt better and, half raising himself on his left hand, saw another line emerge from the scrub and charge.... Baluchis and Gurkhas, friends ... thank God!! And there was Augustus. He'd pass him as, just now, he had passed Terence Brannigan and the two other Baluchi subalterns. Would Augustus feel sick at the sight of him, as *he* had done? ...

With a wild yell, the big Baluchis and little Gurkhas charged, and the line was borne back toward the machine–gunners, who disappeared with wonderful dispatch, in search of a desirable and eligible pitch, preferably on a flank, for their next musical performance.

"Hullo, Priceless Old Thing, stopped one?" asked Augustus, pausing in his rush.

"Bit chipped," Bertram managed to say.

"Oh, poignant! Search—" began Augustus ... and fell across Bertram, causing him horrible agony, a bullet–hole the size of a marble in his forehead, the back of his head blown completely out.

Bertram fainted as his friend's brains oozed and spread across his chest.

Having dodged and manœuvred to a flank position, one of the machine–gunners played a solo to the wounded while waiting a more favourable moment and target. His fellow sons of *kultur* wanted no wounded German *askaris* on their hands, and of course the wounded Sepoys and British were better dead. Dead men don't recover and fight again.... So he did a little neat spraying of twitching, writhing, crawling, wriggling or staggering individuals and groups. Incidentally he hit the two British officers again, riddling the body which was on top of the other, putting one bullet through the left arm of the underneath one.... Then he had to scurry off again, as the fighting–line was getting so far towards his left that he might be cut off.... Anyhow he'd had a very good morning and felt sure his "good old German God" must be feeling quite pleased about it.

---

[42] "The stretcher–bearers will come, brother."

[43] "No doubt, sir. I am waiting."

[44] "Gone, sir. There is nothing."

[45] "Bravo."

[46] "Kill! Kill!"

CHAPTER IV

Baked

§1

When he recovered consciousness, Bertram found himself lying on a stretcher in a little natural clearing in the bush—a tiny square enclosed by acacia, sisal, and mimosa scrub. On a candelabra tree hung a bunch of water–bottles, a helmet, some haversacks, a tunic, and strips of white rag.

An officer of the Royal Army Medical Corps and a *babu* of the Indian Subordinate Medical Service were bending over a medical pannier. Stretcher–bearers brought in another burden as he turned his head to look round. It was a Native Officer. On top of his head was an oblong of bare–shaven skull—some caste–mark apparently. Following them with his eyes Bertram saw the stretcher–bearers place the unconscious (or dead) man at the end of a small row of similar still forms.... There was Brannigan.... There was a man with whom he had shared a tent for a night at Taveta.... What was his name? ... There were the two Baluchi subalterns.... Was that the dead row—the mortuary, so to speak, of this little field ambulance? Was he to join it?

The place stunk of blood, iodine and horrors. He could move neither hand nor foot, and the world seemed to be a Mountain of Pain upon the peak of which he was impaled....

The continued rattle of firing was coming nearer, surely? It was—much nearer. The stretcher–bearers brought in another casualty, the stretcher dripping blood. No "walking wounded" appeared to come to this particular dressing–station.

The firing was getting quite close, and the sound of the cracking of branches was audible. Leaves and twigs, cut from the trees by the bullets, occasionally fell upon the mangled and broken forms as though to hide them....

"Sah—they are coming!" said the *babu* suddenly. His face was a mask of fear, but he continued to perform his duties as dresser, as well as his shaking hands would permit.

Suddenly a ragged line of Gurkhas broke into the clearing, halting to fire, retreating and firing again, fighting from tree to tree and bush to bush.... The mixed, swaying and changing battle–line was going to cross the spot where the wounded lay.... Those of them who were conscious knew what *that* meant...

So did the medical officer, and he shouted to the stretcher–bearers, *babu*, mule–drivers, porters, everybody, to carry the wounded farther into the bush—quick—quick....

As his stretcher was snatched up, Bertram—so sick with pain, and the cruel extra agony of the jolts and jars, that he cared not what befell him—saw a group of *askaris* burst into the clearing, glare around, and rush forward with bayonets poised. He shut his eyes as they reached the other stretchers....

§2

On the terrible journey down the Tanga Railway to M'buyuni, between Taveta and Voi, Bertram kept himself alive with the thought that he would eventually reach Mombasa....

He had forgotten Eva only while he was in the fight and on the stretcher, but when he lay on the floor of the cattle–truck he seemed to wake from a night of bad dreams—to awake again into the brightness and peace of the day of Love.

Of course, the physical agony of being jolted and jerked for a hundred and fifty miles, throughout which every bump of every wheel over every railway joint gave a fresh stab of pain to each aching wound and his throbbing head, was a terrible experience—but he would rather have been lying on the floor of that cattle–truck bumping towards Mombasa, than have been marching in health and strength away from it.

Every bump that racked him afresh meant that he was about forty feet nearer to M'buyuni which was on the line to Voi which is on the line to Mombasa.

What is the pain of a shattered right elbow, a broken left arm, a bullet hole in the right thigh and another in the left calf, when one is on the road to where one's heart is, and one is filled with the divine wonder of first love?

He could afford to pity the poor uninjured Bertram Greene of yesterday, marching farther and farther from where all hope, happiness, joy, peace and plenty lay, where love lay, and where alone in all the world could he know content....

She would not think the less of him that he had temporarily lost the use of his hands and, for a time, was lame.... He had done his duty and was out of it! Blessed wounds! ...

§3

In the hospital at M'buyuni the clean bullet–holes in the flesh of his legs healed quickly. Lucky for him that they had been made by nickel Maxim–bullets and not by the horrible soft–nosed slugs of the *askaris'* rifles. The bone–wounds in his arms were more serious, and he could walk long before he could use his hands.

His patient placidity was remarkable to those who came in contact with him—not knowing that he dwelt in a serene world apart and dreamed love's young age–old dream therein.

Every day was a blessed day in that it brought him much nearer to the moment when he would see her face, hear her voice, touch her hand. What unthinkably exquisite joy was to be his—and was his *now* in the mere contemplation of it!

His left arm began to do well, but the condition of his right arm was less satisfactory.

"Greene, my son," said the O.C. M'buyuni Stationary Hospital to him one day, "you're for the Hospital Ship *Madras*, her next trip. Lucky young dog. Wish I was.... Give my love to Colonel Giffard and Major Symons when you get on board.... You'll get a trip down to Zanzibar, I believe, on your way to Bombay.... You'll be having tea on the lawn at the Yacht Club next month—think of it!"

Bertram thought of something else and radiated joy.

"Aha! That bucks you, does it? Wounded hero with his arm in a sling at the Friday–evening–band–night–tea–on–the–lawn binges, what?"

Bertram smiled.

"Could I stay on in Mombasa a bit, sir?" he asked.

The O.C. M'buyuni Stationary Hospital stared.

"Eh?" said he, doubting that he could have heard aright. Bertram repeated the question, and the O.C., M.S.H., felt his pulse. Was this delirium?

"No," he said shortly in the voice of one who is grieved and disappointed. "You'll go straight on board the *Madras*—and damned lucky too.... You don't deserve to.... I'd give ... "

"What is the procedure when I get to Bombay?" asked Bertram, as the doctor fell into a brown study.

"You'll go before a Medical Board at Colaba Hospital. They may detain you there, give you a period of sick leave, or invalid you out of the Service. Depends on how your right arm shapes.... You'll be all right, I think."

"And if my arm goes on satisfactorily I shall be able to come back to East Africa in a month or two perhaps?" continued Bertram.

"Yes. Nice cheery place, what?" said the Medical Officer and departed. He never could suffer fools gladly and he personally had had enough, for the moment, of heat, dust, stench, monotony, privation, exile, and overwork…. *Hurry* back to East Africa! … Zeal for duty is zeal for duty—and lunacy's lunacy…. But perhaps the lad was just showing off and talking through his hat, what?

§4

The faithful Ali, devoted follower of his old master's peregrinations, saw the muddy, blood–stained greasy bundles, which were that master's kit, safe on board the *Madras* from the launch which had brought the party of wounded officers from the Kilindini pier. Personally he conducted the bundles to the cabin reserved for Second–Lieutenant B. Greene, I.A.R., and then sought their owner where he reclined in a *chaise longue* on deck, none the better for his long journey on the Uganda Railway.

"I'm coming back, Ali," said he as his retainer, a monument of restrained grief, came to him.

"Please God, *Bwana*," was the dignified reply.

"What will you do while I am away?" he asked, for the sake of something to say.

"Go and see my missus and childrens, my little damsels and damsons at Nairobi, sah," was the sad answer. "When *Bwana* sailing now?"

"Not till this evening," answered Bertram, "and the last thing I want you to do for me is to take these two *chits* to Stayne–Brooker Mem–Sahib and Stayne–Brooker Miss–Sahib as quickly as you can. You'll catch them at tiffin if you take a trolley now from Kilindini. They *must* have them quickly.... If they come to see me before the ship sails at six, there'll be an extra present for one Ali Suleiman, what?"

"Oh, sah! *Bwana* not mentioning it by golly," replied Ali and fled.

Mrs. Stayne–Brooker was crossing from the Hospital to Vasco da Gama Street for lunch when, having run quicker than any trolley ever did, he caught sight of her, salaamed and presented the two *chits*, written for Bertram by a hospital friend and companion of his journey, as soon as they got on board. She opened the one addressed to herself.

> "*My Dear Mrs. Stayne–Brooker*," it ran, "*I have just reached the Madras, and sail at six this evening. I cannot tell you how much I should like to see you, if you could take your evening drive in this direction and come on board. How I wish I could stay and convalesce in Mombasa! Very much more than ever words could possibly express. It is just awful to pass through like this.*
>
> "*I do hope you can come.*
> "*Your ever grateful and devoted*
> "BERTRAM GREENE."

The worthy Ali, panting and perspiring, thought the lady was going to fall.

"*Bertram*!" she whispered, and then her heart beat again, and she regained control of her trembling limbs.

"You are Greene *Bwana's* boy!" she said, searching Ali's bedewed but beaming countenance. "Is he—is he ill—hurt—wounded?" (She did not know that the man had been in her husband's service.)

"Yes, Mem," was the cheerful reply. "Shot in all arms and legs. Also quite well, thank you."

"Go and tell him I will come," she said. "Be quick. Here—*baksheesh*. ... Now, *hurry*."

"Oh, Mem! Mem–Sahib not mentioning it, thank you please," murmured Ali as his huge paw engulfed the rupees. Turning, he started forthwith upon the four–mile return run.

Putting the note addressed to her daughter on the lunch–table, beside her plate, she hurried into her room, crying for joy, and, with trembling hands, made her toilette. She must look her best—look her youngest.

He was back! He was safe! He was alive! Oh, the long, long night of silence through the black darkness of which she had miserably groped! The weary, weary weeks of waiting and wondering, hoping and fearing, longing and doubting! But her prayers had been answered—and she was about to *see* him.... And if he were shattered and broken? She could almost find it in her heart to hope he was—that she might spend her life in guarding, helping, comforting him. He would *need* her, and oh, how she yearned to be needed, she who had never yet been really needed by man, woman, or child....

"*Mother*!" said Miss Stayne–Brooker, as she went in to lunch. "*What* a bright, gay girlie you look! ... Here's a note from that Mr. Greene of yours. He says:

> '*Dear Miss Stayne–Brooker,*
>
> '*I am passing through Mombasa, and am now on board the Madras. I can't come and see you—do you think you'd let your mother bring you to see me'—he's crossed that out and put 'see the Hospital Ship Madras'—'it might interest you. I have written to ask if she'd care to come. Do—could you?*
>
> '*Always your grateful servant,*
> 'BERTRAM GREENE.'

But I am playing golf with Reggie and having tea with him at the Club, you know."

"All right, dear. I'll go and see the poor boy."

"That's right, darling. You won't mind if I don't, will you? ... He's *your* friend, you know."

"Yes," said Mrs. Stayne–Brooker, "he's *my* friend," and Miss Stayne–Brooker wondered at the tone of her mother's voice.... (Poor old Mums; she made quite a silly of herself over this Mr. Greene!)

§5

Having blessed and rewarded the worthy Ali, returned dove–like to the *Madras*, Bertram possessed his soul with what patience he could, and sought distraction from the gnawing tooth of anxiety by watching the unfamiliar life of a hospital–ship….

Suppose Eva Stayne–Brooker could not come! Suppose the ship sailed unexpectedly early! …

He could not sit still in that chair and wait, and wait….

A pair of very pretty nurses, with the sallow ivory complexion, black hair and large liquid eyes of the Eurasian, walked up and down.

Another, plain, fat, and superiorly English, walked apart from them.

Two very stout Indian gentlemen, in the uniform of Majors of the Indian Medical Service, promenaded, chattering and gesticulating. The Chief Engineer (a Scot, of course), leaning against the rail and smoking a black Burma cheroot, eyed them with a kind of wonder, and smiled tolerantly upon them…. Travel and much time for philosophical reflection had confairrmed in him the opeenion that it tak's all sorrts to mak' a Univairse….

From time to time, a sick or wounded man was hoisted on board, lying on a platform that dangled from four ropes at the end of a chain and was worked by a crane. From the launch to the deck of the ship he was slung like so much merchandise or luggage, but without jar or jolt. Or a walking–wounded or convalescent sick man would slowly climb the companion that sloped diagonally at an easy angle along the ship's side from the promenade–deck to the water.

On the fore and aft well–decks, crowds of sick or wounded Sepoys crouched huddled in grey blankets, or moved slowly about with every evidence of woe and pain. It takes an Indian Sepoy to do real justice to illness of any kind. He is a born actor and loves acting the dying man better than any part in life's drama. This is not to say that he is a malingerer or a weakling—but that when he is sick he *is* going to get, at any rate, the satisfaction of letting everybody know it and of collecting such sympathy and admiration as he can.

"No, there is no one so sick as a sick Indian," smiled Bertram to himself.

In contrast was the demeanour of a number of British soldiers sitting and lying about the deck allotted to them, adjoining but railed off from that of the officers.

Laughter and jest were the order of the day. One blew into a mouth–organ with more industry than skill; another endeavoured to teach one of the ship's cats to waltz on its hind legs; some played "brag" with a pack of incredibly dirty little cards; and others sat and exchanged experiences, truthfully and otherwise.

Near to where Bertram stood, a couple sprawled on the deck and leaned against a hatch. The smaller of the two appeared to be enjoying the process of annoying the larger, as he tapped his protruding and outlying tracts with a *kiboko*, listening intently after each blow in the manner of a doctor taking soundings as to the thoracic or abdominal condition of a patient.

An extra sharp tap caused the larger man to punch his assailant violently in the ribs, whereupon the latter threw his arms round the puncher's neck, kissed him, and stated, with utter disregard for facts:

"'Erb! In our lives we was werry beautiful, an' in our deafs we wos not diwided." (Evidently a reminiscence of the Chaplain's last sermon.)

But little mollified by the compliment, Herbert smote again, albeit less violently, as he remarked with a sneer:

"Ho, yus! You wouldn't a bin divided all right if you'd stopped one o' them liddle four–point–seven shells at Mikocheni, you would. Not 'arf, you wouldn't...."

But for crutches, splints, slings and bandages, no one would have supposed this to be a collection of sick and wounded men, wreckage of the storm of war, flotsam and jetsam stranded here, broken and useless....

Bertram returned to his chair and tried to control his sick impatience and anxiety. Would she come? What should he say to her if she did? . . . Should he "propose"—(beastly word)? He had not thought much about marriage.... To see her and hear her voice was what he really wanted. Should he tell her he loved her? ... Surely that would be unnecessary.

And then his heart stood still, as Mrs. Stayne–Brooker stepped from the companion–platform on to the deck, and came towards him—her face shining and radiant, her lips quivering, her eyes suffused.

He realised that she was alone, and felt that he had turned pale, as his heart sank like lead. But perhaps *she* was behind.... Perhaps she was in another boat.... Perhaps she was coming later....

He rose to greet her mother—who gently pushed him back on the long cane couch–chair and rested herself on the folding stool that stood beside it.

Still holding his left hand, she sat and tried to find words to ask of his hurts, and could say nothing at all.... She could only point to the sling, as she fought with a desire to gather him to her, and cry and cry and cry for joy and sweet sorrow.

"Yes," said Bertram, "but that's the only bad one.... Shan't lose the use of it, I expect, though.... Would she—would a woman—think it cheek if a maimed man—would she mind his being—if she really ... ?"

"Oh, my dear, my dear! Don't! Oh, don't!" Mrs. Stayne–Brooker broke down. "She'd love him ten thousand times more—you poor, foolish ... "

"Will she come?" he interrupted. "And dare I tell her I ... "

And Mrs. Stayne–Brooker understood.

She was a brave woman, and Life had taught her not to wear her poor heart upon her sleeve, had taught her to expect little (except misery), and to wear a defensive mask.

"*Eva is engaged to marry Mr. Macteith,*" she said in a toneless voice, and rose to go—to go before she broke down, fainted, became hysterical, or went mad....

Had two kind people ever dealt each other two such blows?

She looked at his face, and knew how her own must look....

Why *should* God treat her so? ... To receive so cruel a wound and to have to deal one as cruel to the heart she so loved! ...

He looked like a corpse—save that his eyes stared through her, burning her, seeing nothing. She must go, or disgrace herself—and him.... She felt her way, blindly fumbling, to the companion, realising even then that, when the stunned dullness immediately following this double blow gave place to the keen agony that awaited her recovery of her senses, there would be one spot of balm to her pain, there would be one feeble gleam of light in the Stygian darkness of her life—she would not be aching and yearning for the passionate love of her own son–in–law! ...

And, were this veracious chronicle a piece of war–fiction woven by a romancer's brain, Bertram Greene would have been standing on the deck that evening, looking his last upon the receding shores of the country wherein he had suffered and done so much.

On his breast would have been the Victoria Cross, and by his side the Woman whom he had Also Won.

She would have murmured "Darling!" ... He would have turned to her, as the setting sun, ever obliging, silhouetted the wonderfully lovely palms of the indescribably beautiful Kilindini Creek, and said to her:

"*Darling, life is but beginning.*"

* * * * *

Facts being facts, it is to be stated that Bertram sat instead of standing, as the *Madras* moved majestically down the Creek; that on his breast, instead of the Cross, a sling with a crippled arm; and by his side, instead of the Woman, a Goanese steward, who murmured:

"Master having tea out here, sir, please?" and to whom Bertram turned as the setting sun silhouetted the palms and said: "*Oh, go to hell*!" (and then sincerely apologised.)

* * * * *

Captain Stott passed and recognised him, in spite of changes. He noted the hardened face, the line between the eyes, the hollowed cheeks, the puckers and wrinkles, the steel–trap mouth, and wondered again at how War can make a boy into a Man in a few months....

There was nothing "half–baked" about *that* face.

* * * * *

And so, in ignorance, the despised and rejected boy again avenged his father, this time upon the woman who had done him such bitter, cruel wrong.

CHAPTER V

Finis

After war, peace; after storm, calm; after pain, ease….

Almost the first people whom he met in the Bombay Yacht Club after visiting the Colaba Hospital and being given six months' leave by the Medical Board, were his father and Miranda Walsingham.

Major Walsingham Greene had been severely wounded in Mesopotamia—but he had at last won decoration, promotion, recognition. He was acting Brigadier–General when he fell—and it was considered certain that he would get the Victoria Cross for which he had been recommended.

When he beheld his son, in khaki, war–worn and wounded (like himself, like his father and grandfather, like a true Greene of that ilk), his cup was full and he was a happy man—at last.

And Miranda! She could scarcely contain herself. She almost threw her arms round her old playmate's neck, then and there, in the middle of the Yacht Club lawn…. How splendid he looked! Who said her Bertram might make a scholar and a gentleman—but would never make a *man*?

Oh, joy! She had come out to bring home her "Uncle" Hugh and generally look after him—and now there were *two* patients to look after.

* * * * *

It was a happy voyage Home, and a very happy six months at Leighcombe Priory thereafter….

And when acting Brigadier–General Walsingham Greene and his son returned to India, Miranda Walsingham went with them as Mrs. Bertram Greene.

But Bertram was no longer "Cupid"—he seemed to have left "Cupid" in Africa.

Printed in Great Britain
by Amazon